HOLIDAY READ

HOLIDAY READ

Taylor Cole

An Aria Book

First published in the UK in 2023 by Head of Zeus,
part of Bloomsbury Publishing Plc

A CIP catalogue record for this book is available from the British Library.

ISBN (PB): 9781804545348
ISBN (E): 9781804545324

Cover design: HoZ / Nina Elstad

Typeset by Siliconchips Services Ltd UK

Head of Zeus
First Floor East
5–8 Hardwick Street
London EC1R 4RG

WWW.HEADOFZEUS.COM

For Rachel, Rachel, Rachel, and Lerryn

Prologue

Newquay, June

The beach is ice-cold beneath my sleeping bag and there's a slumbering British guy on either side of me. Alexis and Daniel. Author and agent. Both smart, both handsome, both important to me in different ways. Too important, it's beginning to feel now. I've gotten myself into something that I can't get out of and just the thought of our predicament makes my head hurt.

How did I get here?

There's a song that goes round and round in my head, the one my mom used to sing whenever my dad was leaving for the offshore rig. I can hear it in my mind right this minute as I look up to where vapour-trails criss-cross the clear night sky, because nine months ago I left Oahu on a jet plane, and I might never be back again.

My dad used to get so mad at my mom, say he wasn't leaving on a jet plane, he was getting a ride with his buddy and then they'd be taking a helicopter – or the crew boat if the weather was too rough for them to fly – and she always knew for a fact when he'd be back again, because it was right there on the wall planner, and why was she singing

John Denver songs when she knew he hated that guy, and all of his songs – particularly that one – sucked balls?

But my mom never gave in. She kept singing, through all my dad's complaining, and her voice was beautiful.

I think of Alexis's book. All this work. All this research. All this time together. I wonder if these guys are starting, perhaps, to see things differently? Is this project still just a commercial decision – a 'summer read' to pay the bills? For me, love stories have always meant so much more. While my mother turned to music when things got tough, I turned to stories. I still do.

As I listen to their deep breathing, I sense that I'm not going to be able to escape into a novel and out of this. Because it may all be business on the surface, but I've secretly begun to realise something: One of these men sleeping next to me could just be more than my summer. He could also be my future.

The skin on my upper back and shoulders burns with humiliation. After everything I told myself, promised myself, have I let myself fall in love?

One

May

'So, it turns out he's a limpet,' Makayla announces as she sweeps the crumb-drifts from the many corners of Demigorgons, which maybe wouldn't take long in a regular café, but this place is easily the biggest building in the beach complex and it's been constructed in a star shape, with glass triangles that cut into the outside space to maximise views of the ocean. Plus, the day before had involved two kids' birthday parties, and both had featured movie-style food fights that my boss hadn't had the heart to stop.

Morning light is streaming through the rear windows, illuminating the room with a rich orange glow. I can already feel the heat of that sun, cutting through the chill I had as I walked across the dune trail to work. I'd rubbed my hands together then, blown on them, and thought of Joseph, back in Hawaii, wondering where I'd gone. Not having the first idea where to look for me.

'It's a shame,' Makayla says, exhaling. 'I honestly thought the bloke had potential.'

Her curly hair is making a halo as she sweeps her way across the space, silhouetted by the sunlight.

'Huh, what did you say is wrong with the guy?' I say,

covering my yawn and trying to get my game face on, because I have to deal with eight hours of serving halloumi burgers and deep-fried avocado goujons to tourists who will likely be full of questions about places to go visit and what it costs to use each parking lot.

'He's a tit limpet. In bed.'

I must give her a look because she stops sweeping and hops up on the counter to take a break, patting the countertop for me to join her. On a typical day, I'd have hopped right up, but today I don't think I could haul my butt onto that counter if my life depended on it. And I know if I stop moving now, I'll have trouble getting started again. My insomnia has been brutal lately and my body is screaming out for rest. Even the floorboards of the café look comfy. I'm pretty sure that if I curled up in that warm spot by the window, I could sleep like a cat.

'He's a what now?' I say instead.

'You know, one of those men whose favourite hobby is to just sort of squish your naked breasts together and slide their face into your cleavage.'

I keep on cleaning the espresso machine, wiping away the previous day's coffee-ground spatter, and say, 'That is not a thing.'

'It is totally a thing,' she says. 'They're unstoppable. They don't respond to hints. Move them away and they will just move back. You cannot shake off a tit limpet.'

'Who are we talking about again? The Doberman or the Poet?'

The Doberman is actually a doorman at a nightclub in town, which overlooks one of the smaller beaches, but I misunderstood Makayla's Cornish accent the first time she mentioned him, and the nickname has stuck. The Poet isn't exactly a poet either, but it is true that he once had a piece published in the *Newquay Voice* that caused a sensation. Mostly because it involved a word not commonly printed in local newspapers; that word being *vulvodynia*. Which was the entire final line of his haiku.

It's hard to keep up with Makayla. She seems to have an endless stream of men interested in dating her, which isn't surprising at all, given she's the most fun person I've ever known and she also has legs like a gazelle. I met her on my first day here, when she was passing through the high street with a bag of French fries and pickles and found me weeping outside a real estate agent. She gave me some of those French fries and pickles, and helped me to find a vehicle to live in, putting out an SOS on her social media pages for anyone selling a van that wasn't a shit heap. She found me a place to live and a job in Demigorgons, and I will owe her forever.

'Not the Doberman. He's not a cuddler. He's the silent, emotionless type. He's just *there*. Like a cucumber. All cold and hard.'

I shake my head and smile. 'The limpet thing or whatever you called it sounds better.'

'You must've known a tit limpet, Candice. There's no way you've got to twenty-nine years old without encountering one. It's just not possible.'

She slides off the counter again, clearly disappointed that I've rejected her invitation to flake on our task list.

'What even is a limpet, anyways?'

'For chrissakes, woman. How do you not know that? Is Hawaii not chockful of sea life?'

I shrug. 'Yeah, but none of it reminds me of men I've dated.'

'A limpet is a sea creature. Those tough little bastards you can't pull off a rock. You can't even kick them off. You can basically use them as footholds when you're climbing.'

She consults her phone to pull up the official Google definition.

'*A cone-shaped sea snail.* Well, shit, look at that – I did not know it was a snail. The point is that they glue themselves to the sides of rocks and they are impossible to move. Tit limpets are the same way. They will stay with their face glued to your boobs for, like, *hours.*'

'There's just no way. You're messing with me.'

'I'm deadly serious.'

'How do they breathe?'

'I don't know how they breathe, Candice. But they do. They will sleep with a tit in each hand, face mashed against your ribcage, and wake up two hours later fresh as a daisy.'

'So, you're talking about, like, after sex, right?'

'After. Before. During. Any time really. It doesn't even have to be related to sex. If you're horizontal on any relatively soft surface, that's all it takes for them to start tit-limpeting.'

'Please stop putting those words together,' I say, my head beginning to ache. 'You're gonna give me nightmares.'

'Sorry. My bad.'

'Okay, the Poet is a limpet, the Doberman is a cucumber. Who does that leave?' I ask, flicking on the little white lights that are strung all around the chair rails and window casings of the café.

'The Irishman. But I can't even talk about the Irishman

because it's too bloody embarrassing and, coming from me, that's saying something. Ask me another day.'

Joseph used to say he had Irish blood in him, from a great-great-grandfather somewhere along the line, which he thought explained his love of beer and cursing.

It will just be getting dark in Oahu, seven thousand miles away from here, and eleven hours behind us on Hawaii Standard Time. The sun still hours away from rising again over the house where Joseph and I had loved each other so deeply. Fought so bitterly.

But I can't think about that right now. All I want is to stand in the window and turn my face to the sun, to let the shadows fall behind me.

Which is just what I would do, if there wasn't so much prep work to get through before the tourists arrive for the day. Once the first one comes through the door it will be non-stop crazy running about until the last one leaves. And that's usually the way I prefer things to go, because it makes the time pass quicker, and I want as much time as I can get between the me from now on and the me who was spoken for by Joseph.

The café door opens with a little ding of the bell, and the outline of a man blocks the light streaming in from outside.

'Sorry, mate, we're not open yet,' Makayla says, before she gets a good look at him.

When she does, her eyes widen, and I know exactly what she's thinking because I'm thinking it too.

This man is gorgeous. Beyond gorgeous. He is, as Makayla will tell me later, *horrifically hot*.

His dark hair is damp, he's wearing running shorts with a

creased white T-shirt, and he has a leather laptop bag slung over his shoulder.

'Oh, sorry,' he says, sweeping aviator sunglasses up onto his head. 'Caffeine addiction got me out of bed way too early this morning. What time do you open?'

He has the sort of English accent I've only heard in Hugh Grant movies, but also an edge, like he's trying to sound more 'street' because he thinks that will make him seem cooler to regular people.

'Another fifteen,' I say, glancing at the clock. 'Scratch that. Fourteen.'

He raises an eyebrow at me. Clearly, I don't have the Cornish accent he was expecting. Both of us are visitors to this town.

'Is it okay if I wait in the seating area outside? Will I pick up the Wi-Fi out there? Or should I just hang fire on the internet until I can come in?'

'You know,' Makayla says, pursing her lips as if she's had to think real hard about this, 'I think we can make an exception this one time. What do you say, Candice? Shall we let our customer enter fourteen minutes before opening time?'

'The coffee machine isn't exactly ready right now,' I say smiling tightly, because the teenage temp who'd closed up yesterday had left without doing any of the usual cleaning, claiming a nosebleed when everyone knew he'd actually gone to start an early shift at the cinema. Also, if I had time to spare, I'd use it to read a few more pages of *The Unhoneymooners*. I could probably get through the next two chapters in fourteen minutes.

She breezes past my coffee machine concern like it's no objection, like it's missing the point.

'Come on in, my lover,' she says.

The way that some Cornish people say 'my lover' as a generic term of endearment is still so strange to me, but I've given up questioning it. It's just another one of those unfathomable things that I will never understand about this place.

'Are you sure it's all right?' he says. 'It's totally fine for me to wait outside. I don't want to get under your feet while you're setting up for the day.'

'You could never,' Makayla says. 'Come, come, come.'

I throw up my hands and motion to the espresso machine, which is still at least ten minutes away from being ready: the For-Fuck's-Sake Light is blinking, which means it has to complete a full clean cycle before it will even consider spitting out coffees.

'Coffee machine won't take long. What would you like to order, sir?'

She only says 'sir' when she's flirting. Which is always.

'I'd love a coffee, thanks. Sorry to be an annoying old prick, but do you use decent beans here?'

'Cornwall's finest,' she says, nodding to the Origin bags stacked behind the counter. 'You want real milk?' she asks. 'Or we have oat, almond, soya and coconut. The whole shebang.'

'Black is great.'

'Candice will make your drink while I plug you in.'

She says the last three words with such an evident double entendre that I have to bite my lip.

He grins from dimple to dimple and says, 'Really? Thank you so much.'

'Not a problem,' Makayla says, beaming back at him. 'There's a few tables near power points. I'll show you. You can take your pick.'

. She waves her hands around her face, like she's trying to inhale a smell she really likes. Which is probably exactly what she is trying to do.

Looking Makayla square in the eye, he says, 'I owe you one.'

Nice return innuendo, I think, as Makayla gravitates towards him like an extremely cute moth to an extremely sexy flame.

Here we go again, I think. The start of another of Makayla's great romantic adventures, which I'll experience, once again, as a loveless bystander. But why shouldn't she shoot her shot? Right now, everyone in this little beach town seems to be grabbing at fun like majorette batons, twirling them in their hands, turning somersaults and shrieking with laughter as they march through the high street in tie-dye tees and Bermuda shorts. Except for me. I'm not here for fun. I'm especially not here for romance. I'm here for a different reason altogether.

The guy chooses his table and sits down. He's completely engrossed in unloading his items from his messenger bag, like a little boy arranging his favourite toys in just the right way. Or a person who thinks a café table needs the same ergonomic arrangement as a personal desk.

His head is tilted forward, and his hair is loose, just a little longer than his chin – the man-boy curtains style that was all the rage in 1994, which I know because so many of my aunt's surfer boyfriends rocked it. Or thought they rocked it.

He has a notebook with him, along with his laptop, cell phone and a headset with a mic, presumably so he can take business calls, and maybe personal ones too. Plus a paperback novel. When I catch a glimpse of the cover, it makes me frown. Because it's not the kind I'd expect him to be reading. Not Bukowski. Not even Hemingway. It's the kind with a pink cover and a long cartoon leg wearing a giant red stiletto. The kind that Joseph used to try to make me feel bad for reading when he saw them stacked up on my nightstand. The kind I still have in my van now, as battered and bruised as their owner.

'He's really making himself at home here,' I say to Makayla.

'Bless him,' she says.

The guy plugs his fancy white power cord into the outlet, squeezes in earbuds and starts typing.

'This is not a bless him situation,' I say, smiling tightly. 'This is more of a fuck him situation. And not in a sexual intercourse way.'

'But it could be,' she says. 'A bit of "touch therapy" would do you good.'

Makayla frequently makes a point of telling me that I'm touch-deprived; mostly because she wants to give me a head massage, I suspect. But it's hard to argue with her, because sometimes I find myself longing, yearning, for physical contact. Sometimes at night, my arms still reach for Joseph in bed, even though I know he's on the other side of the world in the middle of the Pacific Ocean, even though I hate his guts.

*

Laptop Guy types steadily for the next two hours, while tourists stream in and out around him. He talks to me just the one time, when he asks me to watch his computer while he uses the bathroom, which, fine – it's not like I have anything else to do. It's not as if I'm here to work.

I stand by his table the whole time he's gone, hands in my back pockets, making a point. But he doesn't seem to notice. When he comes back, he says thanks and plugs his earbuds back in.

I go to collect a bunch of plates and when I return, I see Makayla hovering behind him. She beams her brightest smile at me when I catch her eye and mouths the words, 'Ask him out,' then does the obscenest hand gesture in her repertoire, which involves the V-sign and multiple tongue flicks.

'No,' I mouth back. I ignore Makayla's sad face and double thumbs-down as she goes to deal with a new line of customers.

I'm serving a family from London who have been in every day of their vacation, along with their warring teenage daughters Venetia and Phoenicia, when I see a hand waving about in my peripheral vision.

'Isn't it supposed to be Demogorgon? Spelt with an o in the middle, not an i?' Laptop Guy says, as if he's deeply worried by this. He's staring up at the sign above the counter.

'I don't know,' I say. 'It's our friend's place. She picked the name.'

'And, let me guess, she's a big fan of *Stranger Things*, right?'

'No, she's never seen that show.'

I know this because customers ask her all the time and she always sets them straight.

'She's old-school Dungeons and Dragons,' Makayla says, bringing tall lemonades to Venetia and Phoenicia, who are glaring at each other.

'Dungeons and Dragons?' the guy says, still staring at the sign with a troubled expression. As if he's discovered a fatal flaw; a misspelling that will necessitate the expensive commission of a whole new sign and promotional materials.

'D&D had a Demogorgon and our boss was well into the weird shit back in the eighties,' Makayla says. 'Medusa and the Gorgons too, cos she has mad curly hair. Not as mad as mine but getting there.'

The guy seems a little disappointed. Perhaps he was hoping to get talking on plot points from his favourite TV show.

'Also, and maybe we should have led with this,' I say, 'her name is Demi.'

He finally looks away from the sign and grins, relieved that it's a deliberate choice, not a mistake after all. 'She sounds interesting.'

Demi is more than just interesting. She is the most compassionate person I've ever met. She remembers how it feels to have no money in her account. She remembers it so well that anytime I look the least bit hungry she gives me takeout containers of highly calorific food to take home. Pizza slices, parcels of fries, sticky chicken. The sort of foodstuffs that could build up my fat reserves enough to take me through a Russian winter.

Demi has her own way of doing things that has very little

to do with the best way to make money, which makes it hard to believe her café has been in business for fifteen years. She regularly gives away meals for free – to homeless folks, elderly people who tell her they're struggling, and anyone else who needs a helping hand. Warmth radiates from her like sunshine. My mom was loving, in a tough way, but she was not affectionate. She was not like this. Demi wraps me in a bear hug every day I come into work, and I always want that hug. I look forward to it. Some days, it's the only touch I get from another human being.

'Demi is great,' I say. 'She's basically a genius. She's a member of Mensa.'

'She can finish *The Times* crossword in twenty minutes. Forty tops,' Makayla adds. 'I don't know why she's running a café when she could be running the government. Oh, yeah, I do know why. She was born in Camborne and then moved here.'

'Where?' the guy asks, sounding genuinely interested.

'Camborne. One of the poorest parts of Cornwall,' I say. 'And it doesn't even have a beach.'

'Heck of a mining museum, though,' Makayla says. 'And don't forget Tahiti.'

'What does Tahiti have to do with anything?' I ask. Trying to keep up with Makayla's brain and her conversational switch-ups is always a challenge.

'I said *TEHIDY*. You know, the country park. Full of trees, wildflowers, lily pads, squirrels and all that other nature shit.'

'I'll have to visit,' the guy says, apparently making a note of it on the document he has open on his laptop, which I'm frothing to read over his shoulder, if only I can find a way to do it without him noticing.

I glance at the clock. It's 11 a.m. and our breakfast menu will close in a half-hour. Then there'll be a thirty-minute break while the kitchen staff prepare for lunch.

'Would you like to order something to eat?' I ask him, figuring that if I don't ask, he'll probably try to order eggs benedict the moment the kitchen closes.

'No, thanks.'

'You aren't hungry?' Makayla asks. 'The food here is pretty good. Especially if you like avocados.'

'I don't, unfortunately. To me they taste like, well… pond slime.'

I twitch. Is he trying to be cute? Who doesn't like avocados? And who, for that matter, knows what pond slime tastes like?

Although, given this guy is maybe one of Tom Hiddleston's younger cousins, he probably grew up with a lake in his garden and swam cold water laps before breakfast.

'But it's not that,' he goes on, before I can unruffle my feathers enough to form a reply. 'I don't eat during the day. I'm IF.'

'Oh, sure,' I say, as if I understand what he's talking about; wondering what medical condition he could be referencing with those two letters.

'Pardon me?' Makayla asks, her eyebrows dancing skyward.

'Sorry. Intermittent Fasting. I prefer to fast during the day. It keeps me leaner and makes my brain more alert. I've been on this regime for almost a year now. For a while before that, I was mostly on bone broth. For my gut health,' he explains.

'Oh,' I murmur, which is all I have to say about that.

'Really?' Makayla says, stunned. 'You can go a whole day without eating, like, anything? How are you still standing up?'

And how, I wonder, *are you building all that muscle?*

'Another coffee, then?' I ask.

'No, I'm good and caffeinated now, thanks. I'd love to grab a glass of water, though, if that's okay?'

'Sure thing,' I say. 'Still or sparkling?'

'Tap water is fine.'

'It can be a little cloudy here,' I lie.

'I'm not fussy,' he answers. 'So long as it won't poison me, I'll drink it.'

'No worries,' Makayla says, pouring him a tall glass of faucet water with lemon and taking it to his table. 'Just shout if you need anything else.'

He thanks her and cosies down back at his primo table by the window.

'He's probably going to be typing away over there all day, you know that, right?' I say to Makayla, when she comes to make a face at me and whisper the word 'fasting' in the same hushed tones that somebody might say 'leprosy' or 'cannibal'.

'Yeah, I bet he is,' she says.

'And you don't find that annoying?' I ask.

'No, I hope he's here all day *every* day,' she says, opening a container of yoghurt and managing to eat the entire contents in two gigantic spoonfuls. 'He's the hottest weirdo we've had in a while. I'm crossing my fingers he stays until closing.'

The guy doesn't even seem to notice that we're talking about him. He's completely absorbed in whatever it is he's doing on his laptop.

'Makayla,' I say, when another thirty minutes have passed, without him once looking up from his keyboard. 'We should move him to one of the back tables, don't you think? The one he's on has, like, four place settings and the lunch rush will be starting up soon. People will get mad at him for taking a whole family table to himself.'

'Oh, leave him be. He'll bring in extra customers if people see him in here. Nice little honeypot to attract the thirsty bees.'

'I'm not trying to be unkind to this… strange guy,' I say, meeting her eyes, 'But he seems totally unaware that Demi is operating a business. He's literally never going to order food. By the time he eats, we're closed. We can't even charge him for the water.'

'Yeah, but look at him,' she says, indulgently. 'He's Regulation Hot.'

'What does that *mean*?'

'Ticks all the boxes. Tall, broad, pretty eyes, sensual mouth. Great hair.'

'So what?'

'He's operating under a different instruction manual, isn't he? Normal rules are for normal people.'

'You did not just say that.'

'No, I would never say something that stupid.'

'Seriously, Makayla. Stop indulging the—'

'The hot stranger?'

'The hot *entitled* stranger. Let me set him up on one of the crappy tables. He won't mind. How can he? He's not even appreciating the ocean view. He could be typing in a closet for all he knows.'

'Don't you dare move him,' Makayla says.

'What are you thinking about?' I say, eyeing her suspiciously. 'You have a weird look on your face.'

She shrugs. 'My mind's a filthy place. Worse than Fistral Beach after Boardmasters.'

I've heard all about Boardmasters from almost every local person I've met here. Once a small Fistral Beach surf contest, now a major music festival alongside the surf contest, it attracts tens of thousands of party people. It's this town's Coachella, and the mess it leaves behind is equally epic, which is why the organisation usually offers free tickets to anyone who wants to wake up at the break of dawn and litter-pick the beaches.

'He's perfect where he is,' Makayla says. 'Right in my line of sight.'

Two

Makayla and I run about bussing tables, and the guy types away as if we don't even exist. People come in, eat and leave again all around him, bickering over shared orders of fries or laughing so hard they snort soda out their noses. Some American tourists sit down, giddy with excitement to be in Cornwall. I can hear them geeking out over the fact that they're really truly in the location from *Poldark*, even though none of it was filmed at this beach, but a little further down the coast.

'What's good here?' they ask me, eyes running down the menu.

'The sausage rolls are excellent,' I say.

'I don't think I've ever tasted one of those before. Is it, like, a breakfast food or a lunch food?'

'You can eat one whenever. It's savoury, with black pepper. Sort of like an old-school wiener wrap with ground sausage meat wrapped in puff pastry. It's good.'

I have a sense that I'm being watched and turn to see that Laptop Guy is listening to every word of this exchange, as if we've been discussing something momentous, instead of highly seasoned meat pastries.

When I pass his table, I look down at his open leather-bound notebook and, at the top of a blank page, I see he has written 'wiener wrap' and underlined it twice, which is so bizarre that I don't even know what to do with that, except tell Makayla the first chance I get.

'Don't you think that's weird?' I ask her, shooting her a look.

She twists up her lips, thinking of a way she can make that not weird, then holds her hands up in surrender.

'Okay, that's definitely a little bit unusual.'

*

Laptop Guy types on. He stops every now and again to stretch his arms over his head, revealing neat sweat patches under his arms. Sometimes he mixes things up by massaging his neck and the tops of his shoulders.

There's something about the way he keeps frowning at his computer screen and sighing that makes it seem as if he wants me to ask him what he's doing, so that he can tell me a story that he thinks I'll find impressive.

Which doesn't, unfortunately, dampen my curiosity at all.

'What are you doing over here?' I say, at last, when all the other customers have finally taken the hint and gone back to their vacation rentals. 'Looks kind of intense.'

'It's nothing really. Just a project I have to work on this summer. I'm up against a bit of a deadline. Under the gun, truth be told, although it pains me to admit it.'

'What kind of project would that be, then?' Makayla says, leaving the kitchen where she's been asking the chef Jeremy about his recollections of the Fistral surf scene during the early nineties, most of which seem to revolve around strawberry acid trips and other psychedelics.

'I can't really talk about it yet. It's sort of, well, top secret, if it's not too dickish to say that.'

'Are you an agent for MI5?' Makayla asks. 'Because if so, I'd say you need to work on your spy-craft if you're using Demigorgons' completely hackable guest Wi-Fi.'

'No,' he shakes his head. 'I'm not that cool. I suppose I can say it's a new… commercial venture. I'm just redrafting the proposal at the moment.'

He isn't the only one trying to launch a new commercial venture. Except mine's looking like it's going to start falling earthward right after blast-off. It's looking a lot like I'd barely even clear the Kennedy Space Center before the critical errors kicked in. I've had fifty business cards printed up for my surf lesson business and Demi has agreed to put them by the cash register, where her customers won't be able to help seeing them. So far, this excellent business strategy of mine has resulted in exactly zero bookings. But several little kids have gotten tiny canvases to doodle over.

Part of me wanted to sweep those cards straight into the garbage pail, but another part of me, the part that didn't want Joseph to be right, told me to hang in there. Nobody could make this happen for me. I had to make it happen by myself.

'Oh,' Makayla says, sounding a little disappointed.

Laptop Guy smiles and closes the lid of his laptop.

'So, we'll see you again this week?' Makayla enquires in a neutral tone, as if she's not at all invested in his answer.

'Absolutely. I've actually taken the cottage for the whole summer.'

Jeremy, who's just come out of the kitchen for an end-of-shift bottle of beer, looks impressed by the idea of taking a cottage for a whole season, as if this guy has achieved something remarkable, rather than just being rich enough to block-rent a property in an expensive location.

'Sweet,' Makayla says, punching the air down by her hip, so that I can see it, but Laptop Guy can't. Like she's excited for me.

'Yep, and this is my new favourite workspace.'

I stop myself from pointing out that he's actually talking about our workspace, which he's been invading with his annoying tip-tappy typing and his regular stretching programme, both of which are extremely distracting to servers trying to deal with real customers who order more than coffees and waters they don't pay for.

'He's here all summer, girls,' Jeremy says. 'Lucky us. I wish my husband would stop in. I've worked here over a month now and he won't even come for a coffee. And he walks past every day, the antisocial bastard.'

'Why is he like that?' I ask. I've heard Jeremy grumble a few times about his husband this past week. They're clearly going through something.

'Don't ask me. He hardly ever goes out, except to metal detect. Says he doesn't like eating and drinking in front of strangers. Says it's because his jaw clicks from an old surf injury, but the acoustics in here are terrible. Who would even hear a jaw clicking over all the chatter? He's just a miserable git who hates everyone.'

'Maybe he's just shy?' Makayla says. 'Can't blame him. Demi is pretty intimidating.'

'I really should be going,' the Laptop Guy says, looking

8910

a little uncomfortable now, as if he's fourth-wheeling the Demigorgons comedy act.

'Why don't you walk him home, Candice?' Makayla says suddenly. 'We can lock up. You're both going the same way. You might as well.'

I make 'You are batshit crazy' eyes at her and feel all the blood rush to my face.

'I'm actually getting in the ocean just now, but maybe some other time?' I say, knowing for certain that there'll never be another time because I'll never let myself say yes to this.

This is my chance to find out what I want and who I am, and I won't be able to do that if I get distracted by a hot stranger.

Plus, all my yesses were burnt out in another life. For the rest of this one, however long it lasts, I intend to be all about the *no fucking way*.

Three

I watch Laptop Guy walk away towards the surf complex, and feel a wave of disappointment rise up my throat. On the one hand I'm happy he's finally vacated the table, because the noise of his typing was starting to feel a little like a pneumatic drill to my third eye, the spiritual one my yoga teacher talks about, located right between the eyebrows. But on the other hand, I was curious to see what he was working on, and I guess now I'll never know. Maybe I should have asked him when I had the chance. But the tourists, they come and go, never to be seen again. That's just the nature of a beach resort – something Makayla likes to tell me, in a reassuring way, whenever she's slept with one of the previous day's customers.

She sees me watching him go.

'He must be minted if he's hired one of those Towan Headland cottages, cos they cost like four grand a week in high season.'

'He may have just gotten a good deal from someone he knows,' I say. 'He seems like the type to know fancy people.'

'I reckon he *is* fancy people. We get all sorts in this town.'

She sighs, heavily. So heavily that I stop what I'm doing and turn all my attention to her.

'What's wrong?' I ask.

'Live and learn,' she says, like she's saying something important to me. Something I will instantly understand and recognise to be true.

'How do you figure?'

'The road not taken.'

'Uh, what are you talking about, Makayla?'

'I don't know how I know this, Candice – it might be because my grandmother was an actual witch who read tealeaves – but I'm telling you that guy was your road not taken.'

'That's what you're saying? Some random guy with pretty hair and a fancy laptop is my destiny?'

'I didn't say "destiny". But he was definitely a road that you could have ridden on.'

'So, in this scenario my life is... a bike?'

'Absolutely. A really cool motorbike. Like, a retro Kawasaki. Electric green with black flames sprayed on the body. But the thing is, right now, it's just sat there in the garage, getting all dusty and crusty.'

'Wow, that might be the most insulting thing that any person has ever said to me.'

She puts up her hand for a high-five. 'Well, there you go,' she says, grinning. 'So now you'll always remember me.'

'There is no reality in which I could ever forget you, Makayla, and please tell me you meant rusty, not crusty.'

'I did not,' she says, solemnly, as I limply return her high-five just to make her put her hand down.

'To be clear with you,' I say. 'If my life is a bike, it for sure has pedals because I'm not poisoning the planet with toxic fumes, not if I have a choice in the matter. Don't look at me like that. My van is basically my house. And two, I'm pumping up those tyres, oiling the chain, and taking it for a spin every chance I get.'

'Sure you are,' she says, stroking my head. 'You're oiling your chain every day.'

There's just no arguing with Makayla. Even if I want to be mad at her, she slips past my line of defence and manages to make me laugh. She's the only person who's ever been able to do that.

But I can't shake off the ache in my chest. Something Makayla said has hit a nerve that has somehow run right to my sadness. I can't even figure out what exactly because so much has gotten twisted up in my head. Nothing I feel makes sense to me, and there's only one way I know how to handle that.

I go out back and change.

*

The tiredness of the morning has passed but I can feel it around the corner, waiting to ambush me, and I know that if I go home now, I'll crash out and that will be the end of the day. I need something else. Something to make this day not just about work.

I keep a board and wetsuit out back in the shack, nothing too expensive in case the place gets robbed, which is always a risk in a place that gets so many folks passing by.

The shack belongs to Demi, but we have a special

arrangement, which means I always have the option of paddling out to catch some waves after work.

Surfing is the only thing that has ever freed me from myself. There's no better way to redeem a day, no matter how bad the conditions are, no matter if I don't get a single good ride in a session.

Before I lock my bag and clothes back in the shack, I check my phone and see there's a message from my brother Ricky. My stomach lurches instantly, because I know what he's going to say, what he's going to want to know.

It's a long message and I only read the first sentence.

Are you any closer?

Then, I back out of the message and turn off my phone. I can't deal with that now. I need to surf first.

*

The conditions today are not great; too small for the serious surfers who won't want to be seen paddling out for waves any less than shoulder-high. As if small waves have a direct correlation to the size of something else.

I don't care about the visuals or the judgement of strangers. I don't buy into the ego and competitiveness of surf culture. Just moving with any wave is enough. It soothes my soul in a way I can't explain to people who don't surf. It strips the splinters of the day away, every single time.

I don't know why I let that guy from the café get under my skin the way I did. There's no solid reason for it. My mom used to say that when a new person irritated me past what was rational, it was because they reminded me of a thing I didn't like about myself, some trait I wished I didn't have. A theory she'd picked up from a self-help book she'd read one summer, a book which seemed to have stuck in her head for life. But the guy from the café is nothing like me. All he cares about is his own comfort, the way the world can accommodate him and his very particular needs. Which is not me. Which *can't* be me.

So maybe, then, Makayla is right. Maybe the guy was, in some way I can't imagine right now, my road not taken, which makes no sense at all.

And yet. Something about him made me stop. Not just the way he looked, although that had something to do with it, in the same way that seeing Mr Darcy emerge from the lake at Pemberley made Lizzy Bennet back up in the TV adaptation of *Pride and Prejudice*.

But there was something else, too. There was a moment of recognition. The recognition you feel when you meet the people you were somehow meant to meet in life, not necessarily in a romantic sense, or even a friendship sense, but the ones who make you pivot in some way, toward something new.

Which I would never admit to Makayla, because she would never stop talking about it.

When I'm suited up and have finished waxing diamonds onto the deck of my board, I give Makayla a wave as I pass Demigorgons. She's still in there, holding a dishcloth and flirting with Jeremy, who has been married to his husband for eight years and who is also at least fifty-five years old, which is within Makayla's age bracket for dating, but only just. Her guidelines seem to be no ages that start with a one – not even nineteen-year-olds, even though she's only twenty-four herself – and then all the way up through the ages until the sixes start. The gay and married thing would be a problem, though.

She comes to the door when she sees me.

'Be safe out there,' she hollers. 'Don't get washed away!'

'The waves are twelve inches today. Eighteen on a good set.'

'Might be a freak wave. You never know. My nan used to say, "Never turn your back to the sea."'

'You kind of have to when you're surfing,' I point out.

'All I'm saying is be careful.'

'Didn't we just cover this? I'll be fine. I'm always fine.'

'Watch out for rip currents. Don't forget that one that sucks surfers around the headland there to the beach at Little Fistral.'

'Okay, Mom, I think I got it,' I say, smiling.

I cross the parking lot, weaving through groups of men. It looks to be a large bachelor party. Half of the guys are tattooed and bare-chested, T-shirts tucked into the back pockets of cargo shorts. They're all different ages, from teenage boys right up to guys in their seventies. And they look so happy to be here. So thrilled that they've left their worries and commitments behind and actually made this trip. This town can bring tourists so much happiness. It can leave them memories that will last a lifetime.

I'm smiling to myself when I see the bachelor himself, the man of the hour, turn his head to one side, cough up a bunch of phlegm and shoot it onto the sidewalk.

This is the kind of thing that Demi wouldn't let stand. She would make that guy wait right there while she went into the café for a Tupperware of hot soapy water and a scrubbing brush. She'd make him wash it clean while she watched. I make do with giving him the stink-eye and, to his credit, he at least has the grace to look a little uncomfortable.

Grossness aside, my heart begins to flutter the way it always does when I walk down to a beach, but particularly this one. Fistral Beach.

The saltwater dip will cleanse me of feelings, at least for a little while. Which makes me think of all those shirts I see teenage surfer girls wearing nowadays that say, 'Catch Waves Not Feelings', and how much I love that. I'll always be grateful to my mom for taking me into the waves and teaching me to surf. Surfing gives me a place to belong, because as soon as I'm in the ocean, I feel part of something, something huge and powerful. A thing as big and mysterious as the universe. A thing that makes me realise it's okay to be here. That maybe, in some small way, I have a place in the world.

Once I've paddled through the impact zone – no problem at all in these conditions – I hang out in the line-up, where surfers wait for waves, sitting on my board and breathing deeply, soaking in the energy and beauty of the ocean. Once I catch my first ride, I can feel all my negativity slipping away with the water.

In the end, I only catch a handful of waves, but I get some good rides and come out of the water feeling better than I did when I went in. I can feel the skin of my face glowing from exercise and saltwater and the shallows are warm against the cold skin of my feet. The sky is soft, painted in pastel shades, and everything seems peaceful, as if I'm in the right place at the right time and everything is going to work out just fine. My fears don't have to be real. They could come to nothing. The worst-case scenario doesn't have to be my reality.

I rinse off underneath the giant flipflop shower on the beach and get changed into sweats beneath my dryrobe. There's no wind, the air is still weirdly warm, and the sun is low in the sky. Fistral faces due west and when the sun sets it disappears straight into the water, into the very centre of this bay.

There are people scattered along the sand at regular intervals. Groups of teenagers staring off at other groups of teenagers, wondering if they'll join up before this evening is through. Twenty-something couples, tangled up in each other, kissing like it's their last chance. Beach bunnies, too cold to stay in their bikinis and done for the day with tanning, covering up in long flannel shirts that come down to their knees, which look like they belong to their boyfriends. Boyfriends who are probably still in the ocean, catching just one more good ride, like I have just been trying to do in there with them, before they call it a night. Longboarders and shortboarders, walking in different directions, back to their surf wagons waiting at opposite ends of the beach, to sleep a few hours and return with the sunrise. This moment, this vibe, is the dream that so many people come here to experience. The fizz of being part of something special. They are here to share in the magic of this place. Magic that creeps along the beach like the mist that comes down from the north end of the shore right after the sun sets, making everything softer and hazy and quiet.

I look sideways at the last two groups of young families, headed by surfer moms and dads, taking turns feeding their passion and feeding their kids. One parent in the ocean, one on the sand. The one out just waiting for their next turn to get back in the water between handing out hot dogs from disposable grills and doughnuts warm from the heat of the day. Then, when they know they have to leave, even though they're not ready yet, trying to get everything packed up before the baby wakes and starts yelling, because it's too late to be on the beach, at five minutes past ten on a school night, but they're here all the same because how can they not be, with this sunset happening and these waves? How can they make the sensible choice when the dream choice is right there, just waiting to be snatched out of the air, out of the water, like a gift? A gift from gods who know better than to live by schedules.

I catch wisps of their voices on the still night air, just beyond the reach of the sea's roar, and I can't help wondering if Joseph and I could have been like them, raising a family like this. Free and unencumbered by feeling we had to do everything the right way.

But Joseph never wanted kids, and that was fine, I agreed it was fine whenever we talked about it, which we did a lot at first, before and after we got married. Which made it so much more of a surprise when he got Issy pregnant – a fact I heard from my brother, who informed me in a video call a few months after I arrived in Newquay. Information I didn't need to know right then, but which Ricky thought I absolutely did need to know.

I'd never heard my brother so angry. He almost never uses curse words, but that day he called Joseph a *son of a bitch*, and then immediately apologised for bringing

Joseph's mother into it, when it wasn't her fault that her son was a *piece of shit*.

My mind was spinning out. Issy, my best friend since the first day of elementary school, was pregnant with the child of my husband, who had been my boyfriend since college. Each of them contributing fifty percent of their DNA to make a whole new person.

The thought of the physical stuff between them I can deal with. The anatomy of it all. All animals have sex. But the thought of them cosy on a couch, gazing into each other's eyes, full of hope and dreams, and planning out a whole new life together, raising kids, is still too much for me to handle.

And what is even the point of thinking about that when all it does is hurt? And they are not the people it hurts. They are happy. They are just great together, prepping for their new life as a family by the ocean, just like this family I'm trying not to stare at now.

But Joseph and Issy are beside the point.

I'm not even here because of them. I'm in England, in Cornwall, in this little beach town Newquay, not to run away from them. I am here to try to find something. Something that has nothing to do with them. To locate a thing I need, for me. And I have to find it, because if I don't, I think I will maybe lose my mind.

I take the paperback out of my bag. Now that I'm warm and I can feel my fingers and toes again, I'll read by the golden light of sunset. The tatty novel with turned-down pages and a creased cover that I currently keep in my beach bag is a romance I picked up in a thrift store, about two warring painters who start out as professional rivals and wind up lovers. Who wind up married, but are still professional rivals, just ones who support each other by sharing brushes and paint thinner. I've read it before but that doesn't stop me wanting to soak in the juice of the story again. There's a comfort in reading books when I know how they end. When I know that a happy ending is coming, if the characters just make the right mistakes and learn from them.

When the lowest curve of the setting sun is only minutes from dipping onto the horizon, a young couple walks to the waterline, side by side.

They stand there together, totally still and silent. It takes me a moment to realise what is happening, but then I figure out that they are waiting. And at the very moment the sun begins to set, they start to kiss. They kiss for the whole time it takes the sun falls into the sea, opening their eyes every now and then to check on that setting sun, and when it disappears from sight, they leave too.

They don't look at the ocean for one moment longer. They don't wait for the orange glow to intensify as the sky darkens to an inky blue beyond it. They just turn and walk away, hand in hand, because they've done what they wanted, what they came here to do. They've added this particular moment to their relationship memory bank.

Did Joseph ever kiss me like that?

No, he'd thought that kind of romance was performative, box-checking, though he wouldn't have used those words. Corny is the word he'd have used. Did he kiss Issy like that? And why, after everything, does that even matter to me?

I throw my book in my bag and am starting to walk back to Demi's house, where my van is parked, when I see another person on the beach. Above this person, there are lights glowing in the sky, one hundred feet up.

I frown because it looks so strange there, hovering like a UFO, like the spaceship from the movie *E.T.* Mesmerising, beautiful and completely weird.

It's a drone. A fancy drone that must have cost someone a whole lot of money. The type used by professional photographers to capture breath-taking pictures of this famous beach that people from cities will buy and install above their beds, to remind themselves of their soul home, the dream they are working toward.

The drone pilot must be somewhere around here although I can't see him, and I'd bet my board that it is a him. Maybe that pilot is up in the dunes with the party people and free-campers, who are making the most of the fact that this campsite has the best view in town and no fees to pay, even though it isn't strictly legal or even a little way responsible, because of damage done to the dune ecosystem.

The pilot has flown the drone directly above the person at the water's edge, snapping pictures for an image that will appear on Instagram or Facebook sometime soon. It occurs to me that I'm also in range, I'll be in that photo too, a tiny black outline of a surfer walking with a board, lit up in the sunset, just like the postcards sold to happy tourists who want to take a piece of this place home with them, to stick on their refrigerator when they need help remembering.

As I walk closer, I can see the outline of the person's body against the vivid glow of the horizon and I'm pretty confident that it's a man. He's standing, sneakers still on his feet, right at the very edge of where the water laps, keeping his toes just out of its reach. He doesn't want wet shoes. He definitely doesn't want wet feet. It's important to him that he keeps dry, which makes me wonder why he's standing there at all.

He has long hair and at first I think it's just another surfer who doesn't have his board this time, on a date or coming home from work maybe, but checking out the way the surf is working, because it's ingrained in us to do that, to identify the rip currents and sandbanks, trying to see how it's all coming together. But what surfer would care about keeping their feet dry? Not one I've ever met.

His hand goes to his face and it stays there. He has his back to me, so I can't be sure, but I think he might be crying. Standing alone at the water's edge, crying. Which happens here and at every beach break I've ever surfed. Something about the water moves the emotions in people, bringing them to the surface like air bubbles.

When he turns his head a little, I see that I'm wrong about him. He's not crying at all, he's smoking. Marijuana, going by the smell drifting toward me. He's likely having a moment, thinking about what this all means, like people do when they look at the ocean, hoping, even if we don't say it, to figure out something about this life, maybe what it means to be alive, to be a human person who is living a life that's worth something, a life that matters at all in the grand scheme of things.

Too late, I see the other thing. The man has turned a little and has registered me standing here. He's looking at me, almost like he knows me, or like he expects me to recognise him. Which I don't, at first, but then I notice the great bone structure. The shape of his face is beautiful even from this distance, even in semi-darkness.

I can't be certain of it – that's what I tell myself – but he sure looks like the guy from Demigorgons, although he's dressed different. Mr Tippytappy with the laptop. He raises his hand to me, but only halfway, not a hip wave but not a real wave either. He's not sure that he knows me, not sure that I'm the waitress who served him water all day.

I don't know what to do with his uncertainty. I'm not going to walk right up to him and offer a fist-bump. Ask him if he's had a snack yet and broken his fast.

So, I pretend I don't see him there, that my eyes are too bad to see in this low light, that I can't be expected to notice a thing like a person waving at me from fifty yards away.

I tighten my grip on my board, feeling the tired muscles of my arms flex, and turn my back to him. I'll take the dune path that leads past the golf course. I'll carry my worn-out, dinged-up board and my worn-out, dinged-up self all the way back home.

Just when I'm near the top of the first dune, weaving between the dead Christmas trees that conservationists have used to shore up the bank, I turn around to take one last look at the waterline, half expecting to see the guy still there, watching me walk away. But I don't see him. He's disappeared.

He must have walked fast to get off the main expanse of the beach and over the rocks, where I can't see him. Jogged, maybe. He must have stubbed out his joint and really gone for it. Then my eyes focus on a little bundle of something near the water's edge and I search the waves. Beyond the break, in the deep water of the bay, I see the silhouette of a person sunset swimming. Not playing, not splashing about like a kid and feeling the beat of the waves, but swimming powerfully towards the headland – front crawl, like an athlete. Could it be the man who was keeping his feet dry, the one who may or not be – but probably was – Laptop Guy?

I don't know. Maybe.

I don't stay to watch, a thing I would do if he were a weaker swimmer, just to make sure he was okay and didn't need my help or a call to the emergency services if he got caught in a rip current. I can see just from his swim technique that whoever this swimmer is, he doesn't need someone looking out for him. He knows what he's doing. He's got it all figured out.

Good for you, I think.

Maybe he can give me pointers, because I've got no clue how to get where I need to be.

Four

I feel alone in a way I haven't in a while, and I almost go knock on Demi's door, to ask if she wants company. But I know she'd say that she does. She'd let me in whatever the circumstances, telling me once again that I have an open invitation to join her for movie nights and dinner any time I want. But I never knowingly bother her when she has company over and, judging by the van in her drive, I'd warrant she does have company right now.

Instead, I run my fingers over the battered spines of my pile of paperbacks, most of which I bought from the Cornwall Air Ambulance charity shop in the main part of town. I never just have one book on the go. I like to be in the middle of at least four new stories and old favourites that I dip into, depending on the way I'm feeling that day. Today I want nostalgia and I take my worn copy of *Pride and Prejudice* from its place underneath my pillow. The first time I read it, I was in middle school and the main thing I took away from it was that British people were really hung up on money in a way that just didn't make sense to me. I couldn't believe that they talked actual figures when discussing incomes. I didn't know why that was so important. My mom knew, though.

She sat me down one afternoon, when the weather was too hot and the house was too empty, and explained that money was the reason we'd lost my father. After he was medically discharged from the US Air Force, he couldn't take the stress of having to provide for his family on odd jobs that he could never depend on coming when he needed them. That he would rather be away from us than see us every day and know he was failing to provide. Not long after, he went out to the offshore oil rigs to work as a roughneck. He sent back money, so there was always enough food on the table, but when we needed him, he couldn't be there.

The company determined the accident was of a 'slip, trip and fall' nature, but they left out the part about him being an overworked employee, who hadn't been adequately provided with mandatory rest periods. We learnt that from the broken-up guys who attended his funeral, who were there when the accident happened, who couldn't save him.

His insurance paid out enough that my mom would be comfortable for the rest of her life. But that money was only there because my father lost his life working in a place that was hazardous, work she never wanted him to do in the first place. It made her hate money. Not just the money from his death benefits, but all money. The system of money. It pained her every time she saw a bank statement. She wanted nothing to do with it.

Mr Darcy offered money in a way that meant Elizabeth Bennet would never have to think about it or worry about it. She wouldn't have to look at numbers on a spreadsheet to figure out if she could pay rent that month or buy food for her children. Mr Darcy's 'large income' meant freedom to worry about other things, like what she wanted to do with her life, the kind of person she wanted to be. It also gave her a huge park to walk around in, a string of little dogs trotting behind her. Or so I imagine.

Right now, all I want to do is read. I want to read myself to sleep and read again for at least an hour when I wake up. This is the other way I treat myself, the other way I have fun.

★

For the first time in I don't even know how long, I don't wake every hour of the night, drenched in a cold sweat, panicking about all the things I can't change. I put my head down on my pillow and it stays there until 5 a.m., when I'm woken by the sound of music. There's a second when I wonder where I am, when I almost roll over and reach for Joseph, as if we're together sleeping in our home in Oahu, in the bedroom we painted together in separate shades, three walls my choice and the feature wall his. It's crazy to me that these moments of confusion still happen, even now, all these months on, when my subconscious should know better.

The music gets louder until it seems right outside. Somebody is playing Van Halen's song 'Jump', which is both the best and worst choice for this time of the morning.

I sit up too quickly and bang my head on the metal roof, which I've pretty much stopped doing, but the deep sleep has sunk my brain into a fog. I don't feel like I'm waking up ready to start a new day. It's more like I'm emerging from a coma.

As well as the shriek of music, there's also some kind of voice counting down from ten to one and it keeps repeating. Is this some kind of a joke? Is there a bunch of wasted teenagers in Demi's yard hoping to wake up the neighbourhood?

There's a moment where the music stops and I try to go back to sleep, but then it starts up again and this time there's a definite thudding sound to go with it. I look at the digital display of my watch: 5.04 a.m.

I pull back the little curtain over my van's side window and see a flash of something yellow. My eyes adjust to the light of the dawn, and I realise what I'm looking at. A blonde ponytail. It keeps swishing up and down, right outside. My peripheral vision catches another movement. A brown ponytail. Two ponytails total. No explanation.

I sit there, head in my hands, trying to work out what's happening here. Eventually my brain gets it. Demi's back yard runs up against a tiny patch of grass with a view of the ocean. And two women have chosen this tiny patch of grass to do a very intense HIIT workout, with their own miniature speakers on blast.

Maybe they don't realise that the camper van on the other side of the low fence has a person inside of it. A person who has now been woken up from the best sleep maybe of her whole life.

They are really going for it. They are not holding back, at all. Their jumping jacks are fast and furious. Everything they're doing looks that way. Their high-knee jumps are so high that my weak knee throbs just watching them. How long can they go on like this? Surely they'll soon be through with this insanity exercise, and they'll go home?

Maybe they're tourists, staying in an Airbnb somewhere on this street. I hope they are. Because if they're locals, this could be their new favourite workout spot. This could go on all summer. Perhaps they just don't care that they're disturbing someone. Maybe this is a deliberate provocation. A statement against the van-life crowd, who clutter up passing places and beauty spots with their 'lazy lifestyle choices'.

I let the curtain fall again. They didn't even notice they were being watched. Or maybe they're so into their workout that a tree of Peeping Toms wouldn't stop them.

I might have to rethink my sleeping quarters.

I don't have to sleep in the van. It's a choice I keep making and I'm not even totally sure why.

Demi says it's fine for me to stay in her spare room, that it's 'got my name on it', and when I had food poisoning, I gave in. I loved the ready access to indoor plumbing and the way Demi brought me cups of hot tea with honey and lemon, and cool washcloths. But mostly I prefer to stay outside in the van, which she lets me park behind her house. I think she does this because she has a grown-up daughter who is also travelling the world alone and relying upon the kindness of strangers. She is hoping that with every kindness she does for me or some person else in need, her daughter will receive an act of kindness in return, over there in Australia or Cambodia or wherever she happens to be that week.

Eventually, after a whole hour, the loud music and counting stops. I twitch my curtain again and watch the women tear open Wet-Naps, which they use to wipe the sweat off their faces and underarms, before dabbing at themselves with fluffy white handtowels.

They have a whole process here, I see. An after-workout hygiene regimen.

When I hear them walk away, attempting talk to each other but too breathless to make full sentences, I curl my toes and try to go back to sleep. There's sand in my sheets but I don't brush it away. It's almost cosy to me, this sand, because it's the one constant in my life. There are different-coloured grains at home, made from different kinds of rocks, thrown out by volcanoes and coral. Here it's golden as sunlight, but some version is always with me, wherever I go, because I choose never to be far away from a beach. Joseph never saw it that way. Sand wasn't a comfort to him. He loved to surf, loved the freedom of the lifestyle that went with it, but he thought sand should stay on the beach.

He didn't say it out loud, in words, but he said it other ways, in sighs and eye rolls, that a good woman should make sure the house he lived in was swept clean every day. The house he lived in should be clean and tidy in all ways. And didn't I want to be a good woman to him?

I tried to be what he was looking for, because I liked seeing him happy, I liked seeing him pleased with me. But as time passed and he became less so, it became clear that even if I gave household chores every piece of energy I had, he would not be satisfied with me. Not all the time. And it would be unreasonable for him to expect that. So why did he?

I needed him to understand that I was trying, that I would always try for him, but that I couldn't be his everything. He needed people outside of me, to give him other things. Other types of friendship, of closeness. I didn't expect that he would take me telling him that as a green light to start something with my best friend. That he would even see that as a possibility.

When I was sitting on the airport tarmac, a plane ticket to England in my hand, waiting to leave my life behind, I thought about the grains of sand in my bag, on my skin, between my sheets, and how it was always there between us, like all the other things we couldn't brush away.

I thought he would be reasonable, that he would change, if I just knew how to say the exact right things at the exact right time, but I never could seem to do that. When I finally figured out what I wanted him to know, he was done trying to hear me.

He was unable – unwilling – to make compromises. His way was the right way and he didn't see a need to discuss other points of view, especially not with his wife, who he thought should trust his judgement, like his mom had always trusted his father's. When our surf shop faced tough months, he didn't want to try new ideas – my ideas – for pro-surfer meet-and-greet events, with online marketing spend and aggressive social media engagement. He thought that was selling out, becoming part of the rank commercialisation of surfing, when what he wanted was to provide a service: to get the right gear to the right people. He thought principles mattered more than the bottom line. He thought he knew best. But how could you not think in a commercial way when you were running a shop?

If I had known out of the gate that he had this seam of inflexibility in him, solid as the wooden stringer running from nose to tail down the centre of a surfboard, would it have changed anything? Would I have accepted that it was there forever, or would I have still tried to break it, even though I knew for sure it would ruin the whole thing?

I don't have the answer to that question. And I don't understand why my mind keeps turning all of this over, when it's too late to change anything.

Maybe I should go surf again. My suit's still damp from last night and no one wants to put on cold wet neoprene on a chilly summer morning in Cornwall, but I would, if I wanted the high bad enough.

I think what my body needs today – my head too maybe – is to run. I've always hated running – or more, it hates me – but I've done it enough now to be good at it, and just like surfing, like all the adventures I've had, even the scariest ones, I never regret choosing to do it, once it's over. Even when the weather is terrible, when biblical-seeming rainstorms come off the sea and almost blow me off my feet, I'm always glad that I've done it once I don't have to do it any more.

*

I take the path that leads across the cliffs and towards the sheltered bay where a series of beaches link up at low tide. I pause to stretch at the Huer's Hut, the ancient whitewashed hut once lived in by a hermit – used later by lookouts, huers, who waited to sight shoals of pilchards and yell out to teams of fishermen who'd go and net them in the millions, which apparently led to the phrase 'hue and cry' to mean some kind of a brouhaha. This building's etymological claim to fame.

I'm still stretching when Ricky calls.

I see his name there on my phone and I almost reject the call, but that will only lead to more and longer calls.

'Hey, Ricky,' I say.

'Are you okay? You sound like you've been running.'

'I've been running. It's morning here.'

'Are you making any progress?'

'Maybe. It's too early to know yet. I'm putting out feelers all over the place.'

'Why does this matter so much to you? What is it even going to change?'

'Who said it was about changing something?'

'You're fooling yourself. You think you'll find some big answer there, but you won't. You'll just dig up more questions. She's gone. It's too late for all this.'

'I can't talk now, Ricky.'

I can't go over it all again. I don't have the energy.

'Come home, Candice. Just come home. Today.'

'I can't do that.'

'You can. It's not even a little hard. Drive to the airport and get on the plane. You need money, I'll pay for your ticket. You don't have to be there.'

'I need to be here.'

'We miss you. The girls miss you… I miss you.'

'I miss you guys too. Look, Ricky, I have to jump off now. I have to get to work.'

This is a lie. Today is my day off, although I'll stop by the café when Makayla's on her lunch break.

'Bussing tables?' he says, his voice harsh.

'Yeah, and I could do without the judgement.'

'Promise me you'll be careful,' he says. 'Can you at least just promise me that?'

'I'm almost thirty years old. I'm not your responsibility.'

'You're my little sister.'

'Who grew up. I'll be okay. Send my love to everybody.'

*

I end the call and hear a cough. Someone's here. I walk around the back of the building to the other side and see there's a guy sitting on the very top step of the stair that runs up the exterior of the building. He has his hands around his knees, looking out at the view. No lenses pointed, just drinking it all in. He's bundled up against the morning chill with a stylish wool overcoat that could belong to Dolce & Gabbana's new fall line, and a yellow beanie that could belong to a trawlerman. He's also wearing a scarf and sporty sunglasses, so I have almost no idea what he looks like. On a normal day, I wouldn't interact with him, but right now, after that frustrating, suffocating conversation with my brother, I want to talk to someone else. Anyone. Even a man I don't know. Maybe especially a man I don't know.

'I wasn't eavesdropping,' he says, in a deep voice, and adds, 'Am I allowed to sit up here? I know it's an old building.'

I shrug. 'People do.'

He has a slight Cockney accent – enough for Makayla to privately assign him a 'DFL'.

Down From London.

'There aren't any signs saying not to,' he says.

'Then I guess you won't be arrested and hauled off to jail.'

He thinks about this. Rubs his chin as he mulls it over.

'Maybe I should be wearing a hard hat,' he says. 'This thing is made of rubble, according to the internet. It could collapse under my weight, taking me right down with it.'

'It's one storey tall. And it's been standing seven hundred years so you're probably good for another ten minutes.'

'Those medieval builders really had their shit together,' he says, running his fingers across the bumpy, whitewashed walls, as if appreciating the craftsmanship.

I could walk on now. It's a natural break in the conversation. The normal thing would be to walk away.

'What else did the internet tell you?' I ask.

'Some sad stories about charitable people throwing pound coins through the barred window and door openings, to go towards the restoration efforts, and other – less charitable – people poking handheld fishing nets between the bars to steal those coins. Oh, and something about it originally being either a hermitage or a lighthouse, before the pilchard-spotters commandeered it.'

'I mean, if you leave money within fishing-net-poking distance, shit will happen.'

He nods and goes quiet. I wait for him to turn his back to me and start looking at the view again, but he doesn't.

'So which was it?' he asks, looking up from his shoes.

'Which was what?'

'This place. Before the huers used it as their fish-watching station.'

'You're asking me? Does this accent sound local to you?'

'Half the time tourists know more than locals about the history of a place. They go on the tours and read the guidebooks.'

'I'm not a tourist. I live here.'

'Lucky you,' he says. 'So, nobody actually knows if it was a hermitage or a lighthouse?'

'Maybe it was both,' I say. 'Maybe the person in charge of the lantern was just really antisocial.'

He laughs. 'Even if there's no records, you'd have thought that lore would have been passed down in the oral tradition.'

I bite my lip. 'There's zero oral to speak of. Everything's coming up mute.'

He massages his temples, as if he's trying to self-soothe. When he looks up, he takes off his sunglasses and I see his eyes for the first time. Dark eyes. Tired eyes.

'So, this story is a mystery,' he says.

'Yep.'

He puts his hands above his head.

'I'm getting a message,' he says.

'People use phones for those.'

'I'm getting a message from the universe,' he says. 'I think a witch used to live here. A shunned woman.'

'Did she have an opinion on something? Turn a man down? Own a cat?'

'Those things will definitely get you shunned in some small towns,' he says, seriously. 'But our witch had actual powers.'

'Uh-huh.'

'She could tell the future.'

'So she saw … bachelorette parties? Surf contests? Weddings on the beach?'

'She was a sort of marriage soothsayer. She could see which newly married couples would stick, and which ones would twist.'

'Your witch is a blackjack player?'

'Pontoon player,' he says, knowledgeably. 'A sort of "Love Pontoon". No – "Passion Pontoon" has a better ring to it.'

'Those are honeymoon destinations. Or slang for the phallus.'

He laughs again. 'Nice imagery.'

'You're welcome.'

I sigh. He echoes my sigh. I sigh again.

'If only I lived in a rubble hut,' I say. 'And ate nothing but pilchards. Then I could stay here all day long.'

'If only,' he says. 'Well, it was good to meet you.'

'Good to meet you too,' I say.

And I mean it. I really mean it. This brief flirtation with a stranger has washed away the bad taste left in my mouth by my phone call with Ricky. He would hate me flirting with a random guy. He would say I should be saving my energy for saving my marriage. He would say a lot of things that would make me miserable.

'Have a nice day,' the guy says as I hit the winding road back to the café, and I wave without looking back.

As I make it round the first bend, I get the urge to stop and walk back to him. See if he's still sitting there. To at least ask his name. But I don't do that. I force myself to keep running.

I run the cliff path around the headland, down to the sand on Towan Beach and right across Great Western and Tolcarne Beach, past the secret places where the sea glass searchers are already climbing over jagged rocks to hidden coves only accessible at low tide, sifting through the shingle or searching by eye for their treasures, and on to Lusty Glaze, which is maybe the weirdest name for a beach that I've ever heard and which Demi has told me has come from the Cornish words *Lostyn Glas*, meaning: a place to view blue boats. Which is, I have to admit, a strong visual.

I take the one hundred and thirty-three steps of the private beach exit to the parking lot and then cut across the Barrowfields, a green expanse high on the cliffs, where ancient burial mounds can still be seen, their precious contents cleared away by old-timey farmers who didn't realise the value of what they were throwing in the trash.

I use the public bathroom and splash water on my face, before walking the rest of the way home. There are teenagers in black uniforms heading to the local high schools and I wonder how many of them are counting down the minutes until they can hit the beach after classes are out for the day.

Joseph used to say that the only class he cared about at school was woodshop class. He liked the smell of hot timber and the fact that he could make real things with his hands, which was only a hop away from shaping surfboards. He loved seeing the design in his mind come to life in front of him, as he built a bird-feeding table or planed a foam blank into the exact surfboard contours he wanted. He said he tried but he just couldn't respect people who worked all day typing away on computers. He thought that was a waste of life. Definitely a waste of fingers. About which Makayla would definitely make a smart remark.

I didn't tell him that my dream job was maybe a travel writer, so that I could see the world and spend the weeks after writing about all I'd experienced. Except, becoming a travel writer wasn't an option that was available to me. People like me didn't just get to decide they could have a career like that. People like me lived in vans and flipped burgers for tourists who had more money going into their checking accounts in one month than I would earn in a lifetime.

Walking onward, my joints easing up now, I soak in the view that stretches for miles along this coast.

Joseph doesn't even know where I am. I don't need to ask his opinion about anything. I can try anything I want here. If I want to write an essay on being a Hawaiian in Cornwall, I could do that. I could totally do that.

I won't, but that's not the point. The point is that if I did, Joseph wouldn't be able to stop me. Because he doesn't get to choose for me any more.

*

When I get back to Demi's house, I see she's left a note Blu Tacked to the door of my van, which says:

Gone to meet New Guy for a walk on the beach. I've left fresh towels in your bedroom. There are blueberry and banana muffins cooling on a rack in the kitchen and I've made a pot of coffee. Help yourself. Xx

I'm not sure if I'm imagining it, but I think I actually catch a waft of the muffins drifting through the air, like a cartoon scent trail. Either way, it's too good an offer to refuse.

Demi's notes always make me smile. She insists that her guest bedroom is mine for however long I want it, but I can't accept it. For one thing, I know she's actively dating via various apps, and I don't want to get in her way. I don't want her to feel that every time she walks through her own front door, I could be there, hanging around. On her couch. In her kitchen. Sitting on a lawn chair in her flower garden. It's enough of an imposition letting me permanently park my van on her property, without also roaming all over her home.

Since she's already left for her date, though, I don't feel too bad about letting myself in with her spare key and eating every crumb of one of those totally incredible muffins, or sipping on a blissfully strong coffee.

Her house is gorgeous. Full of flowering plants and art. She's not an artist herself but there's a vibrant art scene in this town and in the thirty years Demi's had this house, inherited from her mother, she's filled it with as many original pieces as she could afford, always wanting to support the Cornish artists whose livelihoods depend on locals keeping them afloat in the winter.

When I'm done breakfasting, I take a long shower and use Demi's coffee grounds, sea salt and shea butter scrub, which she makes herself, and wash my hair in apple-scented shampoo. I blot it with a towel but give Demi's blowdryer a miss. The weather has turned, and it's going to be a hot day; by the time I finish putting on lip gloss and eye make-up, my hair will be almost dry.

I check my phone and there's a message from Makayla.

Your friend is here again.

What friend?

You know who I'm talking about... Laptop Guy.

Why is he my friend? I barely spoke to him.

The look in his eyes when you serve him tap water.

So the guy's thirsty?

He's DEFINITELY thirsty.

He'd better have gone by the time I meet you for lunch.

She responds only with the hands thrown up in confusion 'Who knows?' emoji.

*

I take a moment to check my emails. There's a message to my surf school account from a prospective new student.

I hug my phone to my chest, only just resist kissing it, and hope that the new student will turn out to want at least three sessions, which would just about cover the cost of having the business cards printed and the Facebook ad I blew thirty pounds on.

I message my potential new client back to say that I'm free any time today or on my next day off, which is Friday, and the reply comes straight away.

Would today at 5.30pm work for you?
VB
Sent from my Galaxy

That's great. I'll be waiting at the shack on Fistral, right by Demigorgons. I'll be the one wearing the stripy wetsuit.
C

My best wetsuit. The one that makes me stand out from all the other instructors on this beach. The wetsuit was a present from Joseph, who'd read a feature in a surf magazine that claimed making yourself look like a poisonous sea snake reduced your chances of being attacked by a shark, and he'd then ordered a bunch into inventory at our surf shop. I wasn't sure I believed in the snake theory, but it made him happy to believe it.

I read a few more chapters of *Sense and Sensibility* – which I'm currently ping-ponging with *Pride and Prejudice*, trying to figure out whether Willoughby or Wickham is more toxic, and why the hell I'm still attracted to them both anyhow – and then write down a few potential new leads in my personal planner. I also jot down a few story ideas, for that one day when I'll finally be brave enough to try to write something of my own.

I meet Makayla outside the café for her lunch break, and the first thing she does is motion to Laptop Guy, who's typing away furiously.

'I can't believe he's here again,' I say.

'He asked about you,' Makayla says, mischievously.

'You're making this up.'

'He asked if you'd be coming in today. I said you'd be popping in around lunchtime to keep me company on my break. He seemed... disappointed.'

I shake my head. Refuse to engage. 'Shall we go to our usual date location?'

'Absolutely yes,' she says. 'A taste of luxury without the price tag.'

'Ladies who lunch,' I say. 'Without buying lunch.'

★

We walk up to the Headland Hotel, a red-brick place over a hundred years old that stands on a promontory overlooking the ocean. It's also the location where the original movie of Roald Dahl's *The Witches* with Anjelica Huston was filmed. Makayla likes to come here in her lunch break to use the luxurious bathrooms, ostensibly to poop in peace, but mostly to avail herself of the complimentary spa-style products. She's a particular fan of the scented hand soap, which she uses to refresh her underarm area, and the matching hand lotion, which she also applies to her legs and decolletage. She especially likes coming here when the actors from the Rosamunde Pilcher German TV production are staying in the hotel and propping up the bar. According to Demi, Cornish romance has been huge over there for decades, so huge that it brings hundreds of thousands of German tourists to Cornwall each year. I've read a few Pilcher novels since I arrived here and raced through them. Makayla's appreciation is limited solely to the extreme hotness of the cast.

'One day we'll actually get drinks here,' I say.

'When we can afford eight quid a pint,' she points out, with a sigh. 'So, I've figured out who Laptop Guy reminds me of. It took me a minute, but I got there in the end. Guess who?'

'I have no guesses.'

'Go on, just say a name, Candice. The first one that pops into your mind.'

'Winona Ryder.'

'Sensible guesses only, although they do have the same hair, so I'll allow it.'

'I don't know, Makayla. I can't think of anyone and I don't much care to, if I'm being honest.'

'Want me to tell you who?'

I sigh. 'Shoot.'

'James Bay.'

'I don't know who that is. Should I know who that is?'

'Only the most talented singer-songwriter in the entire universe, according to my baby cousin anyway, who's his biggest fan.'

'You don't think that guy could actually be him? That singer-songwriter person?' I say because, although it seems wildly unlikely that a pop star would hang out in Demigorgons with his laptop, stranger things have happened.

'We do get some famouses in there, but no, the eye colour is different. I did a Google Image search last night. Also, this guy doesn't seem to be into hipster hats. He's definitely someone, though. Not your average Joe.'

'Because your average Joe pays for his cup of joe?' I say.

We take the basket of food and soda that I've brought with me and go to sit outside in the grounds where there are alcoves set into the terraced slope, with stripy lawn chairs. The area is meant solely for the use of paying guests, but nobody's come to interrogate us yet.

I've just finished a slice of some savoury tart thing that was selling for half-off in the superstore, when Makayla clears her throat.

'You just need to take the plunge and do it, Candice,' she says, holding a cold egg in one hand and a buttered roll in the other, taking alternate bites of each.

'I need to do what now?'

'Ask sexy Laptop Guy out. Obviously.'

'How is that at all obvious?'

She pauses to chew.

'Because he's here and so are you.'

'He's not a mountain I'm going to climb.'

'He could be.'

'Why would I ask him out? I'm not interested in him. He's clearly just another selfish asshole. He's Wickham. Or Willoughby.'

'Huh?'

'Austen assholes. And he's probably got a girlfriend. Or a boyfriend. I don't know, but no way he's single. You only have to look at him.'

'I see where you're going with that, because yes indeed look at him,' she says, picking up a cranberry juice-box and draining it in one go. 'But he's single.'

Makayla says this so confidently that I wonder if she's actually asked him to confirm his marital status.

'And you know that how, exactly, Makayla?'

'I can always tell. It's my superpower. Plus, he has the vibe.'

'What vibe?'

She flashes me a sharky grin.

'The *vibe*.'

I shake my head, giving her my blankest look.

'Of being available for a roll in the sand.'

'There's a vibe for that?' I ask, giving her a cynical look, which she ignores.

'Oh, there definitely is, and he has it. To the max.'

'Then you ask him out, Makayla.'

'Me?' She points to her chest, as if this perfectly sensible counter-suggestion of mine is ridiculous. Scandalous, even. 'I can't add another person into the mix. Look at me.'

She looks exactly as she always looks. Tall, willowy and radiant. Long eyelashes framing dark brown eyes sparkling with amusement.

'I'm looking,' I say, giving her the full up and down. 'What am I supposed to be seeing here?'

'I'm a husk of my former self. I'm exhausted, plus I have really brutal cystitis today. And you know the rule.'

I do know the rule. Makayla has rules about everything, and she generally breaks them all before lunch.

'Once I start peeing blood, I force myself to take a week off the horse. It's not easy, believe me, and I've tried to power through in the past. But lived to regret it.'

'How do you "power through" cystitis?'

'A lot of willpower. Some cranberry juice and antibiotics.'

'I think the cranberry juice thing is a myth.'

'The point you're missing, or deliberately dodging, more like, is that you should definitely get in there, Candice. There'll be no shortage of women in this town ready and waiting to snap him up. You wanna make your move before someone else pips you to the post.'

'I'm not just going to proposition a customer. Not even to pip his post.'

'He's not really a customer, though, is he?' Makayla says. 'He's working, just like us. He's practically staff.

Everything he's had at the café I've given him for free. Only coffee and water, mind you, but still.'

'Okay, sure. Good point. I'm not just going to proposition a freeloader.'

'Well, you should. That's all I'm saying. Because you haven't had a hook-up since you arrived in Newquay and there are men literally everywhere, it's stag party central right now, and you haven't let yourself get taken out once.'

'I don't want to be taken out. "Taken out" sounds like the mafia is going to tie concrete blocks to my ankles and drop me in the ocean.'

'We don't get much mafia down here in Cornwall, funnily enough.' She frowns as if trying to scan her memory banks for spaghetti-eating gangsters. 'No. I don't think we're dressy enough for the mafia. Too many scruffbags in piss-soaked wetsuits.'

I smile at the beautiful imagery. Makayla doesn't understand my position on dating, doesn't understand that I need to be alone right now. She doesn't understand it, and I don't know how to explain.

A couple in their twenties sets down their own picnic blanket a little way from us. The girl is unpacking the food, while the guy checks every pocket of his jacket for something. By the time she has her groceries set out the way she wants them, he's down on one knee, holding up a ring box. It takes her a while to notice him, as she's taking photos on her phone of the pretty picnic aesthetic. Then she's saying yes and they're embracing. Kissing. They turn to see if anyone has seen, and we give them a round of applause. Maybe I should've taken a photo of the proposal moment, AirDropped it to them for their grandkids to be shown one day.

'Truly, Makayla, I appreciate the concern, but I'm happy as I am. Hashtag-vanlife all the way.'

'But are you happy, though? Because you're young, pretty, free as a bird and *Hawaiian* for fuck's sake, and you have no social life. You don't do anything for fun.'

The newly engaged couple are drinking champagne, the sea sparkling blue behind them. He takes a bite from a strawberry she's holding out for him.

'Rude. I surf for fun.'

'Which is also work, in your case. And you know what they say about hobbies once they become work?'

'You're cleverly monetising something you enjoy?'

'They become another form of stress.'

'Surfing's not like that, which you'd know, if you ever tried it.'

'Why would I try it? Do I want to break my nose and knock out my teeth on a surfboard? Slice my ears off on one of the fins? No thanks.'

'That would clearly not happen because I'd take you out on a foamie. No way to hurt yourself on a foam board. You won't even break a nail.'

'Nah,' she says, giving her scalp a good scratch, probably on account of it still being full of sand from her most recent roll around in it. 'I can't afford your prices.'

'My prices are fifty percent of the other instructors' working this beach. And come on now: you know I wouldn't charge you, Makayla.'

'I'd have to pay you something,' she says. 'Else I'd feel I was taking advantage.'

'Then pay me something,' I say.

'Can't afford it.'

'A pound? That'll work.'

'That's an insulting amount for your time and expertise.'

'Ten pounds.'

'Too dear. Can't swing it.'

'It would just be a nice thing for us to do together, that's all I'm saying. Hanging out in the waves. Instead of working in a café.'

'Demigorgons is my happy place.'

The young lovers are eating meat pastries now and I wait for it to happen, because there's something about the smell that always draws them in. It's just a matter of time.

'Give surfing a chance. It could change your life,' I say.

'Getting attacked by a shark could change my life. Just... not in a good way.'

It always amazes me how many people go straight from surfing to sharks. As if 'the men in grey suits', as surfers like to call sharks, are always cruising the surf line-up, waiting to pick off any juicy human that catches their eye.

'You don't have those kinds of sharks in Cornwall. Not even close. You have cute little guys here who eat sushi.'

The first seagull lands on the picnic blanket and steals the Cornish pasty right out of the groom-to-be's hand. The bird begins shredding it and starts calling out to its pals, while the guy tries to shoo it away. In less than ten seconds, there are ten gulls fighting over pastry, potato and meat scraps.

'Seals bite people,' Makayla says.

'You've got to be kidding me with this,' I say. 'Who do you know who has ever gotten bit by a pinniped?'

'If that means a seal, then loads of people. Happens all

the time in the mating season. One of the customers said it happened to his mate's brother.'

'Sure, sure. One of his friend's brothers got bit by a harmless sea mammal. That absolutely happened.'

'It did.'

The bride-to-be is freaking out. The gulls have got into her desserts. One of them flies away holding a whole piece of chocolate cake.

'Let's just start over,' I say, wondering if we should go to help, although there's no saving their romantic moment. The situation is too far gone. At least three dozen gulls are involved in the fray now and it won't be over until they've eaten everything, or the couple have run away. 'Look, I promise I won't let you get mauled by any marine animals. And you promise me you'll think about it. Surfing is the thing that makes me feel some real peace here. Makes me feel at home. I want you to experience that.'

'Fine, I'll think about it. Now stop nagging. You're worse than my granny was for guilt-tripping.'

'Okay, okay. "Hang loose,"' I say, throwing her the surf shaka hand sign.

The hand sign she does back is definitely not surf-related.

We watch the couple pack up the remains of their picnic and leave, the girl holding the blanket above her head like a beach parasol, because all that food has started to move things along in the gulls' digestive systems.

Makayla puts her head in her hands and exhales.

'What's wrong?' I ask. 'Are you finally ready to tell me the thing the Irishman did? The thing you were too embarrassed to tell me before. You said to ask you later. It's later.'

'Ask me *even* later. This is about the Doberman. His sister is in town next week and she wants to meet me,' she says.

'How do you feel about that?' I say, hesitantly, because I know her rules include strict boundaries when it comes to families, and this is a rule she never violates. 'Is that a thing that interests you?'

'It does, but mostly because his sister called her kid Libya.'

'Like the country?'

'No. It's spelt with "i"s and an extra "b". Libbia.'

'Does she at least have some connection to the country of Libya?'

'She's tenth-generation Cornish. Is it just me, or is Libbia a bit too close to labia?'

'I mean, it's not far away from it.'

'I tell you this much,' she says. 'By the time that kid sits through a class on reproduction, she'll be going by Libby.'

Makayla sighs again. 'So how do I handle this? Do you think I should say yes to this picnic on the beach with his sister and niece? They're bringing a bat and ball. They're expecting me to play cricket.'

'And you don't want to do that?'

'I love cricket. I would play beach cricket all afternoon long, with the right guy. But it's weird. He's acting like I'm his girlfriend.'

A new lot of folks come along with a picnic blanket, settling a little way off from where the first couple got engaged. Clearly, they didn't see what just went down and haven't noticed the birds watching.

'And you don't want to be his girlfriend?'

'I don't know. It's not a conversation we've had. I've never even really thought about it.'

'He knows you're sleeping with other people, right?'

'Of course he knows I'm sleeping with other people. What do you think this is – amateur hour? He is, too. Or so he says. Men are confusing. Anyway, he also wants to meet me for dinner some time, just the two of us, to talk about where this is going.'

'That sounds serious.'

'It's crossing a line to have a conversation like that after one month. It's throwing a bag of dog turds in a postbox. You just don't do it.'

'Who throws dog crap in a mailbox?' I ask, wincing.

'Nobody. That's my point. He's getting shit all over my nice clean envelopes.'

'Hang on,' I say, and go to warn the new couple about the gull hazard, because they too have a picnic basket. This is why we sit in the alcoves, I tell them, and not on the grass. The gulls swoop from behind so you don't see them coming and they work in teams, with lookout birds alerting the rest. The key is to have your back to a wall, I explain. The couple are so grateful that the girl insists on giving me a can of cider, which I take back to split with Makayla.

'I guess you're not going on the dinner date, then?' I say.

'He's made a reservation for that restaurant on Tolcarne Beach. The Colonial.'

'I've never eaten there but that place looks fancy.'

'Which is why I've said yes.'

'Makayla.'

'What? They do strawberry piña coladas and they're the only place in the whole of Cornwall that does, but I don't

66

know if I should be going. He might not like what I have to say, and he's got a bit of a temper.'

'Back away. Text him right now to say you're not going.'

'I don't mind a bit of a temper usually, especially when it's aimed at tourists driving like knobs, but I'm a bit worried that he'll take the news badly.'

'What news?' I ask.

'That I'm pregnant and he's not the father.'

I turn to her, eyes wide, hardly believing what I'm hearing.

'Just joking,' she says, airily, as if she didn't just almost give me a heart attack. 'God, Candice, lighten up already.'

'You need to work on your comedy routine,' I say, giving her a punch on the shoulder, which she returns with a little too much enthusiasm.

Five

I walk Makayla back to the café and see Demi's car outside. It's her day off too, and there's a full rota of holiday temps hard at work inside, but she stops by anyways – not to check up on Makayla, she insists, but just to say hi.

She's sitting on the bench outside, gazing through the window at Laptop Guy, who she's spotted, even though the café is busy with customers. She points at him and says, 'Who is *he*?'

I shrug. 'Tourist. He was in yesterday. Seems to dig the Demigorgons vibe. How was the second date?'

'Good. Nice bloke. Not much of a talker but what he did say didn't turn my stomach, at least, so that's something.'

'What's he like?' Makayla asks, always keen to hear Demi's dating adventures and swap disaster stories.

'About my age. Divorced three years ago. Didn't do as well out of his divorces as I did, or inherit money from a great-aunt, but he has his own carpentry business, which is doing well.'

The whole time she's saying this, she's staring at Laptop Guy. It's warm, there's sweat on her upper lip, and she fans herself with one of the menus we keep under painted rocks to stop the wind blowing them across the beach.

'Phwoar,' she says.

'Did you really just say phwoar?' I ask. 'I thought people only said that in movies.'

'Couldn't help myself. God, he's pretty. Looks just like a young Eddie Vedder.'

'Who's that?' Makayla asks, biting her fingernails.

'Eddie Vedder? Only the sexiest man who has ever lived,' Demi says. 'Also the frontman of the greatest rock band of all time. Pearl Jam. I was a fan in the nineties. Everyone was.'

'Never heard of them,' Makayla says. 'And their band name sounds like spunk.'

'I think "pearl jam" does in fact refer to semen, yes,' Demi says. 'Although it took me a while to work that out as a teenager. You don't think this chap is an actor, do you? He's got that movie star look about him.'

'He's probably going to be here all day again,' I say to Makayla.

'Let's hope so,' Demi says. 'Bit of eye candy to look at.'

'Demi, we were only telling him yesterday what a genius you are,' I say, exasperated.

'Yes, and now you're making yourself sound all shallow,' Makayla adds, trying to look stern and judgemental, even though she's spent the entire time she's known this guy gazing at him with hearty eyes.

'Hey, geniuses can appreciate male beauty,' Demi says. 'Bloody love a peacock.'

'I don't,' Makayla says, grimacing. 'You can keep your pea-sized cocks to yourself.'

'Guys, enough. Please, I beg of you,' I say.

Makayla goes back inside and starts serving, and I ask Demi about her life in the nineties. She has all these amazing stories about her formative years here and I can't get enough of them.

When I glance up again, I catch the guy looking through the glass pane at me with a weird expression in his eyes. It's not hostility and it's not admiration. It's something like... curiosity.

*

I spend the rest of the afternoon walking from beach to beach, trying to think of the best angle to set a travel magazine story here and coming up short, until it's finally time to go to the shack to meet my new surf school student.

Makayla spots me and comes out of the café to give me an encouraging pat on the back that says, *You got this*.

'What are your plans for later?' I ask, when I see her smiling at her phone.

'I'm meeting the Doberman on the Barrowfields.'

'How come?' It was a nice enough place, but more for tourist kids wanting to use the bounce houses and inflatable slides.

'He's gone and got a puppy.'

She shows me a photo of a baby dog on her cell phone, and I feel my brow wrinkle.

'Uh, that's not a...'

'It is indeed a Doberman, yep. He said we put the idea in his head. Can you believe it? You mishearing me say the word "doorman" has led to me getting to hang out with the world's cutest puppy. This might be the best day of my life.'

'You have fun now,' I say, grinning because her pure joy about this dog is infectious. I also find myself wondering when I'll get a chance to pet it. And also to meet the Doberman himself, who I've only seen from a distance and whose real name I don't even know, because there are so many names to remember that it's easier to rely on nicknames.

I need to get myself set up for the surf lesson, to get into the zone, so I go unlock the shack and try to calm myself. It is only a 'surf shack' in the loosest possible sense of the words. It is, to be precise, the shack that once housed the Demigorgons' trashcans, the industrial ones that get emptied by trucks, as well as smaller ones for customers wanting to recycle soda cans and plastic bottles.

It's about twenty feet by ten and its original purpose was to keep the wind from sending garbage everywhere during the worst of the Atlantic storms that blow over this little Cornish town, but all the café trashcans were moved to a purpose-built brick shelter for the whole complex, all the way over by the entrance to the parking lot, which left Demi's old garbage shack empty.

I'd looked at that garbage shack and thought: *Hmm, there is my future, there is my chance, and I am here to take my shot.*

Demi could easily tear it down and used it for firewood, no questions asked. She put it up, so it's her right to do whatever she wants with it. But there's something about me that she relates to. We seemed to sense right away that we share the same warped sense of humour, the same cynicism about our love lives, the same existential dread of getting pooped on by seabirds.

She's let me take the shack, on a trial-run basis. I've placed a sign, of my own design and painting, in there, along with three chairs, two for customers and one for me. I'm not a surf school so much as a surf tutor. I have the right qualifications and insurance, but I have no equipment other than the surfboards I already have stacked on the roof on my van. I can hire suits and anything else I need from the main surf hire place on the beach. They know me there now and give me a decent discount. The only thing I am selling is my time and expertise. And I know I'm good at teaching people to surf. People told me so all the time back home. I've gotten hundreds of people up and riding waves. If I get a few clients here who spread the word, maybe I can branch out, buy some equipment. Pay for a professional sign. Maybe I can even put out enough feelers to find the person I'm looking for.

I've made Demi promise me that if I haven't made a go of it after three months, she'll take a two-pound sledgehammer and set to it, bundling up the wood for whichever locals want to collect it for their burners and beach fires. That's the deal.

'Are you sure about this?' she'd asked me.

'No. I'm never sure about anything, but I think I have to try.'

'You're not going to be asking me for another week, another month, while the business is "turning a corner"?' She'd used scare quotes so effectively that I'd had to laugh.

'Nope.'

'You know I have to charge you rent. It wouldn't be fair on the other businesses in the beach complex if I didn't.'

'Sure thing,' I'd said, beginning to sweat, because I had

no idea what business rents were like in this town, but I was pretty sure I couldn't afford even a small one.

'But…' she'd said. 'Nobody needs to know how much that rent is. Let's call it a token amount, but we'll make everything official and above board, so that we both know you're serious about this.'

'Thank you,' I'd said, waiting for the figure to spring out of her mouth. 'How "above board" are we talking?'

'I'll give you receipts, which you can keep for your files, but those receipts will be written in hieroglyphics.'

'Great,' I'd said, laughing. 'And that receipt will be for how much money exactly?'

'Two pounds fifty a week.'

I'd given her a hug, pulling her to me and returning her squeeze. 'You are the best owner of a café anywhere on the whole planet.'

'Flirt,' she'd said, walking away with a smile.

'Hey there,' a male voice says now, startling me. When I look up, my eyes do not meet my new surf student. Instead, they fall once again on Laptop Guy.

Six

He's wearing blue Adidas track pants and a white muscle vest. He looks like an extra from a Spice Girls music video.

But also, undeniably hot.

'Did you leave something behind in the café?' I ask, trying not to sound rude but also not deferential either, because I'm not his server now. I'm a person who has other things to do than talk with him. A person with a failing business to run.

'I think maybe I have an appointment with you for a surf lesson?' he says, looking uncomfortable. 'I saw the business cards in the café and grabbed one. I didn't actually realise when I emailed that you were the instructor. I didn't put two and two together.'

'Oh,' I say, icy realisation dawning. I'll have to spend time with this man. Not only in Demigorgons, but in the ocean as well. There will be no getting away from him in any part of my day. He will be like a very committed stalker who is also paying my wages.

Terrific.

My feeling of displeasure must translate onto my face.

'Am I late?' he says, suddenly, looking at his empty wrist. 'I left my watch at home.'

'No, you're actually a little early.'

'Turning up early is a bad habit I had drilled into me at boarding school. I'm Alexis, by the way. I can't remember if I told you already.'

'No, you didn't. And you didn't sign off your email message, other than with a VB, which I guess means Very Best, and not the acronym for volleyball? Oh, and also that you were emailing from your own Galaxy.'

'Oh right. Yeah, I was typing on my phone and I forgot it doesn't have my proper email signature.'

And his Gmail address, which I don't want to let on I've even noticed is the beautifully weird 'SlainByASmurf'.

He doesn't ask me for my name, but I volunteer it.

'I'm Candice. If you didn't know that. If Makayla didn't already mention it.'

'Really?' he asks, looking up and down the beach. 'I thought Makayla said your name was Candy.'

'*Candice*,' I say. 'Emphasis on the diss.'

He smiles and it catches in my throat. I have to stop being so reactive to him like this. It's throwing me off my game.

'Did I see you on the beach last night?' he asks.

'Maybe. I went to surf. You were there, too?' I ask, even though I know he was there. I thought it was him and now I know it for sure.

He nods. 'I went for a swim.'

'Cool.'

'And I saw you. I wasn't sure it was you, though, so I didn't come over. The neoprene, the wet hair, the sunset. It was hard to tell.'

He seems to think he's been rude to me for not coming over to say hi. Why does he care? He doesn't know me. He's perfectly entitled to ignore me if he sees me on a public beach. We're strangers to each other.

'No sweat,' I say.

'Have you always surfed?'

'Since I was a little kid. Surfing helps me feel a little more...' I trail off. More what? Stable? Grounded? Happy? None of those seem exactly right. 'Me.'

'Interesting,' he says, and I have the distinct impression that he's making some kind of mental note.

'Don't you feel like that when you swim in the ocean?' I ask.

'I don't think so. No, in fact, I'm sure I don't.'

'No?' I say, surprised that he hasn't even attempted a confirmation of my weird statement, not even for the sake of politeness.

'I'm mostly in it for the cardio. I don't really enjoy the taste of saltwater in my mouth or the sensation of kelp shackling my ankles. And, if I'm honest, I kept worrying about jellyfish. Didn't help that I saw several Portuguese man o'wars swimming around the rockpools on my way in. I didn't realise they'd even got those things here.'

'Oh yeah, we do. They can kill you if you're allergic to the venom. Pretty much shut your lungs right down.'

'This is what I'm talking about,' he says. 'There's just too much alive stuff in the ocean. It's like wanting to go for a swim in an aquarium, knowing for a fact that there are going to be eels and squid zipping around you. Not to mention sharks. Not really my scene.'

'Huh,' I say, trying not to judge, because why would

anyone let the thought of a rich ecosystem spoil an ocean swim? 'Well, at least you gave it a try.'

'I felt like I had to. I don't get the chance to go sea swimming in my normal life, I'm more of a pool person, but I thought I should make the effort while I'm down here.'

'For sure,' I say. 'The ocean is free. No entry fees to pay.'

He looks momentarily confused, as if entry fees are something he's never even considered worrying about.

'So, I probably shouldn't admit this, but I was expecting somebody, well, older,' he says.

'Than what? I'm not far off thirty years old. Not exactly a teenager here.'

'It's just your name. You never go by Candy?'

'No.'

Not ever.

'Candice somehow suggests, I don't know... older than twenty-nine.'

'Um, thanks, I guess.'

'I've never met anyone younger than fifty with your name.'

'My mom was named Janice. Candice isn't too far away.'

He thinks about this and nods. 'Not that it's a bad thing to be younger than people expect, of course.'

'I mean, for sure there aren't too many elderly surf instructors running around these parts. Not that I've seen.'

This seems to trigger a thought in him.

'I meant to ask in my email: what is your surf proficiency?'

'What is *my* surf proficiency?' I say, smiling a little too tightly. 'Because that's just what I was about to ask you.'

'I know that must seem like an odd question. I just wanted to know what level you're at. So, like, intermediate?

Advanced? Roughly, I mean. If you had to put a number to it, on a scale of one to ten, with a ten being Kerry Slater.'

'KELLY Slater,' I say, a little too vehemently.

'That's the one. So, if you had to put a number to it?'

I can feel the colour rising in my cheeks. 'I wouldn't. But I've been surfing a long time,' I answer, not mentioning the championships I competed in as a teenager. Absolutely not mentioning the ones I won. I don't want him to think that I have something to prove. I don't care about his opinion of me. He can think whatever he wants to think. He has no idea what my relationship is with surfing.

He smiles, like I've just made his day. 'You're pretty good, then?'

'If we are being precise about it,' I say. 'Yes, I am pretty good.'

He looks at me, waiting for further elaboration.

I'm not sure what more he's expecting me to say, or even what sort of situation this is. Is he flirting in some strange way? Is this a very bizarre kind of negging? Is he trying to make me feel badly about myself, trying to make me justify myself for setting up as a surf instructor?

'What's *your* surf proficiency? Are you still in the white water or are you able to surf green waves?' I say.

'Oh, I have no proficiency. I've never even tried bodyboarding, let alone stand-up surfing. I'm a decent swimmer but a total beginner when it comes to catching waves. A thirty-two-year-old noob.'

A kook, I think, but I don't much want to get into a conversation about surf lingo. So how come he wants to learn now? *Is it a bucket list thing?* I wonder. Or is he just killing time while he's in Cornwall? Not that it makes any difference to me, just so long as he keeps paying me for lessons.

As if reading my thoughts, he says, 'When I was looking at holiday lets in Cornwall, I read that Fistral Beach is the surf capital of the UK, which surprised me.'

'That surprised you?' I say, looking out at the break, where the other surf schools are out with literally hundreds of customers.

'My parents always used to talk about Cornwall as God's Acre.'

I look at him blankly.

'You know, like the burial ground in a churchyard. People come to Cornwall to retire and die. I didn't realise there was a whole California-style surf industry thriving down here.'

'Kernowfornia,' I say, and he takes a second to connect the dots. Kernow, the Cornish word for Cornwall.

'Exactly,' he said. 'I wanted to get a look at that. So, I thought I might as well learn to surf, while I was here. It seemed like a missed opportunity not to. I'd hate to be in my nursing home bed thinking, *I wonder what it's like to ride a wave on my head?*'

'I'm pretty confident when I say that we're not going to be doing any headstand surfing today,' I say. 'What's your fitness? Any injuries I should know about?'

'Nothing worth mentioning.' He pauses to flick a blowfly off his forearm. 'Do you have any injuries? I mean, does surfing do anything bad to your body? Wear out the joints in the same way running does?'

Why is he asking me these questions? What is his deal? Do my janky knees and stiff hips have anything at all to do with him?

'I don't think you need to worry about getting injuries today. You'll be on a foamie and we'll be in the white water. Nice crumbling baby waves. Nothing to worry about at all.'

'Of course. I trust you,' he says, looking me dead in the eye, and man, his eyes are pretty. His eyes are so pretty that it makes my stomach flip.

My stomach is a goddamn traitor to my brain, which knows for one hundred percent certain that this guy is an asshat.

'Great. I have all the qualifications and I've been doing this for a long, long time,' I say. 'I started surfing when I was a kid. I began teaching when I was in my teens.'

I've been riding waves since my mom first took me out on a board when I was three. Not that I'll ever tell him that.

'It's just that surfing is a lifestyle, or at least that's the impression I get from reading the surf magazines in my cottage,' he says. 'I wanted to learn more about the entire thing. Get an idea of what's going on. Holistically, so to speak.'

'Maybe let's take this down onto the sand,' I say, trying to stop looking at his eyes, which only makes me drop my gaze to his mouth, which is somehow even worse in terms of the effect it has on my stomach.

He's the first adult customer I've had in weeks and he's here for the whole summer. If this goes well, he'll book more sessions. I can't afford to screw this up, I can't afford to let any kind of embarrassing physical chemistry get in the way of this.

It's just that he's unnerving me. He's so in my face.

I hear Makayla's creeper voice in my head.

You wish you were sitting on his *face…*

Shut up, my inner voice snaps back. *There's no way that this is going... there.*

'Right, let's do this,' I say, hoping he'll put my flushed cheeks down to the heat of the afternoon.

*

I've already brought my eight-foot foamie, but Alexis doesn't have his own wetsuit, so I take him to rent one from the surf hire joint, down by the pasty shed.

'Don't people wee in these?' he asks.

'Depends.'

'On what?'

'How long they're in the water. More than ninety minutes and I would guess yes.'

'Oh.'

'It's fine, though. The suit rental places hose them down between customers.'

'Do I need to wear something underneath it? I've brought swimming trunks.'

'Personal decision.'

I choose not to, because there's nothing worse than getting a bikini wedgie under skin-tight neoprene. But he doesn't need to know that.

'You can use the surf shack to get changed if you want privacy,' I say.

'No, it's fine. I'll use my towel.'

He retrieves a too-small beach towel printed with purple hibiscus flowers from his backpack. It still has the price tag on it. He must have remembered he needed one and bought it from one of the surf stores on the way down to the beach.

He does his best to squeeze his body into the medium

wetsuit that the hire guy recommended, but he has a swimmer's physique and I think he maybe should have gone up a size. I can't help getting a glimpse of butt as his towel flips in the wind and he wrestles his way into the damp suit.

'Uggh,' he says, when he's finally worked his arms and shoulders in and is ready to pull the zipper up the back. 'It's horribly wet and cold.'

'Welcome to surfing.'

'Do I need to take off my chain?' he says, motioning to the tiny crucifix at his chest.

'I would recommend taking off all jewellery, yes,' I say. 'It's too easy for things to get broken or lost when you're out there in the ocean.'

But you're wearing a ring, I can see him thinking, as he looks down at the third finger of my left hand.

The one ring to fool them all. Because if they think I'm taken, they'll leave me alone.

'Could you give me a hand zipping this thing up?' he asks, sweating.

'There's a cord on the back of the zipper,' I say, placing the cord in his hand. 'So you can do it yourself.'

When he's finally all suited up, and I've helped him with the Velcro neck strap, he's sweating so heavily it's running off the end of his nose.

'This is awful. I can hardly breathe it's so tight. Is it supposed to be like that?'

'Pretty much. Maybe it's a little snugger than it could be, but you don't need it flapping around like a jumpsuit while you're trying to catch waves.'

'So, what now?'

I take him through the motions of paddling out, popping

up on the board and correct surf stance, and get him to practise on the sand. He's in good shape and he insists he's strong and flexible enough to jump up from prone without having to go through the kneeling stage. Insists he wants to at least try, anyways, so that he doesn't pick up bad habits straight out of the gate.

'Let's get out there,' I say. I don't have a board of my own with me, because I'm going to be pushing him onto waves, until he gets the hang of basic paddle technique and can build up enough speed on his own.

He wipes out a couple of times but on his third wave he stands up on his board. He remembers to keep low, and he even turns the board a little. The look on his face is pure joy. If the best surfer is the one having the most fun, he's acing it.

There's one hairy moment when he wipes out, gets held down for a couple seconds and then nailed in the impact zone, where the waves break so powerfully that it's hard to battle through to the calmer water out back. He emerges streaming salt-snot, hair plastered all down his face, his breathing coming raspingly. But I take the long leash of his board, steady the deck and help him back on. The set passes, he catches his breath, and we wait for another one.

'This is incredible,' he shouts to me, over the roar of the approaching set waves. 'It's the most alive I've felt… ever.'

I nod and motion him to paddle for the wave again. He hasn't got the hang of basic paddle technique yet and the board rocks haphazardly as he panics for the wave, instead of keeping the board smoothly gliding through the water. It doesn't matter though. He's committed to focusing on this one thing, to trying to get it right, and I can already see he'll get there.

Most people love surfing once they try it. Because ultimately, it's just play and it's a really fun way to spend time, so long as you manage not to get swept up in the ego and competitiveness.

After another thirty minutes of the lesson has passed, I can see he's beginning to tire so I motion him to head back to the beach.

'You can body-surf the next wave all the way into shore,' I say. But he doesn't want to. He wants to walk his board onto land, cosplaying a seasoned surfer, maybe, even though seasoned surfers would be riding sleek fibreglass boards, not foamies.

We're walking together through the warm ankle-busters where elderly folks are paddling up to their knees, when I see a spasm cross his face.

'Ow,' he says.

'What's up? Have you pulled a muscle?'

'I think I just stood on a sharp piece of shell. Or maybe it was broken glass.'

He's limping a little, so I lead him up onto the wet sand and motion for him to sit down. He's biting his lip and I can tell he's in pain. I take his foot in my hand and see the problem.

'Have I cut it on something? It doesn't feel like it's bleeding, but it hurts like hell.'

There's a small puncture mark on the soft part of his foot, halfway between the ball of his foot and his heel.

'Oh boy.'

'What is it? Have I been stung by a jellyfish?'

'Um, I don't know for sure.'

'If you had to guess?'

'Then I'd say you just stood on a weever fish.'

'On a what? Jesus, it's really starting to burn.'

I can see his foot is beginning to swell. 'Hang in there,' I say. 'It's past six, so the lifeguards are gonna be off duty now but there might be a few of them still around on the beach. Just wait here and I'll be right back.'

The lifeguards don't usually head home right away. Some of them will be getting in the water for a surf or swim practice. I manage to track down Arianna, who's sitting with her arms over her knees, gazing out at the surf. I've chatted with her a lot since I arrived in Cornwall, for various reasons, and she's always been supportive of me in the ocean, whooped and hollered when I caught good rides.

'How's it going, Candice?' she says. 'Got any new leads?'

I shake my head no. 'One of my surf students has just gotten stung by a weever fish.'

I should've made him hire boots as well as the wetsuit, I think, kicking myself. Rookie error. But if he'd listened to me and body-surfed that last wave to shore, he'd be fine now.

'Don't worry. It happens. I'll sort him out. He can come up and sit on the deck of the lifeguard building. We'll have a catch-up too,' she adds kindly. 'I've been asking around for you, but no joy yet.'

The way that people here have been willing to help me find what I'm looking for has warmed my heart. Everyone warned me about localism in prime surfing locations, about small-town hostility toward outsiders, but the surf community here has wrapped its arms around me.

Arianna follows me back to Alexis, whose pain is obvious in the line of his mouth.

She looks a little dazzled when she sees him and catches his gaze.

'This is your student?' she asks, and I nod.

'I hear you stepped on the spine of a weever fish, mate,' she says. 'Unlucky.'

'I've never even heard of them before today,' he groans.

'Pesky little blighters,' she says. 'They're only about two inches long but they burrow into the sand and leave their spines sticking up. Accidentally stand on them and expect to be envenomated.'

'Superb. Just my luck.'

We haul him to his feet, and he tries to keep a lid on the pain.

'Easy,' I say. 'Just take your time.'

He leans on me heavily and hops the distance to the lifeguard building, while Arianna goes ahead and unlocks the door. I manage to get him up the metal staircase, but it's slow going. When we're finally up there, Arianna motions us to the balcony, before disappearing and returning holding a pair of tweezers.

'I'd better just check that there are no spines left in your foot,' she says, cheerfully.

'I didn't see any,' I say.

But then, my close-up vision is terrible.

Especially when it comes to men.

Moments later, Arianna announces that Alexis's foot is clear of spines now; there had just been one tiny broken-off piece inside, which she ripped out without him even noticing, since his whole foot was already a burning ball of pain.

She disappears into the room at the back before reappearing with a metal pail of water, which is insanely hot, judging by the steam coming off of it.

'You're gonna need to put your foot in this,' she says to Alexis, sympathetically. 'Ideally for forty-five minutes. I'll reheat it when the temperature drops.'

'It looks like it's just off the boil,' Alexis says, looking at the bucket with evident alarm.

'It needs to be as hot as you can bear,' Arianna explains patiently. 'In order to break down the neurotoxin venom. There's really no point to any of this otherwise. If you make the water the temperature of a baby's bath, you might as well not bother.'

'I don't want to end up with third-degree burns on my foot.'

'I've put my hand in,' she says. 'It's bearable. At least, I can bear it.'

'Man, this is not the way I wanted your surf lesson to go,' I say, as Alexis plunges his foot into the hot water. I was expecting him to go quarter-inch by quarter-inch, but he just goes for it, right up to his shin.

'Shit,' he says, closing his eyes tightly. 'Do you have any painkillers on you?'

'I don't,' I say.

Arianna comes to the rescue, rooting through her bag and handing him a white tablet and a half-drunk bottle of water. 'Ibuprofen,' she says. 'Should take the edge off the pain.'

'I'm really sorry about all this,' I say.

'It's not your fault,' he says. 'I'm the plonker who stepped on the toxic fish that was hiding in the fucking sand.'

'What did you just call yourself?' I say, sure I've never heard that word before.

'Plonker? Sorry, my father used to say that all the time. I don't know why it just popped out of my mouth. It's not a term I normally use. I suppose I'm just thinking of him because he was also extremely accident-prone. If there was a sharp carpet gripper to stand on, his foot would find it. He was always getting injured by household implements. Electrocuted by our doorbell once. I think it was probably just a combination of dyspraxia and bad luck.'

I can relate, but I don't ask any questions because I don't want to pry. Families are a minefield. I should know.

He shakes his head as if shaking away difficult memories.

'You must think I'm more trouble than I'm worth,' he says. 'I was hoping to have another lesson tomorrow and the next day, but I don't suppose I can now.'

'No sweat. We can reschedule your other surf lessons for another time. It'll take about a week for your foot to feel better.'

'I really loved it out there,' he says, crossing his arms tightly over his chest. 'It was the happiest I've felt in I don't even know how long.'

I think of what my mom always used to say – *Surfing heals the sad boys* – and I wonder if it will be true for this one. Because sadness lingers over him, I can see that now, and I wonder how I didn't pick up on that before.

'We need to get your wetsuit back to the hire place tonight,' I say. 'And we should probably take it off you before your foot swells up any more.'

'I'll help,' Arianna says, piping up from the other room, where she's evidently been listening to our conversation.

'Oh God,' he says. 'I'm not wearing anything underneath it. It was so tight.'

'It's all right, mate,' Arianna says, coming into the room, looking delighted. 'We'll avert our eyes.'

Which is not all that easy, in the event, because peeling the world's tightest neoprene off of a swollen foot takes some work. And some of Arianna's coconut hair oil, which I rub over his foot as gently as I can manage, to add a little lubrication.

When we finally get the suit off him, and he's cupping himself to preserve his modesty, Arianna hands him a pair of lifeguard shorts and tells him to put them on, which he does while evil-eyeing the crumpled wetsuit lying on the floor, as if he'll never be wearing one of those again.

'Foot back in the bucket, please,' Arianna orders, before going into the other room again. Alexis does it obediently, like a child afraid of a particularly fierce teacher.

'Can we start over?' he says, suddenly. 'I feel like I've made a shit first impression. I mean, I usually make a shit first impression, so nothing new there, but not usually this bad.'

There's a strong smell of cooked meat wafting up the late-day beach, presumably from all the barbecue grills, but maybe from some of the fiercer sunburns, also.

'It's fine. Don't worry. You haven't made any kind of impression,' I lie, brazenly.

'Oh God, no impression at all is probably worse, isn't it? Like a nondescript wallpaper.'

I smile. 'I wouldn't say that, exactly.'

'It's just… well, I haven't been entirely honest with you, Candice,' he says.

Here we go, I think.

Seven

I look over at Alexis, sitting with his foot in a steaming hot pail of water, staring out at the ocean.

'So, first I should say that I really value my privacy, my anonymity.'

'Oh?' I say, ears pricking up, because maybe Makayla's had it right all along. Maybe this guy is one of her 'famouses'. But then, why hasn't he been recognised by the other customers? It's not as if he hasn't been attracting attention.

'I'm a writer,' he says.

'The commercial endeavour is a book?' I ask.

'Yes, that's right. A novel. It has a surf element, which is the real reason I need lessons. For research. Not just in case I happen to regret never learning when I'm an old duffer in my nursing home...'

'Why didn't you say anything before?'

'I generally don't tell people that I'm an author. Not if I can help it. Obviously, once I get to know them, I do. Or once I get envenomated. But at first, it's just easier not to disclose that information.'

'Really? Why?'

He sighs, deeply. 'A lot of factors.'

'It sounds like such a cool job. Work from home. Be creative on a daily basis. See your name on a book cover.'

I don't mention the joy of books, how stories can find you when you need them most and hold your pain at bay.

'People make assumptions, is the problem. They think I'm a millionaire. A success. And that's just not true. I wrote two novellas, the second one of which sold eight hundred copies.'

Eight hundred copies?

'That's too bad.'

'I mean, it wasn't all bad. It was reviewed well in some papers, but, when all's said and done, who buys novellas?'

'I'd have thought novellas would be perfect for today's world. Shorter than a novel, require less of a concentration span. Like volumes of short stories. You can dip in and out.'

'Do *you* buy novellas? Collections of short stories?'

I shake my head. 'Except for in college.'

And only because they were on the reading list.

'You went to college?'

'Why do you sound surprised about that? Wait staff and surf instructors don't go to college in this country?'

'Of course they do. I'm just surprised anyone can afford to go to college in the States. Doesn't it cost, like, a hundred grand a year?'

'Depends. It can do. You don't have to pay upfront, though. I have a lot of loans.' Not as many as some of my friends, but enough to stress me out whenever I'm stupid enough to think about them. My Sallie Mae student debt repayment is there in my bank account every month, debiting hundreds of dollars and pushing me further into the red. 'I try to block all that out, though, since there's not much I can do about it right now. It's sort of out of my control.'

'Yeah, I hear you. I have an advance that I need to earn out.'

'I don't know how the book industry works, I'm sorry.'

'An advance is just what the publisher gives the writer up front. It's an advance against royalties, so that the writer can keep the lights on and buy food while they're working on the book. Otherwise, you'd be working for two years with no money until the book is released.'

'It takes that long between getting a deal and the book hitting the market? *Two years?*'

'Mostly, yeah.'

'Bummer.'

'So, the bigger the advance, the more the pressure is off the writer financially, but on the other hand you then have shitloads of other pressure, because you need to sell enough copies of the book to make the publisher feel they've made a good investment in you.'

'That sounds very stressful,' I say, while thinking: *Nice problem to have.*

Alexis is on a roll, though, and doesn't pick up on my hint of sarcasm. 'And, remember, you need to earn out that advance before you get any royalties, which is hard when the cut most writers get from a paperback sale in a bookshop is about twenty-five pence. Four sales and I've paid off one pound of my advance. Forty sales – a massive stack of books – and I've still only paid off a tenner. Most bookshops might carry one or two copies of a title. You see the problem?'

'I'm beginning to. I'm also pretty good at math.'

He gives me an apologetic smile.

'It took me about thirty seconds to do that sum in my head,' he says. 'What I need now, what I have to find a way to write, is a *hit*. I can't afford to put my name to another book that's a critical success but a commercial failure. My agent got me a great deal on three chapters and a synopsis. Editors loved it. It went to auction. People were fighting over me.'

'Yeah, that blows.'

He grins.

'I know it sounds amazing but it's a mixed blessing. All those years I spent as a kid dreaming of being an author and getting a big book deal and now I have it, I feel like I have the sword of Damocles hanging over me by a single hair and sooner or later it's going to drop and that will be the end of me as a writer.'

'I don't think writing a book is exactly like sitting on a throne with a sword hanging from the ceiling,' I say, because I know the story about Damocles too and I don't want him to think I don't. I don't want him to think that I needed his explanation.

'Okay, maybe that was a stretch, but this is my one shot to hit a mass market readership. If I fail, that's me done as an author, which would delight my parents because then I'd have to go back to being a serious journalist.'

'Being a journalist is also cool. I mean, it's not working the mines.'

'It's not right for me. Too much pressure. Too few jobs.'

'So, you chose Cornwall as the place to come and write your hit novel?'

'It's where most of the romances I see on supermarket shelves are set, so it seemed like a sensible choice.'

'You're writing a *romance*?'

This didn't even occur to me as a possibility. Alexis seems like the antithesis of romance. The cloth he's made from is woven from sensible choices. He thinks about his gut health. He has lived on bone broth alone.

'Now who sounds surprised?' he says.

Everything about this is surprising to me. Including why he's telling me all of this in the first place, when this is clearly something he usually keeps to himself. Maybe it's just easier to talk to a stranger than the people in his life. People get so weird about romance fiction. As if it's something shameful, a guilty pleasure that should be hidden within the dust jacket of Serious Literature and read in secret.

'Can you say more about it?'

'A little bit but not too much, or else I'll lose the spark and I won't want to write the thing. That's happened to me before and I don't want to risk it again.'

'So tell me what you can.'

'It's simple enough. Everyone loves romance. It's a huge slice of the bookselling market, but bigger than ever now. First there's the whole "TikTok Made Me Buy It" movement, with huge sales generated by people using the platform to shout about books. Then there's what my agent calls the "*Bridgerton* effect". You know that TV series, the one that's supposed to be Regency England but a flashier, more diverse version of it?'

I'm not on TikTok, but I have seen every episode of *Bridgerton* and I loved every minute of that show. It's the best thing I've watched in years. The only reason I was able to watch it was because Demi strongly encouraged me to log into her Netflix account on my laptop. I'd inhaled the whole thing over two days, like an intoxicating drug. It left me feeling a little lonely and more than a little sexually frustrated, but also ravenous for the next season, which I guessed was the point.

'Who doesn't love a flashier and more diverse Regency England?' I say. 'I loved that show. It's very smart and sexy.'

'Oh, I know. But so are a lot of books and when you see how many copies those *Bridgerton* books sold, it just makes you wonder why some things that are good, but not amazing by any metric, seem to fly to these giddy heights while others, objectively better in every sense, sort of sink without trace.'

'Who's objective about books? It's all subjective, right? It's opinion. It's how a certain story, a certain voice resonates with a reader.'

'I know. I don't mean to be a snob and I have a lot of time for women's fiction, Margaret Atwood, et cetera. But there is a lowest common denominator element to these mass market romance books that I just can't quite... fathom.'

'Margaret Atwood is not "women's fiction". She is a woman who writes fiction, true, but most of her stuff is speculative. And *Bridgerton* is fucking great.'

'Of course it is. I'm not knocking it. It's so funny, though, the way that half the costumes are completely wrong for the time, covered in sequins and plastic flowers, and they have this wisteria that grows all year long, apparently, and the sets look like they were designed by the team behind Sylvanian Families.'

'Man, I love that wisteria,' I say, ignoring his criticisms, and letting my mind fall back to a particularly raunchy scene. 'And also Sylvanian Families.'

'Everyone loves *Bridgerton*,' he says, sighing. 'You can never talk women out of it. It's that mix of sexy and romantic, and the actors are excellent. But I'm getting sidetracked... I want to write a modern version. Obviously, I'm not going to set a Regency novel in Newquay, because fuck all was happening here back in the Regency period, but I think there's a way of getting the same feel, embracing the cottagecore movement in a more current way. Sexy seaside cottagecore.'

'Did you say *cottagecore*? Because I have no idea what that is.'

'Right, yes, it is still a bit niche. It's like the modern version of pastoralism. You know pastoralism, I suppose, if you went to college?'

I can't tell if he's trolling me or if he is actually this oblivious to how he is coming across.

'Pastoralism? Sure. When wealthy Romantic-era poets and authors idealised life as a shepherd, right? There were no bad smells, cow dung or mosquitoes to worry about. It was all sunshine meadows and cloud-watching from plaid picnic blankets and hand-stitched quilts.'

'Exactly. Cottagecore is the Instagram version of that. It's nostalgic and beautiful, all gorgeous gardens and awe-inspiring views, but cool as hell. Aspirational.'

'That's why you rented such an expensive cottage on Towan headland?'

'I thought it would give me the necessary inspiration for this project. It was a calculated risk. It's my shot at getting this right. Writing from London wasn't really working for me. I couldn't seem to enter the right mind-frame there.'

'Hang on,' I say, as I look up 'cottagecore' online and see

a lot of very pretty women with gorgeous houses, perfect lawns and rose gardens. The people who live in these places must be millionaires. Yet they all seem to be so young. Women in their mid-twenties dressed in flowy cotton dresses with hand-embroidered pink flowers, and sleeves capped to show off arms decorated with amazing tattoos. Much chintz. China dolls posed on beds, wearing flowing skirts to match their owners' outfits. Women who kiss passionately as the sun sets behind them. Wildflowers. Fields of corn. Leather-bound journals full of romantic poetry.

I can see the appeal. I can see it so clearly that I kind of want to ditch my van and run into the sunset with these women.

If Alexis can write about this, can really tap into this movement, write it in a beach cottage setting, and add in some *Bridgerton* chemistry and sexiness, maybe he is onto a winner. As a city guy with an eye for what city folk care about and know about, I'd put down money that he has a decent shot of nailing it. Anybody who's grown up in the country, who realises that farmhouses go with farm *work*, probably couldn't write the book he wants to write, but he won't be held back by real-life experiences. By reality. He's free to develop any fantasy world he likes.

'Are you disappointed?' he says. 'That I'm writing, well, glorified chick-lit?'

'First off, you need to cut that shit out. Chick-lit is a derogatory term intended to diminish women's voices and experiences.'

'I couldn't agree more, actually. It's just that the reaction from my friends and family hasn't exactly been supportive. There's been a lot of judgement.'

'Then they're being assholes. Personally, I love romance novels. They are the absolute best kind of books.'

My grandmother used to bring them whenever she came to visit us from Florida. Once I reached middle school, I couldn't resist reading her books, my heart rate picking up every time I got to a scene featuring any kind of passion. Or nudity.

'Wait, you read a lot of romance novels?'

'They're pretty much all I read.'

He frowns. 'But *why* are you reading them?' he says. 'That's what I'm still trying to work out about the readership. Is it purely for the escapism or is there something more to it?'

'For the truth,' I say. 'Romance novels shine a light on human nature.'

'Lowest common denominator human nature,' he says, in a way that has no hint of a sneer but couldn't be more offensive.

'Hey,' I say. 'Universal truth should be acknowledged. There's value in that. Just ask Jane Austen.'

'So you're not dreaming of running away with a knight on horseback? You're looking for something more from these stories.'

'That's kind of an insulting question. Romance is not just having some rich guy carry you away on a horse. There's a little more to it than that.'

'You're right,' he says. 'I need to change the way I think about this.'

'I don't disagree. I think you do have a problem here. You seem to be embarrassed, no, ashamed of the book you're being paid to write. That will show up in the text. That will shine through more than any insights into human nature that you try to crowbar in there.'

'You're absolutely right,' he says, looking a little shaken. 'What makes a good romance? I don't think I even know. In its essence, I mean.'

'I know what it is for me.'

'Then could you share?' he says, smiling ruefully. 'Because I have no idea.'

'I guess for me it boils down to the trope that we so often see in Austen novels.'

'Which is?'

'Two people longing for each other, not able to have each other, suffering in silence. They share this huge intense thing that they can't talk about. And nobody knows, except them. Like Anne Elliot and Captain Wentworth in *Persuasion*.'

'That makes sense... I respect that. It's just... whenever I sit down and try to write a paragraph of this, I feel like Joan Wilder from that film *Romancing the Stone*, dreaming up handsome hunks for buxom prairie ladies to run away with into the sunset, as I sob over my keyboard at the beauty of it all.'

'You wish you were Joan Wilder,' I say. 'Joan Wilder has it all. The great city apartment, the amazing career, the financial means to take a long exotic vacation and meet a smoking hot anti-hero. Literary fans in non-English-speaking countries. A chonk cat.'

'Was the cat very chonk?' he asks, biting his lip, trying to remember.

'It wasn't *not* chonk. It had some girth.'

'I'm more of a dog person.'

'Why write a romance if you don't love romance?'

He starts tugging at his hair, drying now in the evening sun, curling into waves. He takes a strand and pulls it out, then another, and goes on.

'Desperation. I thought I'd give it a punt and it paid off. As I said, I ended up selling the project on three chapters and a synopsis. Three very short chapters. It's rare that publishers go for that these days, but they really liked the sample material and they're trusting me to deliver. God only knows why, because the book they've bought is going to be nothing like anything I've published before.'

'So why are they trusting you?'

'Daniel – my agent – whipped up a lot of excitement. The editor who ended up winning the auction was a massive fan of my debut novella, especially the strand that dealt with doomed love. She said she thought I wrote women really well, which made me so happy. But writing about doomed love is pretty different from writing a romance with a happy fucking ending. What do I know about happy endings?'

I feel like Makayla would have a smart remark just waiting to go here, but I come up blank, and nod for him to continue.

'My life hasn't been full of great romance,' he says. 'I don't think I've ever actually been in love. Not pure love. Not even in my serious relationships. I've never let myself be. I've never wanted to be so out of control.'

I stare at him. Of everything he's told me about himself, this is the thing that makes me most uncomfortable. That he would rather experience no love than risk being hurt by it is just unfathomable to me.

'And now you're writing a whole book about falling in love?'

'You don't have to have experienced a thing to know how to write about it,' he says. 'That's what imagination is for, right? Isn't that the whole point?'

'You've never fallen head over heels for someone?'

'I've loved people, but I've never loved someone so much they were the only thing I could think about. I've always been able to keep my feelings in perspective. I've never let them colour the other aspects of my life. I'm probably coming off a bit like a sociopath, but it's just the way my brain works. Everything is divided into different sections and the sections don't touch.'

Whereas, when I fell in love, it was all-consuming. Catastrophic. It took over my mind, my body, my soul.

'That hasn't been my experience,' I say. 'I have pretty much always gone all in. Maybe your way of thinking, of keeping things separate, is the smarter approach.'

'Not great for writing romantic fiction, though.'

'I did notice you're reading some,' I say, thinking of the paperback with the giant red stiletto on the cover that he'd brought into Demigorgons.

'That's how I've been spending most of my evenings. Agent's orders.'

'Nice work if you can get it. What kind of stuff have you covered so far?'

'Quite an eclectic mix. I've been swerving between Regency classics, steamy bonkbusters from the eighties, noughties chicklit and this year's big romance hits. Anything with a happy ending. That's the thing Daniel's most concerned about. He doesn't think I can pull a happy ending out of the bag. He doesn't think I have it in me.'

'Did you finish the red stiletto book?'

'Yes. It was surprisingly gripping.'

'Why surprising?'

'I don't know... I just didn't think you could squeeze that much tension out of a story that is essentially boy meets girl and everyone lives happily ever after. But it really had me turning the pages. I finished *Persuasion*, *Emma* and *Mansfield Park* and now I'm racing through *Pride and Prejudice*. First time I've ever read it, although obviously I've seen the films with girlfriends.'

I love that story heart and soul, and I brace myself for whatever he has to say about it.

'What do you think? Are you a fan?' I ask.

'Austen is a genius, no doubt. Brilliant sense of humour, understanding of human nature and very shrewd social commentary, but mostly I find it interesting to think about what's not on the page.'

'How do you mean?' I say, looking at his lips, which he's pressing together, as if he's thinking deep thoughts, like a Harvard professor. A professor who has one foot wedged in a pail of steaming hot water.

'Elizabeth might not know it, but it's clear that Mr Darcy has a mistress waiting in a flat in some city. London. Maybe Manchester.'

'What?' I say, outraged.

'Oh, at least one mistress. She's probably in Cheapside, with Lizzy's aunt and uncle. She'll be at that sort of social level. More bohemian than them, though. Long wavy hair and fine eyes. Probably a fine arse too. Just like Lizzy. I'm pretty confident that fine eyes is shorthand for fine arse.'

'Oh, you're confident about that?' I say.

He's brightened now, cheerfully espousing his philosophy, the most animated that I've seen him.

'Yes, and his father almost certainly introduced Mr Darcy to brothels at the age of fourteen. Maybe even on his fourteenth birthday.'

'What are you even talking about?' I say. 'None of that is true. You're tripping.'

'It was true of most men of his class at the time. So why not Mr Darcy?'

'Darcy is not that kind of guy. He's a gentleman.'

'Gentlemen were the worst. They had more routes to deviancy open to them. More time for debauchery.'

'You're insane,' I say, trying not to smile as I look out at the kids playing on the beach and the late evening sunbathers reading paperbacks. 'I can't even believe I'm listening to this garbage.'

'Okay, have it your way. But if you're seriously telling me that super-rich Mr Darcy of sodding Pemberley is a virgin until he meets and marries Elizabeth Bennet, then you're the one who's tripping.'

'Maybe he is. He could be.'

He gives me a look that clearly says, *You are deluding yourself, woman, and I think you know that.*

'One thing I will say though,' he continues. 'Is that Austen understood sex and sexual compatibility, no question. Sex oozes from the page in her work.'

'Where are you getting that from? Because I definitely do not remember any steamy scenes in *Pride and Prejudice*.'

'Jane and Bingley? Loads of giggly sex. No blowjobs.'

'You are. You're crazy.'

'Lizzy Bennet and Darcy? All about the foreplay. Their whole courtship is a precursor to their sex life. All that knocking the pride out of Mr Darcy is basically about getting him down on his knees for cunnilingus.'

I laugh, and look up at the sky, which is still blue without even the tiniest wisp of cloud, and try to imagine Jane Austen's characters walking along this beach with their parasols. Trying to imagine what they'd make of the concept of surfing.

'I don't think it was *exactly* about cunnilingus,' I say, no longer able to maintain my expression of what Makayla would call 'serious offence taken'. I can feel myself blushing, because it's not exactly normal to talk about this subject in your first real conversation with a person, especially when that person is an extremely hot guy you seem to be attracted to, despite your logical brain telling you not to be, because it *knows* this is a bad idea.

'It's there in the text. Austen always lets us know what kind of sexual relationship her characters are in for. *Mansfield Park* is a great example. The cousins, Edmund and Fanny Price. No sex at all. They don't end up having kids and there's not the merest allusion to chemistry between them. It's all spiritual love. We're not even talking Bed Death here, because their marital bed was never alive, you see? Those sheets are semen-free.'

'Okay, the first cousins thing is weird,' I admit. 'But different times. Different laws... What about Mr Knightley in *Emma*? What's your take on him? I always found him a little tight-wound and sexless.'

'Not at all. He's a sex maniac. Austen's clue is in the name. Mr Nightly. Twice-nightly, more like.'

'It's with a K,' I say, laughing. 'As in a noble knight of the realm.'

'True but that's just the surface meaning. The secret meaning is that he goes like a champ.'

'Mr Knightley does not go like a champ. He has respectful sex with no eye contact and minimal exchange of bodily fluids.'

'He has raw sexual power. Good dancer too, like Mr Darcy. That's another way you know he's sexually sophisticated. He's got the moves.'

'You're ruining the books for me.'

'Okay, but imagine readers in two hundred years' time looking over the sexy romance novels on the bestseller lists today. You don't think they'd have things to say? Objections to make?'

'Is that what you're worried about? Being judged by romance readers two centuries from now?'

'No, I'm worried that my editor will read my manuscript and realise she's made a huge fucking mistake. That I've bitten off more than I can chew.'

'You can chew this just fine,' I say. 'Just don't rush your bite, okay? Give yourself time to, um, swallow.'

He smiles again, that big, beautiful dimple-to-dimple smile that makes me go a little weak at the knees despite my better judgement.

'When I'm cleared to get my foot out of the bucket, would you like to go for a drink with me? A coffee, a beer, whatever you fancy.'

'Now?'

The truth is I'm not keen on the idea of going anywhere right now except home to my van, because I'm tired from a long day and salty from the ocean, but buying him a beer is probably the least I can do since I led him into the lair of the weever fish and got him maimed. I just hope he doesn't have a delayed allergic reaction to the sting and go into anaphylaxis. Besides the potential lethality element, it would look really bad on my Tripadvisor reviews.

'Okay then,' I say. 'That'll work.'

'Really? You don't mind?'

'Why would I mind?' I say, narrowing my eyes at him because he is just so weird in his reactions to the things I say. 'Do you think I'm so busy that I can't make time for one drink?'

'You just have this very busy vibe. You seem like you always have people to see and places to be.'

That may be my vibe, but his vibe, according to Makayla at least, is being perpetually available for a roll in the sand. Which is worse than my vibe.

'My evening is wide open. Say the word when you want to go, and we'll go.'

'Can we go now? I can't take much more of this foot burning. I think it's done all the good it's going to do me.'

'You think you can make it to the beach bar?' I say, motioning to Arianna that we're leaving. 'It's not far. I can give you a ride on my back if you need me to do that.'

He shakes his head. 'I'd be too heavy for you to carry.'

'Hey, let me be the judge of that. I'm a surfer. I have muscles.'

'I think I can limp my way over there, but I appreciate the offer.'

There's no denying that he has a great smile. One of

those genuinely warm smiles that make the recipient feel all luminous inside.

'Let me run over to the shack and get your clothes,' I say. 'I have to return your suit anyhow.'

'Thanks,' he says, handing me the damp wetsuit. 'I really don't want to rock up at a beach bar wearing red lifeguard shorts, like I think I'm David Hasselhoff in *Baywatch*.'

'Don't hate on the Hoff. He's a god,' I say, and I smile all the way to the shack.

*

When we finally limp into the bar, it's full of tourists and locals, throwing back bottles of artisan beers brewed in the local vicinity and pints of something called Rattler, which I've learnt from prior experience is a highly alcoholic cider, with a rattlesnake as its logo, and not to be confused with the cloudy apple juice 'cider' that American children drink at the fairground.

Within moments, Alexis is causing something of a stir. There are already a few women staring directly at him, not even trying to hide it, but he seems completely unaware of what's happening. Maybe he's so used to being stared at that he doesn't even notice it any more.

He limps to the last free booth, the one by the door to the bathrooms that nobody wants to take because of the constant stream of customers passing by. And because of the smell.

'Ready for that drink?' I ask. 'My treat. Did you want coffee, beer, or something else?'

'Definitely something with a high alcohol content. I need to revive my tissues.'

'Your poisoned tissues?'

'Exactly. I'll have whatever's on special.'

He opens a battered leather billfold wallet and offers me a ten-pound note, which I wave away, even though I could really use the money. He slumps down onto a chair under a flatscreen TV showing footage of a surfer riding a heavy wave. I turn away from the screen and go up to order our drinks from the bartender: a young woman I recognise with feathery eyelashes and two strawberry-blonde French braids that stretch down her back. When I return holding two bottles of Rattler, Alexis seems to be in even more pain than before.

'Maybe I should have done the bucket treatment for longer. God, I feel like a massive twat,' he says, suddenly. 'Getting stung by a tiny little toxic fish on my first ever surf lesson. How bloody embarrassing.'

'It could happen to anybody. Wrong foot, wrong patch of sandy seafloor. You know how they tell you to do the stingray shuffle in the States, so that you can scare them off when they're hiding in the sand? That doesn't work on weever fish – these assholes just sting your big toe.'

He smiles again and his face lights up. Some of his brooding artist persona lifts away and I see a flash of the carefree kid he must have been once, before the world got to him and made him the way he is.

'This might seem weird, but what I'd really like...' he says, 'is to take you out for lunch. To say thank you for teaching me how to ride a wave. Even though it was just one. And I ended up in hot water, quite literally.'

I stare at him. There's something about his body language which seems off. As if he's nervous. He hasn't seemed that way at all until now. Quite the opposite.

'You're inviting me to lunch?'

'Not interested?'

'But you don't eat lunch. Am I supposed to eat a footlong sandwich while you watch and maintain your fast?'

'I think I can make an exception this one time,' he says. 'I mean it. If you're up for it, I'd like to take you somewhere really decent.'

'Not Demigorgons, then, huh? Is that a slam on my place of work?'

'No, not at all. I didn't mean that. Demigorgons is great. Excellent. The food looks… good.'

'But you can't vouch for it. Because you never bought any. Not while I was working, anyways.'

'The thing is, and I don't want this to sound judgemental of anyone's dietary choices, but there's a lot of carbohydrates on those plates. I've seen three different types of carb on one starter dish.'

'We have an arugula salad. It comes with carrot-ginger dressing. Also, um… croutons. But on Saturday there's Korean food on the menu. We have tteok-bokki.'

'Which is savoury cakes made of… rice.'

I'm about to point out to him that it comes with spicy cucumber salad and hard-boiled egg, but he speaks first.

'I'm more of a paleo guy.'

'Paleo and fasting,' I say, with a low whistle. 'Wow. You'd have got on great with my mom. She and her friends loved to talk about both those things. They could keep on for hours.'

'Your mum's no longer with us?' he asks, looking as if he's just stepped onto a landmine and heard a distinct click.

I shake my head. 'She's been gone nearly a year now. I came to Newquay not long after she passed.'

'I'm so sorry to hear that. Really, Candice. That's awful.'

I blink back tears. I cannot cry now.

'So how about that lunch?' he says, sensing I don't want to have the conversation about my mom, or perhaps just as a Pavlovian response to the scent of hamburgers, which is coming in strong through all the open doors.

'Where are you thinking?'

'I'm not sure. I haven't eaten out here yet.'

'Not at all?'

He shakes his head. 'And, let me tell you: it's hard to fast in this town. Seems like around every corner there's a shop selling Cornish pasties or cod and chips. And, dear God, the smells from the bakeries.'

'Why don't you just stop doing the IF thing then? Live a little.'

'My digestive system would hate me. I've been cooking myself healthy three-course meals every night. I feast within a four-hour window, and then fall sleep around 1 a.m. That routine seems to work best for me.'

'Yikes,' I say. 'That sounds tough. Are you sure you want to do lunch, then? Risk messing up the system like that?'

'I'll eat something nutritious and low on the glycaemic index that won't cause a flare-up. I could use your input on restaurants, though.'

I shrug. 'I have no preference.'

As soon as I say it, I realise that I sound completely indifferent, or worse, like I'm being forced into something I'd prefer not to do at all.

'It's really okay if you don't want to come out with me. I know I can come across as a bit annoying,' he says, flashing me another one of those smiles.

'Oh, so you know that?'

'It has been mentioned, once or twice, yes.'

I think about it and come to a decision. 'I am plenty busy, I have a job and a new business, but a girl's got to eat. This girl anyway. Usually every two hours if we're being honest, so yes, I'll go to lunch with you.'

'Amazing. There's actually an adults-only boutique hotel, just up the coast.'

'A hotel?'

'Oh, I just meant the restaurant. It's apparently on the way to getting a Michelin star.'

'I can't afford that. I probably couldn't even afford a dessert in that place.'

'It's on me. Like I said, it's a thank you.'

'A thank you is two words, not a three-course lunch in a bougie hotel.'

'It's a *five*-course lunch, actually.'

'That for sure is breaking your fast,' I say, feeling some real concern about the effect this might have on his large intestine.

'In for a penny, in for a pound,' he says. 'Anyway, once won't hurt.'

And yet, once so often did turn out to hurt. Once had hurt me plenty.

Once was the whole reason I was here.

'So,' I say, because I need to change the subject. 'You've given me the setting, but what's the story?'

Eight

'You have to promise you won't tell anyone else. I'm not supposed to discuss it at all. It's sort of "high concept".'

Alexis does air quotes.

'As in...' I say, keeping a straight face, 'you were high when you came up with the concept?'

He laughs. 'Accurate, actually. Okay, so it's these two surf-bum kids who grew up in the same neighbourhood. All run-down fishermen's cottages with roses around the door and marijuana in the herb garden. The book is set in Cornwall, obviously, but a more aspirational Cornwall than reality. A Cornwall with huge California-style apartments and swimming pools. I'm going to leave out the factory assembly line jobs and sheep-gutting, because I just don't think that's right for the genre.'

'Go figure.'

'So Janie and Bryce have always been friends.'

'These Cornish kids are called *Janie and Bryce*?'

'Absolutely. It's the wannabe California culture, you know. People call their kids those kind of American-sounding names in places like this. So, the pair of them have always been friends, always spent early mornings surfing together when conditions were good, but now they're grown up.'

'They don't surf any more?'

A gorgeous girl in a gold thong bikini and gladiator sandals walks through the bar to order something at the food counter, and I wait for Alexis to start staring, along with half the other guys in the place, but he's so absorbed in his story that he doesn't even seem to notice her.

'They still surf. Which is why I need to learn how to, so that I can write about it convincingly. But they don't talk on the beach after their surf, they don't hang out with each other, not like they used to. They keep secrets from each other now. They've drifted apart.'

'Bummer.'

'Both of them are gorgeous, obviously, but they've never gone out. Everyone else in their town is sort of plain but these two had major glow-ups when they hit their teens. The girl, Janie, has slept with all of Bryce's friends, but never him. She's never even kissed him. The only time she ever touches him is to hold him up when he's drunk.'

'I think I see where this is going.'

'One day, when she's realised she's broke again, and so is he, she comes up with this ingenious plan. She's seen a gap in the market. The gap between middle-aged married people with bags of money who no longer want to have sex with each other. They're looking for something to spice up their marriage and they're willing to pay for that thing.'

'This is a story about prostitution? Okay, I take it back, I did not see where this was going.'

Alexis shakes his head. 'No, not prostitution. Close, but no. They take one evening class on massage therapy at the local college and set up as high-class masseurs. They get a loan and do up one of the cottages, so they have premises, but they also offer house calls. Janie takes the male clients and Bryce takes the female clients. It's not really about the massage. It's about their hot surfer bodies. The muscles. The strength. The all-over tan. That's the dream they're selling.'

'Most cold-water surfers in Europe have a farmer's tan. Tanned hands, feet and face and that's it. It's the wetsuits. Even in Hawaii, where people surf in boardshorts, butts are never tan.'

He looks me directly in the eye, seeming surprised by this.

'Okay,' he says, opening the Notes feature of his cell phone and writing something down, while murmuring, 'Butts are never tanned'. 'But readers can suspend their disbelief. Anyway, these middle-aged marrieds get to be touched by the hottest, coolest couple they've ever seen. They get to be rubbed down.'

'Couple? I thought you said Bryce and Janie never dated.'

'Correct. But for their business enterprise, for their brand, they pretend they're a couple. To build on the fantasy. And maybe there's a hint that they'd be open to swinging, in the right circumstances, but it's only implied, it's never explicitly said. It's very sexy. All hot breath and moaning as they hit the right spots.'

'Uh-huh.'

'Too much?' he says.

'It depends what kind of romance this is. If this was a TV show, what kind of rating would it have?'

He bites his lip, and a flash of panic comes into his eyes.

'I haven't quite nailed that down yet. There are indecent

proposal moments from some of the clients, male and female, but Janie and Bryce always turn them down. They say that although they're interested, of course, if they cross the professional line then they can no longer give massages, and people really love getting these massages by our gorgeous protagonists.'

My eyes fix on a guy in a sport jacket, who is absentmindedly digging earwax out with his pinky finger. He meets my gaze and reddens.

'What do you think so far?'

'It's sounding a little like a seventies porn movie.'

'Is it?' Alexis says, biting his lip again, so hard that a little dot of blood blooms there. 'I might have to reassess certain parts. Remember, the potential for sex is just part of the act. It's not real. Just dangled like a carrot.'

'It's all going swell. Where's the conflict?'

'I'm getting there. One of the clients, a rich guy with three sports cars and a yacht, wants to leave his wife and marry Janie.'

'How rich are we talking?'

'Skirting a billion. He's a media mogul. Started off as a journalist but is giving Rupert Murdoch a run for his money now. He has several properties in Cornwall, including one penthouse apartment on Fistral Beach.'

'Good for him.'

'No, not good for him. He's a prick. He gets obsessed with Janie, and he won't take no for an answer.'

'This is a romance? You're sure this book is not actually a thriller being forced into a romance Halloween outfit?'

'It's a romance. Things get crazy. Bryce has to step in and fight the rich guy. He has to save Janie from this creep with all the money and none of the moves. He breaks the guy's nose and tells him that if he ever troubles Janie again, he'll kill him.'

'You're quite sure this book is not a thriller?'

'It's not a thriller. Bryce is not really going to kill the billionaire. He's a surfer. He's laid back. He's all about the chilled vibes.'

I think of all the fist fights I've seen on beaches here and home. Angry guys taking out their frustration on each other, squaring up on the sand after poor surf etiquette and dangerous dropping in on waves. I've seen punches thrown in the water. My brother was assaulted by an elderly bodyboarder, who took his flipper off and hit Ricky over the head with it, after he inadvertently dropped in on the guy's wave. Ricky kept apologising – as he dodged the rubber swim-fin – but the guy was too incensed to hear it.

'Surfers can be some of the biggest assholes out there. Pumped up on steroids and aggressive as hell, swinging dicks looking for a fight, scratching for the biggest wave.'

'Really?' Alexis asks, sounding disappointed, as if he was expecting some fraternity of love and mutual support. 'Well, Bryce isn't like that. Bryce is a mellow guy. But after the fight, when he sends billionaire guy packing, he looks down at his bloody knuckles and realises that all this time he thought he and Janie were just friends when she was always the one for him.'

'And what are her thoughts on this?'

He blinks, as if this is a new question.

'She realises he was her one. They take their business over to Florida, where they can charge even more because of their poshed-up English accents, and the book ends with them having sex in this lagoon that runs behind a beach and is fed by the ocean. It's hot, sweaty and sexy as hell. It's paradise.'

'There are no alligators in this lagoon?'

'No alligators.'

'Bull sharks? Bull sharks *love* swimming in brackish water.'

'No sharks. Just warm turquoise water and multiple orgasms.'

I nod and try to picture the scene. 'Way to go, Bryce and Janie.'

'What do you think? Does it sound commercial to you, as a hardened fan of the genre?'

'Let me make sure I have this straight. The book is about two gorgeous Cornish kids getting rich by manipulating horny boomers out of their money, finding love and leaving Cornwall to go live the American dream in Florida? That's it?'

'That's it.'

'How long do they keep up their sexy massage business? Are they still doing it when they're married and expecting their fourth kid?'

'I'm not sure yet. I've got a lot of decisions to make. I might lose the contemporary setting altogether and make it all happen in the Regency era. Cash in more obviously on the *Bridgerton* thing I was talking about.'

'Were house-calling cottagecore massage therapists a thing in that era?' I ask, while realising that I would totally read that book.

'I haven't dived into the research yet, but it's definitely possible. Maybe that kind of massage was marketed as a medical procedure. To relieve non-specific malaise. To cure indisposition. Whenever I set it though, it's got to be as sexy as I can make it. I'm aiming for a book that will make women readers want to sleep with their husbands. That night. That's basically the whole *raison d'être* of the book. It's in the official proposal.'

'Please tell me you're kidding.'

'Not at all. My agent said that was the key to the success of *Fifty Shades*. It turned on readers so much that they were happy to jump their own spouses, just so they could get some.'

'Huh, I wonder if you can work that into the blurb?'

'*Will make you enjoy sex with your husband* is quite the jacket copy,' he says, cleaning sand out of his thumbnail with a toothpick that a stranger has left on the table.

'Do you have a title yet?' I say, hoping he'll quit it with the toothpick.

'No, it's still untitled at present. The people at the publishing house can't agree on one.'

'You have *Fifty Shades* with a friends-to-lovers element and a massage theme?' I say, pondering it. 'How about *Fifty Shades of Effleurage*?'

'Isn't effleurage, like, sewage?' he says, wrinkling his nose. 'Because that doesn't sound very sexy. That sounds like a leaflet put out by a water company to warn beach users when the faeces level is so severe they need to get out of the sea.'

'You're thinking of effluence. "Effleurage" is a common massage technique,' I say. 'It means "light touch" in French. Something like that.'

'You know massage, too?' Alexis says, his face lighting

up. 'Because that would be massively helpful from a research point of view.'

'A bit,' I say, thinking about the hours I spent on Joseph's muscles, after an intense workout or long surf session. He was always so incredibly grateful, amazed at how I could reduce his pain, at how I could make him feel better, until he wasn't grateful any more. Until it became just another service he expected me to perform as part of the marriage deal.

All that massage left my body aching, drained the energy out of me, but I told myself it was okay. That the slow touch sent me into a meditation of my own, one I needed, so that the act benefitted me too.

'Could you show me?' Alexis says. 'I'll pay you for your time. For the lesson.'

I blink. This request could seem a little flirty, coming from somebody else, but I'm not sure someone like him would flirt with someone like me, so this is all in the name of research, I guess.

'Sure I'll show you. You don't have to pay me to show you basic massage technique, but there is something you can do for me.'

'Anything.'

'Switch tables at the café.'

'I picked a bad one?'

'You picked the best one. Then didn't order anything the whole time you were there.'

'Your friend said it was fine.'

'Makayla is nicer than me.'

'God, I'm a prick sometimes.'

'Only sometimes,' I say, smiling. 'For the other ten percent of the time, you're doing just great.'

He looks at me differently and, for the first time since we met, I can see a flicker of desire. Something in this conversation has made him want me. It's right there in his eyes and I know that look. It's the same hunger I'd seen so many times in Joseph's eyes.

If I asked Alexis to follow me back to my van now, he'd follow, poisoned foot or not. And maybe I'd want him to. Which is totally inappropriate. Which is crazy.

'I don't think I can walk all the way to my cottage,' he says, suddenly, and I realise he will in fact have to come into my van, which is parked right across from this beach bar, at the back of Demigorgons. On a typical day, I'd walk to the beach, but not today. Today I had to bring my quiver of boards with me, because I had a new surf client to meet and I didn't know what surf level he was at, so I needed to bring them all.

'I can give you a ride,' I say.

'You have a car here?'

'I have my van over by the café.'

'Are you sure?' he says. 'I can get a cab. It's not a problem.'

'It's a two-minute drive. I can swing it.'

He picks up his bottle of Rattler and drains it, putting his hand over his mouth afterwards, because of the insane amount of fizz. I set my own bottle aside, half-drunk.

He only has a shoe on one foot and, when I look down, I see that his injured foot has swollen even more.

'I think I have some antihistamines in my glovebox,' I say. 'Might be worth a try. Could help the swelling go down.'

'Do you have any painkillers?' he asks. 'That single ibuprofen tablet isn't really cutting it.'

'Only the herbal kind,' I say, giving him a look.

'I love the herbal kind,' he says, breaking into a huge smile. 'I just started smoking – research for this project – and I've been reading all about the health benefits.'

'What did you do to your boyfriend?' a senior citizen in a neon pink vest calls from his stool at the bar. 'His leg looks like the Elephant Man.'

'He's not my boyfriend. And he stood on a weever fish.'

Old guy makes a face. 'Nasty little bastards. He'll feel it even worse tomorrow.'

'Great,' Alexis says, wincing as he hobbles through the bar. We go slow and he leans on me heavily as we walk to my van. I've seen a few people with weever fish stings before, but Alexis seems to be responding worse than any of them. Maybe his pain tolerance level is just set lower or maybe he's having some sort of allergic reaction.

'Do you want to go to the hospital and get checked over?' I ask.

'No, I Googled it already. It's not serious. I'm just being a drama queen.'

I unlock the van and put the board I lent him back on the roof with the others, while he climbs awkwardly into the passenger side.

Buckling myself in, I see the moment when he notices my pillows and the blue comforter rolled up in the corner. The moment when he realises this van is my home.

'Does it have a name?' he asks.

'Hal,' I say.

'Like *2001: A Space Odyssey*?'

'Short for Halen.'

He looks at me confused and then breaks into that smile.

'Van Halen. Nice. Is it yours or are you borrowing it from someone local?'

'I own it. I had enough money to buy an old, beat-up van when I arrived here, but that was all I could swing. There were no rentals available on any of the real estate websites I visited and when I visited the offices in person, I was told that there were huge waiting lists and that places got snapped up within minutes of them becoming available, and those people were able to put down a year's rent in advance. Which wasn't me.'

I wait for him to ask how it is that I'm here in the first place, how it is that I got the necessary documents to work here and start a life here, but he doesn't. He just takes it all at face value. As if a girl from Hawaii emigrating to Cornwall is a totally run-of-the-mill thing.

'That's... I can't even imagine how tough.'

'Where's your place?' I say. 'How close is the parking lot to your cottage?'

'You can park at Little Fistral. My cottage is down there.'

It takes a while to get out of the Fistral Beach parking lot on account of all the tourists circling, trying to find a space, desperately hoping I've just vacated one they can slide into. I do the throat-slitting motion, to try to explain I've come out of the Demigorgons space, which they can't use without getting clamped.

Driving past the private entrance to the Headland Hotel, I hit the blinker, hang a left and take the lane to Little Fistral, past dozens of camper vans and their lounging, music-playing owners.

When we arrive in the parking lot, I realise that this cottage he's been talking about is not just any cottage.

It's the place by the old lifeboat house, just down the hill from the whitewashed coastguard lookout at the top of the headland, newly painted and refurbished for the Airbnb market, just like most of the other empty properties in this town.

'This is the place?' I say. 'You have all this space just for you?'

'I got a good deal,' he says, with a casual shrug, that seems to gloss over the fact that he's probably dropped something like ten thousand pounds to hire this place. 'Do you want to come in?'

'You're inviting me inside?'

'It feels like the least I can do, given you taught me how to surf and saved me from a toxic fish.'

Taught him how to surf is a little strong when he caught one wave before wiping out horribly over the nose of the board. He's probably going to be covered in bruises tomorrow and have a stiff neck from that one bad wipe-out alone.

'I also put you in the path of the toxic fish.'

He looks over at me and I feel the strings of my heart twitch toward him. Him and his sweet oceanside home.

I look down at my bare, still-sandy feet and try to make a decision. If I go inside, that could lead to something that might not be so easy to get out of.

This way, staying outside, he's just a guy who has money to burn this summer for surf lessons and I'm the first instructor who's crossed his path. I shouldn't do anything to jeopardise that arrangement.

I'm quiet for a long, awkward minute before I look up and meet his eyes.

'I could say I have stuff to do tonight but that wouldn't be the truth because I don't. I don't want to make this situation complicated. Do you know what I'm saying?'

Alexis nods, but I can see the disappointment there in those pretty eyes of his and I don't like that I've put it there. Something within me wants to please him, in the same way that something within me wanted to please Joseph.

'No problem,' he says, warmly, apparently not offended. 'Have a nice night, Candice.'

'Hey, I really hope your foot feels better tomorrow. Let me know when you want to reschedule that surf lesson. If you still do, that is. If you don't, I'll give you your money back. That won't be a problem.'

The crisp twenty-pound bills are still there in my pocketbook.

'I definitely still want to learn how to surf. But until we can do that, let's do that lunch, yeah?'

I look out at the deep turquoise of the shallow water behind him. Even though it's evening, the sun is still pushing down hard, and I can feel sweat running in cool little beads the whole way down my arms, off of my wrists and onto the warm asphalt.

Is this lunch really just a thank you, or is he asking me on a date? Or is it somehow something else?

'I'm working tomorrow,' I say.

'The next day, then? Or whenever you want. If you want. Your decision.'

My decision. Great. Except, historically, most of my decisions have been lousy, maybe even including the one to come to Newquay.

Then, I hear Makayla's voice in my head, telling me to live a little.

'Friday might work.'

He lights up like a pinball machine, and man, he is nice to look at when he's smiling.

'Excellent. I'll arrange everything,' he says. 'All you have to do is turn up and eat. Oh, and wear flat shoes. And trousers. Pants, I mean.'

'Why?'

'You'll see.'

Getting to wear flats is always a plus, since I've never had a date in stilettos that I enjoyed. I've always been too worried about wobbling over – breaking a heel or an ankle. Throughout all my best times I've always been wearing my sneakers.

'Count me in.'

*

As I drive back up the lane from Little Fistral, I look out at the lights from boats dotted in the bay, over the rows of fishermen's cottages, to the bright floodlights of the tiny soccer stadium on the hill.

Newquay, I have come to realise, has all the fixings of a traditional small town, with a resort feel that has something for nearly everyone. It brings bucket-and-spade families, senior citizens on bus tours, bachelor and bachelorette parties who stay in the cheap lodges in the centre of the town, and a hardened surf crew who come from all over the world, chasing endless summer and the world-class waves that hit the shore when all the conditions line up right. International surfers have moved through here, up-and-coming chargers and old-timers alike. I was aware of this place before I had any idea of how it would figure in my own life. Even Kelly Slater put up a picture of himself standing on Fistral Beach when he was just a teenage grom, surfboard under his arm and a full head of hair. There is also a new demographic of super-rich second-homers who'll drop a million pounds on a new oceanside condo that they'll visit once a year. Some would argue that all the new construction work and financial investment from city folks is making the town worse. It has for sure made it more expensive.

That someone like Alexis, a city guy with money, would want to experience this place is not surprising, but what I can't get past is his interest in me. There are plenty of surf instructors working this beach, who have all the gear and hundreds of glowing online reviews. If he's just looking for a hook-up, why would he choose someone wearing a wedding ring, when he could likely have his pick of any one of the beautiful girls around?

I'm not a good-on-paper person. I have barely three hundred pounds of small bills hidden in stashes around my van, no savings and no prospects of building any. All I have is student debt and extremely bad credit. I'm not even particularly nice to be around, as Joseph so often reminded me. So what does Alexis want from me?

Nine

I have work the next day and I get up early to run. All along my route, I can't help hoping I'll see the guy from the Huer's Hut, although it's rare to see a holidaymaker twice. There have been a few occasions where I've had good conversations with new folks and wished I'd been able to see them again, but that's not the way it goes in a resort town.

When I get back I get dressed in the van, put on my Demigorgons shirt with some shorts, apply sunblock and tinted lip balm and head to the café. I get there a half-hour before opening time and notice that there are no early-bird guys with laptops hanging around outside.

It's busy from the off, so the time should go fast. But it drags. I'm not waiting for Alexis to come in, I'm not expecting him to walk through the door, because he's probably tucked up in his cottage, resting his swollen foot. But, even so, I keep looking around to check.

I shouldn't care that he's not here, because it's not as if I have feelings for him. At least, not romantic ones. But him not coming into the café doesn't make me feel relieved. All it does is leave me feeling depressed, like I've wound up being rejected by somebody I didn't even want in the first place.

'How was your date with the Doberman?' I ask Makayla. 'Did you go?'

'Yeah. I think I'm starting to like him a bit more, now he's dropped the cold cucumber act.'

'That sounds… promising?'

'I dunno. I think it's mostly because he keeps sending me photos of the puppy – it's like he's constantly microdosing me with happy. I can't go cold turkey now.'

'Did you meet the puppy?'

'Not yet,' she says, looking glum. 'He can't go out until he's had his jabs.'

'Sure, but can't you go see him at the guy's apartment?'

'He says the puppy's too young to meet people, in case we give him coronavirus or something. I don't know. Maybe he's bullshitting me.'

Makayla tells me everything she knows about this baby dog, and I try to listen, but I'm distracted. Maybe Alexis did go into some kind of anaphylaxis and is lying dead in his cottage right now? Or maybe he's decided to leave me shitty reviews online? Maybe he's creating me a local business profile right now and is about to award me one sad little star.

Crappy surf instruction. Doesn't even tell you to wear boots to fend off weever fish attack.

Makayla doesn't seem to pick up on my awkwardness. She's too high on the thought of puppy parenthood and doesn't ask any questions at all about my day off.

'What's the puppy's name?' I ask. 'You haven't told me yet.'

'Major.'

'That's quite the alpha-male name.'

'Yeah, but his second name undercuts it quite a lot.'

'What's his second name?'

'Slobber.'

*

I'm just returning from a quick surf on my afternoon break when I see a broad-shouldered guy with a messenger bag standing outside the café. I watch him from the beach; I can't seem to bring myself to walk any closer. He's standing to one side of the entrance, staring up at the sky – at a pattern of clouds, I think at first. But I'm wrong because what he's actually looking at is the nest of herring gulls on the flat roof of the surf shack. Three floofy chicks with black spots on their heads are hopping about bugging their mom for food, tapping at a red dot on her yellow beak, waiting for her to throw up her lunch.

I watch until I'm sure it's Alexis, then I head a different way, doubling back and taking the dune path. If I go the parking lot route, I can enter the café through the rear door where he won't see me. I haven't had a chance to catch Makayla up on what happened and I want a minute to get myself together before I see him.

Ahead of me, there are two crows hopping around, feeding each other what look like bugs, and a small group of people has stopped to watch them, as if this is a sight to see.

'Cool crows,' I say to the woman next to me.

'They're not just crows,' she says. 'You haven't noticed anything different about them?'

I take another look at the birds, which both appear to be wearing red lipstick with matching boots.

'Red bills and feet,' she says, talking to me as if I'm dimmer than the usual strangers she meets.

'Okay, so what is it – some sort of redneck raven?'

She laughs and says, 'No, it's a chough.'

I pause, trying to think of a way to say this diplomatically. 'I thought that word was British slang for a woman's, um…'

'No, love, you're thinking of C-H-U-F-F,' she says. 'Pronounced the same, true, but very different things. Choughs are on the Cornish coat of arms. They're magical birds, that's why it's so unlucky to kill one. King Arthur didn't die – he was transformed into a Cornish chough. His spirit is still haunting the cliffs where he lived, in the shape of a chough, even today. So the legend goes, anyway. The red bill and feet on account of his horrible bloody death.'

'Nice symbolism,' I say. 'You know, this bird would make one heck of a witch's familiar. Hollywood needs to get on that.'

'Look at all these people walking by,' she goes on, shaking her head, as if I haven't spoken. 'I bet they think we're just looking at crows, as well. But crows would fly off. Choughs aren't afraid of people at all. It's amazing, given how rare they are,' she says. 'Only three hundred pairs left in the whole world. I never thought I'd see one in my lifetime.'

A man standing close to her and holding binoculars looks away from the birds, surprised.

'Really?' he says. 'I've seen quite a few pairs along this coastline. You want to go to Specsavers, Anne.'

'You carry binoculars on your walks,' she says, a touch of acerbity in her voice. 'Look, that's another load of people just gone past without looking twice. Can't they see these birds aren't crows?'

The man with the binoculars clears his throat. 'Technically, they are members of the same family.'

She gives him a sharp look, but he carries on talking.

'Choughs are also known as the Crow of Cornwall. The Ancient Greeks called them the Sea Crow.'

She sighs and says, 'No one likes a smart arse, Elliott.'

Which just makes me think of Makayla – the smartest of all the smart asses, but who I like more than any friend I've ever had.

Demi emerges from a car, spots me and starts hollering my name at one hundred decibels. Then Alexis appears and looks directly at me.

'Hi,' I say as he comes over. 'How's the foot?'

'Bit better today,' he says. 'Still sore as hell, but less so.'

'Did you sleep?' I say, looking at his tired eyes.

'Not much,' he says, as Demi walks past us, ostentatiously making it clear that she wouldn't dream of intruding on our conversation. She's accompanied by a sandy-coloured dog with shaggy hair and droopy ears.

She must think better of giving us space, because after going inside to say hi to everyone, she pokes her head out of the door again.

'Come on, kids,' she says. 'I'll shout you a free coffee… And maybe some of Jeremy's finest millionaire's shortbread.'

'So, that's Demi,' I say to Alexis, as we head to the counter. I can see through to the kitchen and spot Makayla in there giving Jeremy a hand clearing the dishes. Before I can give

Demi's dog companion one of the canine-friendly cookies we keep behind the cash register, Alexis is on his knees and the dog is showing him his belly, waiting for a scritch. Then the dog is jumping up and licking his neck. And licking it. I'm surprised Alexis has any neck skin left.

'You two know each other?' I ask, as the dog branches out and sticks his tongue in Alexis's ear, making him screw up his face.

'No,' he says, laughing as the dog picks up a black napkin and presents it to Alexis as if he thinks it's a dead bird. 'But I do love dogs.'

'They seem to like you too.'

'Who's your friend?' I ask Demi, as Alexis takes his laptop out of his bag and places it on the table.

'Koda,' is what I think she answers. 'He's the carpenter's dog. I asked if I could take him for an afternoon stroll, to make friends, just the two of us, and he bit my hand off. The carpenter, I mean. Not the dog.'

'Cool,' Alexis says. 'Koda means "friend", doesn't it? In a Native American language? Like in the *Brother Bear* movie?'

'Not Koda with a K,' she says. 'I already asked that. It's spelt with a C.'

'Oh, like the other movie?' I say. '*CODA*? The one that won the Academy Award. *Child of Deaf Adults*? Weird name for a dog, unless the Carpenter is going deaf, I guess.'

Demi shakes her head at us. We seem to be missing whatever she's trying to get at here.

'He is a bit deaf, but no. The carpenter's son chose the name and his job is in IT. This is *Coder*.'

I laugh. 'He does have coder hair,' I say, looking at the

long shaggy waves falling to the dog's shoulders, waves which don't seem to have seen a grooming brush in a while. There's a definite resemblance to my brother, Ricky, who has a great job working as a runtime engineer for an AI software firm, and who never seems to have time for a haircut.

'I really miss having a dog,' Alexis says, a look of longing in his eyes. 'Mine died a few years ago. Could I maybe give Coder a quick run on the beach? Throw his ball a few times?' he asks. 'Or would that be too weird?'

'I don't know,' Demi says. 'Depends if you're going to dognap him.'

'I mean, I might have to,' Alexis says. 'He is very tempting.'

'Well, he's not my dog, so I'm not that invested, to be honest. Plus, you seem like a nice bloke who'd look after him.'

'So, I can take him for a run on the beach?'

'How about this…' Demi says. 'You leave your fancy laptop with me, and you can have it back when you hand over the dog. Deal or no deal?'

'Deal,' he says. 'There's no dog ban on this beach during summer?'

'Nope. Not at any time of the year. It's dog central. Fill your boots, love. Just watch out for anyone flying a kite. He's a bit freaked out by them. Seems to think they're pterodactyls.'

'No problem. What's his recall word?'

'It's more of a phrase, really,' Demi says.

'Which is?'

'*Get back here, you little shit.*'

Alexis looks appalled and Demi smiles. 'Just call his name and he comes back.'

Demi hands Alexis a bunch of treats, tennis balls and poop bags, Alexis hands over his laptop, and we watch him and Coder walk off together down the beach, like they've known each other forever, Alexis limping a little. The dog doesn't just like Alexis, he is in love.

'Nice lad,' Demi says. 'I thought he might be a bit up himself, looking like he does, but he seems all right, doesn't he?'

'Up himself?' I enquire.

'You know, up his own arse,' she says, as if this explains anything.

'What a delightful phrase,' I say, grinning. 'Can't imagine how I never read it in *Pride and Prejudice*.'

'I just mean he doesn't seem arrogant. A bit away with the fairies. Off in his own world. But nice.'

Makayla comes out of the kitchen and places her hand on the lid of Alexis's shiny silver laptop.

I mentioned that Alexis is writing a novel, which has only increased her curiosity about him.

'What if I just opened this and we had the quickest little look at what he's writing? He has his font so tiny I haven't been able to read more than about three words that were in all caps. I'm dying to know if he's any good.'

'Writers hate people reading their early drafts, don't they?' Demi says, stepping into the kitchen to talk to Jeremy about an overdue order. She pops her head out again to add, 'But I suppose a quick look wouldn't hurt.'

'Guys, we cannot look at his laptop screen,' I say. 'That is a total invasion of privacy. He's trusting us to keep his equipment safe.'

Makayla snorts with laughter when I say the word 'equipment'.

'We're not going to run it through the dishwasher,' she says. 'We're just going to have a quick little read of one page.'

She starts pulling up the lid and I yank it away from her.

'No,' I say. 'Just no. I'm guarding this thing with my life.'

I take the laptop to one of the back tables and sit there eating the banana chips I keep in my purse for emergencies.

'Spoilsport,' Makayla says.

Alexis brings Coder back after twenty minutes.

'He was sniffing some flotsam and jetsam on the tideline, and I think he might have bolted a few crab legs before I could stop him. Sorry.'

'Don't worry, love,' Demi says. 'I was warned he has a taste for shellfish. Keeps his coat glossy.'

When the afternoon shift is finally over, Makayla and Demi tactfully leave me to lock up and I see them wander across the dune path, Coder running between them.

Alexis takes a hard look at me. The kind of look people give you when they're about to say something they find difficult.

'Do you want to come to my cottage?'

'Now?'

'Yes.'

'Don't you have writing to do?'

'I haven't been able to write all day. I think company is the one thing that might actually help to get the creative juices flowing.'

My instinct is to say no, but maybe that's just fear of

the unknown talking, and aren't you supposed to feel the fear and do the thing anyway? A professional writer, who is also going to pay me handsomely for surf lessons, wants to hang out with me. I'm a grown woman. I should be able to handle the nuances of this situation.

'Are you sure you want company?'

'I'm sure. Come on.'

We walk the little path around the headland, across the cliffs and into his cottage, which is just beautiful. It's been recently remodelled, judging by the scent of paint, and decorated in that minimalist style that hosts think impresses guests with money. Blond-wood floors, real paintings on the white walls, gorgeous and startling, not generic prints. Everything has a place and there's a place for everything. Nothing is superfluous. The decor could have leapt out of the pages of an interiors magazine. Somewhere along the line, I had come to believe that I hated this style of decoration. That it's soulless and fake, made for Instagram influencers and rich mommies and daddies who want to impress the other rich mommies and daddies at their children's elementary schools. But there's a part of me that craves this simple elegance, that wants to live like this too, in the beauty and the quiet.

I run my fingers along the cool granite of the kitchen island and walk to the end, through a door to a butler's pantry equipped with mason jars of pulses and grains. Vases of flowers are dotted around the house, and I wonder if Alexis has put them here or if they were ordered in advance and included in the deal. Expensive hothouse flowers that give off a sickly-sweet scent.

Alexis watches me as I walk around, looking at everything.

Eventually, when I'm through with being nosy, I sit on the couch and feel the squish of shaggy throw pillows under my fingertips and the rug between my toes. So many nights I've been cold in the van. So many times I've wanted to accept Demi's offer to stay in her guest bedroom, but I haven't because I can't admit I need help from anyone. I want to be able to do it all alone. If that means freezing my ass off in a tin can, then that's just what I'll have to do.

'Is this weird?' Alexis says to me, suddenly.

'Your place? No, it's nice.' I get up and walk to the windows, which look out over the ocean. 'Great views. You must have been thrilled when you saw the place.'

'Yeah, there's a pod of dolphins that sometimes comes close to shore with the high tide. So I'm told. I've been looking but I haven't seen them yet.'

'Wouldn't you rather work on your book here than in Demigorgons?'

He shakes his head. 'Not really. I like the atmosphere in there. The bustle, I suppose.'

'Seriously? This place is beyond gorgeous.'

'I don't disagree.'

'It's crazy to pay so much money for a rental and then spend all your time in a local café. You're not even in it for the food.'

'That's true.'

'So, why don't you work here?'

'You're not here.'

'I'm not here?' I say, looking around, as if I might be hallucinating this whole experience.

'I mean, you're here now, but you wouldn't be, if I hadn't

booked a surf lesson and stepped on a toxic fucking fish. That's what broke the ice.'

'And that's a factor?'

'Is you being around a factor? In my decision to sit all day on the hard chairs in Demigorgons? Yes, that's a factor. Don't you already know that? I thought I'd made myself pretty clear.'

'What are you saying right now?'

Because he has not been making himself clear. At all.

'I was hoping you might go out on a date with me. A proper date. I asked your friend Makayla if you were single the first chance I had. Didn't she mention that? She seems like the type of girl who would tell you, if I'm honest.'

'She dropped some hints.'

But she didn't tell me outright because she knew I'd react badly. She knew I'd slip right back into my shell and hide there until the danger had passed, until Alexis had stopped coming into the café. But now something has changed. He's not just a pretty stranger with a laptop any more. He's interesting to me. More than that.

I like him.

'Do you want anything to drink?' he says. 'There's soft drinks, beers and mixers in the fridge. Spirits are by the bread bin. I don't have any wine, I'm afraid. Bastard sulphites in it give me migraines.'

'Shall I just go and help myself?'

'Please. If you don't mind. And could you pass me a can of slimline tonic, a glass and that big bottle of vodka? I really need to get shitfaced.'

'Is that a need?' I laugh. 'Because it kind of sounds more like a want.'

'Today, it is definitely a need.'

He pours himself a triple shot of Grey Goose vodka and adds what looks like a thimbleful of soda.

'You always drink triple shots?'

'It's frowned on in pubs, but at home, yeah, occasionally.'

'And how's that working out for you?'

'Great. I've improved my wrist strength,' he says, wiggling the fingers of his hands. 'All that pouring is good exercise.'

'Triple shots are basically physical therapy, is what you're saying.'

'Exactly. But you haven't got yourself a drink,' he says, downing the rest of his.

'I'm still considering it.'

'Considering which drink you're in the mood for?'

'Considering if I want to stay.'

'It's okay if you don't. I'll be fine here. All alone.'

'Hey, guilt trips don't work on me, Writer Guy.'

'It's obviously fine if you want to go, but I was hoping we could talk a bit more about surfing. I'd love to hear more about your experiences.'

Which is irresistible to me.

He holds up the bottle above my empty glass, waiting for me to decide.

'Hit me,' I say.

*

I talk about the places I've surfed, the boat trips to offshore reef breaks and the first summers I spent learning to ride waves in a more technical way, learning to compete tactically, learning the principles of wave selection, and coming to love the ocean beneath my board.

When I pause, he sighs deeply.

'Something troubling you, Alexis?'

'I just need to shake myself out of this… strange mood. I need to pull up my socks and just do the fucking work. I need to force myself to do it.'

'Is writing supposed to feel like that?'

'I don't know. I don't think other writers struggle like this. It's not like I'm being sent into a warzone. I'm being paid to type words onto a laptop. This shouldn't be too taxing, even for me.'

'Okay, maybe you just need a reset. A redirect. Find an angle you can get excited about.'

'Like what?' he says.

'You're asking me for ideas?'

'Maybe…' He looks at me hopefully.

'Okay, well my first thought is that instead of Bryce and Janie being best buddies since childhood, how about you make them childhood enemies? Enemies to lovers stories are hot at the moment. They could transform from kids who couldn't stand each other, to adults who can't stand to be apart from each other.'

He lights up, then closes his eyes and exhales.

'Shit, I think you've found it,' he says.

'What?'

'My way in. Please keep talking…'

He listens as if he really cares about what I have to say. He lights candles and plays music and the whole thing feels warm and dreamlike, and the drinks slip by one after another until I can't remember how many there have been, but I know the room is beginning to spin a little, and I know for a fact that it's good I walked here because I'm not fit to drive.

I wouldn't be able to get the key in the door to the van. I'd stagger off a cliff-edge on the way to the parking lot.

The sun has gone down and he hasn't made a move to turn on a lamp or pull the window shades. We sit together in the shadows of the room, in the flickering light of the last candle, which sputters and goes dark, drinking liquor and watching seabirds that swoop from corner to corner of his epic window wall.

Even though it's dark now and I can't see a whole lot of anything, I know he's turned to look at me. One of those looks where if there was light and I met his gaze for more than three seconds, we'd both know it was on. But it's too dark to be sure and I don't know what I want, anyhow. I reach out my hand a little way from my hip and let it settle on the couch, a short distance from his. If he just reaches out to touch my hand now, I'll know everything I need to.

He does nothing and I close my eyes, trying to steady my breathing, trying to convince myself that this is all a big mistake anyhow. Haven't I been telling myself a version of that since he first walked through the door of Demigorgons? Because didn't I know I would end up here, wanting a man who is unsuitable, impermanent, flighty as these birds we're still watching in silence, like it means something?

Then I feel the warmth of his skin. His hand is touching my wrist. My body tenses up and I'm incapable of moving either toward or away from him.

Why am I like this? Why can't I just know what I want and do that? Why do I always have to react to what the other person decides to do?

I make the decision, gather my courage in the same way I do every time I make the decision to paddle for a big wave, and slide my hand underneath his. Interlink our fingers. He tightens his grip and pulls me towards him.

He's not as delicate as I first thought. He's lean, but wide across the shoulders and chest. Like a surfer, and yet he only just caught his first wave in our lesson. Swimmer. That's right. He told me he's a pool swimmer. The delts show it. The abs.

I think of the term Makayla used for him: 'Regulation Hot'. The type of look that's used to sell cologne in magazines. To sell couture in Paris. He's strong enough to pick me up but he would never do that. It would never occur to him to lay hands on a woman like that.

Joseph would hate him. Call him a soy boy, a simp. He wouldn't understand this version of masculinity. He would never allow himself to be caught looking like that, looking so vulnerable.

I could say no. I could stand up and Alexis would let me leave. He wouldn't even make an issue of it. Leaving would be the simplest thing to do. The only course of action that makes any kind of sense, so why do I use my other hand to touch his thigh instead, gripping his quadriceps muscle, waiting to see if he'll stop me?

When I look up at his face, his eyes are liquid with desire and it would be so easy now to seduce him, I would hardly even need to try. One word, one breath would do it.

I can't. He's my client. My student.

But couldn't I just touch my lips to his, just for a second, to see what happens? To see how it feels? Because then I'll know for sure, one way or another. It doesn't mean I have to sleep with him. It doesn't even mean I have to open my mouth and really kiss him, not if it doesn't feel right.

Maybe I let my prejudice against him as a rich, successful guy stop me from seeing that he is more than surface gloss. He has damage underneath, too.

Whatever I do next will be significant. It will direct the course of our relationship from here on out. I could keep this professional; I could broaden it into a friendship. Or I could do something else.

One move and this will be over. Another move and it will just be getting started. And he is so beautiful that it takes the breath all out of me.

I stare into his eyes, and he looks so nervous that I want to make it all better, to put him at ease here with me.

'I don't know what to do,' I say, the strength going out of my knees, and with that he kisses me.

I'm kissing a man who is not my husband, the first man other than Joseph I've kissed since I was at college.

At first, I'm not sure Alexis even wants to kiss me, he's so gentle. I keep waiting for him to stop, to tell me that he's made a mistake, and this is not what he wants from me. That all he wants is to learn to surf and discuss romance novels while we're drying off on the beach or hanging out waiting for waves in the line-up.

I open my eyes as we kiss and tangle my fingers in that soft hair, which I've wanted to touch since the very first moment he walked into Demigorgons. I run my fingers across those deltoid muscles and he shudders, knocks my hand away.

'Don't,' he says. 'Gentle hurts.'

'It hurts?' I say, taking both my hands off him, like my hands have burnt his skin.

'It's... torture. Like insects running over me.'

'Okay,' I say, thinking that this is the time to walk away, a little surprised it even took this long.

'It's the way I'm wired,' he says, eyes clouded with concern, maybe sensing I'm about to run away from this. 'The way I've always been. Even when I was a kid, I couldn't stand light touch.'

'What do you need?'

'I need you to desensitise me. Can you touch me harder, be rougher with me?'

'Okay,' I say, not knowing how to even start. Forgetting how my hands even work.

'Here,' he says, making my hand into a fist, placing it on his chest, forcing it down with his own hand, which is flat and hard. I can feel his heart beating. Racing. Whatever this is, he's into it.

He drags my fist up to his neck, pushes it into his throat, and then unfurls my fingers and pulls my hand down his ribcage, pushing my fingers hard into the soft tissue between his ribs, every one, and dragging my hand down to his stomach. He's intent. Focused. He groans as he relaxes, like the pressure of a slow punch is all he wants, all he needs from me.

I haven't even taken him in my hands, I don't even know what he feels like. I could keep moving down. Stop him from wanting this strange pressure. I could take him out of his underwear, roll it down his legs and toss it across the room. Do every little thing that Joseph taught me, I could do it all for Alexis.

I lean back into the couch and feel the heat and strength of his chest push into mine. So what if I'm still technically married? This guy is interesting, and smart, and he's got into my head in a way that nobody has since I got together with Joseph. He's also sexy as hell.

So what if I've always made terrible decisions when it comes to men? Why shouldn't I let myself have this experience? Joseph wouldn't think twice about taking something he wanted. He took my best friend.

My hand goes to the button of Alexis's fly, and I can feel the heat of him, straining towards me.

His mouth is on my neck now, teeth grazing skin, sending shivers down the string within me that ends between my legs.

I'm still in my clothes, but I'm tugging on his shorts and boxers, and he's raising his hips to let me. They hitch on his ankles and he leaves them there, waiting for me to take them. I tangle my toes in the fabric and kick them away, leaving him exposed, vulnerable. Waiting for me.

He sits up in the middle of the couch, puts his hands on my waist and lifts me, settling me on top of him.

I lower myself onto him, gently, so that we miss, so that he doesn't get what he wants right away. He meets my eyes, and his blue gaze is wide with longing. His need sucks the air out of my lungs. I touch the curve of his cheekbones and my fingertips are alive with the feel of his skin, already glistening in the low light, already beginning to sweat. His lips are parted a little and, as I look at them, they settle together again, so softly I barely see them move.

I still haven't kissed him with my mouth open. Through all of this touching, this intimacy, I still don't know how his mouth tastes today. How any part of him tastes.

I lean in to kiss him and smell the sweetness of soda on his breath, the tang of alcohol right behind it.

'Please,' he says, softly.

My hands push lower, over the fine line of dark hair, and I wonder if this will be too much for him, if I'll hit a nerve, if he'll ask me to stop. I wonder if the places that were Joseph's erogenous zones will turn out to be torture buttons for Alexis. But he doesn't flinch, he groans with pleasure.

My phone rings, shrill in the softness of our heavy breathing.

It's probably a spam caller asking me if I've recently been in a road traffic accident. I've been getting a ton of them at all hours since I got this burner phone, which is why I usually put it on silent when I remember.

But the interruption does something to my brain. Diverts it off the stretch of tracks it's been careening down. I need to stop and think about this. I also have a sudden, urgent need to pee.

'Point me in the direction of your bathroom,' I say.

I need to splash my face with water, think my way to the end of this thought sequence.

'Down the hall. It's the third door on the left. Shall I pour us another drink?'

I throw up my hands. 'Sure.'

I'm drunk already. Getting more drunk doesn't feel like a problem.

I just need to find the third door on the left. Except I can't seem to count to three because the door I open leads to a bedroom so small it can barely fit the bed. I'm just about to close the door when I spot the leather-bound journal, in which Alexis wrote that weird little note about wiener wraps and I'm still desperate to know what that was all about. With so much alcohol running through my veins, corroding my principles, a quick peek at his work doesn't seem like such a big deal after all. Maybe if I can find the right page, all will become clear, and I'll put that mystery to bed forever.

I pick up the notebook and something catches my eye. The word 'CANDY'. At first, I think chocolate and wonder if he's developing some junk-food subplot in the narrative.

Except, the word is circled neatly and there are ruled lines radiating out of it like a porcupine. And there are subcategories that include the words: 'beseeching eyes', 'honey skin' and 'sexy surfer shoulders'. There is also this.

Change Janie's name to Candy? Or just base Janie on Candice and keep the original name?

There is a list of questions, too, that include:

How to convey vocal fry without making the character seem dim?

Where to set sex scenes to maximise visuals of the Cornish locale?

Make female protagonist Hawaiian to appeal to American audiences?

Make Bryce a Londoner. Easier to nail the voice.

And, perhaps worst of all:

Nipples – how to describe them poking out of her work shirt without sounding too pervy?

On the next page over, he's bullet-pointed an entire novel's plot arc in which Bryce is now a handsome city journalist who's had enough of townie life and has resigned and moved to Cornwall for an adventure. He comes to Newquay and romances 'Candy the sexy surf instructor' in various locations around Newquay before he convinces her to be part of his erotic massage business.

I take it from the nightstand and walk back into the lounge area, where Alexis is standing at the window, looking out at the scatter of stars above the ocean and listening to the crash of waves, still naked from the waist down.

He turns to me with a look of confusion, not understanding why I'm holding a book in my hand.

'You fucking asshole,' I say.

I consider throwing the journal directly at his now flaccid penis.

'Candice, it's not what you think,' he says, picking up his shorts and trying to hop back into them. He winces as he fastens his fly without underwear and catches pubic hair in the zipper.

'It's exactly what I think,' I say, pulling down on my T-shirt and wishing I hadn't opted for the most cropped one I own because now I have to have this argument while my belly button is showing.

'I was going to change your name,' he insists. 'These are just notes for me. While I'm getting everything straight in my head.'

'That is so not the point,' I say.

'I'm sorry,' he says. 'Please just listen to me a minute. I have something I want to talk to you about. A proposal.'

Our words keep running up against each other in a car crash of speech, but neither of us stops so that most of what we're saying is lost.

'I'm not interested,' I say, putting out my hand in the universal sign for *shut the hell up before I jab you in the throat with a closed fist*. 'Whatever you're trying to sell here, I'm not buying.'

'Please. Hear me out. My idea could work for both of us.'

'There is no us.'

'That's not what I meant.'

'Don't you see you can't come back from this?'

'But if you'd just listen, you'd realise this could be a great opportunity for someone like you.'

'For someone like *me*? You don't know the first thing about me. You don't know why I'm here in Newquay. You never even asked. So don't make like you have some kind of insight into my life. You can't even fucking describe my nipples.'

'But I want insight into your life. That's what I'm trying to say, if you'd just let me get a word in, I could explain.'

'Go find some other waitress to write about.'

'You're not just some waitress.'

'Oh, you think so? I'm touched,' I say, holding his notebook at arm's length and wondering if I should let it catch on one of the fancy scented candles he's just lit, but then I'd probably wind up burning the place down and getting thrown in jail for arson.

'Look, Candice. Let's just take it easy, okay?' he says. 'I should have been honest from the start. I made a mistake and I admit that.'

'You made a whole fucking bunch of mistakes.'

His hands go to the top of his head and he interlaces his fingers over the crown, like a little boy who knows he's about to get grounded for the whole summer. 'What can I say to make this right? There must be something.'

I look at him, completely taken aback.

'There is nothing you can say to me that can make this right,' I say, walking to the door and taking his fancy leather-bound journal with me.

'Hey, you can't take that,' he says. 'It's got all my notes in it. I need it.'

'Boo-fucking-hoo. Write something else and leave me and my life alone.'

'Candice, don't go.'

'I am so out of here.'

Ten

I push my way out of his cottage, taking a faceful of cold night air, feeling the thud of my heart.

My chest is burning with humiliation. What Alexis has written about me is disgusting but I'm equally disgusted with myself because, against all my instincts, I allowed someone I didn't fully trust in the first place to stab me in the back.

I slam the door and he doesn't come after me. He just lets me go.

I still need to use the bathroom, so I head for the public washrooms, but they're bolted and padlocked. Instead, I take the metal stairway down to Little Fistral to pee behind one of the rocks that get rewashed with every tide.

I'm alone. So completely alone. And I've been such a fool. I've been Marianne Dashwood in *Sense and Sensibility* mooning after a selfish S-O-B, just because he was rakishly handsome and told her everything she wanted to hear, right before throwing her over to get a little money. But Marianne Dashwood was sixteen when she fell for Willoughby. I should be old enough to see past a dashing exterior, I should be able to see through to the rot.

I take Alexis's journal to the water's edge and wait there for a sign. I could throw it into the current because fuck him.

But something stops me, and I slide it into my bag instead.

I can't even be mad at him. I knew there was something off about him, but I didn't trust my gut enough to listen to it. He was never interested in me, the person. All he wanted was content for his garbage romance novel.

My phone rings again and I take it out of my back pocket and see Demi's name on the display.

She never calls late. Something is wrong.

'Is everything okay?' I ask.

'Where are you? You're not here.'

'I'm out. What's wrong?'

'It's Makayla,' she says, her voice quivering. 'She's in trouble.'

'What happened?' I say, blood rushing to my ears, white blocks appearing in front of my eyes, so that I can barely see anything at all.

'I don't know. She's hurt. She was with a man. She's on the way to Treliske Hospital. Can you come?'

'I'll be there. Wait, no. I've been drinking.'

'Where are you? I'll come and pick you up.'

'Little Fistral. I, um… I was with a client.'

She's silent. I know what she's thinking. A client? At this hour? What kind of client are we talking here?

'It's Alexis. The writer guy from the café. You know, I've been giving him surf lessons.'

'It's a quarter to midnight.'

'It… ran late.'

'I'll be there as soon as I can.'

She ends the call and I look up at Alexis's cottage, candlelight still flickering inside, until he walks up to the windows and pulls the shades.

★

'Is Makayla okay?' I yell out when Demi pulls up, my voice jarring in the still night air. I'm riding shotgun before the vehicle has even stopped.

'All I know is she's badly hurt.'

'What the hell happened?'

'I don't have all the details. Her sister Misha was down as her next of kin, but she's living in Spain, and when she called me she was obviously in a real state. I couldn't make out half of what she was saying,' Demi says. 'But I think Makayla was on a date when she got hurt.'

'A guy hurt her?' I say, panic rising in my throat.

'I don't know, Candice. I just don't know.'

'Where were they?'

'When I was with her earlier, she said she was planning on going down to one of the beaches. I don't know which one. I think her sister said she has broken bones and some sort of head injury. They don't know about her spine yet.'

'Holy shit,' I say.

Demi keeps talking at a rapid pace, like if she slows down, she'll break down.

'They have her in surgery. We'll go straight to the hospital and be there when she wakes up.'

'Who was she with?'

'Misha rang Makayla's phone after the hospital called. The guy who answered had an Irish accent. She said he kept apologising to her. Said he sounded pissed up, and as if he was crying.'

My hands are in my lap, and I put them in prayer position, close my eyes and beg any deity who's listening to help Makayla.

'I think a helicopter might have been involved,' Demi says. 'The search and rescue guys were circling around earlier.'

I heard rotor blades as I was kissing Alexis. It didn't even register as something to concern me, because of the major Royal Air Force base just a couple miles from here, on the outskirts of town. I thought it was just a military aircraft. I wasn't thinking at all.

My head is spinning. I've had way too much to drink and none of this is making sense. How could anyone hurt Makayla?

Eleven

We stay all night in the waiting room, waiting for someone to bring us news, and I realise how much Makayla means to me.

I need someone to come and tell us that she is going to be okay, that her head injury isn't serious, that she'll bounce back from this, that she'll be just fine.

Demi sits next to me, acting now as if this is all perfectly normal and nothing to be concerned about. At one point, she takes knitting from her purse and starts up clickety-clacking, while watching the all-night news show that's playing on the small TV screen in the corner of the waiting room. Like she might be at home in her living room.

I think again about the day I met Makayla, how if she had just kept walking and eating her French fries instead of stopping for a crying stranger, she would never have been in my life. Without a place to stay and a job, I would have had to go back home. I would have failed before I'd even gotten started, but her kindness set me on my feet again.

'Why don't you read?' Demi says, suddenly. 'There are paperbacks on the table if you don't have one in your bag.'

The only book I currently have in my bag is Alexis's

notebook and I would rather read my own funeral notice than that.

I walk to a small coffee table stacked with books and pre-schooler toys and pick up a copy of *Rebecca*. I don't think I'm up to reading about love, even the twisted kind. I put it down and choose a battered paperback edition of Stephen King's *Misery*. I flick through it, looking for the chapter where the Kathy Bates character breaks the author's ankles with a sledgehammer, vowing that this is what I'll do to the Irishman if he's responsible for hurting Makayla. But it's all different in the book. In the novel, Annie Wilkes doesn't break Paul's ankles – instead she cuts off his left foot with an axe and cauterises the wound with a propane torch.

That would work too.

Demi jumps as her phone beeps. She reads the message and types out two words.

No news.

'Percy,' she says, as if that means something to me.

I look blank and she continues. 'The carpenter.'

Like Makayla, Demi never mentions the real names of the men she's dating until she's halfway sure about them. Says there are too many time-wasters, and way too many Johns.

'Percy,' I say. 'Like the little pig candies?'

'Yes,' she says, thoughtfully. 'And also Percy Bysshe Shelley.'

'His parents really chose that name for a baby?'

Demi nods. 'He grew up on an estate in Devon where

people were dirt poor, but all the streets were very grandly named after famous poets, authors and playwrights. Hence, in Chaucer Way, loads of the baby boys got called Geoffrey. Ditto all the Williams in Shakespeare Road, and the Taylors and Samuels in Coleridge Close.'

'Aspirational names,' I say. I can tell that Demi is doing everything in her power to distract me from worry and I could hug her for it.

'The powers that be obviously thought some blatant literary marketing would make the housing estates seem more salubrious. The carpenter grew up in Shelley Street, and he was damned close to being called Shelley. One of his mates got landed with the name Bysshe.'

'Bish? As in – slang for "bitch"?' I say, blinking.

'Yes,' Demi says. 'Poor little Bysshe really pulled the short straw. Percy got off lightly, all things considered.'

★

Eventually, at dawn, a woman comes to give us an update.

'Your friend has a bad compound fracture of her ankle, and a serious concussion, but she's out of the woods.'

The relief floors me. I've hardly cried since I left Joseph, but all the tears that have built up come flowing out like a burst dam, except this dam is made of toxic waste and it's poisoned all the water that ever touched it.

'She's just waking up now,' the woman says. 'Give it another hour or so and then you can come and see her.'

★

'What happened?' I ask Makayla, hours later, when she finally feels up to talking about the particulars of the night.

'It's so stupid,' she says. 'It was my fault totally. Travis was just going along with me.'

'The Irishman's name is Travis?'

She almost never tells me their real names, and I don't ask.

'Trevor is his birth name, but he goes by Travis because he thinks it sounds less like a trainspotter.'

'What did he do?'

'He didn't do anything. It was me. I convinced him that we needed to visit the pirate cove. It's the best cove for, uh, romance. Gorgeous views, quiet, not overlooked.'

'Back up. The pirate cove?'

'It's this tiny cove that you can only get to when the tide's right out. It has loads of black sea glass, from old rum bottles. The sort of thing that sailors would drink hundreds of years ago, so they call it pirate glass. We checked the tides on his phone. It should have been fine. We should have had at least two hours before the tide cut us off.'

'But you didn't,' I say, reaching out to hold her hand.

'It came in way too fast. The swell picked up, there must have been an offshore storm or something, and we were cut off, our backs against the cliff.'

'Jesus, Makayla. You could have been killed.'

'I mean, I was starting to panic. I thought we could scramble over the rocks to the next beach, but the rocks were high up and I lost my balance.'

'You fell?'

'About twenty feet, yeah.'

Demi visibly winces at the thought of Makayla falling so badly, but she tries to keep the mood light and says, 'Bet that hurt like a mother trucker.'

Makayla nods her head. 'It was pretty bad. Worse than getting my left nipple pierced. Nowhere near as bad as the right nipple, mind – she's always been too sensitive.'

'You don't have to joke,' I say. 'You must have been terrified.'

'It sounds dramatic, but I did actually think that I might die.'

I stroke her hand, careful not to touch the deep grazes on her forearms and wrists.

'Travis called the emergency services, and he was great. He couldn't go in the helicopter to the hospital with me, and he was too pissed to drive, and no way was I letting him pay forty quid for a taxi when he's skint, and it was just broken bones, so I made him go home.'

'I bet he loved that,' Demi says, shaking her head.

'He threatened to walk all the way here but it's twelve miles and I told him if he did, he was dumped. Plus, he'd have probably drunkenly staggered into the road and got hit by a cement lorry or something.'

She's trying to keep her tone light but there's a quaver in her voice.

'As we were waiting, it made me realise that I don't have any family here now that Misha's working in the Costa del Sol. I don't have a safety net to fall back on.'

'Yes, you do,' Demi says, firmly. 'Us.'

Makayla starts to cry.

'It's all right,' Demi says, giving her a gentle hug. 'I'll go and get you some clothes and toiletries. Are you okay to stay here for a bit longer, Candice?'

'Of course. There is no place else I'm going.'

'I'll swing by the café and put a note on the door to

say that due to an emergency we'll be closed today and tomorrow. I've already texted the kitchen staff. We could all use a little break. Paid time off, obviously, so you don't need to worry about your wages.'

'You don't need to do that,' Makayla says, eyes still streaming, despite her best attempts to make them stop. 'I'll stay here on my own. You guys get back to Demigorgons. All your regulars will be freaking out if you're closed. The tourists will be leaving angry reviews online.'

'Don't worry about that,' Demi says. 'When you get out of hospital, you'll come and stay with me in my big empty house, and we'll look after you. There's no way you can take care of yourself alone in a flat. You can have my daughter's bedroom since it has the ensuite bathroom. Candice will be in the guest room. Does that sound all right, girls?'

Makayla gasps through her tears. 'That sounds amazing. Thank you.'

I give her hand a squeeze. 'You have family here,' I say. 'We both do.'

Twelve

Alexis gets wind of the accident and sends expensive-looking floral arrangements: one for Makayla, which arrives first, and then one 'care of Makayla' – for me – which arrives while she's sleeping and fills me with rage the moment I see the card.

In her card, which Makayla reads out happily to me, Alexis says he wishes her a speedy recovery and that he'll miss seeing her at Demigorgons.

In my card, which I hide from Makayla, it just says:

So sorry, Candice. I'm a massive twat.

I ask an older nurse to take my flowers to the waiting room, because I don't need them, don't even really like cut flowers, and other people could benefit. I think she must understand what's behind this aversion, because without asking a single question she does as I ask, holding the cheap vase away from her body as if it's full of poison ivy and black widows.

'Thank you,' I say to her retreating back, the flower

heads springing out either side of her head, like a different kind of Gorgon.

She nods. 'The consultant doesn't really approve of too many flowers in patient rooms anyway, because of allergies and such, triggered by all the pollen. Plus, there's a whole world of disgusting bacteria that multiplies in fusty water, which could get spilled. And who wants that in a clinical environment?' She says all of this in a broad Irish accent, turning to look at me briefly. I see piercing blue eyes and white hair cut into a neat bob with thick bangs, just like my mom always wore hers.

She pauses before continuing. 'And if I'm reading you right, I don't suppose you'll mind me saying there's little in this world that's more irritating than flowers from a man you don't want reminding of?'

'You might be right about that,' I say, missing my mom so much that all the strength goes out of my legs.

*

It's another day before Makayla is released from hospital, hopped up on painkillers and majorly plaster-cast, but she's in good spirits. Her curly hair is piled on the top of her head.

'The broken bones suck, but you really suit a messy bun,' I say, as she grimaces her way into the front seat of Demi's car. 'It's actually a classic romcom heroine hairstyle, stretching right back to the Regency era. I think Lizzy Bennet rocked it whenever she was out of bobby pins.'

'This?' she says, motioning to the top of her head. 'Is a pineapple.'

'It's a what now?' I say, raising my eyebrows.

'A pineapple. That's what curlies call it when they wear their hair like this. None of your messy bun malarkey. That's for straights.'

'I stand corrected,' I say, smiling.

Demi drives us back to Newquay, through the lush and vibrant farm country that lies between the south and north Cornish coasts. It's like some dream of England, all green fields, ancient barns and lounging cattle, so different from the California vibes of the north coast.

'Can you feel it?' Makayla says.

'What?'

'The fizzing sensation. I always get it as I come into Newquay. I've heard tourists talk about it too. It's like rushing before you get high.'

'Or those lovely seconds before you orgasm,' Demi says, very primly, in her high school principal voice. 'You know something nice is coming, but you're not quite there yet.'

Makayla nods and repeats Demi's words, as if she's trying to absorb them into her psyche. Then, just as we reach the Gannel roundabout, a tourist wearing both a lei and a Stetson cuts us off and Demi pumps the brakes.

'Although one can't always guarantee an orgasm,' she says, sighing. 'Sometimes you're just left looking at a prick.'

Thirteen

When we get back to Demi's house, the Irishman is there waiting with a bouquet of daisies and a box of chocolates.

'I'm an idiot,' he says.

'You are,' Makayla says. 'But I forgive you.'

'It's all my fault,' he says, turning to me.

'How do you figure?'

'I read the tide times wrong,' he says, groaning. 'I googled it and read out the first search result, instead of clicking on the page. I somehow read out the wrong day.'

He looks terrible, as if he'll never forgive himself for this mistake.

'I should have checked them too,' Makayla says. 'And it was my idea to go down there in the first place. No point wondering what if.'

He helps her into the house and into Demi's daughter's room and I make myself scarce. I left my best hoodie in Demigorgons, so I take the keys to the restaurant, with a view to swinging by to pick it up, and maybe informing any of our regular customers I run into about Makayla's condition, so they don't think the worst.

When I get there, I see Alexis sitting morosely on one of the tables outside. He doesn't have his laptop bag with him, he's just sitting there like a lost boy, staring out to sea. He seems to have dressed himself entirely from the gift shop near his place. His T-shirt says 'Sea-Sing the Day' and his socks have gone for a different tone altogether. One of them says 'SAME' and the other says simply 'SHIT'.

'Why are you here?' I say, startling him.

My tone is hostile, and he looks alarmed.

He gets to his feet and stands in front of me, eyes pleading.

'I was waiting to see if you'd come,' he says.

'Why? You knew Makayla was in hospital. Didn't you read Demi's note on the door saying Demigorgons is closed?'

'I hoped you'd stop by at some point. I need to explain. And I know I owe you a massive apology.'

'Sure you're not just here for your notebook?'

'I don't care about that. Can you give me a minute?'

'One minute,' I say. 'I need to get back to Makayla.'

'Is she okay?' he says.

'She will be, but she's got six weeks of living in a plaster cast ahead of her. She had a real bad fall on the rocks and she's pretty upset.'

'Fucking hell, I'm really sorry to hear that,' he says, running his fingers through his hair. He's sweating hard. There are damp patches under his arms and around his neckline.

'So, you'll understand when I say that whatever it is you're doing, it doesn't seem that important. Do you get that? I don't have capacity to deal with you.'

'Okay, I get it. Let me explain and you'll never see me again. Can you just sit down?'

I do so reluctantly, clutching my bag to my chest.

'I should never have treated you – used you – like that.'

'Then why did you, Alexis?'

'The short answer is that my literary agent encouraged me to have a summer romance.'

'What are you saying? That you were just trying to seduce me as some form of, what, research?'

'It's not like that. My agent thought it might help with the book. But I thought I had no chance of finding someone who interested me here. And I'm not the summer romance type, at all. Then I met you and you were cool and interesting, and I thought maybe Daniel was onto something. I made some stupid notes. I was so blocked creatively, and I wrote the first thing that came into my head, which was you.'

'Am I supposed to be flattered?'

'No, I'm just trying to explain what happened. I'm really sorry.'

'Fine. I accept your apology. Can you leave now?'

He nods. 'Please send Makayla my best. If there's anything I can do to help her in any way, please just let me know.'

He hands me his business card, in which his full name is written – Alexis Chancery-Mordaunt – and in which he describes himself, without irony, as Journalist/Author/ Wanderer.

I get up, holding the business card between two fingers, not sure whether to drop it in a trashcan or put it in my pocket.

If the card was meant for me, I'd go for the former option, but since it's for Makayla, I slide it into the back pocket of my jean shorts.

'I wasn't thinking straight,' he says. 'I was panicking

because I don't know what I'm doing. I went into this project thinking it would be easy but it's not. I'm out of my depth and it impaired my judgement. Badly.'

'I have to go,' I say and turn my back to him. I can feel the anger rising up in me and there's so much of it. Alexis is part of that anger, but the smallest part. He's a liar and a user, but his ability to hurt me is limited by the fact that I am already hurting. Broken is broken.

I hear the scuff of his loafers on the sand as he walks away. I exhale with relief that the final confrontation is over now, and I'm through with ever having to see him again.

I go around to the back of the café and unlock the door that leads to the kitchen. When I open it, it swings into my face and a torrent of water hits me so hard I'm knocked off my feet.

Fourteen

The café is flooded. When Demi stopped by to put a note on the door, still majorly worried about Makayla, she popped inside to have a look around and make sure everything was okay. She must have also decided to wash up a few cups and saucers or clean her hands. In her distracted state, she left the faucet running. Which wouldn't have been a problem ordinarily – other than the water bill – but the stopper was in.

I can see at first glance that all the wooden flooring is warped and will probably need to be torn out. There's already a smell of mildew and the baseboards and lower-down cabinets have absorbed water and begun to swell. The appliances will need to be inspected for water damage, and maybe replaced. Then there's the electrics, the walls. Even if Demi can get people in here right away, Demigorgons is going to be out of business for weeks at least, maybe months. In peak season. It's going to be disastrous.

I feel as if I'm going to have a panic attack and rush outside to sit where the ocean breeze can blow over me. Everything is messed up. Everything is getting worse and

I'm no nearer to finding the thing I came here for in the first place.

Which is my father.

★

Joseph would be so happy if he knew my life was falling apart, if he knew how badly I was failing.

What people don't understand about Joseph is that he wasn't always like this. When I met him, he seemed like just another laidback surfer. I didn't know then that he had a dark side. He kept it so well hidden that most people didn't know – not even his closest friends, not even his college roommate.

My mother knew, though, and she tried to warn me off him, although I wasn't able to hear that warning, because the love I had for Joseph was absorbent cotton wound tight about my head and no criticism of him could get past the layers.

The first inkling I had that anything about him was off was at our wedding, when he got into a screaming match with a guest who'd thrown some shade about the whiteness of my wedding gown, as if I'd dated half the football team at college, when the truth was humiliatingly different.

Joseph could take any joke at his own expense, or so it had seemed, but there was something about me being mocked that he could not suffer. Perhaps it was because I was his wife now, albeit of three hours, but that apparently was enough of a reason.

My virtue had been questioned and my honour was at stake. And that, it turned out, was a slam on him. He wasn't just a man any more, he was a husband, and his duty was to protect his wife. Even though I never asked that of him. Even though I never cared about my sexual history being joked about – if anything, I was embarrassed that it was so limited.

Even though, ultimately, it was Joseph I needed protecting from.

But he couldn't do that. He couldn't protect me from himself because he didn't have control over himself. What he had was a fiery temper that pushed up through the bedrock and exploded like lava. And once that route had been established, once the surface had been breached, the lava just kept coming, over and over, until I was burnt through to my soul and there was nothing left of me for him to hurt.

'I've never hit you, not once,' he'd say, as if that made his behaviour acceptable. As if that meant I should believe he never would. He thought it was okay for him to leave me afraid, just so long as I was unbruised. He slammed his fists on the dinner table so hard that one of the legs broke, threw food I'd made in the trash and shouted himself hoarse in critiques of my personality. Later, when he'd calmed down, he told me everything I did wrong, why I had made him lose his temper and how he expected me to correct my behaviour going forward.

My love for him made me stay, even when my feelings were a festering wound.

I'd scrape out the infection, the poison, but if even the tiniest part was left over – and there was always love left over – it would take hold and start to multiply. Before long the wound would be weeping and oozing as bad as ever.

It was only when my mother died of a pulmonary embolism – so young, with so much life left to live, only just into her fucking fifties – that I knew I had to make a different choice.

He tried to say the right things, but I could tell he was just waiting until I got hold of myself and went back to being productive. He needed me at the shop, he needed me to cook the food he liked, he needed me to smile at him when he walked through the door. What he didn't need was a woman who shut herself in her bedroom and cried in great juddering sobs.

I couldn't read, I couldn't eat. The only thing I could drink was a few sips of water. I kept the bedroom TV on all day and night, soothing background noise, and Joseph slept on the couch in the living room. I watched a TV show I'd seen before because nothing else seemed to help. *Gilmore Girls* got me through the first six days. While the show was playing, I could dial down my feelings enough to stop crying and just watch two people fall in love. When the credits rolled, I'd skip to the next episode before my grief sucker-punched me again.

On the sixth day, Joseph came into the room carrying two mugs of coffee, which he set on the nightstand. He looked at my swollen tear-stained face and frowned.

'This has to stop, Candice. You need to eat something. Walk in fresh air. You can't live your life in a bedroom like some kind of hermit. You have to keep living, Candice. Life goes on.'

'It hasn't even been a week since my mom died,' I said, anger welling up past the sadness.

'But you're getting worse, not better. And I don't think

this trash show you're watching is helping. You need to come back to the real world. Deal with this and move past it.'

I looked at him then and saw him, really saw him. Maybe for the first time ever.

This wasn't concern for me, at least not mostly. This was concern for him. I was messing up his plans with my inconvenient grief. I had to function as he needed me to, otherwise I was no use to him.

'I don't want to come back to the real world,' I said. 'Because in the real world my mom is dead.'

He ran his fingers through his hair, which I noticed he'd buzzcut himself – presumably because I was unavailable, and he refused to pay for haircuts. There were long strands behind his ear and a tuft just below the crown.

'Death is part of life. Parents get old and die. It's sad but it happens. And it wasn't as if your mom looked after herself. I never saw her exercise the whole time we've been together.'

'She wasn't old,' I said, my voice cracking.

'Well, she wasn't twenty-five.' He paused. 'Come give me a hug,' he said, his manner softening. There was pain in his eyes. Maybe he realised he'd gone too far.

He got up from where he'd been sitting at the side of our marriage bed and waited for me to come to him.

I almost said no, but I knew how he would take that. As a rejection of his affection. As a provocation.

I went to him and he drew me in close and pressed our foreheads together. It should have been a tender gesture, but it didn't feel that way. He was too strong. He was holding my head against his, and I couldn't pull away unless he released me.

'I can't do this any more,' I whispered.

'*You* can't do this any more?' he replied, laughing in my face.

'We're not making each other happy,' I said, catching a glimpse of my exhausted face in the vintage porthole mirror he had given me for our first wedding anniversary.

'You want out?' he said. 'You think you can find somebody else better than me?'

I didn't know how to answer, how to fill the silence left by his question.

'You know, Candice. It's not like I don't have options here. I was trying to be the good guy, but fine. Let's get into this.'

'What options?' I said, looking him square in the eye. And it all came out. What Joseph wanted wasn't me. It was Issy, my oldest friend. For months now they'd been hanging out behind my back, meeting in secret and messaging through the long hours of the night. Joseph swore that they hadn't slept together yet.

Yet.

But they'd done other stuff. They'd kissed, they'd gotten naked, they'd fallen in love.

And, as it turned out, in just a few short months they would make a baby.

Fifteen

Demi is up with the sun to begin the long process of sorting out the flood damage. She's made enquiries with various local tradesmen about the renovation and has already signed up one contractor, who is going to fit her new kitchen for a one-off, knock-down price. Percy.

She's also begun battle with her insurance company.

'Do you think they'll pay out?' I ask her. 'Since you left the water running yourself?'

She sighs, like she has the weight of the world on her shoulders, and replies in a gloomy voice, 'Anxiety and hope oppress me in equal degrees.'

'I recognise that quote from somewhere,' I say, trying to put my finger on it.

'You should do. I read it in that copy of *Sense and Sensibility* you keep leaving around. Say what you like about Austen, but she'd be great at writing menacing emails to insurance companies. Exquisitely polite, yet devastatingly caustic.'

'She really would,' I say, wishing we could manifest her into Demi's house with the power of worship.

When I go to check on Makayla, she's also awake and

wide-eyed. I don't know if it's the effect of the drugs the doctors gave her in hospital, but it's only 6.30 a.m. and she's full of energy, asking me, weirdly, if I know that summers last forty-two years at the south pole of the planet Uranus.

'Well, no, I didn't know that, Makayla,' I say. 'How again is it that you do?'

'Demi's got a book on planets in the bog. Gawd, a summer that lasted the whole length of the Doberman's life so far. Imagine the chub rub.'

I look at her blankly.

'You know, when your inner thighs get all sweaty and rub together so you get that horrible itchy rash that burns every time your legs touch.'

'I think even in summer, Uranus is probably pretty cold.'

She laughs but doesn't make the obvious joke.

'Bit crap that the winters of Uranus also last forty-two years,' she says, scratching a tiny zit on the bridge of her nose. 'But how easy would it be to park up? No bloody holidaymakers anywhere.'

'The winters of Uranus?' I say, finally giving in. 'Are you trolling me?'

She waves this away and continues to spray me with facts about the rest of the solar system, while I wonder what's put her in such a good mood. She still has a broken leg and soft tissue damage all over, but she's acting like she's walking on air. I think of how I've gone through the world the past year, moping over every little thing, slipping into quagmires of sadness through the long dark hours of the night. Makayla has dealt with a life-threatening situation, dusted herself off, and got on with things. Part of me wants to tell her and Demi about what happened with Alexis, but the whole thing is so embarrassing, so humiliating, that I can't bring myself to do it. Especially not now, when she has real challenges to deal with that make my experience with yet another toxic, lying man seem like nothing at all.

Later that day, I take an hour to walk the waterline of the bay where Makayla had her accident, picking up any fragments of black pirate glass gleaming in the wet shingle, so that if she wants to, she can use her craft supplies to make something as she convalesces. Maybe more jewellery that she can sell at the local car boot sale to make some extra money, which she always does during the peak season when the tourists are down, as a side hustle.

I'm just in the process of pulling some sea glass out of a rockpool when I hear the squawk of seabirds around me and look down at the low-water mark to see thousands of tiny silver fish flipping about on the sand.

There's one other person down here with me, an old guy with a metal detector. We look at each other and then both start picking up fish and throwing them back into the water.

'Pilchards,' he says. 'A wave must have caught them out.'

'We can't get them all,' I say, still flipping fish into the backwash. 'The tide's going out. They'll be stranded.'

'We'll do what we can,' he says, and we work together until it's too late and the ones we haven't reached yet have already died.

'Out of time,' I say, feeling a hot tear slide down my face. The seabirds are here in their hundreds now, pecking away at the small silver bodies on the sand.

'Circle of life, man,' he says, like some old Californian hippie. 'We live and then we die.'

'Sure,' I say. 'But today I really didn't need the reminder.'

Sixteen

When I finally get to Fistral Beach, my pockets heavy with sea glass for Makayla, there's already a bachelorette party setting up their towels and pop-up shelters on the beach. I keep hearing snatches of their conversations, which seem to involve visiting one of the town's tattoo parlours later in the day.

'A mermaid's tail on my ankle is what I'm thinking,' one girl with a Welsh accent announces to her friend, who nods approvingly.

'That's sexy,' she says.

'So sexy,' another girl chimes in.

An older woman in horn-rimmed glasses and a rollneck sweater clears her throat. 'The thing is, love, how will anyone know it's a mermaid's tail? Could be a haddock tail for all they can tell.'

'Shit, I don't want a haddock on my ankle,' the first girl says, laughing. 'Fuck it, I'll get a pink dolphin.'

'A *pink* dolphin?' the older woman says. 'I don't think they come that colour, dear.'

'It's a river dolphin from China,' Makayla says, appearing from one of the beach shelters, where she looks like she's been applying sunblock, given the greasy cream coating all over her arms.

'I thought you were at home resting?' I say, surprised but happy to see her here.

'Demi took pity on me and hired me a beach wheelchair, with the thick tyres. I can't stay in that house any more. It's driving me bananas. It started to feel like bloody lockdown again.'

'So, you're... tanning?'

'Only my limbs that aren't broken. The smashed-up one has a really high sun protection factor. Plaster.'

I smile. 'Aren't you worried about sand getting under the cast?'

'Aha,' she says, brandishing a roll of saran wrap. 'I come prepared. The Irishman is going to be here any minute to help with cling film application.'

'Hey, I got you some treasure,' I say, emptying my pockets and making a little pile of shining sea glass on the towel in front of her.

She gasps and points to her chest. 'For me? All of this?'

'Yes,' I say, smiling. 'Make necklaces and prosper.'

Then I take myself off to the shack, psyching myself up to interact with anyone who might be a potential new surf lesson customer. Except, it doesn't go exactly to plan.

By the time the sun is overhead, the beach is covered with tents, all of them sailcloth white and none of them emblazoned with the logos of big-name surf sponsors. Which is unheard of on this beach, or any big surf beach, where sand real estate is worth all kinds of big money.

But this is a fundraising event, a joint one, for both the Air Ambulance and for a local charity that helps children with disabilities to enjoy the ocean safely, for the therapeutic benefits.

There's a gazebo filled with something that's making the whole beach smell like heaven and which is apparently a Get Baked competition, which is nothing to do with tanning or marijuana, and everything to do with cakes. Everyone gets to try the cakes for free, so long as they vote for the one they like best and put a donation of whatever they can afford in a charity box.

I think of Alexis, tortured by the smell of baked goods, and wish I hadn't, because the thought manifests him. He's here walking between the tents with a man I don't recognise. All I can see of the other man is that he has dark hair and a body type that says weights, never cardio.

As they get closer, I can see from the way the guy is walking that he's wound tight. He's talking to Alexis about something important, I would guess, something that's making both of them uncomfortable. They don't look up and see me and I don't give them a chance to. I duck into the shack and hide. As they go past, Alexis murmurs something and the man says, in a tone of surprise, 'This is the surf school you told me about?'

'Yeah,' Alexis says. 'The sign is hand-painted. How cool is that?'

'Professionally made signs are expensive. Hand-painted is cheaper,' the other man says. There's something about his voice that I recognise. Maybe he visited the café before the flood.

'True, but I think in this case it was more about the shabby chic aesthetic.'

It absolutely was not about that. Even the cheapest

option for a professionally made sign would have blown my budget, which was a few dollars above zero.

Alexis and the new guy walk on, and I don't hear any more, because I stay inside the shack and read an ebook on my phone for the next two hours, in case they pass again, which is not ideal when I'm supposed to be actively promoting my surf lesson business, not hiding in a shack that used to house literal garbage.

The flooding of Demigorgons should have been a disaster for me. With no income, I knew I'd run out of money in less than ten days, and then I'd have to use my return ticket to go home to Hawaii. A failure. Just another one in a long string of failures.

But Demi wouldn't have it.

'I'll pay you for your missed shifts at the café,' she'd told me as soon as she arrived at the café to inspect the damage.

'You don't have to do that,' I'd said, handing her the box of snickerdoodles I'd bought from the coffee van while I was waiting for her.

'What kind of biscuit is this?' she'd asked, biting into one.

'A classic. How do you like it?'

'I'm going to need to eat a lot more of them before I decide,' she'd said, cramming in the remaining half of the cookie. 'And I meant what I said about paying you for the missed shifts.'

'And I meant it when I said it's not necessary.'

'It's necessary to me. For all of the staff. It's my fault the place is flooded, not yours. I still can't believe I left the tap running when I popped in to check on things.'

I'd felt for her. Because Demi is always on top of things,

always double and triple checking. The idea of her leaving a faucet running is worryingly out of character.

'I've been a bit out of it lately,' she'd said. 'Probably my menopause, but when I told my father what happened, he suggested I change the name of the café to Demensha.'

'Sheesh,' I'd said, wincing on her behalf.

'Oh, it cheered him up no end. Very bad taste really, given he's just been diagnosed with the early stages of dementia. Ever the joker.'

'I'm sorry about your father. But how can you afford to pay us if you're not open for business?'

'Firstly, that's not your problem. Secondly, I'm not short of a bob or two. You are. Use this time to focus on your surf school. The café is going to be out of action for a while, as I'm thinking of ripping out the whole kitchen and redesigning it from scratch. That's Jeremy's preference, anyway. He says everything's in the wrong place as it is.'

'You're doing a full kitchen remodel? That's going to take a minute.'

'I know. A month or two. So, go get new surf clients. Make your mark. Shoot your shot, Candice. This is the time to do it.'

Which is all very good in theory, but not so good when people keep reading my sign and walking past, even when I hear them say they're actively looking for surf tuition.

Thankfully, Alexis and his friend seem to have gone, plus I have my headphones and a new audiobook, which is about two city women who move to adjacent lakeside beach houses to find themselves, along with lesbianism and the G-spot.

It's too hot to sit in neoprene, so I have on my backless

yellow bathing suit and cut-off jean shorts. I also have a huge straw sunhat, which is casting perfect shade onto my phone screen, so I can rewind whenever I get to a sexy part.

'Not very busy today, then?' a gruff voice says, startling me.

I look up from my book to see a man frowning at me. He looks familiar but I can't quite figure out how I know him. He has tightly curled brown hair cut too short, so that all the curls are semi-circles, and dark eyes. He's wearing tailored pants and a dark blue button-down shirt, two buttons open at the neck. His jacket is undone but he's still wearing it, even in this heat. He looks undone in general; he's sweating, and his beard is coming through on his jawline, like he's just done twelve hours on a flight.

'Just means I have more time to listen to my audiobook,' I say, giving my cell phone a little wave in his general direction, while still hovering my index finger over the play button. I wait for him to move on, to make his way down the beach with all the other tourists, because if he was here for a surf lesson, he'd have led with that, which means he's probably just bored and thinks I must be, too.

He smiles awkwardly and takes a breath, as if working out what to say, and I catch the smell of him on the breeze. He has a warm woodsy scent mixed with a tang of sweat. Eau de Lumberjack.

'Nice to meet you,' he says, putting out a hand that's wet with perspiration because it's one of the hottest days of the summer and he is standing in the full glare of the midday sun, wearing a suit. A dark suit. One made of finely woven wool, by the looks of it. Not a linen suit. Not seersucker.

Sheep fibres. He's wearing something any sane person would only wear on a cold day in a big city.

'Everyone says it always rains in Cornwall,' he says, as if reading my mind.

'Not today. What we have here is a bona fide heatwave.'

'Just my luck,' he says.

'If you visit one of the surf stores in the complex, they'll hook you up with a T-shirt and boardshorts. Maybe some sandals.'

'I don't think I can pull off sandals,' he says, steeling himself for something. 'People would stop and point.'

'They'd point at your feet?'

'Probably.'

'Why?'

'Lost half a toe when I was younger.'

'In battle?'

He smiles and shakes his head. 'Frostbite.'

'Did you get stranded on a mountain or something?'

'Sort of. Lake District. Duke of Edinburgh Award.' He narrows his lips and shifts his weight a little. 'I'd have thought this would be peak season for surf lessons,' he says.

I wave my hand towards the beach, where the tide is at an extreme low of 0.3 metres thanks to the full moon effect, and the waves are tiny.

'Who can be bothered to walk all that way to the ocean? It's like a quarter-mile of walking on hot sand before you even get to the water's edge. And look at those waves. I've seen better dribble in the mouths of babies.'

'The small waves I get, but the walk to the water really puts the punters off?'

He seems nice. Friendly, but not creepy. He looks as if he's around my age and he has fine lines around his eyes, as if he's spent too much time in the sun. Maybe he's a beach bum who happens to have a white-collar day job, or maybe he grew up on a farm.

'Sure, it puts people off. You know, lugging a board all that way when you're not used to carrying one. It's not a problem we have back home.'

'And where's home?'

'I can't tell you that,' I say.

'Why not?'

'You're a stranger,' I say. I almost wink at him, which is so weird, because I'm pretty sure I've never wanted to wink at a stranger my whole life.

He nods and looks out at the beach, his eyes searching for something to settle on.

'Where are you from?' I ask, just for something to say.

'All over,' he says. 'But I work in London now.'

'Good for you,' I say. 'Let me guess – you have a great job in finance.'

I'm surprised by my own level of sass, but he smiles – a real smile – not the tight half-smile he managed earlier.

'Okay, I'll narrow it down for you,' I say, thinking *what the hell*. 'I'm from some place in Hawaii.'

I wait for him to fall over himself to tell me how lucky I am to call Hawaii home, but what he actually says – in a tone of total incredulity – is, 'They don't have tides in Hawaii?'

'Of course they have tides in Hawaii. But the tidal swing is more like ten inches than ten yards.'

He shoots me a look of confusion.

'So basically nothing, then?' he says.

'Not nothing. You feel the difference when you surf.'

'But why's it so small?'

'You tell me,' I say – only just stopping myself from asking if that's a question he hears a lot. Where is this flirting instinct coming from? What the hell is wrong with me? Maybe it's a reaction to Alexis's betrayal but it's as if something has clicked in my brain and I've engaged Makayla Mode.

He shrugs. 'I literally have no idea. I never did well at Geography.'

'Hawaii is in the middle of the Pacific Ocean,' I say. 'Which is pretty big.'

'That I did know.'

'Do you know about amphidromic points?'

He looks at me blankly.

'Okay, I'm no expert but I read online that it's something like this. Imagine the ocean is like two guys holding a rope and swinging it at both ends. Big movement at the edges of the rope, as their arms go up and down, but not so much happening in the middle, right? Also, we don't have those crazy big bays you guys get here, which funnel in the water. We have igneous rock from all the volcanic shit.'

'That's the technical term? Volcanic shit.'

'Yep.'

'Well, Candice, thanks for the lesson.'

I flinch. 'How do you know my name?' I'm sure I didn't mention it.

He sighs. 'Alexis. You're the girl from the café. The one who also owns the surf shack. The one who hates his guts.'

This hits me like a surfboard to the face. This must be

the man I saw Alexis walking with in the distance, the one I heard him talking with. How did I miss that?

'Bye now,' I say, looking down at my phone and pressing play.

'You're giving me the brush-off, eh?' he says, before I can return to a very sweet scene between my favourite fictional lesbians.

'Yes, that's exactly what I'm doing.'

'I can't say I blame you,' he says, with another deep sigh.

'And yet you're still standing here.'

'Give me the brush-off, by all means, but I was just wondering if you could say something cheery and American-sounding as you do it?'

'Are you serious?' I say, and he nods hopefully.

'What kind of thing do you have in mind?'

'I don't know. Something classic. How about, *Have a nice day, sir*?'

'Hey, asshole – I'm not calling you sir. And I don't give two shits if you have a nice day.'

'Fair enough,' he says, grinning. 'But I once had a waitress in Florida say this really bizarre thing to me after I gave her a ten-dollar tip and I couldn't stop thinking about it for ages afterwards.'

'What did she say?' I ask, because how can I not. This is information I need to know.

'She said: "I hope you make good memories today." And the thing was, she really did seem as if she hoped I'd make good memories that day. I'd never come across anything like it before. It unnerved me.'

'You're weird,' I say. 'Who are you exactly?'

'Daniel Burns,' he says.

'You're a friend of Alexis?'

'Worse. I'm his no-good literary agent. The son-of-a-bitch who told him to run away to Cornwall for inspiration. To have a summer fling with a beautiful girl who made him go weak at the knees.'

'Weak at the knees?' I say, with a derisive snort. 'I don't think Alexis is capable of reducing his knee strength for anyone. You really said that?'

'Yeah, sorry,' he says, taking a half step back, as if I'm going to get up and slap him.

'Then it's a good thing I'm not the girl he's looking for,' I say.

'Are you sure?' he says. 'Because Alexis really thinks you could be.'

'Then he shouldn't have written about me behind my back. All he cares about is himself and his book.'

'Oh, he freely admits he's been a selfish arsehole,' he says, making eye contact. He looks worried. 'For what it's worth, though, I think he genuinely is sorry and ashamed of himself.'

'I'm glad this has been a learning moment for him,' I say, exasperated. 'But he clearly doesn't give a crap about me.'

'I don't know about that... It's been ages since Alexis was interested in someone and, the way he's been talking, I'd say he's totally intrigued by you.'

Seventeen

I should tell Daniel to fuck off, but I don't, because suddenly I'm hit by a wave of pure exhaustion.

I get out of my lawn chair and lie down on my back, feeling the heat of sand grains hit my skin.

'I don't think I can have this conversation right now,' I say.

'Are you okay?'

'I need a minute.'

I pat the sand beside me, just like something Makayla would do, and he sits down, unbuttons his cuffs and rolls his shirt sleeves up, pushing them all the way to the beginning of his biceps.

'I know Alexis can come over a bit self-absorbed, but he's not an arsehole, really. He just sometimes...'

'Sometimes what?' I interrupt.

'Forgets that other people are real.'

'That's pretty damning. Coming from his literary agent, especially.'

'This is going to sound strange, but you didn't happen to be running around the Huer's Hut last week and see a weirdo sitting on the steps, did you?'

'That was you in the trawlerman beanie?' I ask.

'It was a cold morning,' he says, defensively. 'Although, I'm flattered you remember me.'

'You didn't get arrested?'

'No, but an old lady with a very fierce Pomeranian did give me a telling-off for disrespecting Cornish heritage.'

I nod and there's a beat when neither of us speaks. I should end this conversation. Go inside the shack and close the doors.

'Alexis wants me to see him again to talk about something,' I say. 'He says he has a business proposition for me.'

'Oh, does he?'

'I mean, I would think his agent would already know that.'

His jaw tenses. 'He doesn't tell me things until they're a *fait accompli*, so that I can't scupper them. It's quite annoying.'

'What are you doing here then?' I ask. 'Is this trip business or pleasure?'

'Both, which is a problem, I admit. Alexis called in a panic about the book and told me he'd rented a cottage. I was due some time off at work so I thought a break in Cornwall might be nice.'

'You're staying in the cottage with him?'

'God, no. I stayed two days and that was enough. I'm in the Travelodge now. They have a sea view and decent Wi-Fi but I'm mainly catching up on my submissions.'

'Submissions?'

'From writers who want me to represent them. Lord knows why they do – I fear I'm pretty shit as a literary agent. There are certainly more dynamic ones out there.'

'Well, you're here for Alexis. You can't be too terrible.'

'Thought I could talk him back from the brink. He's talking about ending his contract with his publisher. Giving back the advance money.'

'His choice to make,' I say, with a shrug.

Daniel scratches his head. 'I've already spent my commission.'

'Buy anything nice?'

'Paid off an old credit card from when I first moved to London.'

'I was expecting you to say you'd bought a Lamborghini.'

'My commission is fifteen percent, which wouldn't buy the wing mirror of a Lambo.'

'Sucks,' I say. 'But at least you paid off your MasterCard.'

'It was actually a Visa, but I do have two MasterCards with five-figure balances and a chunky little American Express.'

'I didn't know you guys could get Amex here.'

'Yeah, they offer a comprehensive range of products for Brits who want to expand their debt portfolio.'

'Nice. So not so great for you if Alexis goes back on the deal?'

'It would be frankly disastrous if Alexis backs out of this deal. And I think he might.'

'What's got him so freaked out?'

'It's a standard author crisis of confidence. He doesn't think he has a romance in him. I've been trying to tell him to give it a try, get some real-life experience, but that... hasn't worked out.'

'Hey, there's plenty more "real-life experience" to be had in this town. I'm far from his only option, believe me.'

'He says you interest him.'

'I'm not interested in his interest,' I say, aware that I sound like a petulant pre-teen, but just the thought of Alexis's interest in me makes me so uncomfortable that I want to hide in a burrow and never come out.

'How did you end up in Newquay?' Daniel asks, an abrupt turn of conversation I wasn't expecting.

'Do you know Alexis has never asked me that? He just accepts that I'm here and has no curiosity whatsoever about how I got here. Why I wanted to be here in the first place.'

'You didn't answer my question,' he says.

'Ask me another time. I'm not ready to share my pain with a rando who just accosted me on behalf of his dickwad client.'

'Fair enough.'

He wiggles his feet back and forth as if stretching out his ankle muscles, and moves a little further away from me, trying to get a more comfortable position on the sand.

'Since I have precisely zero customers,' I say, 'and a pretty low likelihood of getting any more today, how would you like to take a very long walk along the ocean?'

I surprise even myself with this. It's more forward than I've maybe ever been in my life, but there's something about Daniel that makes me feel somehow comforted, and safe. Plus, there are at least two thousand tourists on the beach today, so if he's an axe-murderer there are going to be plenty of witnesses.

'How long a walk are we talking?' he says. 'Because I'm wearing brogues.'

'So go buy sandals in the surf shop. Also,' I say, 'I should make clear that this walk will be in silence. Does that work for you?'

'I think it actually might,' he says, as I pack up my things and lock the double doors to the shack. 'Give me two secs to hit up the surf shop and I'll be right back.'

It takes him almost thirty minutes before he reappears, time in which I sit on the sand wondering if I've been ditched.

When he eventually appears, he's wearing blue sliders, one of which says 'Trop' and the other of which says 'Ical'.

'Only ones they had in my size. Hardly any stock left in there. Like a plague of locusts had passed through.'

'What size are your feet?' I ask, shooting a look at his gigantic big toes, as well as the missing tip of his baby toe.

'Size twelve,' he says. 'Why?'

'Nothing.'

'Twelve is a perfectly normal size for an adult human.'

'I didn't say anything.'

'Talking of giant pasties, I got these,' he says, handing me a plastic bag containing two Cornish pasties, two bottles of water and two chocolate chip cookies. 'I thought we'd need sustenance on our silent travels through the heat haze.'

I take a pasty gratefully and take a huge bite.

'People back home do not know what they're missing,' I say, as he takes a matching gigantic bite of his. He matches me bite for bite, like we're in a race, which I win because I've perfected the art of scarfing scorching hot pastry.

'Blimey,' he says, taking a sip of water to cool his mouth down. 'You demolished that.'

'Not my first rodeo,' I reply, eating a bite of chocolate chip cookie.

*

When we finish our food, we take our waters and walk the full length of the beach, climbing the stone steps to the esplanade and around to Pentire headland.

'What's that?' Daniel says, pointing to an art deco Italian-style villa down on the rocks, so close to the ocean that it has its own saltwater swimming pool, which is getting topped up by waves as we watch.

'Baker's Folly.'

'Who's the baker? And what's with the folly?'

'Frederick Baker, who built it on the wrong side of the headland, like a hundred years ago. Catches the worst of the weather and the full force of storms.'

'My kind of folly,' he says. 'Drink?'

He points to the other building up here, the fancy place right on the cliff, so close to the edge that when you're out on the terrace it feels like you're sailing in a cruise liner.

'This was supposed to be a *really* long hike,' I say. 'And we've been walking thirty minutes.'

'I'm paying for the drinks,' he says. 'In case that changes your answer.'

'Lead the way.'

I go to use the bathroom and, when I come out, I see Daniel at the bar. The first thing I notice is that the bartenders are talking to him with warm genuine smiles. He's so at ease with himself, and people appear to like him. Alexis, for all his flashy looks, sets people on edge, but Daniel seems to have the opposite effect. People talk to him like he's their buddy.

Everything is simple. There's no battle, no tortured soul at his centre.

He seems to have nothing in common with Alexis. If it weren't for the fact that I know they have a professional relationship, I would put Alexis in a different category altogether. I should put him out of my head completely.

'What are you drinking?' Daniel says to me, when he's finished discussing tennis players and the upcoming Wimbledon contest with the bartender.

'We walked so I guess we don't need to worry about being over the limit.'

'So… Jack Daniel's?'

'No,' I say. 'But I'd say yes to a rum and Coke.'

'If you like coconut, I'll do you a Koko Kanu special,' the bartender says, hopefully, as if he's personally invested in my drink choice.

'Tell me more,' I say, settling my elbows on the bar and propping my chin in my hands, which Daniel seems to find amusing.

'It's a cocktail of my own invention.'

'Keep talking.'

'There are secret ingredients, but I can't tell you what they are.'

'Why not?'

'You might patent the recipe and be the next Ronald McDonald.'

'I don't think Ronald McDonald was the founder of that brand,' I say, but the bartender is already picking out the right glass.

'I think you're just going to have to trust him,' Daniel says. 'Kristoff knows what he's doing.'

'I really do,' the bartender says. 'But thanks for the vote of confidence, Daniel, mate.'

'You guys have already swapped names? Sweet.'

'And football teams,' Kristoff says. 'We hate all the same ones. It's uncanny.'

'You've bonded over the teams you hate?'

They both *yep* at the exact same moment.

'Not the ones you like? Is that a soccer thing?'

'Definitely,' they both reply, again in unison.

'Okay, let's unpack that later,' I say, as Daniel beams at Kristoff, who seems to be flirting with both of us, and who leans forward to whisper something in my ear.

'Your boyfriend is a keeper.'

I shake my head and mouth, 'Not my boyfriend.'

Kristoff looks surprised, like Daniel and I have led him to believe that we're together, which is crazy given we've known each other for one hour.

We sit down in an alcove by the window, sparkling sea stretching out ahead of us, and Daniel takes a deep breath.

'So, you had something going with Alexis?'

I squeeze my eyes shut. Here it is. The conversation I knew would be coming, sooner or later.

'I did. Kind of. Not exactly.'

'But you freaked out when you saw what he was writing? That's when it all went wrong...'

I sink half of my rum cocktail and say nothing. Because that question is more complicated than I know how to answer. The thing Alexis and I had never 'went wrong'. It was wrong from straight out of the gate. All my instincts told me to steer clear of him, but I ignored them, because he was so different to Joseph. Because I was lonely and he acted interested in me. None of which I want to admit to his literary agent.

'The thing that's wrong is that Alexis is an asshole. An asshole who treats people like laboratory rats, so that he can write about them in his little notebook,' I say, with an aggressive smile.

'Ah, so you have formed a firm opinion about my star writer.'

'Kinda,' I say, taking another sip and looking to heaven.

'And there's really nothing I can say to shift you on that opinion?'

'Really, really.'

'I bet there is,' he says, a twinkle in his eye. 'I bet you the next two rounds that there is.'

'Save it. And you already told me you were paying for the drinks.'

'Whatever. I shouldn't tell you this thing anyway…'

I drain the rest of my cocktail and consider.

'Why shouldn't you tell me?'

'It would be unprofessional. I'd be breaking the writer–agent code of confidentiality. Alexis would be pissed off. He'd cut up rough.'

'Cut up rough? What is that?'

'Slang. Very hot in the 1920s.'

'When you went to school? You're looking pretty decent, considering.'

'I like to think so.'

'Time traveller?'

'No, just a literary agent who's thinking of betraying his star client by spreading malicious rumours that could end his career.'

'Okay, so now I need to hear it.'

'Can you keep a secret, though? Are you trustworthy?'

'Somewhat. On a good day.'

'And you're certain you want to hear this?'

'Shoot.'

He looks me in the eye, dead-ass serious, and says, 'I have one word for you.'

'I'm listening.'

'Exclosure.'

Eighteen

'Exclosure is not a word,' I say. 'At least I'm pretty sure it's not.'

'It's the name of Alexis's very first novel,' Daniel says. 'The one he self-published anonymously as an ebook on Amazon.'

'What's it about?'

'A solid question. On the surface it's about an alcoholic writer who has really bad irritable bowel syndrome.'

'I'm going to need more.'

'He lives on bone broth.'

'Huh, no kidding,' I say, realising that I still haven't looked up bone broth, and wondering if it can possibly be as bad as it sounds.

'This writer's only goal is to get published by telling the story of his life. And he does that. But once he's done that, he decides he needs to cover his back. He needs to track down all the exes who wronged him, the ones he slagged off in the book.'

'Got it,' I say, looking around to catch Kristoff's eye in the hope he'll let us start a tab. 'They are the *exes* in the title, and now he's looking for *closure*.'

'Exactly. Ultimate closure. He decides he needs to kill them so that they can't stir up trouble. Because he's so sure that the book will sell a million copies and the tabloids will come hunting for dirt and tell-all interviews with the women of his past, just to bring him down.'

'He's a creep.'

'Oh, one of the worst.'

'We're still talking about the character, right? Not Alexis?'

'The character.'

Daniel breaks to go up to the bar and order us another round of drinks.

'I'm on the edge of my seat here,' I say. 'Does the book-in-the-book sell a million copies?'

He shakes his head. 'No, it does not. In the novel, the book sinks. It isn't available in bookshops, it isn't reviewed anywhere – not even on book blogs – and the crazy author isn't invited to literary festivals. Not even dotty old lady book groups.'

'So, he's killed all the ex-girlfriends he wrote about? Got his "ex closure" and it was not even necessary?'

'Precisely. All three of them murdered in suitably gruesome ways.'

'An essential part of the narrative,' I say, starting to feel a warm glow from the alcohol.

'That's Alexis's literary fiction masterpiece. The one he talks about as being the only thing he's truly proud of writing, but which he could never put his real name to, because that would be career suicide, given the level of misogyny spouting from his protagonist.'

'Which first spouted out of Alexis's brain.'

'Unfortunately, yes. He admits to it, though. Says that

there's a well of misogyny deep inside of him and sometimes he dips into it without even meaning to. He dipped into it a lot for that book.'

'Did Alexis sell many ebooks on Amazon?'

'Two. He bought one, his flatmate bought one, and then he got cold feet and took the book off the site. I think it was live on there for about twenty minutes before he took it down.'

'Why did he get cold feet so quickly?' I say, leaning forward in my chair, because I'm so into this now.

'He realised the risk wasn't worth the reward. And he'd done what he needed to do; he'd got the story out of his system.'

'Writers are weird.'

'You have no idea. Alexis is one of the more normal ones on my list, if you can believe it.'

I snort and Koko Kanu shoots out of my nostrils.

'What was Alexis's pseudonym for his Amazon ebook?'

Daniel bites his lip.

'Are you ready for this? Steel yourself.'

I nod. 'I'm steeled.'

'It was... Persephone Dudd.'

I sink some more of my cocktail and ponder.

'Alexis's fake name was... Phony Dud?'

'I never said he doesn't have a sense of humour.'

'Okay, so if I tell Alexis that you spilled the beans and told me all this, he'll fire you?'

'Not exactly,' he says, motioning to Kristoff for another round. We're drinking way too fast, but I don't want to slow down.

'The truth is that he told me I could tell you.'

'*Why?*'

'He thought it might make you realise he's a broad-spectrum dickhead. Not just making a special effort for you. Did it make you feel better?'

'Maybe a little,' I admit.

Daniel holds up his whisky glass, clinks my glass and glances down at my wedding ring.

'So is your husband going to be joining you in Cornwall?' he says, in an unnaturally neutral voice.

Which is when Makayla swings up to us on her crutches.

Nineteen

She's wearing white linen pants and a striped blue vest top with a matching scarf tied in her hair and oversize sunglasses. Even with the blue plaster boot, she looks like she's just stepped off a yacht in Saint-Tropez. She looks like a million dollars, and then some.

'I thought you were meeting the Irishman on the beach?' I say. 'And why have you changed your outfit?'

'His mum's car broke down outside Morrisons, so he went to rescue her, and try to fix the car, like the good boy he is. And I changed because I always wear my fanciest shit to this place. If I'm paying seven quid for a glass of wine, I'm wearing a statement outfit. Why are you here?' she asks me, hopping into a chair and leaning forward to give me European-style kisses on both cheeks. 'And who's your friend?'

'Daniel, this is Makayla, my colleague from Demigorgons. Makayla, this is Daniel. He's an agent from London.'

Her eyes widen as she takes in this information. She thinks I'm here on some Tinder date. That I've met up with a tourist who's just passing through this town. That I'm making room in my life for a one-nighter. For some touch therapy. She doesn't know that I've recently had some with Alexis. Partly because she has enough to worry about without me taking my problems to her, but mostly because the whole thing is still too humiliating to admit.

'Cool job,' she says to Daniel.

'It has its moments,' he answers, his gaze catching on the scarf in her hair, as if he's wondering how it's sitting there so perfectly.

'Makayla has also met your star client Alexis,' I tell Daniel.

'Wait, wait, wait,' Makayla says, staring at us in turn. 'Am I butting in on two-thirds of a three-way?'

I ignore this and say, 'Makayla loves Alexis. He's been one of her favourite customers this summer.'

'Really?' Daniel says, turning to look at her with renewed curiosity. 'You get on with Alexis?'

'We're pals,' she says. 'So, he works for you as a writer?'

'Technically, I work for him,' Daniel says. 'I help him get deals and he pays me commission on whatever he earns.'

'Fifteen percent,' I say.

'Twenty percent for film and foreign deals,' Daniel says, as if that's important information.

'You must be minted,' Makayla says.

'Yep, I shit on a golden toilet.'

'Me too,' Makayla says, high-fiving him.

'So why do you like Alexis?' Daniel asks her, and I wonder why he's asking her this.

'I mean, what's not to like?' she says, waving to Kristoff, who brings her a glass of red wine without even being asked. 'He's gorgeous, he's talented, he's weird as fuck. If it wasn't for him taking a shine to Candice, I'd have been right in there.'

'He never took a shine to me,' I correct her. 'He just thought he could use me for his creepy little story about a rich guy who spends a summer fucking a surf instructor.'

'What?' Daniel says. 'That isn't in the proposal he wrote. The book he's supposed to be writing is about two Cornish twenty-somethings who fall in love and start a sexy business.'

'Janie and Bryce. Except Janie is now Candy and Bryce is the media mogul version of Alexis.'

'This is bad,' Daniel says, with a low whistle. 'This is breach of contract.'

'You're the literary expert,' I say, a rush of schadenfreude filling my body. I want Alexis to get into trouble. I want him to piss off his publisher, even if it does mean his literary agent won't get to pay off his Amex.

'He hasn't sent me material yet. I had a bad feeling it was something like this. Why can't writers ever just stick to the fucking brief?'

Makayla has gone suspiciously quiet. She's also taken the scarf out of her hair and is using it to cover her eyes. Which is when the questions I should have already asked occur to me.

'Makayla, why are you here? You're supposed to be at home, resting. And why do you not seem surprised to hear that Alexis was writing shady shit about me?'

Which is also when Alexis walks through the door.

Twenty

'You're here to meet Alexis?' I say, filled with a sense of betrayal, because how could she?

But then, I shouldn't be surprised, because I know Makayla's liked him from the start. She made no secret of that. If anyone should have been on that couch in the cottage with him, it was her, not me.

'Keep your knickers on,' Makayla says. 'I'm here because he wanted to talk about you. I didn't know you'd be here too.'

'When did you two even swap numbers?'

'You passed his business card on to me, remember? I thought I should text him to say thank you for the flowers. Wish I hadn't bothered now, to be honest.'

'What did he tell you?' I ask, not able to meet her gaze.

'Not a lot. He knows he messed up and he wants to make things right.'

'How? Can he go back in time and not start writing a cringe story about me?'

Alexis has taken one look at us and swerved to the bar, where Kristoff does not engage him in conversation, but instead serves another customer. Maybe it's the boyband looks or Alexis's penetrating stare, but something is throwing Kristoff off his bartending game. Was this what I looked like when Alexis first walked into Demigorgons? Did he push me off balance like this?

Alexis gets his drink eventually and walks sheepishly to our table and sits down.

Makayla goes to him, gives him a peck on the cheek, in the same way she might kiss her grandmother, and then looks at the three of us, sitting in silence, and turns to go.

'Don't even think about leaving,' I say, and she shushes me, and goes to a bar stool to talk to Kristoff.

'Why are you here?' I say to Alexis, before Daniel can try to smooth things over.

'Firstly, to say sorry again. I'll always be sorry about how I handled things with you. I shouldn't have got naked with you. At least, not without talking to you about all this first.'

'I'll just go up to the bar too, I think,' Daniel says, suddenly flushed. 'Give you guys some time to talk.'

I go to say something to Daniel, to tell him he has no reason to feel awkward because what happened with Alexis is in the past, it will never happen again and we didn't even have sex, if that is at all relevant, but which also feels like extreme overshare.

Alexis puts up his hand. 'Okay, mate. I'll see you at the bar in a bit. Candice, please let me finish.'

'Sure,' I say. 'Go right ahead. I'd hate to interrupt the author's flow.'

'The truth is I was in a bad way. Drunk and depressed. It's that old adage, really: hurt people hurt people.'

This is how Alexis is excusing his behaviour?

But why shouldn't he? That was how I excused Joseph's

behaviour. The damage flows through toxic men like radiation, distorting cells, flowing right out of them into the person standing by them.

Joseph had been troubled and for the longest time I didn't even know, because when he was in a good patch, he functioned great. And I met him in a good patch. But the bad patch was always around a corner.

Later, when it became clear he had serious unaddressed emotional issues, and a temper he couldn't control, I knew the bad patch would always be there, somewhere, and every time there was a bend in the road, I wondered.

That state of alert made me more anxious than I'd ever been in my life, but I loved him. I thought I was strong enough to deal with whatever his demons threw in our way. Because hurt people hurt people, and Joseph was hurt all the way through.

Alexis is making the same argument for himself. A man I've known a few days, who has already betrayed my trust.

'The truth is I want you to help me,' he says. 'Not for free.'

'Then for what? What exactly are you offering? Exposure? Creative writing coaching?'

'Money. What I'm offering you is a cut.'

And then he details his whole crazy plan while I look at him, at the pretty eyes, the perfect waves of his hair and the gorgeous mouth, and I realise that maybe this was the thing I sensed in him all along. Maybe this was my road not travelled. It wasn't Alexis I was interested in; it was his book. It was the fact that he got to write one.

I didn't want to be with Alexis.

What I wanted was to *be* Alexis.

Twenty-One

We do a switch around after our next round of drinks. Alexis goes to the bar to sit with Daniel, who is laughing again with Kristoff, and Makayla comes back to the table to sit with me.

'What's happening? That looked intense.'

'Alexis wants my help.'

'With what? Surfing lessons?'

'Not just surfing. He wants help with his book.'

'He wants you to help him write his book?' she asks, her eyes widening.

'Maybe.'

'So, you'd be his, what, co-writer?'

'I guess. But I don't think I'll be doing much writing. Just pointing him in the right direction.'

'But your name will be on the cover, along with his?'

'I don't know. I think I'd be more of a freelance creative. But it would be a paid gig.'

'Well, you know the golden rule about freelances,' Makayla says, raising her eyebrows.

I wait for her to elaborate.

'If a lance is going to be doing its best jabbing, its owner needs paying upfront. How much is he going to pay you?'

'He didn't mention a figure, but he implied it would be decent. He used this weird phrase. When he was talking about the offer, he said, "I'll put some welly behind it", so that's got to be good, right?'

'How much is a welly?' Makayla asks. 'Because he could be talking about a teeny tiny toddler's wellington boot, or a farmer's massive bog-trotting one.'

'Okay, so I didn't ask him to define wellies as a unit of monetary value, but I would guess he means four figures. Don't you think?'

'What you need is a day rate. You're providing him with help and your day rate is two hundred pounds.'

'What? I can't charge that. That's crazy.'

'Don't sell yourself short. He can afford it if he can afford a fancy seafront cottage in high season.'

'It's actually that really sweet place by the old lifeboat house,' I say.

'How do you know that?' she asks, eyes like a hawk.

'I gave him a ride after his surf lesson when he'd injured his foot,' I say, looking sheepish. Makayla is so open about everything that it seems wrong, or at least rude, to keep something like this from her, but I'm not the same way she is. I need protective walls to hold me up. 'Then I went over again.'

'What exactly will you be doing for him? Apart from giving him rides at his place.'

'*To* his place, Makayla.'

'Slip of the tongue.'

'I'm going to help him understand what appeals to romance readers, go through the key cues of the genre. We'll brainstorm plotlines, character motivation and turning points. I'll also show him around Cornwall, take him – and maybe Daniel, too – to see things and locations that I think will appeal to a romance readership. It's going to be like a guidebook to Cornwall, as well as a romance that appeals to fans of the genre, so I'm going to need to include all of the greatest hits.'

'Of Cornwall or the romance genre?'

'Both. Where can Alexis set scenes, do you think? Where around here would be good for that?'

'Isles of Scilly. Bryher is unspoilt and wild. Mermaid of Zennor is romantic. Fowey for Daphne du Maurier. The caves where *Poldark* was filmed. I had sex in one of them. Sorry, two of them. I usually think of caves on Cornish beaches as, well, toilets – especially during the pandemic when all the facilities were closed – but they're tidal so it smelt fine, and it was actually quite romantic.'

'Keep going, I'm writing this down,' I say, glancing down to my phone where the Notes feature is up, then out at the panoramic view of the ocean. Sitting here in this incredible oceanside building that feels like it really could be a boat, I have a sense that this is right. Like I'm on a ship that's steering me on a fresh course, taking me somewhere new, somewhere better.

'The woods near Ponsanooth are romantic. Oh, and I had sex with the Poet at Chapel Porth,' Makayla says, jolting me out of my reverie. 'Heck of a view from up there. That was before he told me what his real job was. There was no more sex after that.'

'What's his real job?'

'I can't even bring myself to say it. Oh, and the car park at Jamaica Inn is weirdly sexy. Bit of a hot spot for first-date action.'

'I can't take an author and his agent to a parking lot for some second base action.'

'Who said second base? And don't forget Tintagel. You'll definitely want to include a kiss, maybe some heavy petting, under the statue of King Arthur. You can pretend you're Guinevere as you snog Alexis.'

'I don't think Guinevere was into heavy petting, and I'm not going to be kissing Alexis. Or anybody. My kissing days are over.'

'Not forever.'

'Yes forever. I'm a tour guide to Cornwall, a research assistant, and maybe a co-writer.'

'It seems like a lot of work to help a writer you only just met. Someone who has only mentioned wellies. Maybe you should go with three hundred a day. When are you getting the contract?'

'I don't know. Alexis has only just run this idea past me, but he says, if it goes well, I'll get a cut of the royalties and a credit.'

'How much of a cut?'

'Halfsies, I think. He didn't say that outright, but that was what he hinted.'

'Why is he hinting? Why can't he just tell you?'

'You know how posh people feel about talking about money. What's the word – *uncouth*.'

'Uncouth,' she says, laughing. 'Where did you dig that up? Another one of your Regency romance novels? It's not uncouth to discuss terms. It's smart and businesslike. And you're both those things. Has Alexis had any money from the publisher upfront?'

'Some.'

'Because maybe you should be getting a cut of that too if he's serious about this arrangement. You should look into it. See how it normally works with book deals. The information is bound to be out there on the internet.'

'Maybe I'll talk more to Daniel.'

'So...' she says, chewing her thumbnail thoughtfully. 'This *is* basically a threesome situation, isn't it? You show them a good time and they make it worth your while in a financial sense.'

'You're making it sound a little sketchy there, Makayla.'

'Deliberately so, yes.'

'It's not going to be sexual. It's purely a business relationship.'

'What if it was sexual? Could be a fun way to spend a summer...'

'You're recommending that I enter a three-way romantic relationship with an author and his literary agent? Because that does not sound like a fun time to me. That sounds stressful.'

'Fair enough. Threesomes are tricky. I don't recommend them. Now foursomes, on the other hand, are absolutely fucking great.'

'Please stop. I can't deal with this visual imagery right now.'

'I'm serious. Nobody gets left out. Everybody has someone to play with and then snuggle with afterwards for the chill-out sesh.'

A thought suddenly occurs to me. 'Makayla, this is not your way of suggesting yourself as the fourth member of this illicit liaison, is it? Because I don't think I'm okay with that.'

'Pu-leaze,' she says. 'You are like a sister to me. Gross.'

She shudders as she walks away to the bar and I can't help thinking about how much Joseph and my ex-best friend Issy would like her, and how glad I am that they'll never get to meet her, because they don't deserve Makayla in their lives. I'm not even sure I do.

When we're done drinking and Daniel has settled up with Kristoff, the four of us go to walk a few yards along the headland trail – Makayla swinging too wildly on her crutches – to sit on an outcrop of rocks and watch the sun go down. Daniel stops as soon as we get up onto the ridge and looks across Crantock Bay to a rectangle of farmland glowing bright crimson in the sunset.

'What's that?' he says, pointing across the water.

'That,' Makayla says. 'Is pure magic.'

'The poppy fields of West Pentire,' I say. 'I'll take you there, but right now I have to get Makayla home. She's had enough crutch work for one day.'

'It's true,' she says. 'I'm getting blisters in my armpits.'

'Road trip soon?' Daniel says. 'You up for it, Candice?'

He gives me a look and I take a moment to answer.

Wherever this winds up, I'm in for the journey.

'Sure,' I say.

We walk back to the parking lot and call a cab. Makayla sits in the front with the cabbie, who she's given the nickname 'Drive' – a nickname she keeps using whenever she talks to him, for some unfathomable reason. 'How's your night been, Drive?' 'Any dodgy customers, Drive?' and Alexis, Daniel and I sit in the back in silence. Daniel has chivalrously taken the middle seat, even though his legs are longer than mine, and our knees keep touching.

Before the cab drops Makayla and me at Demi's house, Daniel passes me his business card.

'If you need to get hold of me,' he says, 'don't hesitate to call. Or send me a message. A WhatsApp. I know this agreement you've come to with Alexis is a bit unusual and you'll have questions. Contact me whenever you want to.'

'I think she gets it,' Alexis says, staring out into the night.

I take the business card, put Daniel's number into my phone and hand him back the card.

'Save it for some talented stranger looking for literary representation,' I say, and he laughs and slides it back into his billfold.

I tap out a message and hit send.

His phone buzzes, he opens the message and smiles.

'What did she write?' Alexis asks, straining to see.

'Nothing important,' I say, handing Alexis three shiny pound coins. 'That's for our share of the cab,' I tell him.

'Don't be a dickhead,' Makayla says from the front seat. 'Let the rich Londoners pay for the taxi. It's the least they can do.'

'She has a point,' Daniel says, looking serious. 'I'll expense it.'

I hold out my hand and Alexis drops the coins back into my palm.

Just before I slam the car door, I hear Alexis say something.

'What did she text you?' he asks.

'Just hi,' I hear Daniel lie, and then the car moves off.

Twenty-Two

'Weird day,' Makayla says, as we walk slowly up the driveway to Demi's house.

'And then some.'

I feel my phone vibrate in my pocket and when I open the message, I see that Daniel has replied to me.

I'll see what I can do, but no promises!

I show the screen to Makayla.

'What did you ask him for?' she asks.

'An e-copy of Alexis's first novel. Secretly published on Amazon.'

'You want to read that?'

'I think it might make me feel better about my own first shot at working on a novel.'

Makayla smiles, then stumbles on her crutches and groans. She talks a good game, but I can tell she's tired and feeling pain.

'Meds and bed,' I say to her, and she doesn't argue.

*

But, when we get inside Demi's house, music is blaring. I recognise the song 'Temple' by Kings of Leon, which I've always found deeply romantic, since the lyrics are about someone being willing to 'take one in the temple' to save their lover's life.

'God, I love this song,' Makayla says, having a little headbang on her crutches.

'It's the ultimate declaration of love, isn't it?' I say. 'Being willing to take a bullet in the head for someone?'

'That's what this song is about?' Makayla says. 'I thought it was about butt stuff.'

'How could this song possibly be about... *that*?' I say, turning to stare at her, waiting for her to make this make sense.

'Hello? The "temple"?'

'Which is the flat part at the sides of the forehead, right?'

'Maybe *literally*. In the song, it's clearly a euphemism. So, taking one in the temple...'

'Oh my gosh, Makayla. Please do not tell me you call your – y'know – the temple?'

'Doesn't everybody?' she says. 'Temple of Doom if you do it wrong.'

Demi's in the living room, ironing the wrinkles out of a cornflower cotton summer dress and having a full-blown danceathon with herself. It looks a lot like the iron is her dance partner because she keeps waving it around at eye level and I'm both concerned that she's going to get third-degree burns to her nose and amused that she is still able to dance so sexily while holding a domestic implement that is literally pouring steam into her eyes.

The dress has a row of blue buttons running up the

middle and I can already tell it's going to look fabulous against Demi's skin tone.

'Hello girls!' she says, delighted to see us. 'Can you believe that these boys are going to be playing in our little town in two months' time? Kings of Leon in the Quay!'

'Bit late for ironing, isn't it?' Makayla says.

'I have a breakfast date. Pays to be organised. Seven "P"s and all that.'

'Huh?' I say, yawning.

'Weren't you a military brat, Candice?' she says. 'You should know the seven "P"s. "Prior Planning and Preparation Prevents Piss-Poor Performance".'

'You're going to be performing on your date?' I ask.

'Of course,' she says with a wink.

'Do you mind if I use the iron when you're finished?' I say. 'I have linen pants I want to get the creases out of, although I don't know why I'm bothering when they're just going to wrinkle again the second I sit down.'

'You're going to iron something?' Makayla says. 'You never iron.'

'I mostly don't need to. All my favourite clothing stretches, which is also my username on Reddit.'

'You're deflecting,' Demi says. 'Tell us more about why you need to iron. Do you have a date? I hope it's not a job interview because Demigorgons needs you. At least, it will need you as soon as we reopen, which it will, you know.'

'I'm not totally sure what it is,' I shrug. 'It could be a lead, but I don't want to get my hopes up.'

She pats me on the back and goes to flip the kettle on.

'Arianna wants me to meet an older guy who worked

here as a lifeguard in the nineties,' I say to Makayla. 'She thinks he might know something about my father. The guy still surfs and trains, twenty miles up the coast. He's coming to Newquay just to meet me.'

'How old are we talking?' she asks, innocently.

'In his sixties.'

'Damn,' she says, grinning.

★

Later that night, just as I'm on the brink of falling asleep, I hear a noise outside the door of Demi's guest bedroom. The floor creaks and I see the outline of Makayla standing there, without her crutches. She's wearing a long white nightdress that I would guess belongs to Demi and she's leaning on the doorframe.

'Candice, are you awake?' she whispers.

'What's wrong?'

'I think I'm coming on my period and I don't have stuff here. Do you have any pads?'

'Yeah. Time of the month for me too. I just started this morning.'

'Aww, we synched up,' she says, beaming.

I throw her the pack of sanitary napkins that I have on my nightstand.

She doesn't hobble outside to use the bathroom, she just drops her underwear, sticks the pad down, and uses the nightdress as a beach-style changing robe. Then she gets into bed with me.

'You know,' I say. 'You never did tell me what the embarrassing thing was with the Irishman? Can you speak about it now that you've broken your leg in front of him and had to be airlifted off the beach?'

She nods slowly. 'I think I'm finally ready to share my secret shame.'

And then she goes silent.

'Don't leave me hanging, Makayla.'

'So, he wanted to do something nice, book a hotel room somewhere, maybe the Headland Hotel even, check out the new spa with all the pools, but it was five hundred quid a night. He wanted to put it on his credit card, but that's an insane amount of money. You and me could do a week in Tenerife for that. So we went to the Travelodge. Still a nice view over the sea. Romantic as chuff but only eighty quid a night. We went halves.'

'Okay, still not seeing the problem.'

'So we were going for it, but he'd put this "Netflix and Chill" playlist on his phone and just as I was really getting going, a song came on and it totally ruined the vibe.'

'What was the song?'

'Fucking Kings of Leon. Every bastard in this town is listening to them cos of Boardmasters coming up.'

'But what was the song?'

She buries her face in her hands. 'It was bloody "Sex on Fire", and it was too much pressure. The boner fizzled.'

'That's all? That's totally normal.'

I say this knowledgeably, as if my two partners to date have made me quite the sexual sophisticate.

'Well, it's not normal for me!'

'It's no reflection on you. Travis probably just got psyched out. Or had too much to drink.'

She shakes her head. 'I'm saying I lost my lady boner. My sex drive vanished.'

'Oh,' I say, finally catching up. 'Well, I'm sure he would have understood.'

'He was fine about it, but I'm still not over it. The lyrics made me weirdly self-conscious, like our sex *had to be fire*, and then I just couldn't get there. I had to climb off him and have a soothing cup of tea.'

'What kind of tea?'

'Who asks what kind of tea after hearing that story? You always want to hear the weirdest details, Candice. Maybe you should be writing your own novels.'

'So…?'

'Lady Grey.'

'That's a classy tea.'

'I'm a classy lady,' she says, finally managing to smile.

I can feel the warmth of her arm next to mine and I hope she doesn't move it. Maybe she's right and I am touch-deprived.

'Look, I know you'll be busy with all this book stuff now,' she says, slowly. 'But don't forget to prioritise your own needs, will you?'

'How do you mean?' I ask.

'Your journey led you here to Newquay. Don't forget why, just because some guy needs your help.'

'I see your point, but I'm hoping it will be like when you're searching for something important that you've lost.'

'How do you mean?' she asks.

'You can't find it anywhere. Then the second you stop looking, there it is,' I say, and add, '*Knock on wood*.'

'Well, I hope you're right,' she says, getting quiet.

'What are you worried about, Makayla?'

'For all my dating experience – my "high body count" as the Tinder dickheads call it – I don't know much about men, but I know this: I know that you learn who they *really* are when you say no to them.'

'Okay. What are you saying exactly?'

'What did Alexis do when you said you wanted nothing more to do with him?'

'He... got his agent on the case.'

'Exactly. He brought in the big guns. I know he comes across as a bit clueless and dopey, and maybe he is, but he's also determined. Resourceful.'

'You say that like these are bad qualities.'

'Not necessarily, but he's the sort of bloke who's used to getting his own way. Just be careful. If this project doesn't go well, I'm worried it could blow up in your face and leave you hurt.'

'Don't say that. I'm just getting to feel excited.'

This is the problem with allowing myself to hope. The moment my happiness balloon begins to soar, some sharp object comes along to pop it.

'I'm sorry. I don't want to piss on your chips. I just hate the thought of some rich prick ruining your life here and making you want to leave Newquay. Do the project but make sure your interests are protected.'

There's a long silence and I wonder if she's fallen asleep. I turn to look at her and see a glint of moonlight in her eyes.

'Makayla,' I say. 'When was the new quay built?'

'Huh?'

'The new quay of Newquay. I feel like I should know, if I'm living here.'

'Don't ask me. Like, a hundred years ago maybe?'

I take my phone from under my pillow. No new messages from Daniel. Nothing from Ricky either.

'Wow,' I say, reading from Google. 'Six hundred years ago – 1439, when the Bishop of Exeter granted permission for a new stone quay to be built.'

'Oh right,' Makayla says, with a huge yawn.

'Not so new, then, at all,' I say. 'And it's not even the oldest thing about this town. There's been a cliffside fort settlement here for sixteen hundred years. Early people smelted iron ore here for tools and weapons.'

'You mean like Stone Age man? Like in *The Croods*?'

'I guess more like Iron Age man,' I say, trying to imagine how they'd felt living here, how they'd arranged their lives. What they'd wanted. What they'd gotten.

'I don't like thinking about it,' Makayla says, yawning again.

'I love thinking about it,' I say. 'It makes me feel part of something. A progression.'

'Well, thanks for the history lesson,' she says. 'Now stop talking and go to sleep.'

But I don't sleep for hours. I think about all the stories that led people to this town, about the story Alexis wants me to help him write, and about all the choices that led me here.

And then I think about my mother.

Twenty-Three

D emi is up early to make us all breakfast. She seems so happy to have us under her roof that I feel a little guilty for holding out so long and staying in my van.

'I thought you had a breakfast date?' Makayla says to her, skewering a rasher of bacon.

'That's second breakfast. I need to line my stomach first. So, I hear you have some news, Candice? Makayla wouldn't give me any details. She said I have to ask you. Have you found your answer?'

'Not about that. This is something else. So, I met a literary agent yesterday. Alexis's literary agent.'

'He's in Newquay?'

I nod. 'Visiting Alexis. Who actually thinks I might be able to help him with the book and get a writing credit. Can you believe that?'

'Of course I can believe that. I've snooped in your jotter plenty, read all your poems and short stories. You write beautifully,' Demi says, matter-of-factly.

'Demi!'

'What? I assumed if you were worried about people

reading it you wouldn't have left it on the break room table in Demigorgons.'

'Also my reasoning for reading it,' Makayla says, tapping her temple with an index finger.

I laugh. 'That's just daydreaming. I'm not a professional. I've never had anything published. Even Makayla's booty call had something printed in the *Newquay Voice*.'

'That's because he inundated them with stuff until they finally printed something on condition that he'd go away and leave them alone,' Makayla says. 'Do not compare yourself to that bloke.'

'Okay, but I'm a surfer and a waitress, not a writer.'

'How do you know you can't be a writer? Have you ever actually tried to be one? To make a career of it?' Demi says, handing me a coffee.

'No, because what do I have to say that somebody else couldn't say better?'

'Don't think of it that way,' Demi says. 'Nobody can write your story – the one in your heart – except you. If you don't write it, nobody else will.'

'You have…' Makayla says, mopping up her egg yolk with a crust of bread, 'what most women have.'

'An accurate notion of my abilities?'

'An inaccurate notion. You have imposter syndrome. You don't believe you deserve success, but you do. You are talented and you have an opportunity. What you have to do now is go for it.'

'What if I'm no good? What if Alexis and I don't work well together?'

'You'll never know unless you try. This is opportunity that's come knocking on your door, my girl,' Demi says.

'And you would be a fool to send her packing. Take your shot, Candice. Nobody else can take it for you.'

Makayla has finished her breakfast, washed up her silverware and dishes and I've barely got through one broiled tomato.

She brings this week's copy of the *Newquay Voice* back to the table and begins doodling on the front page, which is a photograph of the Prime Minister on a visit to Cornwall. Behind him she draws some planets and a spaceship with a tractor beam radiating towards him.

Demi looks over her shoulder, assesses Makayla's picture and puts her finger on a planet that sort of resembles Saturn.

'Well, that is just a perfect example,' Demi says, cheerfully. 'Everyone always thinks "Saturn" when you say "planet". But it's had a lot of help to get where it is.'

'How has Saturn had help?' I ask, tomato juice running down my chin.

'The rings are new and they're a temporary feature, at that.'

'What are you going on about, Demi?' Makayla asks, laughing.

'Saturn's rings. They've only been there for a few million years. Before that? Totally ringless. It was just your bog-standard spherical planet with no bling.'

'How do you even know this?' I ask, loading my fork with fried mushrooms.

'I read books. It's allowed,' Demi says, her tone beginning to sound a little defensive.

'Okay, I'll play. How did Saturn get blinged up?' Makayla says.

'It's a bit complicated, but they think there was this really icy moon, sort of lurking nearby.'

'Awesome,' Makayla says. 'I already love this. Carry on.'

'And it got too close to Saturn, past the Roche limit, and Saturn sort of nicked all the ice off it. Saturn saw its opportunity to get fancy and went for it. Gimme all the ice, baby.'

'That is the most radical thing I've ever heard,' Makayla says, shaking her head and then adding, 'Bit weird that the limit thing was named after a village in the arse-end of Cornwall.'

'Not Roche the parish,' Demi says, laughing. 'It's named after Édouard Roche – French astronomer and mathematician, who worked out how close a moon could get to a planet before it got all messed up by tidal forces and disintegrated.'

'Is that really true about Saturn?' I ask. 'Because I've never heard anything like that.'

'That's what the experts think now. They think it took a couple of days for Saturn to get her rings, that's all. Stripped the ice off that moon like a string of candy floss.'

'And wound it round her gut like a belly chain,' Makayla contributes.

'So, now everyone loves Saturn,' Demi says. 'Because she was a cheeky bitch who took her shot.'

'So, what happened to the ice-covered moon?' I ask, because that seems important too. 'Is it still up there, just naked?'

'I don't know. I haven't got to that part yet, but I imagine it didn't end well for it. The point is that one day those rings will be gone again, because all the fancy goes eventually and we all end up ordinary old ladies, even Hollywood stars and the planet Saturn.'

'Okay then,' I say, trying to keep up with Demi's thought processes. 'You're saying that I should help Alexis to write his book?'

'Yes, but make sure you're the planet. Not the icy moon getting stripped,' she says, and goes out back to her flower garden to stare up at the day moon.

I've never met women like these before, who are so unapologetically strange and so happy to be just who they are.

It strikes me that whatever happens from here on out, these women are my bolt of good luck, and I am more fortunate than I have any right to be that they walked up into my life.

Twenty-Four

Arianna's lifeguard contact remembers the names of most of the guys he worked with in the nineties, but my story doesn't ring any bells. He'd need more details to connect the dots, and not all the guys talked to him about their private lives. As he tells me, a little bluntly: he was their boss, not their best mate.

'It's a shame that things have stalled with your search,' Makayla says, when I go back home to tell her it was a dead end, just like all the other potential leads I've followed since I arrived in Newquay. But it wasn't as if I ever had a solid plan. I never had a clear strategy for finding him. I naively thought just being here would be enough. That by placing myself at the heart of this beach community, I would somehow find him. But I didn't have a name. All I had was dates and a vague physical description.

'Yeah, I'm no closer than I was the first day I got here.'

'That sucks. But think of all the other things you've achieved. All the truly amazing friends you've made.'

'I actually was just thinking about that,' I say, and just then my phone beeps and I look down to see a new message from Daniel.

Hi Candice, Sorry to bother you. I wondered if you were
free to meet at some point today? Maybe grab lunch at
the beach? I'm paying. It's to do with the book.

I feel a strange, warm sensation when I reply saying yes,
but I bury that and turn back to Makayla asking, 'So how
are things going with the Irishman?'

'Pretty good, all things considered.'

'And the Doberman?'

Her face changes. She looks like she smells rotten eggs.

'I think I may have the ick. The start of the ick. Ick-onset.'

'Why?'

'We finally went out for dinner.'

'It didn't go so well?'

'You know how whales, when they're feeding, take, like,
seventy-five thousand litres of water into their mouth and
then slam their jaws together and the plankton gets stuck
at the roof of their mouth and all the water comes gushing
out of the sides?'

'If you say so.'

'That was the Doberman trying to eat soup. He wouldn't
stop talking. It went everywhere. It was on his chin. It was
on his shirt. Some of it actually got onto the top of his head.'

'Soup was in his hair?'

'Worse, he has a shaved head.'

'Are you a snob, Makayla? Because you're sounding a
little snobby right now. Are table manners so important to
you that a lack of them would give you the ick?'

'I just don't think I can continue to have sex with someone
who eats soup like that.'

'You could see it as sensual. All that slurping...'

'No, it wasn't sensual. I wanted to stop at Asda on the way home and buy him some Vanish for the stains. That was a nice shirt. It was his only nice shirt. Those green splodges are never coming out.'

'But you still haven't seen the puppy yet.'

'I can't believe it,' she says, putting her head in her hands. 'I'm going to have to keep seeing a man who gives me the ick because he's holding his puppy hostage from me.'

'It's a good plan he's got going,' I say.

'Too good. I'm seeing him again tonight.'

Twenty-Five

I spot Daniel pacing in front of a surf shop and answering messages on his phone. He's ditched his wool suit and is wearing an unusual combination of blue boardshorts, a striped sweater vest and a varsity jacket.

'Nice outfit,' I say.

'Borrowed from Alexis. It was all he had that was clean. His cottage doesn't come with a washing machine.'

'And he can't use a laundromat?' I say.

'He wouldn't be able to get his head around the small change. He thinks coin money is for charity boxes and wishing wells.'

'Okay, but why don't you just hit up one of surf shops and buy yourself some new clothes? There's one literally right next to you.'

'I can't bring myself to walk in there again. Everyone in there is so young and hip, even the sales staff. Especially the sales staff. I'm intimidated. Just by their hair, if I'm honest.'

'Shall we go order lunch?' I say, feeling the gurgle of my stomach. 'Or do you want to talk first?'

'Food first, talk later,' he says.

*

'I just want to make sure you understand what you're signing up for. Do you understand all the terms Alexis mentioned?'

We've finished our lunch and Daniel is talking to me like I'm a baby who grew up in a cowrie shell.

'I'm not naïve. I've travelled. I went to college. It's where I met Joseph.'

'Your husband?'

'Yes.'

'Who still lives in Hawaii?'

'With my best friend. Who is also pregnant with his child.'

'Shiiit,' he says. 'You've *lived*.'

'Lived and been shivved.'

He looks at me appraisingly. 'I'm stealing that. So, about your day rate.'

'A hundred is too much?'

'It's not enough. Two hundred, minimum, and you never work more than eight hours, and that's to include research. You never write more than four.'

'Alexis wants me to write with him?'

'He does. Makayla gave him your jotter and he was blown away. He's talking to his editor about bringing you on as a co-writer.'

I stare at him, wanting to pinch myself, because how can this be happening? What have I ever done in my life to deserve this?

'Thank you,' I say, only just holding onto my tears.

Twenty-Six

When I get back to the house, Makayla is in the living room watching the 1995 *Pride and Prejudice* on TV, the scene with Mr Darcy coming out of the lake. She's also doodling planets onto her own leg cast with a selection of different-coloured sharpies.

'What did he want?' she says.

'You gave Alexis my jotter.'

'He wanted to see a sample of your writing and I knew you'd never have the gumption to hand it over. You're welcome.'

'Gumption?'

'What? My best mate is an author.'

'Not yet,' I say, trying not to panic at the thought of all the work I have ahead.

'I was talking about Alexis,' she says, with a grin.

She pauses and looks grave, as if thinking about something momentous.

'I've been thinking about your touch-deprivation,' she says.

Because it turns out that it's not just a ruse to give me a head massage – Makayla is really, truly worried at the thought of my being touch-deprived. As if I'm stuck in one of those grotesque 1950s science experiments, where sadist scientists gave baby monkeys the choice between a fake cloth mother and a fake wire mother and the baby monkeys always chose to cling to the cloth mother, even though the wire one had all the milk. Makayla thinks I have chosen the wire mother when what I really need is a big warm man in my bed.

'I'm not touch-deprived,' I tell her, for the umpteenth time.

'Do you even have a personal massage device?'

'What do you mean?'

'A vibrator.'

'Negative on the sex toys.'

'Why not?' she says, aghast.

'Joseph would have taken it as an insult.'

'Because he's a knobhead. You need to buy one.'

'Right now, I can't afford to buy anything that isn't food or gas.'

'Well, what do you have already?'

She gets up on her crutches, hobbles to my room and starts poking around the few possessions I've left lying around.

After going through all the drawers in my nightstand and looking on the shelves, she selects two things. She holds up the first thing. A handheld fan, which vibrates a little when it's turned on.

'Hold the end of this one over the clitoris.'

I groan and cover my eyes. I can feel myself blushing like a schoolgirl.

'It has rotor blades,' I say, opening one eye. 'I'm not putting that thing anywhere near my lady garden.'

'Hmm, how bad are the weeds down there? Maybe give them a bit of a strim first.'

'Definitely overgrown,' I say.

Then she hands me the second object, which is a battery-powered foot file that I use to keep down the calluses on my heels, which come of so much beach-walking. It has a thick, bulbous handle.

'This is your dildo.'

'It has glass sandpaper on the rotating part!' I say. 'It is literally intended to grind off skin.'

'You won't be anywhere near that part.'

'Wouldn't I be holding that part? Since the handle would be... elsewhere.'

'It won't be turned on, Candice.'

'Neither will I. Nothing that you just said sounds remotely erotic.'

'Fine. It was just an idea. Just to get things going down there. A bit of a helping hand for your, um, hands.'

'My "down there" is fine as she is, thank you. Please never think of her again.'

'I love the way you've assigned your vulva a gender,' she says, grinning.

'Okay, fine,' I say, returning her smile. 'Let's cover our bases and go with they/them.'

There's a long silence.

'I just worry about you, Candice, being so far from home,' she says, quietly.

'I know you do, but I'll be okay,' I say, grateful, but also a little guilty for making my friend worry like this about me.

'Just promise me one thing,' she says, sighing, before she gets up and goes back to *Pride and Prejudice*.

'Lay it on me,' I say, and she rests her head on my shoulder. 'I meant tell me the thing. Not literally lay your head on me.'

'Oh right,' she says, and begins to laugh with increasing helplessness, which I can't help joining in with. By the time we've got ourselves together, we're too weak to talk any more, and we both have to take a nap.

When we wake up, she's big spoon, I'm little spoon, and I have a third text message from Daniel.

Can we do a road trip tomorrow morning?

Works for me, I reply.

Great. We'll take my hire car. You can be navigator.

Twenty-Seven

I don't sleep well and I'm glad to get out of bed once morning comes. I jog down the dirt road that runs in front of Alexis's cottage. He's standing in the garden, staring out to sea, wearing nothing but boxer shorts. I slow my pace, about to raise my hand and yell hi. Before I can do that, he throws up both his hands and goes through a sun salutation, ushering in the morning, not even using a yoga mat, hands and feet bare against the gravel path. When he's finished, he segues into a series of push-ups and stomach crunches. So many that I lose count.

He looks up and sees me and doesn't even blush. He seems completely unfazed, as if this is how he goes through the world, doing yoga and weight-bearing exercises in his underwear, right here in public, as if it's no big deal. As if he doesn't understand the concept of embarrassment.

How, I wonder, can somebody go through the world like that? Not seeming to know or care that people are always watching? And I can't help wishing I had that sort of self-confidence. Half of it, even.

Daniel comes out of the cottage and waves.

'Are you ready for our research road trip?' he says.

'As I'll ever be,' I say.

*

We've been driving for fifteen whole minutes, working our way through Daniel's Taylor Swift playlist on Spotify as it turns out he's another mega fan, when Alexis sees a sign at the side of the road for pick-your-own strawberries.

'We have to go to that,' he says. 'It's the sort of thing my parents used to do when they were kids, growing up in the sticks. I hope they use wicker baskets. It won't be the same with plastic tubs. We need maximum cottagecore-meets-*Bridgerton* vibes.'

'You sound excited about this strawberry idea,' I say. 'Are you even allowed to eat them?'

'Who cares? I've always dreamt of spending a summer day on a strawberry farm.'

'Really, mate?' Daniel says, laughing and hitting the blinker to take the turning to the farm. 'Because that does not sound like you.'

'It's because my parents never took me. They made it off limits, which made me want it even more, you know?'

'If they liked it so much when they were kids in the sticks or whatever, why didn't they ever take you?' I ask. 'That seems kind of mean.'

'Dad is basically a hermit who won't leave the city unless it's an absolute emergency, preferably life-threatening, and my mother's been on the Atkins diet for as long as I remember. Way too much sugar in strawberries for her taste.'

'What's the plan?' I say. 'For the characters, I mean.'

'I'm thinking they either buy or weave their own wicker

baskets,' Alexis muses. 'Then pick as many strawberries as they can manage. Fuck it, we'll throw in some raspberries and tayberries too. Then they go back to Bryce's done-up cottage and let the romance commence.'

'It could work, if we get the balance right,' Daniel says. 'And you've absolutely got to have a fuck-off big kitchen in the leading man's house. Bryce has never cooked in it, obviously.'

'Why hasn't he cooked in it?' I ask, genuinely perplexed.

'Because it's a show kitchen,' Daniel says. 'To make clients buy into the lifestyle they're selling. Also, he thinks he hasn't met "the one" yet.'

'And "the one" is a woman who will use his kitchen to cook meals for him? Is that what you're selling in this scene?'

'Bryce doesn't realise yet that Janie is his one. His forever girl,' Alexis cuts in.

'And what is he eating until then?' I ask. 'Cans of soup and crackers?'

'We're going off topic,' Alexis says. 'The kitchen is important but it's not the most important thing. The most important thing is the jars. There needs to be a row of empty glass mason jars on the windowsill.'

'Why?' I ask, at exactly the same moment that Daniel steers the car out from a pothole and says, 'I love it!'

'Don't you see where I'm going with this, Candice?'

'Oh,' I say. 'You're making sexy preserves.'

'We're making preserves sexy. A hot and sticky jam-making session. Emphasis on the hot.'

'Like the potter's wheel scene from *Ghost*,' I say. 'But with strawberry preserves.'

'Exactly,' Alexis says. 'Pot-throwing wasn't sexy until Demi Moore and Patrick Swayze started squeezing grey clay in their greasy little hands.'

'Don't you throw shade at Swayze,' I say. 'Those were the hands of a god.'

Daniel nods, like he knows exactly where I'm coming from on this, which it turns out he does.

'Not only was Swayze a world-class dancer, who trained in ballet, he was also an accomplished cowboy with his own ranch,' he says.

'YES,' I say, only just refraining from punching the air. 'And what a voice.'

'Oh, I think I did hear he was a singer,' Alexis says, sounding uninterested.

'"She's Like the Wind" is the best song on the *Dirty Dancing* soundtrack,' I say, with absolute conviction. 'And he was a gymnast. And a licensed airplane pilot. So was his dancer wife of thirty years. She flew him to his cancer appointments. Now that is a romance for the ages.'

'What I don't understand,' says Daniel, 'is how he ever found time to shoot movies between all the gymnastics, ballet-dancing, plane-flying and horse-wrangling. He also smoked sixty cigarettes a day.'

'No way was he a smoker,' Alexis says. 'He was in peak physical condition.'

'He said in interviews he was a chain-smoker and a heavy drinker,' Daniel says, looking at me for back-up, and I can't believe this is our bonding moment. This is the thing we have in common. Our mutual love for Swayze.

'Daniel's right. He talked about his addiction and mental health battles openly. He went to rehab after his father died.'

'How do you two know so much about the bloke?' Alexis asks. 'It's a bit weird, actually.'

'Swayze was in all the best movies,' I say. 'Who wouldn't want to know more about him?'

'I read a biography,' Daniel says. 'But seriously, that is a leading man.'

Alexis sighs. 'And if this book doesn't have a leading man to rival Swayze, what's the bloody point. Is that what you're saying?'

Daniel nods. 'If you give me Swayze,' he says, hanging a left. 'I'll get you six-figure royalties. *Bridgerton*'s got nothing on *Dirty Dancing*.'

Alexis claps his hands together, as if to signal he's decided we need a change of topic.

'Right. Do you know how to make jam?' he asks, turning to me.

'Why are you looking at me? Do not look at me. I serve food. I do not make food. Jam is super hard to get right, from what I hear.'

'Well, we don't have to actually make it, do we?' Alexis says. 'We just have to know enough to write about making it. And if we try it, and it goes wrong, we can write about that too. But how do we explain the fact that our leading man has all those empty jars?'

'I mean, people do keep jelly jars, for wildflowers, or tealights,' I say. 'Could that work?'

'No,' Alexis says. 'I've thought of a better idea. He loves eating marmalade on toast and the windowsill is where he keeps his recycling.'

'The windowsill of his beautiful, picturesque kitchen is where he keeps his garbage?' I say.

'Yeah, so that he doesn't forget to put it out. He lives alone and he doesn't have enough glass to fill the recycling box, so he lets the jars build up and when he has enough, say ten, he puts them out to be taken away by the binmen.'

'That is very specific,' I say.

'That's writing. It's the specificity that lends the authenticity. Right, Daniel?'

*

Unfortunately, though, when we pull up to the strawberry farm, it's closed and there's a real estate sign, the size of a city billboard, detailing plans for a new housing development.

'That blows,' I say. 'There goes your sexy jelly scene, Alexis.'

Which is when Daniel jumps about three feet backwards.

'Fuck,' he says.

I look down to where he's pointing. There's a small dark snake curled up in a patch of sunshine by the hedgerow.

'Oh, an adder,' Alexis says, leaning down to take a closer look.

'Jesus,' Daniel says. 'I almost stepped on it. I could've been killed!'

'It's not a death adder. Anyway, he's not bothered,' Alexis says. 'He hasn't warmed up enough yet to be sprightly. He's still all cold and dazed.'

'He does look a bit derpy,' I say. 'Like he's sunk too many Rattlers.'

'Even so, I'd move back a bit, mate,' Daniel says. 'It could, like, jump up and bite you. What's the word – *strike*. They're poisonous, aren't they?'

'Venomous,' Alexis says. 'But I don't think I'm likely to get envenomated twice in one holiday to Cornwall. I've already stood on a weever fish. This is great, actually. I haven't seen an adder since I was a kid. I always wanted a pet snake, but my parents would never allow it. Seeing one in the wild is even better. I'm totally going to put this in the book.'

'There's hardly any snakes in Hawaii,' I say, conversationally. 'There's a tiny little species the size of an earthworm that eats ants, and a type of yellow sea snake, but I've never seen either so they can't be too common.'

'Yet another good reason to move to Hawaii,' Daniel says, shuddering.

'There's really no need to be afraid of snakes,' Alexis says. 'They have tiny little brains. All they care about is food, sex and a place in the sun.'

'Sounds like the perfect life,' I say, and they both turn their heads to look at me, as if I've said something shocking. 'And also, a pretty great foundation for a romance novel.'

Alexis is about to say something when there's a sudden rush of noise and a group of teenage boys on dirt bikes swing in from the road to the abandoned strawberry farm.

'Let's get out of here, before we get mugged and I lose my Rolex,' Daniel says.

'You have a Rolex?' I say, as we traipse back to the car.

'I have a very nice Casio,' he says. 'But when Alexis makes me a millionaire, I'm going to upgrade to a Seiko Kinetic.'

'No pressure, then,' Alexis says, crossing himself.

'No pressure,' Daniel answers. 'But I genuinely do think you're onto a winner here. If the publisher markets it in the right way, gives it enough of a push and gets it under enough readers' noses, this book could really open doors for you. It could change your life. All of our lives.'

'I'd better make a good job of it, then,' Alexis says.

He's smiling while he says it, but as Daniel was talking, there was a moment when I thought another emotion flashed across Alexis's face.

Despair.

*

We stop at a farm shop on the way back and Daniel insists on buying every flavour of jam that they have, maintaining that he'll expense it to the company, along with all the other dubious purchases he's made on this trip.

We sit on a pinewood bench outside the farm shop and spoon splodges of preserves onto paper plates that the ladies in the store gave us for free.

Then we begin to eat.

Alexis eats way too much of it and gives himself a stomach cramp so intense that he has to lie down on the back seat of Daniel's rental car all the way back to the cottage.

Then I start cramping up too and have to take the couch for an hour, before I can psych myself up to walk back to Demi's house, because I'm way too gassy to get in Daniel's car and at least Alexis has music playing in the cottage, which drowns out the noises coming from me.

'Maybe there was mould or something in that stuff?' I say, groaning and clutching my stomach.

'All in all, not a great start,' Alexis says.

'I dunno,' Daniel says. 'Look at all this material you've got to work with.'

Twenty-Eight

The next day, Daniel texts me to meet him and Alexis at the Blue Reef Aquarium, down on Towan Beach. I'd mentioned the place to Alexis, as somewhere he could potentially set a scene – thinking of the *Romeo + Juliet* movie, where Leonardo DiCaprio and Claire Danes have the most gorgeous meet-cute through a fish tank – but the aquarium is tiny, so maybe it won't work after all.

When Makayla hears the plan, she immediately invites herself along.

'But maybe I should have suggested we go visit the National Marine Aquarium in Plymouth?' I say. 'It's only an hour up the road and it's the biggest one in the whole UK.'

'No, because that's in Devon, and this is a Cornwall book,' Makayla points out, patiently, like I'm her daughter.

'The aquarium here is the size of a teacup,' I say. 'I went in there to use the bathroom once. It's tiny. You see bigger fish tanks in malls in Dubai.'

'Well, this is not Dubai, is it?' Makayla says. 'And that, my dear, is the whole point of this book. You're going for quaint fish-and-chips holiday destinations. You're going for charming small-town life. What you're not going for is gigantic shopping centres in the desert.'

'Fair point,' I say.

*

Alexis and Daniel are standing outside the aquarium, finishing ice creams – intermittent fasting and low glycaemic index foods be damned – when we arrive, and there is something boyish about them there together, looking over their shoulders and guarding their cones against seagull attacks, creamy smears around their mouths.

Daniel insists on paying our entrance fees, and we go in together, Alexis with a notebook and pencil in hand.

The aquarium smells, unsurprisingly, of fish. This is something that should not have snuck up on me, and yet, when we get here, I find that it's all I can seem to notice. There's something about the smell of fish that is like the antithesis of romance. The antidote to romance. Start off in love and after ten minutes of fish stink, you're over it.

We walk around the various displays, pushing through clear plastic doors between rooms and actually it's pretty cool. There are baby jellyfish floating around like aliens and an octopus that looks into your eyes as if seeing into your soul.

'So, what are you thinking?' Daniel asks Alexis. 'Could you set something here?'

'Yeah, I reckon there's enough dark corners to make it work. Staring at those jellyfish could get the sparks flying. What do you think, Candice?'

'I think don't mention the smell.'

'What about you, Makayla? What effect does this place have on you?'

'I probably shouldn't admit it,' she mumbles, eyes darting away from mine.

'Why?' I say. 'You have to tell us now. Don't leave us hanging.'

'Well, the truth is, and I know this is bad, but it's really made me fancy a crab sandwich.'

Twenty-Nine

'Okay, so the aquarium was a bust. Let's go to the poppy fields,' I say.

'Great,' Daniel says. 'I've looked at Google Maps, but I can't quite figure out how to get to West Pentire.'

'I know how,' I say. 'You coming too, Makayla?'

'I think I need to get back home and rest my leg a bit, if that's all right. Get some grub too.'

I eye her, suspiciously. 'You're stopping somewhere on the way for a crab sandwich, aren't you?'

She gives me a sheepish smile. 'Possibly.'

'I can't go now,' Alexis says. 'I'm doing a research interview with one of the Fistral lifeguards. Trying to get a better sense of the Cornish surf culture.'

'Arianna?' I ask.

'No, her girlfriend's brother. He's planning to paddle all the way from the Isles of Scilly to Newquay on a stand-up paddleboard. Twenty-eight miles. All for charity. He knows every surfer in this town, and he says he'll share some stories if I chip in twenty quid for his fundraiser.'

'Generous,' Makayla says, before picking up a cab at the taxi rank. 'Say hi to Ben from me.'

'You know him?' Alexis asks, surprised.

'I know all the interesting boys,' she says, throwing a shaka.

I wave her cab off and turn back to Alexis and Daniel.

'Shall we go to the poppy fields tonight or tomorrow?' Alexis asks.

'It'll be tourist central if we go near sunset,' I say. 'Or on the weekend. We probably won't be able to park. People go just to do Instagram shoots there. It's a whole thing. Who gives a hell if they crush tons of the poppies in the process?'

'That's social media culture in a nutshell,' Alexis says. 'However, for our purposes it would work. Janie and Bryce could have a picnic there when they're planning out their business. Roll around in the silky petals instead of in hay.'

'You cannot have them rolling around on the flowers,' I say, appalled.

'It'll be romantic,' Alexis insists.

'How is the wanton destruction of wildflowers going to get your leading lady in the mood for seduction?'

'Okay, writers,' Daniel says, putting up a placating hand. 'Perhaps they could have a significant moment of understanding, with poppies waving in the background and the sun setting over the water?'

'So long as they're standing on a designated path,' I say. 'That would be fine.'

'Where is the sexy spontaneity?' Alexis says, sighing. 'And it's fiction. Who cares if fictional poppies are flattened?'

'Because you can guarantee that if you put it in a book, somebody will want to go to the exact same spot and do the exact same thing. Then you have a crime scene. The remains of poppies, crushed and bloody in the dirt.'

'That's quite poetic,' Daniel says. 'When should we go?'

'I'm free all day today,' I say. 'But I'm planning on working on my surf lesson business tomorrow.'

'Just go ahead without me,' Alexis says. 'But can you get me notes and photos?'

'Sure, no problem,' I say, awkwardly, looking at Daniel, because it seems it's going to be just the two of us in those wildflower meadows.

*

In the end, we don't wind up going until later in the afternoon and the parking lot is full. I have never seen so many elderly folks on a coastal trail. We can barely get ten feet before running into another group of them.

'Have we stumbled upon a pensioners' pilgrimage?' Daniel asks, too loudly.

'Perhaps it's more like a Levelling Up Station,' I say. 'Like, you can't achieve peak senior-citizenship unless you've seen the West Pentire poppies in all their glory.'

'What's that bloke up to over there?' Daniel asks, squinting.

We slow our pace as we pass him. He has a spray can in his hand, and appears to be spraying some kind of pink graffiti onto the ground.

Daniel suddenly puts his hand over his mouth and says, 'Brilliant.'

'What?' I whisper. 'What's he doing?'

'He's spraying all the dog shit.'

We overtake him and see that the man has spray-painted piles of dog faeces in a shade of bright cerise all along this pathway. As we look down the dirt path to the fields beyond, we see other pink patches of poop, and where irresponsible owners have left little black baggies of their dog's leavings, the man has spray-painted, in all caps, the word NO.

Daniel widens his eyes when he looks at me, struggling to contain a laugh, but he can't. For some reason he seems to find this the funniest thing he's seen all year, and his laughter is contagious, because I can't seem to stop laughing either, at least not until the old man catches us up and taps Daniel on the shoulder.

'Not really a laughing matter,' he says. 'This is just making a point.'

'A point?' I say, breathing hard.

'To shame people. If they come back tomorrow and see their dog's mess painted pink, they'll realise that it's been noticed. It's been marked.'

'Does it work?' I say, mostly to take the focus off of Daniel, who is still wiping tears of mirth from his eyes.

'It's going to take time,' the guy says. 'But at least the filthy swine will know we're watching and if we catch them in the act, we'll have the dog warden issue a fine.'

'How many dog wardens are there?' Daniel asks, his voice still weird from laughing so much.

'Three.'

'Just here?' I say, looking around.

'No,' the guy says. 'Three in Cornwall.'

'In the whole of the county?' Daniel asks, incredulous.

The man nods.

'So, the odds are that no one's getting fined?' Daniel says, his voice beginning to crack again.

'But they could be,' the man says, holding up a finger to the wind. 'And there lies the deterrent. Imagine the shame of being prosecuted for leaving a pile of stinking turds in a poppy field.'

★

We follow the paint-spotted path, which has a few thousand flowers in bloom, but nothing compared to the photos I've seen in my Google Image searches.

'I mean, it's nice,' Daniel says, looking at a skylark hovering a hundred feet above us and singing at top volume. 'But I expected more.'

'Same here. I keep waiting for the wow factor,' I say. 'Let's keep going and see where the path leads.'

It leads us around a bend and into another field, which is absolutely ablaze with red.

'Sweet Jesus,' I say, and I see the same wonder reflected in Daniel's eyes.

'How is this real?' he asks.

We've stopped too abruptly and we're standing too close to each other. As I turn to look at him, my hand grazes his and he looks down at it.

'This is the place,' he says.

'For a scene in the book?'

'Absolutely. A set piece. Something momentous should happen here.'

'The first kiss,' I say, definitively. 'This should be where our hero takes his girl by the hand, gazes into her eyes and kisses her like she's never been kissed before.'

I squeeze my eyes closed.

'What are you doing?' he says.

'Imagining it. What Janie would be thinking in this moment. What she'd be feeling.'

'And?'

'She'd be worried that people were looking. Judging. She'd be worried that she wasn't feeling the right things.'

'And is she?' he asks me, his voice quiet.

'She's feeling everything, all the things she's kept hidden, pushed down too deep, and now they're all surging up to the surface.'

'How does Bryce handle that?'

'That little beach down there?' I say, motioning to the grassy slope which falls away to a narrow cove of golden sand, unspoilt and totally natural. 'He takes her by the hand and leads her into the water. The water calms her down. Brings her back to the moment.'

'And then?'

'Let's see.'

We walk in silence down to the beach, where another elderly man is walking his geriatric dog back to the footpath that will lead them home.

The beach is in shadow now. I drop my bag, kick off my shoes and wade into the water. I don't look behind because I can feel Daniel there, following in my footsteps.

When I get up to my knees, the water heavy on my dress, I stop and look at him.

'They stop here?' he says. 'This is where they kiss for the first time?'

'This is where it happens,' I say, as a wave washes in around my calves and swirls at my dress hem. 'Maybe more than a kiss. Maybe they get naked here.'

'What are they doing with their clothes?' he asks.

'Janie throws her dress and underwear back onto the sand. Bryce takes off his shirt, pants and boxers,' I say. 'It's the work of five seconds. Then they can do whatever they want in this water.'

'People would see,' Daniel says, looking back at the footpath.

'They'd just see two people in the water with their arms wrapped around each other. They'd see two people in love.'

'Okay,' Daniel says. 'Now what?'

'Now we include this in our chapter plan for Alexis.'

'That's not what I meant.'

Which I'm beginning to know.

'Why are you here, Candice?' he says. 'Why are you really in Newquay? Will you tell me now? Do you even have a work permit?'

'I'm fully documented,' I say. 'You don't need to worry about me.'

The tide is surging forward, pulling us into deeper water, but I don't want to be the first one to move. I want him to be the one to call it a day and lead the way home. It feels like a moment is happening here, some sort of vibe, which is probably just because all the thinking and talking about romance is warping my neural pathways, but it's confusing.

'The tide's coming in fast,' he says, saltwater darkening the thighs of his pants.

The water is so cold as it hits my legs that it makes me gasp.

He looks at me, concerned. 'Do you want to leave now?' he says.

'A little longer,' I say, as the tide pushes against us, soaking our clothes and setting us up for a cold, dripping walk back to the car. I try so hard not to be pushed backwards, to stand my ground, but eventually the water is just too deep, too strong.

I can't keep my balance. I have to go.

'This is where I was born,' I say. 'My father was in the American Air Force, stationed at the huge military base on the edge of Newquay.'

'RAF St Mawgan?' he asks.

I nod.

'Small world,' he says. 'My grandfather served there as a warrant officer, right before he retired. He said there were always Americans around, drinking in the NAAFI. They even had their own cinema.'

'My father, at least the man I always thought was my father, lived four years in military quarters at the base here. I was born right here in this town because I came too fast for my mother to make it to the hospital.'

He's gazing at me, transfixed.

'Do you remember living here?'

I shake my head. 'I was a toddler when my dad transferred to Hickam Air Force base in Oahu. My brother Ricky is a few years older, but he barely remembers it either.'

'Your mother was a military wife?'

'An unhappy one, especially so in the early days. She stepped out on my dad with a local guy one time and that's when she got pregnant with me.'

'You're here looking for your father,' he says. A statement. Not a question.

I catch his eye, nod, and we turn together, just as a huge breaking wave surges towards us.

He reaches out a hand, offers to anchor me, and I take it as the wave hits us, neck-high, his strength holding us both steady.

Thirty

Over a week of intensive writing later, it's Sunday night and Ricky calls, as he always does. Daniel is with me in Demi's kitchen, thrashing out scene ideas for Alexis's novel, which he seems to be growing more excited about by the day. Demi has raised her eyebrows a few times about Daniel involving himself so closely in the creative process, hinting he might be enjoying my company as much as my ideas, but it's not like that. Daniel is invested in this book being a success. His whole financial situation is dependent upon it.

Mine too. At Daniel's suggestion, Alexis and I had agreed a day rate of two hundred pounds, which seemed like a crazy amount of money, but I'd emailed my first invoice to Alexis and the money had arrived in my bank account by the end of the day. I'd stared at the screen, tears in my eyes, hardly believing it. The first time I'd ever been paid to write. I was already way over my overdraft limit and I'm still not out of the red, but at least now there's hope that one day I will be.

Ricky asks me all the usual questions and seems disappointed when I maintain my boundaries by telling him everything is fine, I haven't met anyone who can help me, and I haven't taken up bungee-jumping or wing-walking.

'I take it that was family?' Daniel asks, inspecting one of the amazing hand-turned bowls that have appeared in Demi's house lately. Homemade gifts from the carpenter.

'How did you guess?'

'The general evasion of answering any question was mostly what gave it away. Was it your brother?'

'Yes.'

'He's your only family?'

'We have a grandmother, but she's busy with her own life. She has Roger to think about.'

'Boyfriend?'

'Brussels Griffon.'

'I don't know what that is.'

'Google is your friend.'

He duly types it into his phone and flashes me an image of a crazy-looking fluffball. 'Is that a... dog?'

'It's actually a pedigree.'

'It looks like a muppet. No, it looks like one of those critters from that film, *Critters*.'

'He's a very lovely soul who brings my grandma a great deal of joy, thank you very much.'

'Wait, did you say it's called Roger? As in: Roger the dog?'

'That's correct, yes. She named him after her favourite James Bond. The only 007 worth talking about. What's wrong with Roger?'

'Nothing...'

'I know you want to say something about it,' I say, bracing myself. 'So go right ahead.'

'It's just that roger, in British parlance, can also mean to sleep with…'

'As in…'

'To have sexual intercourse with. So "Roger the dog" does somewhat bring to mind bestiality with man's best friend.'

'Huh,' I say. 'Thank you so much for sharing.'

Suddenly, an electronic voice booms around us and we both jump. Demi has linked up her smart doorbell to her entire home sound system, and then used the facial recognition feature of the doorcam to program in the faces of her regular visitors.

The doorbell doesn't just ring, it announces:

SEXY ALEXY IS AT THE FRONT DOOR
DOORBELL.

When I catch sight of Daniel's face, there's a second when he looks not only startled, but something else. Envious? Or perhaps guilty?

'I suppose he is pretty sexy,' Daniel says, ruefully. 'Like a young Eddie Vedder from Pearl Jam.'

'That's exactly what I said,' Demi answers, delighted. She goes to answer the door and ushers in Alexis with a wide sweep of her hand. In her other hand, there's a glass jar full of foamy beige gunk. The whole time she's asking Alexis questions about the progress he's making with the book, he keeps glancing down at the jar, waiting for her to explain what the heck that foamy stuff is and why she's holding it.

Eventually, Demi seems to notice that her jar of yuck is making Alexis a little uncomfortable.

'It's okay,' she reassures him, holding up the jar. 'This is just my mother.'

The expression that crosses Alexis's face is pure, unadulterated horror.

Demi begins to laugh, which is so infectious that I can't keep a straight face either, and wind up doubled over the kitchen table laughing so hard that my stomach hurts.

Daniel and Alexis just stand there staring at each other, thinking maybe that they've stumbled into a house of witches or serial killers. Eventually, Makayla comes out of the bathroom, holding a book.

'What's all the commotion?' she says.

'Demi's just been refreshing her sourdough starter,' I say, turning to the men. 'Guys, it's just flour and water with a little bacteria and natural yeasts from the air. It combines and ferments. The yeasts eat the carbs in the flour and convert them to carbon dioxide, which make the bubbles.'

'I knew that,' Daniel says, narrowing his eyes and nodding. Fronting.

'I had no idea the process looked so foul,' Alexis says, turning his back on the jar as if even the sight of it is too much for his delicate constitution.

'It requires a lot of patience and TLC,' Demi says, sighing deeply. 'Like most mothers.'

Thirty-One

Alexis and I are going chapter for chapter – he's writing from Bryce's point of view and I'm taking Janie. Our chapter plan has been given the green light by Daniel and each time we finish a new one, we email it to each other and mark it up with notes. Then we add our suggestions in bubbles in the margins and when we both agree the chapter is *tolerable* – not great, striving for great can wait for the edit, apparently – we send it to Daniel, and he emails back with his own notes. In this way, we sail through a fortnight and at the end of it we have forty thousand words. I've never felt so tired in my life, but I've also never felt so exhilarated either, because I'm getting paid to write and I'm going to be credited in a real book. Maybe even on the cover, although I'm not sure about that, as Alexis has been a little vague and says he needs further guidance from his publisher. Likewise, Daniel isn't sure either – he only represents Alexis, not me, so it's up to us how to decide how the partnership works, but he says he'll do all he can to make sure it's fair.

Alexis prefers to work at Demi's house, saying he's starting to find the blandness of his luxury holiday cottage 'intellectually stultifying' and prefers the potted palms and modernist art jungle vibe of Demi's place to get his creativity flowing. Demi is only too happy to oblige. She misses the bustle of Demigorgons but having a houseful of guests is helping to keep her spirits up.

We're just taking a potato chips and milkshake break, Alexis's strict fasting regime having gone completely out of the window on the first day we started writing intensively, when I hear Makayla's sneaker squeaking on the hall tile. Just the one sneaker, as she still has her plaster boot.

'What up, Flow Bear?' she says, drumming her fingers on the kitchen counter.

'Huh?' I say, looking up from my notepad. 'Who's "Flow Bear"?'

'Was he one of the Care Bears?' Daniel asks. 'A really laidback one?'

'He's a writer, ain't he?' Makayla says, doubting herself. 'French bloke. *Madame Butterfly* or something? Demi's left his book in the bog.'

'Oh, Flaubert,' Alexis says, his look of confusion dissipating. 'His debut novel was *Madame Bovary*. Sorry, I missed that completely.'

'Me too,' I say. 'Sorry, Makayla. You know – your accent.'

'You can talk, Donald Trump.'

Alexis excuses himself, takes something out of his pocket and goes through the French doors to the garden.

'Where's he off?' Makayla says. 'Gone to find an outdoor privy?'

'Gone to smoke,' Daniel says, his dark eyes sparkling.

'No effing way,' Makayla says. 'So many toxins. Does he know about the toxins?'

'It's cannabis,' Daniel says. 'Apparently he's using it both creatively and medicinally now.'

'Medicinally, huh? He clearly doesn't have a pharmacy prescription,' I point out. 'Since he told me he had to score it from the guy by the mini-mart.'

'If I knew he wanted weed,' Demi says. 'I'd have put an order in with Eileen. She's always willing to drop round at a moment's notice. Puts plenty of freebies in the bag too.'

'Narcotics samples?' I ask, kind of shocked that Demi is friends with the type of drug-dealer who offers free samples.

'Hand cream,' Demi says. 'She deals Avon as well as cannabis. Services all the mums and grannies in the neighbourhood.'

'You're messing with us,' I say.

'It's the perfect operation. She can come to any door, with any amount of hash in the bottom of those white paper bags, and nobody is any the wiser.'

'What do you put on the order form if you want drugs?' Daniel asks. 'Is there a special code?'

'You do a pen drawing of a marijuana leaf in the margin,' Makayla says.

'Daniel, dear – it doesn't go on the Avon form,' Demi says. 'If I don't see Eileen around, I just text her.'

'Oh,' he says, reddening. 'I thought – I dunno – you could have written *Come on Eileen* or something.'

'I wouldn't recommend it,' Demi says. 'Eileen despises that song.'

'She hasn't ever been caught?' I ask, marvelling at the entrepreneurial spirit of this Avon lady.

'Not in fifteen years of trade. It was my mother who

first put me onto her,' Demi says. 'They met at the Women's Institute. Eileen only deals to women she trusts.'

'I suppose it's the *sine qua non* of drug-dealing, isn't it?' Daniel says. 'Judging who you can and can't safely supply with product.'

'Did you just drop a Latin phrase on us, Daniel?' Makayla says. 'Because it made you sound like a right dickhead.'

'Sorry. One of my authors is writing from the perspective of an Oxford don and the voice has wormed its way into the woodwork. It just means something essential to the plan.'

'Which you know because…?' I ask.

'Because I had to look it up, yes,' he says, grinning at me.

Alexis appears from the French doors that lead to the vegetable garden, smelling strongly of weed and looking happy.

'Cannabis is quite the toxin,' Demi says. 'For a man of such wholesome proclivities.'

'Bryce smokes weed constantly,' Alexis says, in explanation. 'And I really feel I have to get in his headspace, you know?'

'Naturally,' Demi says, turning away to smile.

Thirty-Two

Demi and Daniel have their heads together, scrolling Daniel's Spotify list and talking about their favourite grunge tunes from the mid-nineties. Daniel was just a little kid back then, but Demi was an older teenager and experienced the grunge movement to the max.

'According to my daughter, Sennen – who's just texted the bombshell that she's currently visiting her hopeless hippie father in Goa – in terms of live vocals, Kings of Leon are the new Pearl Jam,' Demi says. 'But that remains to be seen.'

'Ever see them live?' Daniel asks.

She beams at him. 'Pearl Jam? Absolutely. Wembley Arena. Monday, October twenty-eighth 1996.'

'I bet they were incredible,' Daniel says, gazing at Demi in awe.

She nods. 'I'd have to say my favourite part was when Eddie Vedder went to change his sweaty shirt, and then came back drinking a cup of tea and talking about a programme he'd seen on telly the night before about the upgrading of London's sewage system. You just don't get that kind of showmanship these days.'

'Sounds like my kind of guy,' Daniel says, grinning, and I feel warmth rising within me at the sight of my friends bonding, even if it is over grunge bands from thirty years ago.

'It was the best day of my life, no question,' Demi says. 'No other high has ever come close.'

'Demi,' I say, with a questioning look. 'You've had a kid and been married a bunch of times.'

'Giving birth was horrible. My answer,' she says, pursing her lips, 'stands.'

★

Ever since we started the writing, Alexis has been completely focused on the book, and he hasn't made any kind of move. I assume he still feels embarrassed that I saw the awful notes he made about me, and is trying hard to impress me with his professionalism. Or maybe he's lost interest now that I'm no longer just a research subject for his book. He's treated me as a colleague and a friend and I'm not sure how I feel about that, but my brain has been so tired from so much writing that I haven't had a chance to overthink anything else. The line between my emotions and Janie's has started to blur and in the dark hours of the night, when I'm sitting alone in bed, scribbling in a notepad, I've started to feel as if everything I knew about myself is unravelling. As if I didn't understand myself at all, until I tried to write my way into someone else.

By the time we've got through another chapter of the book, the last of the evening has slipped away.

'So how would you feel about visiting an astronomy

class?' I say, fired up by the clear night sky, which I've just been gazing at in deep reflection while taking Coder out for a late-night bathroom break and sniff-fest along the beach.

'Uh...' Makayla says, looking at the dog. 'What's that in his mouth? Looks like he's trying to eat something.'

'Not again,' Demi says. 'Not another bloody dead thing. If it's not crabs, it's birds with intestines full of maggots. When it comes to snacking, that dog has the self-restraint of a headlouse.'

Coder drops the thing in his mouth gently at my feet and we all stare down at something translucent and slimy.

'Oh my God,' Demi says, putting her hand over her mouth and looking as if she's about to throw up the enchiladas she just ate.

'What is it? An eel?' I say, trying to get a closer look, which is hard because Coder keeps picking up the mysterious dead thing and dropping it again.

'It's a condom,' Makayla says, matter-of-factly. She bends down. 'And judging by the knot in the end, it's been used.'

'Jesus Christ,' Daniel says, wincing and closing his eyes. 'I hope the poor bastard's teeth didn't pierce the latex.'

'This,' Demi says, 'is why I only ever have budgies.'

'And why horny tourists should not have sex on the beach if they're not willing to take their manky used rubbers home with them,' Makayla adds.

'Or at least to a trashcan,' I say, trying not to think about the nature of any residue currently residing in Coder's mouth.

When the short straw has been pulled by Daniel and he's disposed of the condom with gardening gloves and some gagging, and Demi has gone to brush Coder's teeth and throw away the toothbrush, we get back to business.

'So, the astronomy class,' I say. 'That could be romantic, right? Looking up at the stars, our protagonists holding hands in the dark of a planetarium, moving them away before someone sees?'

'Is there a fuck-off big telescope involved?' Daniel asks. 'Or are we just looking at slides? Because if it's slides, I'm out.'

'Does it matter?' I say. 'Remember the dark lecture hall? Amazing visuals of the cosmos. Only a few people in the audience. So much sexual tension.'

'Yes,' Makayla says, tightening a fist. 'Like that Alanis Morissette song about going down on someone in a theatre. But in a space auditorium.'

But when I turn to Google, it turns out that there are no astronomy classes anywhere in Cornwall.

'Guys, why not do the obvious thing?' I say. 'Why don't we camp out on Fistral Beach under the stars and see what happens?'

'That'll work,' Daniel says.

'You in, Makayla?' Alexis asks.

'Nope. You can have all those bitey little night sand fleas to yourself.'

'Yuck,' Alexis says. 'But great detail for the book.'

'Demi probably has sleeping bags you can borrow and the Irishman is into all that outdoor camping shit, if you want a tent as well?'

'No tent,' Alexis says, immediately. 'Just wide-open skies.'

Thirty-Three

I'm cool with sleeping on the beach. I don't mind how cold the sand gets, or what insects crawl over my face in the dark. I like the constant thrum of the waves hitting the shore.

But when we get down there – Alexis dressed for a winter in the Arctic in a padded coat he probably picked up from one of the surf shops, Daniel in a grey sweatsuit with matching hoodie, there's a starlight party happening in the dunes.

'I'm going up there,' Alexis says. 'You guys in?'

'You're just crashing somebody's dune party?' I ask, incredulous.

'It's too good a research opportunity not to,' he says. 'I'll ask if I can edge in on their fire.' He reaches into his backpack. 'I have vodka. They'll love me. You coming?'

I shake my head and Daniel says, 'No, I'm okay here, mate. Go get that research.'

Alexis wanders off, leaving Daniel and me alone.

'So, this is weird,' Daniel says.

'All part of the beach town experience,' I say, as somebody

lets off a rocket in the dunes, which is followed by a host of other loud fireworks that make it hard to talk.

'I'm feeling pretty tired,' I say, when the fireworks have finally stopped and the pauses in our conversation have gotten too long. 'I think I'm just going to turn in.'

'Okay,' he says, taking a sip from a Thermos cup of coffee.

I take my roll-mat and sleeping bag from my backpack and try to find a stone-free patch on the hard, cold sand. It's not easy to get comfortable and the sense that Daniel's watching me isn't making it easier.

When he finishes his coffee, he gets into his own sleeping bag, a few feet away from mine. I can hear his breathing; it goes from shallow to deep before I've even started to relax. I'm not sure if he's asleep or just pretending to be.

'Daniel, are you awake?'

'Yeah,' he says.

'You sounded like you were sleeping.'

'I thought it might help you get to sleep if you thought I was. Like contagious yawning.'

'Thanks,' I say. 'That's nice of you. A little creepy, but nice.'

'It's really uncomfortable to sleep on sand, isn't it?' he says.

'Yeah. Doesn't help that the beach is so sloped.'

'I keep sliding down in my sleeping bag,' he says. 'My chin keeps going under. I'm worried I might suffocate. Death by polyester.'

'Maybe turn on your side a bit, so your shoulder digs in?'

I hear a rustling.

'But now I can't see all the stars.'

'Life is compromise,' I say.

There's a pause.

'When do you think Alexis will be back?' I ask.

'Christ only knows. He's probably tapping into a rich seam of scandalous behaviour and local folklore. He might be a while if he's taking notes.'

'Figures,' I say.

Without Alexis here, the whole thing feels awkward as hell, but this is what I signed on for. *I have to put myself out of my comfort zone. I have to be ready to deal with awkwardness*, I think as I finally drift off.

What I'm definitely not ready for, however, is being woken at 3 a.m. by a wild fox sniffing my nose.

I keep still and close my eyes again, but I can feel it looking at me. I hazard opening one eye and see that it is indeed still watching me, and one of its buddies is scratching the backpack at the foot of my sleeping bag.

Alexis is back now, and he and Daniel are both asleep on either side of me, both snoring, but apparently not loudly enough to intimidate wild canines.

Part of me is thrilled that this is happening, and the other part is worried I'm about to get bitten in the face and wind up with rabies, if they have that here, or some other disease if they don't. Tetanus. Hepatitis. Red fox flu.

Alexis has rolled away from me a little, but my hand is not far from Daniel's shoulder.

I wiggle my fingers and manage to make contact with his T-shirt sleeve. He opens his eyes and looks straight into mine. 'Shhh,' I mouth and motion to the group of foxes, which have moved to the other side of me.

'Amazing,' he whispers, so softly that I can barely hear him.

It occurs to me that he might feel he has to do something to control this situation. To stand up and try to frighten them away. To throw a backpack at them. It's what Joseph would have done. To 'protect me'. Believing that it was necessary. Believing that being a man meant you had to scare away the wild things.

But Daniel doesn't do anything like that. He just watches the foxes darting from point to point around us, gulping down broken-off crab legs that have washed up with the tide and any other edible trash they can find. Just like Coder would do.

Eventually they scatter down to the low-water mark and skip back and forth along the line until they move, as one, back to their dens in the dunes, tired after their beach dinner and dance.

Finally, I feel as if I can breathe deeply again, instead of the shallow breathing I've been doing the past two hours.

'Well, that was incredible,' Daniel whispers. 'Shame Alexis slept right through it. He could've put it in the book.'

'We could've woken him,' I whisper back.

Daniel goes silent for a minute.

'We could've woken him,' he agrees. 'But I didn't want to scare the foxes. They're so beautiful. I never really noticed before how elegantly they move.'

'Aren't there tons of foxes in London?' I whisper.

'Not like these. These were magnificent. Magical, almost. The ones in the city are dirty, mangy little things. Hmm, maybe I've got a book in me after all. *The Manky Fox.*'

'That's elitist,' I whisper. 'Your country-living, crab-fed, beach foxes are beautiful, but your hard-living, street-running, city foxes are ugly. That is classist as hell.'

'Stand down,' he says, in a fierce whisper. 'I'm as working class as they come.'

'Really? You look so put together.'

'Now who's being elitist?'

'And the way you speak. Like a commercial for life insurance or assisted living apartments.'

'Thanks. You sound like Rainbow Brite.'

'I don't even know who that is,' I whisper.

'Cartoon character devised by Hallmark. You're just like her. Wild yellow hair. Dresses like a Pride flag.'

'Okay, my hair is brown with a couple of highlights and just because I happen to like bright colours and have a cheerful disposition, that doesn't make me Rainbow goddamn whatever.'

'Brite. Also like you.'

I clutch my neck and whisper as dramatically as I can manage, 'Oh my God. Was that... actually... a compliment? Are you trying to insinuate I'm intelligent? Because, if so, gee thanks. Now I feel good about myself.'

'Sorry,' he says, smiling. 'I'm not very good at this stuff.'

'Talking to women?'

'Talking to you.'

I slide deeper into my sleeping bag. 'Am I so scary?'

But he's already rolled over, turning away from me, and in another few minutes, I hear that he's already sleeping.

*

When I wake up again, it's still dark and my head is burning up.

I had one of my regular dreams – a dream about the men I couldn't save from their hurt. My father working in dangerous conditions on the offshore oil rig. And Joseph, eaten away by bitterness that our surf shop couldn't seem to turn a decent profit, no matter what we threw at it.

I had once made the mistake of insinuating he wasn't making smart business decisions, because he was too stubborn to try something new, too proud to rethink his personally preferred approach, and I'll never forget the look on his face.

'What did you say to me?' he'd murmured in a menacing voice that put me on edge right away.

'Nothing.'

'Say it again.'

'It was just a quote from *Wuthering Heights*.'

'That terrible British movie you made me sit through? Where everyone is awful and you don't know who to root for?'

'Yes. I mean, it's not terrible and the people aren't awful, they're just complicated and flawed. Like us.'

'So now I'm flawed?'

'Everyone's flawed, Joseph! It's part of being human.'

'Tell me what you said.'

'It doesn't matter.'

But it did matter to him. He wouldn't let it go.

Proud people breed sad sorrows for themselves. A pearl of wisdom from *Wuthering Heights*' main narrator: salt of the earth housekeeper, Nelly Dean. Joseph didn't think it was a wise thing to say, though. Joseph thought it was the most insulting sentence I'd ever said to him. His eyes burned with fury, as if I had betrayed our love, our marriage, by suggesting he was making business mistakes.

The sweat is all over me and my sleeping bag is wet through.

I can't handle any more of this, any more of lying next to these men in the dark. I need cold ocean waves to touch my skin and take away my throbbing headache. I need to swim where there might be dolphins or sharks or turtles or sunfish, or any of the other amazing things that have been spotted in this little English bay this summer.

Demi would say I'm delirious and ought to know better than running into the ocean when I'm not feeling well, but Demi's at home asleep, snuggled up next to the carpenter.

I have on a T-shirt and underwear, but there's a change of clothes and a towel in my backpack. If I need anything else, I'll take my keys and get it from the shack.

The beach is spooky in the light of the moon that's risen and something large has washed up on the sand. For a moment, my heart skips, as I think I'm looking at a dead whale, but when I get nearer, I see that it's only the trunk of a hollow tree that must have fallen into the water some place. It's rotten through. Like Joseph. Maybe like me, too.

I step into the water and let the cold wash over me. I lean back in the water and wet my hair. Straight away the ache in my head recedes, working just like Demi's migraine cold cap that she keeps in the freezer and uses to see off a headache before it can really set in. The tide is on the way out and the waves are small but clean. I think about the planet book in Demi's bathroom, about how the moon and Earth have a complex relationship, how it's not just our planet that feels tidal forces. The moon feels ours too and has its own large tide rises, but formed of rocks instead of water.

I'm standing in chest-high water when I see the jellyfish go by. It's the size of a trashcan lid, inky dark against the moonlit water. Its tentacles graze my hand and I cry out in pain, my voice harsh on the night air. I'm still cursing when I turn to shore and see a person watching me from the beach.

Thirty-Four

'You hurt?' the voice from the beach shouts. He's bundled up in a padded jacket and I can't tell whose silhouette it is. I also can't hear over the roar of the surf whose voice it is.

Is it one of the guys I'm here with, or some stranger?

'Who's there?' I yell, wondering if I'm going to need to scream for help in the hope of waking one of the others.

'It's me. Daniel.'

I wade ashore and find him casually holding the spine of a cuttlefish, which he seems to have forgotten because when I ask him about it, he looks momentarily confused.

'I'm taking it for Henry,' he says. 'Demi was asking people to look out for them while they were on the beach.'

Henry is Demi's parakeet. Or 'budgie' as she calls it.

'Did you follow me?' I ask, my voice grouchy.

'Couldn't sleep. What was with all the swearing?'

'Jellyfish kiss,' I say.

'You should wee on it. Supposed to take the sting out.'

'Um, no.'

The idea of dropping my underwear and peeing in front

of anyone, let alone Daniel the fancy London literary agent, makes the sick feeling start to come back.

'It's supposed to stop it hurting so much. Just saying.'

'No way am I ever peeing on my own hand. At least, not on purpose.'

'Are you asking me to do the honours? Because I'd probably consider it my duty as a gentleman.'

'Sure, knock yourself out.'

He makes to unzip his fly, then gets embarrassed. 'Shall we go back to our little camp?' he asks, waiting to follow my lead.

He has my towel, which I left a little way back up the beach, out of reach of the waves.

'You know,' I say, taking it from him. 'Alexis is one hell of a sleeper.'

'Apparently so.'

Over Daniel's head in the west there's a shooting star, followed by another and another.

'Look,' I say, pointing to the flashes.

'NO WAY!' he says. 'This is basically a YA novel we're living in. I honestly don't think I've ever seen a shooting star before.'

'You didn't spend your formative years gazing at stars from the bed of a pick-up truck?'

'Can't say I did. Fair bit of light pollution in Croydon. Is there some sort of meteor shower on tonight or was that a fluke?'

'Bootid meteor shower,' I say. 'They've been going a while. Only the size of a grain of rice but they put on quite a show.'

Suddenly, I feel a little woozy and Daniel takes my arm to steady me.

'What's it like – Hawaii?' he asks, suddenly. 'Have you ever seen a wild turtle?'

'Not what I was expecting you to say, but okay, and yes, I've seen plenty of wild turtles. It wasn't always magical.'

'How so?'

'The last time I saw a wild turtle, it was so gassy from eating plastic that its whole body was out of balance. Its butt was up on the surface and that was pushing its head into the water, so that it couldn't breathe right.'

'Jesus Christ. That's awful. You just think of Hawaii as paradise. You don't think of poisoned turtles who can't get their bums down.'

'It's the same as everywhere. It's all connected. The Pacific Ocean has as much plastic pollution as anywhere else.'

'What happened to the turtle?'

'The local fishermen who spotted it got some surfers to take it to a veterinarian. If they hadn't have seen it in time, it would have been turtle soup. But it was okay. The veterinarian gave it medicine to flush through its system. It lived. I mean, it probably ate a bunch more plastic the day it was released, so maybe this is not a happy ending, after all.'

'I'm sort of glad I've never seen one now. It sounds too sad.'

'It can be. It's crazy, but they can't throw up. Once they start eating plastic, they're committed. It just goes down and down. Same when they're eating jellyfish. Once they pop, they can't stop.'

'You were one of those surfers who saved it?'

'It took a whole bunch of us to lift it.'

'You're thawing me out with your heroism. This is extremely heart-warming stuff, Candice.'

'You wouldn't say that if you saw the state of my truck afterward. The turtle had a long piece of plastic garbage bag hanging out of its butt. It came out on the way to the veterinarian's office.'

'Hmm,' Daniel says. 'That would be quite the ending for a picture book.'

'Tell me about it.'

'*That's Not My Turtle: It's Shitting a Plastic Bag.*'

I try not to laugh.

'Do you have any nice stories about Hawaii?' he asks. 'Maybe something Alexis can include in the book?'

'I had some nice times with hammerhead sharks.'

'Friends of yours?'

'I wish. They are the most skittish sharks I've ever dived with. Everyone thinks they're so big and scary, but they're terrified of divers. They see you and they're out of there. They're basically the scaredy cats of the shark world. Sometimes we even dived at night. Floodlights from the boat.'

'Let me get this straight. You have dived at night with sharks?'

'Brainwave of my husband.'

He flinches at the word. I could clarify. I could explain my situation, but why do I feel I have to? What makes me think that would be a good idea? I wear my ring for a reason. To keep men away. All it would do is make this situation two degrees more complicated.

And yet... I want to tell Daniel everything, all the gruesome details about my relationship with Joseph. How we came together. How we fell apart.

'I've never even been night swimming,' Daniel says, suddenly. 'Which is weird because it was always my favourite REM song. I listened to it so much that the tape wore out from rewinding it so often. I had to listen on my dad's old Walkman, obviously, because my brothers would have never stopped taking the piss.'

'Come in the ocean now,' I say. 'Strip down to your shorts, walk into the water like we did the other day. Swim.'

'No way,' he says. 'Didn't we already establish there are jellyfish?'

'Yeah,' I say, holding up my wrist. He reaches out his hand as if he's going to take mine, to look at the sting maybe, but he changes his mind, clicks on his flashlight, and sends beams shooting up the beach to where Alexis is sleeping.

'Yeah, I don't think night swimming is for me,' he says, looking at the dark form of his friend – his client – motionless on the sand, like something that has washed up from the depths.

Thirty-Five

The squawk of seabirds wakes us up just as the sun is rising behind us, bringing the first grey light of day. Alexis stretches and groans.

'My back,' he says, momentously, 'is fucked.'

'Not a fun adventure?' I ask.

'No. At least you have a van to camp in. The guys up in the dunes were bragging about their tricked-out campers, which made me realise I should probably experience a bit of van life, since so many surfer dudes have them. Could I come and see yours?'

'Yeah, you can come right now, if you'd like.'

And that is how it comes to be that the three of us are squashed in my van. Alexis is sitting on the bunk and Daniel and I are side by side on a folded quilt on the floor. I've shown them my pile of romance novels and asked if Alexis wants to borrow any, but he's politely declined, saying he 'wouldn't want his narratorial voice to be polluted another author's' now that he's actually drafting and making progress. Daniel has taken a book, though, on my strong recommendation – *Rebecca*, since he's somehow got through life without reading a single du Maurier. Practically a criminal offence for a literary agent, he told me, as well as his secret shame.

'That quilt you're sitting on is really quite cottagecore,' Alexis says, looking appreciatively at the little blue and white squares covered in sailboats and seabirds. 'Did you make it?'

'Demi gave it to me.'

'She's like an honorary mother to you, isn't she?' Alexis says, not waiting for an answer before asking if I know that a place on the outskirts of Newquay, up near McDonald's, is listed in the Domesday Book.

'*Doomsday* Book, did you say? As in doom?' I ask.

'Sounds like that but spelt different,' Daniel says. 'I think it was basically some sort of *Yellow Pages* written a thousand years ago.'

Alexis clears his throat derisively at Daniel's explanation.

'It was a survey of the country, ordered by William the Conqueror,' Alexis says. '1086. No adverts for plumbers or iPhone repair.'

He's still talking about the Domesday Book when I'm suddenly aware that the side of my hand is touching the side of Daniel's hand. Little finger to little finger.

He didn't move to me, I didn't reach for his hand, not that I remember, but somehow we've come together and a tiny part of our skin is touching. And there's chemistry. Undeniable sparks of electricity. And for a moment, I don't want to stop at his hand.

Are we going to be sitting this way forever? Eventually one of us is going to have to move. One of us is going to have to make the decision to end this, whatever this is.

Except we don't. Until Alexis sits bolt upright and hits his head on the roof of the van, and our hands shoot apart.

'Ow,' he says.

'You okay, mate?' Daniel asks.

'Not really. Did you hear that noise just then?'

'What noise?' Daniel says, his voice tight.

'How did you not hear it? Sounded like a fucking lion.'

'It was a lion,' I say. 'There's three of them in Newquay Zoo. The sound carries more some days. You can hear them up to five miles away. They're a local landmark. Like, you know you're really here when you hear the lions roar. I'm surprised it's taken you this long to notice them.'

'I'm usually asleep at this time of morning, not hanging out in a tin can.'

'Do tin cans have cottagecore interiors?' I say. 'I don't think so.'

'I'm busting for a pee and now I have to go out into the cold to use the loo,' Alexis says. 'I don't think van life is ever going to be for me, if I'm honest.'

'It doesn't have to be right for you,' Daniel points out. 'Is it right for your leading man, that's the question, isn't it?'

'Or your leading lady,' I offer. 'Van life can be great for women too.'

'It doesn't seem very secure,' Alexis says, in a grumbling tone.

'What do you mean by that?'

'My mum wouldn't even let my sister take a bedroom on the ground floor when we rented holiday houses. In case burglars and rapists climbed through the windows.'

'Nobody's climbing through these windows,' I say, motioning to the front of the van. 'And it's not as if there's room for anyone to hide under the bed or in the closets without me noticing. It's actually a very secure space.'

'What about those tourists in France?' Alexis asks.

'Oh, yeah,' Daniel says, nodding, as if this is something I should know about.

'What happened?'

'They were in motorhomes,' Alexis says, authoritatively. 'And a gang of thieves piped some sort of sleeping gas into the vehicles at night. To knock out the people inside, so that they could break in as noisily as they liked and steal all their money. Passports and stuff too. Whatever they could lay their hands on.'

'That's horrible,' I say, feeling a cold shiver run up my spine.

'Yeah, they just travelled from camping ground to camping ground,' Daniel says, looking worried. 'They got away with a fortune. I don't think they were ever caught.'

'It's not even really about the loss of property, though,' Alexis says, which is easy for him to say, when everything he owns is probably insured ten ways from Sunday. 'It's the entitlement. It's breaking into somebody else's property like that's an acceptable thing to do.'

I shake my head. 'It's the violation,' I say. 'Somebody entering your space and moving among your things, as you just lie there, unconscious.'

'Like a home invasion, I suppose,' Daniel offers.

'Exactly like that. Until Makayla got hurt, this was my home. My only living space. Not just somewhere I hung out on weekends because I was sick of the sight of the same four walls and the view from my kitchen window as I washed the dishes. This van is all I have.'

'I'm building a subplot into the book about the housing crisis here,' Alexis says. 'So many locals have raised it with me as a problem. I had no idea it was so difficult for people to find affordable accommodation in Cornwall.'

'This van was my only option when I got here,' I say. 'And I could only afford it because it's so old and beat-up.'

'You know,' Daniel says. 'If this book does well, things are going to change for you, Candice. Doors will open. You'll have options about where you go and what you do. If it's a bestseller, you might even be able to buy a starter flat or something.'

'Well, money would be great, but I'm not sure I'd ever buy an apartment here. The prices are crazy.'

'Second-home market drives them up,' Alexis says, authoritatively.

'I feel bad for the locals,' Daniel says. 'But at the same time, I'm seriously thinking it would be good to get a little place here. If I ever pay off my credit cards, I mean.'

'Me too, actually,' Alexis says. 'About moving here, I mean. I don't believe in credit cards.'

'Are you guys serious, right now? You're going to produce a romcom novel that includes a subplot about the evils of second homes, how they make things harder for the local population, while hoping to use money from the sales of that book to buy yourselves second homes that will make things harder for the local population you have just been writing about?'

'Pretty much, yep,' Daniel says.

'I think that's quite unfair, actually,' Alexis says, frostily. 'The Cornish people don't own this little peninsula, any more than Londoners own the capital. Just because they happen to have been born here, it doesn't mean they get to dictate who else can live here.'

'I don't think that's what they're trying to do,' Daniel says. 'It's just that for every rich second-homer who comes to live here, there's a consequence for local people. I don't think anyone can deny that, mate. It's a very difficult reality for the people who already live here. There's only a finite number of houses and if seventy percent of them are owned by people who don't live here most of the time – which they are, in some villages – who perhaps only spend two weeks a year down here, that has a very real impact on the community.'

'So maybe they need to build more houses,' Alexis says, in an 'I am the reasonable person here' tone of voice.

'Sure, but then you have a place where every cliff and field is a new development or a building site,' I say. 'Is that even a Cornwall that offers the dream that these second-homers are looking for?'

'Well, they can't build on the beaches, can they?' Alexis says. 'That's all people come here for.'

'I don't think that's true,' I say. 'There's a lot more to this area than just sandy beaches. And think of Florida. Properties built on every plot of land backing onto the beach. Every piece privately owned. You can't just take a walk along the coast path. There is no coast path. It's all property. Extremely expensive property enjoyed only by the super-rich.'

'Well, that could never happen here. We have ancient rights of way. Ramblers' rights. All that shit,' Alexis says, getting a little mad that we're both disagreeing with him and not backing down.

'It just seems a little too on the nose,' I say. 'To buy a

second home here after writing about this issue. But what do I know? I am the most emmetty of emmets, as Makayla likes to point out.'

'What's an emmet?' Alexis asks, finger poised over the Notes app on his cell phone.

'I'm not too sure,' I say. 'But I know it's disparaging, and it means tourist or second-homer. Something like that.'

'It means ant, in Cornish,' Daniel says. 'I looked it up the first day I was here when a local at Fistral Beach car park called me an 'emmet prick' for parking too close to his clapped-out car with a 2002 plate. As if he was afraid my brand-new BMW hire car might scratch his shit-heap.'

'You're a jerk,' I say. 'You know that?'

He nods. 'I've been told. Frequently.'

Alexis finally goes off – with a bad case of the sulks – to use the bathroom and when he comes back, he says that Makayla and Demi are boiling eggs and frying bacon, and he goes to lend a hand.

'So that hand thing...' Daniel says. 'Sorry about that.'

'No worries,' I say. 'The tin can is small.'

'It's just...'

'What?'

A pained expression comes into his eyes.

'Nothing. I'd better go help with breakfast. Alexis is probably just getting in the way.'

'Okay,' I say, disappointed, because it seemed like he wanted to say something real, something important.

As he goes, though, I hear him talking to somebody right outside and when I pop my head out to see who's here, I gape.

Standing right outside, with a gas station bouquet of daisies in his hands, is my husband.

Thirty-Six

'Who the fuck was that guy?' is the first thing Joseph says to me, after all this hurt, after all this time.

'Which guy are you talking about?' I ask, emboldened by the knowledge that my friends are just in the house. 'There were two.'

He's so shocked that he doesn't speak. He takes his bouquet of daisies and tosses them into the garbage pail that Demi uses for Coder's shit.

'How did you find me?' I ask, trying to keep my voice straight, which is hard because I'm shaking like a leaf. *Trembling like an aspen*, Demi would say, and the thought of her gives me strength.

'Ricky,' he says, spitting out the name like old gum.

'My brother told you I was here? I just don't believe that, Joseph.'

'I told him I was trying to save my marriage. What else was he going to do?'

'Why would you say that to him?' Why would Ricky believe it?

'I want to try again,' he says, 'with my wife.'

'What?' I say, hardly believing I'm hearing these words

from him. Is he for real? He wants to try again? Try to make our marriage work after all that's happened?

'That's what I want.'

'What you want isn't the most important thing. You blew it, Joseph. I trusted you and you blew it.'

'I made a mistake. I don't know what I was thinking, fooling around with Issy. I lost my damn mind.'

'You lost your mind? I was at the lowest point of my whole life. I was grieving my mom, I was crying all day, and you were hooking up with Issy.'

There's no coming back from that kind of betrayal – how doesn't he know that?

'We were just friends, Issy and me, to begin with. I didn't even sleep with her until after I'd finished things with you.'

'What *did* you do, Joseph?'

He doesn't answer. He doesn't want to spell out all the things they did that weren't sex but were still cheating. Were still a betrayal.

'Who's running the shop while you're here?' I ask sharply.

'Nobody. It didn't make it. There was just too much bad debt racked up. I couldn't come back from it.' He pauses before adding, 'I hear you have a great new business, though. Ricky tells me you have a good thing going here. You have your own surf school?'

'Our shop is closed?' I say, too shocked to mention the fact that my surf school has barely seen an ounce of action in weeks.

'You walked out. How am I gonna keep going by myself, Candice?'

'You weren't by yourself, though. Which has been fully established. By way of sonogram.'

'Yeah, Issy's pregnant. It's high-risk and she needs rest, not store work. I'll start up the shop again. Find a cheaper location. I need to talk to you about that. Five minutes, that's all I'm asking.'

*

I can see silhouettes in the kitchen window. Everyone in Demi's house is probably watching me as I walk past Joseph and in through the back door.

'Don't ask,' I say, and they don't. Demi just puts a plate of food in front of me and Makayla hands me a cup of coffee.

'It'll be okay,' Daniel says.

'Don't even,' I say. 'You don't know him. You don't know what he's like when he doesn't get his way.'

'If he's threatening you, you need to get the police involved,' Demi says.

'He won't hurt me,' I say. 'All he wants from me is money and I don't have any. He blames me for our surf shop going under. He thinks I have some lucrative surf school here and he wants a piece of it. Probably half of everything I've made, which is nothing.'

'Oh, love,' Demi says, laying her warm hand on the top of my head.

'If he finds out I'm helping you guys with the book…' I say, turning to Daniel.

'Let me call my friend at the agency,' Daniel says. 'She's a lawyer. She deals with shitheads all the time.'

'You don't have to do that,' I say. 'This is not your problem. My husband, my mess.'

'That was your husband?' Alexis says, drifting into

the room, eating a piece of white toast spread thick with Nutella. 'That chap who was over by the van?'

'Yes,' I say. 'That was Joseph.'

'Huh,' Alexis says. 'I expected him to be taller.'

'Why don't you go for a surf?' Makayla says, in her soothing voice. 'Calm yourself down.'

'It's like a lake out there,' Demi says, a washing basket on her hip. 'Haven't you heard? There's no swell due all week.'

'Kill me now,' I say, then head back outside, to where, thankfully, Joseph has made himself scarce.

I shut myself back in my van, bring my beach towel to my face and cry until my ribs ache.

Thirty-Seven

When the worst of the juddering sobs have subsided, I turn off my phone and pick up a book. I have one that Daniel loaned me a few days ago. His favourite book of all time, apparently, which I was expecting to be something by Stephen King, or maybe *Fear and Loathing in Las Vegas*, or even *Fight Club* – the sort of books that all the cool guys from college used to carry around. But it's nothing like that. Daniel's favourite book of all time turns out to be a British sci-fi comedy novel called *Red Dwarf: Infinity Welcomes Careful Drivers*. It manages to stop me crying and even makes me laugh. It also makes me want to ask Daniel how he ever discovered this weird comic masterpiece.

I try to time my bathroom breaks for when Demi and Makayla are out of the house. I don't want to see anyone; I don't want to talk – I just want to be left alone.

I read so long that my eyes go fuzzy and my head aches, but I don't care. I'm not stopping till I've inhaled the whole story.

★

When I wake up the next day, it's past 9 a.m. The first message I read when I turn my cell phone on is from Daniel.

Are you ok?

I type out my reply.

I'm fine.

I know you have a lot going on. Do you still think you want to work on the project? I know you haven't signed a contract yet, so you're not legally obliged and we'll still pay you for the time you've spent helping already.

I still want to work on the project. I just needed a minute to get myself together. That's why you're messaging me? For Alexis?

No. I wanted to make sure you were okay. That your husband hadn't come back to hassle you.

He hasn't. I think he's still dealing with the fact that two guys came out of my van.

If you need me to come over, just say the word and I'll be there.

Thanks, but I'm good. Just a little tired.

Then, after a pause, I add:

I love the book you gave me. I don't think any book has made me laugh like that before. I especially like the cat.

Cat is very cool.

I have one more chapter and I'll return it to you.

Keep it. Might come in handy for some other time you need a laugh.

*

I feel tired all the way through to my bones, but calmer. The composed feeling lasts until I leave the van and look over to the patch of grass where the two women with ponytails did their HIIT workout. There's a pop-up beach tent there, the kind you can buy for ten dollars from any store in town. The favourite move of the only man I know who thinks hotel rooms are for suckers and camping tents are for pussies, but who is actually just too cheap to spend his money.

When I walk out of Demi's yard and around to the road, I see him sitting in the tent opening, trying to make sense of a bus route leaflet.

'Babe, you'll never guess who's playing at a music festival in Cornwall today,' Joseph says, like he hasn't been absent from my life for the best part of a year, like he wasn't just a douche to me yesterday.

I look at him, waiting for him to show his hand, tell me where he's going with this.

'Samantha Crain. You love Samantha Crain. You were always singing "Sante Fe" when you washed dishes. You listened to her albums so much I thought I'd go crazy.'

Of all the things he could have said to make me listen to him, he's landed on maybe the only one that could work.

'She's here?' I say.

'Twenty minutes down the road, at something called Kernowfornia Dreaming,' he says, struggling a little with the name. 'I was thinking I buy us day tickets. We can take a bus right to the festival ground.'

'You want us to go to a concert together?'

I can feel that I'm shaking. The strength has gone out of my legs, but I need to do everything I can to stop him seeing my weakness. Joseph needs to believe I'm stronger now. I need to believe it, too.

'It's not a concert. It's a festival. A public place. Thousands of other people around. Somewhere you'll feel safe. You can leave any time you want. I just want a little time to talk with you. I had to borrow money off my mom for my plane ticket, so you could at least listen. If you don't like what I have to say, I'll go back to Oahu, and you'll never see me again. I give you my word.'

He thrusts his phone in my face and I scroll down the page for the music festival, which is billed as 'The Most Mellow Garden Fête'.

'I'm not sure what that last word even is,' Joseph says. 'Feet?'

'It's pronounced "fate",' I say. 'It's a kind of summer fayre.'

'I don't know how people build a hip music festival around that brand,' he says. 'But whatever – I guess we'll find out.'

'What time is Samantha Crain's set?'

'Noon.'

'You can take the bus if you'd like,' I say. 'But I'll drive there in my van.'

'You're not giving me a ride?' he says, a note of hurt in his voice. 'I was going to buy the tickets now on my cell phone.'

'Are there tickets available from the box office?'

'Yeah.'

'I think it's better if I buy my own when I get there,' I say, determined not to give him anything to hold over me.

'Gates open at ten and it's nine fifteen now,' he says.

'I can be there for half ten. Your bus might take longer.'

Joseph pouts, turns away to look behind him, tries to compose his face so that the anger doesn't show.

'You're really not giving me a ride?'

I am so close to caving that it physically hurts to say the next words. To stand up to him. But the thought of sitting alone with him in the van makes my stomach churn.

'Not when you've gone to all the trouble of buying a bus route pamphlet,' I say, shaking, wondering when I'll cross his line, when he'll lash out and call me a bitch. I have to force myself to stand strong, because if he knows how weak I feel, he won't leave me alone, ever.

'Would you at least give me your new cell phone number?' he says. 'So I can call you when I get there?'

'I'll wait for you in the parking lot,' I say, quietly. 'I have one of my trashy romance novels – the ones you hate so much – to finish reading. You can take as long as you need.'

'There's going to be thousands of vehicles there, Candice.'

'Head for the orange van with the pineapple farm painted on the side.'

'Sure, I'll just walk around like an asshole checking out every orange van for fruit.'

'I guess you will,' I say, bracing myself for his anger.

'Okay,' he says, looking confused. Hurt, even. Completely knocked off balance by this limited resistance from a woman who has always been so willing to accommodate his needs.

'The farm you painted – is it the one near our place?' he calls after me as I walk away back to Demi's house.

I turn. 'Yes, Joseph. That one.'

'You homesick?'

'No.'

'Then why'd you paint it?'

'It's where I was standing when I decided I was done with you forever.'

Thirty-Eight

'Don't go,' Makayla says.

'My favourite singer is playing. Why should I miss out on seeing her just because Joseph is going? He'll be one of, like, ten thousand people.'

'I don't like it. He's manipulating you.'

'Oh, he's definitely trying. But if I do this, I get to appreciate some incredible music and flip him the bird in a safe location. He says that if I hear him out and I don't like what he has to say, he'll go home.'

'He says that. It doesn't mean he'll keep to it.'

'He gave me his word. He won't break it.'

Makayla makes a face. 'I mean, I don't want to be that dickhead who always has to point out the obvious, but he gave you his word before, didn't he? When you made marriage vows. He had no problem breaking those.'

'I hear you,' I say, 'but I feel like this is really something I'm meant to do. A place I'm supposed to go.'

She gets quiet.

'All right, I get it,' she says. 'And the more I think about it, the more I feel the same.'

'Really? You think I'm right to go talk with him today?'

'No, I just meant I'm supposed to go with you.'

'Makayla, you don't need to do that. You don't want to hobble all over a festival site with a broken leg. I'll be fine.'

'I know you will,' she says. 'Because if he tries anything, I'll brain him with my crutches.'

*

Forty five minutes later, we enter the parking lot and pay the attendant. There's no sign of Joseph.

'I said I'd wait for him in the van,' I say to Makayla. 'I said I'd read a book.'

'It's too hot to wait in the van. Let him come and find you inside.'

'But I said I'd wait,' I say again.

'I'm sure when he sees your van is empty, he'll figure out that you've changed your mind.'

'Joseph hates it when plans change.'

'Then this is an opportunity for personal growth,' she says, firmly.

She hops out of the passenger side and slams the door.

'What are you waiting for?' she yells. 'Some of us are standing up on broken legs.'

We walk past glamping tents, through woods in full leaf, strewn with fairy lights, to an Airstream Silver Bullet trailer. There's a line but it moves quickly. We pay, get given our wristbands, then go through security, who check our bags and take a good long look at Makayla's bullet-shaped personal massage device.

'Why do you have that in your bag?' I hiss, through gritted teeth.

'Never know when I might need it,' she answers, dreamily.

'Outdoor shenanigans happen. Not everything fun goes down in a four-poster bed, Grandma.'

The security woman, who has kind but extremely tired eyes, laughs and motions us through.

We go through a literal closet, just like the one from *The Lion, the Witch and the Wardrobe*, and into the main site, which is buzzing with throngs of happy festivalgoers, some of whom appear to be dressed like the Queen of England.

We walk winding paths through the trees, books hanging down from twine all around us, and we come, at last, to a woman painted green, with a long mermaid tail. She jolts into motion with a flip of her tail as we approach and begins playing a harp so beautifully that I could cry.

We get a blissful half-hour to ourselves, sitting on swing chairs in an old walled garden, before we move to the stage area. Makayla joins a long queue for cotton candy and then Joseph appears.

When I see him, my heart sinks.

'Why are you here, Joseph?' I say, with resignation. Because maybe I should hear him out. There's a chance, however small, that he's changed. 'What's really going on?'

'I acted badly,' he says. 'I know that, but that doesn't mean I'm some kind of toxic jerk you need to cut out of your life forever. You don't have to be toxic to do hurtful shit. Good people can fuck up too.'

'I don't think I believe that,' I say.

'That good people make mistakes? Or that I'm a good person?'

'That you can divide people into good and bad. I don't think it's so simple.'

This answer seems to make him happier, give him some kind of hope.

'So then, forgive me already.'

'Except, I no longer believe in that either.'

'How can you not believe in forgiveness? Who even says that?'

'What I'm saying is this: I no longer believe in forgiveness for men who don't deserve it.'

'Okay, well, maybe I don't believe in giving you the divorce you want,' he says, his face clouding with anger. 'Maybe I stall it for as long as I can.'

This is when the Irishman arrives. He's red-faced and flustered, and he appears to be wearing dinosaur-print dungarees.

'Wait here,' I say to Joseph. 'I'll just be a minute. I have to speak to someone.'

'Exactly how many men are you fucking, Candice?' I hear him say, in a low voice, as I walk to Travis.

'Nice threads,' I say.

'Makayla got them for me and told me to wear them. Apparently dino-dungas are what you're supposed to wear at festivals. Is she around?' he asks. 'She told me to meet her here. Said it was "essential".'

'Ah, she might be using you as a heavy in case there's trouble. My ex is here. Sorry.'

'I'm not much of a scrapper,' he says, looking nervous. 'Especially not in this get-up. But I'll give it a go. Where is Makayla, by the way?'

'In line for snacks,' I say. 'And it's okay, my husband's a jackass, but violence won't be necessary.'

I feel a tap on my shoulder and turn to see Demi.

'How are you here too?' I say to her. 'Let me guess, Makayla told you to come.'

'She didn't tell me to come. She… invited me to come. The carpenter's outside too, but he can't come in because he brought Coder and the site's not dog-friendly.'

'Bummer.'

'Assistance dogs only. And he can't leave him in the car because the poor mutt would cook, so he's walking him in the woods across the road. No doubt they'll shortly find their way to a pub for a medicinal shandy and some pork scratchings.'

'That's too bad,' I say, already feeling stronger now that I have my friends around me.

Joseph comes over to us, but stops a little way off, motioning for me to walk to him.

'Who are all these people?' he asks, pissed off, I guess, that it's not just the two of us. That there will be witnesses to whatever move he's going to pull.

'These people?' I say, turning to look at Demi, and Makayla – who has several bags of cotton candy hooked onto her wrist and is also carrying a scooped-out pineapple full of piña colada. 'Are my people.'

They walk over to stand right beside us.

'I need a minute with my wife,' Joseph says. 'Can you give us some privacy?'

'Sure,' Makayla says. She motions to three empty wooden picnic benches near a haybale area, where a bunch of kids are throwing hay into the air and turning cartwheels as it rains down around them. 'Pick a bench. We'll take the other ones.'

'That's not going to work for me,' Joseph says, something like hatred flashing into his eyes as he looks Makayla up and down. She's wearing a pink sparkly festival hat, a button-down vest, short-shorts and a red cowboy boot, which really sets off her blue plaster boot.

'That's too bad,' she says. 'Because that's where you're sitting.'

I sit down at a bench, overwhelmingly grateful that Makayla is taking charge of this situation. She sets my drink on the table in front of me, and takes the other bench, six feet away, where she sits with the Irishman and drinks her own piña colada.

Demi goes to stand in line at a street food stall, but she keeps looking around, checking on us.

'Where's Issy?' I say, watching the Ferris wheel turn round and round. Joseph looks pained, and stares at the big tent where my favourite singer of all time will soon appear and maybe start singing my favourite song of all time.

'You know I'm a straight shooter, so I'm just going to tell you. Issy's gone home to her folks.'

'Isn't the baby due in, like, a month or something?'

'Five weeks.'

'Then why has she gone home, Joseph?'

'She thinks they can look after her better than I can, I guess, which just means they have more money. It means they have a guesthouse with a pool, and they'll get a night nurse to help her through the worst of it.'

'That's not what that means, Joseph. If she's left you, it's because you weren't good to her.'

'Don't come at me with that, Candice. You don't know anything about how Issy feels.'

'I know you weren't good to me, and I think, Joseph, that maybe you can't be good to anybody. Not long-term. Not when it counts.'

'Okay, that's your opinion, but it's wrong.'

'I don't think so. Because I know you. And I know what your love is like.'

'What does that even mean, Candice?' he says. He's getting into the red zone of anger. The vein on his forehead is bulging, and the one at the side of his neck. His voice is turning to a dog's snarl.

I could back down, change the subject. But I have all my people here, so if I'm ever going to say it, the thing I've been wanting to say for the past year, it's now.

I take a deep breath. What the hell.

'Your love is like this soft little moth.'

'The hell are you talking about?' he says.

'It's always there fluttering around a woman, getting in the way of everything she tries to do, leaving its dust all over.'

'You're talking like a crazy person,' he says, wiping his nose with the back of his hand.

I carry on. I have to get through this.

'But when she's so devastated, so lonely, that she actually wants that little bug with her, because everything is going dark and she's afraid to be alone in the dark, that soft little moth flies away to a brighter light.'

'Fuck, Candice. Don't say that. Don't even think that. That's not what happened.'

'That's what happened to me, Joseph. And now you're back here sitting in front of me, telling me that the moth flew straight into a bug zapper and got all burnt up, and what I have to tell you is this. I am glad you got burnt. I am glad you felt pain. I hope you never get over it. Because then, just maybe, you'll have some idea of what you've done to me, what you continue to do to me.'

I've stepped over his line and he loses his temper. With one quick motion, he knocks my cored pineapple drink from the picnic table in front of me.

'Woah,' Makayla says, at the same time as the Irishman says, 'Easy there, mate.'

But I don't seem able to say anything at all.

'I'm easy,' Joseph says. 'Just blowing off a little steam. I'll buy Candice another goddamn pineapple.'

'Ten quid that cost,' Makayla says. Then very audibly adds the word, 'Prick.'

I put out my hand like a stop-sign, try to warn her from coming over.

'Do you want to go home, Candice?' Demi says, balancing various polystyrene food containers on her arm, while also midway through eating a huge rolled crepe from a brown paper bag.

'Not until I get what *I* came here for,' I say.

'What's that – signed divorce papers?' Joseph says, bitterly.

'If you have them on your person,' I answer, feeling more strongly than I ever have before that this is exactly what I want.

'You know, like I said before,' Joseph says with a sneer. 'Ricky told me you've got yourself a nice life here. A new surf school business. But, guess what, Candice, whatever you have is fifty percent mine, because we are still married. You don't just get to walk away, leave our business to fail and start a new one without me.'

Then Makayla is beside me, pointing one of her crutches at Joseph and demanding ten pounds to cover the cost of the drink he tossed. He takes his wallet out of his back pocket and hands over a bill.

'Do you have change?' he asks her. 'I only have twenties.'

'What you have,' Makayla says, taking the twenty and tucking it into her vest pocket, 'is halitosis.'

'Your friend is a little bitch,' Joseph says, raising his arm to run his hand through his hair, but too quickly, so that maybe, from where Travis is standing, it looks as if he's going to backhand her.

What happens next happens so fast that my brain can't keep up with my eyes. The gist of it, though, is that the Irishman punches Joseph. Not hard enough to lay him out, just hard enough to make Joseph start punching back. Then they're on the floor, rolling around like a pair of teenage boys, with Makayla jabbing at them with her crutches, trying to break up the fight, getting nowhere. Then Demi is pouring a bottle of Evian over them, like a person might go at fighting dogs with a water hose.

Demi's approach works better, and they roll away from each other, get to their feet, but then Joseph swings again at Travis.

Out of nowhere, Daniel is here, in between them, a hand on either chest, keeping them apart.

My heart is racing, and I can feel tears welling in my eyes.

Neither Joseph nor Travis is bloody, but Joseph is having trouble opening one of his eyes.

Makayla shakes her head, takes Joseph's money out of her vest pocket and hands it back to him. 'You know what? Keep it. You need it more than me. Use it to buy some Listerine. Now fuck off.'

I hear Demi sigh and I feel her hand on my shoulder.

'This is not the last you'll hear from me,' Joseph hisses at me. 'You better start mailing cheques, or you'll be hearing from my attorneys.'

'You gave me your word,' I say, 'that if I heard you out and I didn't like what you had to say, you'd leave me alone. And my surf business is a bust. There is no money for you to take. If I mail you cheques, they'll bounce.'

'Bullshit,' he says, spitting on the ground.

'Classic emotional vampire,' Demi says, authoritatively, and Joseph doesn't seem to know what to do with that.

'Would you just fuck off already?' Makayla says to him, exasperated.

And just like that, he walks away.

'Sorry we're late,' Daniel says. 'Makayla invited us but Alexis wanted to stop to look at Tehidy Country Park, since we're so close. Not the best idea, apparently.'

'That's okay, I'm just thankful you're here,' I say, and I mean it.

Makayla turns to the Irishman and says, 'You don't need to fight my battles, Travis. I had it under control.'

'He looked like he was about to hit you!'

'I was about to hit *him*. And if I'd hit him, he would have gone down and *stayed* down.'

A sentence which seems to throw Daniel so off balance that he starts laughing helplessly.

Alexis wanders up, holding a stick of powder-blue cotton candy. Daniel's mentioned that a lot of his clients exist on junk food once they're deeply in the flow of writing, all their virtuous health rules out of the window, and Alexis seems to really be running with that.

'What did I miss?' he says, looking interested.

'Nothing much,' Makayla says. 'Just my bloke punching Candice's husband. Quite weakly.'

'Shit – really? A real fight!' Alexis says, sounding disappointed. 'That would have been great material for the book. Daniel, can you tell me everything while it's fresh in your head? I'll buy you a beer.'

Daniel shoots me a look of pure exasperation, as he's led off by his star client to the beer tent.

'Sorry for not being a better fighter,' Travis says, turning to Makayla with a dejected expression. 'I did warn Candice I wasn't much of a scrapper.'

'Luckily that's not a quality I'm looking for in my boyfriend. Which you are, by the way, if you still want to be.'

'I've wanted that since I first met you!'

'Well, obviously,' she says, smiling. 'But I think I'm finally ready for a serious relationship. Maybe in a few years we'll get married and have a kid or five. It could just be hormones or the clock ticking, but I'm broody as fuck.'

Travis turns, it seems, to stone.

I hear Demi choke a little on the last of her crepe and then glug the rest of her Evian.

'You told me you don't do boyfriends?' I say.

'I said I hadn't had a boyfriend that lasted longer than a month *yet*. I didn't say I never wanted one.'

'You live in fear of getting pregnant,' I add. 'You told me you'd been on birth control since you were old enough to ride your bike across town and get your family doctor to write you a prescription. You said your parents' marriage put you off the whole concept of monogamy.'

'My parents were just so... religious. They weren't awful

– or they didn't mean to be – but they were very into shame. And, as you know, I reject shame.'

She's smiling as she says this, but I know this conversation is hurting her. Not long after we met, she told me how her only contact with her parents is for one afternoon around the holidays, when they all try not to offend each other and the strain of it takes a year to recover from. How the last three times she went to visit, she wound up with a huge eyebrow zit – indisputably the most painful of all the zits – which she believed was her body's way of voicing its displeasure at being there. She's showed me the birthday cards they send her, featuring religious scenes, and the enclosed twenty-pound note, which she makes sure to spend only on alcohol and condoms.

'Come on,' she says. 'I'm taking you for a few spins on the Ferris wheel. Demi, you in?'

'No, thank you. I'd like to keep my crepe down and I've just drunk half a litre of water, so I need to start queuing for the Portaloo. Will they even let you on the ride with a broken leg?' Demi asks, looking concerned.

'I'd like to see them try to stop me. Fuck, it's four quid each. Maybe just one go. Travis, you okay to stay here and watch our stuff?'

'Sure,' he says, still looking dazed.

*

We're on our first revolution when Makayla rests her head on my shoulder, and we look in silence out to the festival ground stretching away beneath us.

'You know,' I say, 'your rejection of shame is one of the things I like best about you.'

'Me too,' she says, trying to smile. 'But I was a great disappointment to my mum and dad. I was pretty much the opposite of what they wanted in a daughter, and although they were too polite to say it in words, they still said it – just in non-verbal ways that cut even deeper.'

'I'm sorry, Makayla. That must have been incredibly tough. They sound hard to be around.'

'They don't know they're hard to be around. They think it's everyone else who has the problem. In their minds, their way is the only way that can possibly be right.'

Which makes me think of Joseph. So many people seem to have this kind of certainty. That their way is the only way. The only thing I'm certain about is that I don't know the way.

She puffs out her cheeks and exhales.

'Even as a kid, I knew their life choices weren't for me. And when I got older, I knew I wouldn't be abstaining from sex until marriage, but I didn't want to get knocked up either.'

'And now you do?' I ask, as the ride slows to a halt. Our car touches the ground and the guy comes to release us first. Demi and Travis are waiting a few feet away with trays of hot doughnuts.

'Maybe one day,' she says. 'I'm almost twenty-five. I'm not a rebellious teenager any more. I've played the field and got a lot of angst out of my system. I'm ready for something else.'

'You've definitely played the field,' Demi says, patting her on the head.

'Every inch of it,' Makayla says. 'Played, ploughed, thoroughly watered…'

'Fertilised with the finest dung?' I offer.

'Don't make this weird, Candice,' she says, smiling, but also giving me a fist-bump. 'It's taken me a while to get here, but I'm ready for something else. I'd love to be a mother.'

I turn to look at Travis, who is stock-still and slack-jawed, eyes like marbles.

'Travis, are you in there?' Makayla says.

'I'm here,' he says. 'Can't believe my ears but I'm here.'

I glance in the other direction, where my cored pineapple is still lying on the ground, a reminder of Joseph's anger. Joseph will soon be a parent too.

'You want to have a baby? With *me*? I'm going to be a father?' Travis says, turning back to flesh.

'I mean, if it goes well. There's no guarantees. I could be shooting blanks,' Makayla says, shrugging.

'Or I might be,' he says.

She shakes her head and grimaces. 'I've tasted your spunk. That stuff is full of healthy swimmers.'

'This seems like a private conversation,' Demi says, trying not to laugh.

But neither Makayla nor Travis seem perturbed.

'Do you want to get married?' he says. 'Because I'd marry you today, Makayla. I've already told my mam about you.'

Makayla shakes her head, tells him to calm down, but she doesn't have time to answer fully because a woman a little way off is pointing at the Irishman.

Two security guys come over and we all get escorted out. Very politely, Travis making cheerful conversation with the security guys the whole way, beaming like they're the best men at his wedding.

As we're going, I hear Samantha Crain singing the first verse of 'Santa Fe', and I figure things could definitely be worse.

Thirty-Nine

I message Alexis and Daniel to tell them we're outside and
Demi rings the carpenter, who meets us in the parking lot.
He's swaying a little as he walks and almost falls over when
Coder jumps up on his leash to greet us.

'I'll be driving us home then, will I?' Demi says, giving
him the once-over. And then Daniel and Alexis are standing
beside us, Alexis seeming a little salty about having to leave
the festival so soon.

Over Daniel's shoulder, I spot Joseph lingering,
presumably waiting for us to leave. He's uncomfortably
alone, shifting his weight. Waiting for me to go over.

'Give me a second to handle this,' I say, walking over to
him.

'Why are you still here?' I say.

'The bus isn't due for another hour. Where am I supposed
to go?'

'I don't know, Joseph. Take a cab. Or start walking.'

'What happened to you, Candice? When did you get so...
mean?'

'I'm not mean,' I say, but I feel the sting of that, because maybe I am mean. Maybe I have to be sometimes. 'I'm just looking out for myself.'

Daniel comes over and points his keys at his rental BMW. 'I can give him a lift back to Newquay. Or, I don't know, drop him off at a train station.'

The relief I feel almost floors me. Seeing Daniel standing there next to Joseph, I realise that he has a quality Joseph has never had. Kindness. There is something within Daniel that makes him reach out to others and try to help them. He's not a bystander. He tries to make things better, easier for people.

'Drop him off a train station bridge,' Makayla says, pleasantly, and Travis high-fives her.

'Who the hell are you, buddy?' Joseph asks Daniel, his voice thick with hostility and suspicion.

'Daniel Burns. I'm here for work, but I don't need to be. Alexis, you can carry on without me, right?'

'Fine,' Alexis says, sighing. 'I'd come with you, but I really can't turn down this research opportunity. I'll get a cab back to the cottage.'

'A taxi will set you back the best part of forty quid,' Demi says, and Alexis visibly winces.

'I'll expense it,' Daniel says, sighing.

Then he leads Joseph away from me. Forever, I hope.

*

Demi leaves with the carpenter and Coder, and Makayla and Travis pile into my van, because Travis took the same bus here as Joseph, so that he could get merry in The Secret Gin Garden. Which sucks for him, as the only drink he's taken is one sip of Makayla's piña colada.

On the ride back to Demi's place, I try to give them space to talk but it's difficult when we're all squished up together in the front seat of my van, because Travis won't hear of Makayla riding in the back without a rear seatbelt to buckle up, and my van is too old to have that option, and Makayla insists on him sitting right beside her.

We drop him back to his apartment and Makayla sighs as he walks away.

'There goes my boyfriend,' she says.

'So you're not choosing the Poet or the Doberman?'

'There're two things I haven't told you about the Poet. One: he can only poop naked.'

'Stop.'

'It's true. He has to strip off every single time he needs to go, and hang his clothes from the door-hook.'

'How do you even know this? Did you walk in on him in the bathroom?'

'No, he told me. He considers it his USP. Luckily, he only poops once a fortnight, so it's not too disruptive to his daily life.'

'What's the second thing?'

'He works in an abattoir.'

'The tit limpet works in an abattoir?'

'He had another job offer but he said he liked the idea of working with knives. Thought it would make him seem more macho. I didn't know that when I agreed to go out with him. Obviously. I couldn't have his laundry touching mine, even if I could get over the Shaun the Sheep slaughter.'

'And you're definitely over the Doberman?'

'I've scratched that itch to death. Believe me.'

'So… you're happy?'

'Yeah. Travis might not be forever, but he's nice and I think he'll make a decent boyfriend. Maybe one day a good father, if it comes to that.'

'He has kind eyes,' I say.

'Right? He really does,' she says. 'I thought that the first time I saw him.'

'He has a trustworthy vibe,' I say. 'He seems solid, you know? Like he won't just disappear on you.'

'Well, even if he doesn't stick around,' she says, brightly, 'any baby of mine will have a family of women to look out for her.'

'You're only having girls?'

'I don't know for sure, but I have a feeling.'

I smile. 'Then you'll probably have all boys.'

'Hey, my grandmother was a witch, remember. That's where I get my great intuition.'

I look at her.

'It could be where you got that wisdom whisker on your chin,' I say.

'Fuck sake,' she says, yanking it out. 'But I appreciate the honesty.'

Forty

I get up with the herring gulls and can't get back to sleep. My head is pounding and I don't know how to feel about anything.

Joseph is gone. And, as Daniel led him away, I could see the difference between the two of them so starkly.

One selfish, one selfless.

One helpless, one helpful.

The difference between the world's Willoughbys and Colonel Brandons.

I should do something useful, I could exercise or read, but instead I eat a handful of Pringles, climb into the rainbow-striped hammock in Demi's yard and allow myself to dream.

I press my face into the loosely woven fabric and look at the filtered sun, the heat of which is already fierce. There's enough fabric to close the gap above me, and I keep getting flashes of a man lying next to me, both of us hidden from the world, the warmth of his body up against mine, the touch of skin against skin.

I close my eyes and feel the pound of my heart.

Could the man I'm daydreaming of be... Daniel?

Am I crushing on him?

That is insane. I hardly know him. He is Alexis's literary agent and I'm nearly thirty years old, which is too old for daydreaming in a hammock about a cute guy.

But every time my mind wanders, I get a new image of me and that man together. Walking hand in hand along island beaches, phrasebook in my pocket, no idea of where we're going except that it will end each night in a bed that he will share with me, and in the morning we'll wake up tangled in each other and head out on a new adventure.

No.

Red light.

I have to guard against these kinds of daydreams, because they're not based in reality. They're a distraction from what I'm here to do. All of this has been a distraction, because otherwise I have to face up to the fact that I'm failing.

Suddenly, I hear a *yoo-hoo!* and look up to see a group of smiling senior citizens, waving to get my attention.

'Are you a local girl?' one says, and it takes a beat for me to answer.

'Yes,' I say.

'Then can you give us directions to Newquay Zoo? We're off to see the African lions.'

I can smell incense drifting from the open window of Makayla's room, and she chooses this exact moment to start playing music with explicit lyrics, so that I have to shout directions over the blare of 'WAP'.

I'm not sure if she's making a point with the choice of song or if she's just enjoying the music, but no amount of me yelling for her to turn it down, or at least 'CLOSE THE DAMN WINDOW' seems to make any difference to her.

'What?' she says, her head poking out. 'I've just officially broken up with the Doberman. Told him we will never be hanging out again. Like *ever*.'

'That's very Taylor Swift of you,' I say, smiling, and thinking of Taylor Swift's classic break-up anthem, 'We Are Never Ever Getting Back Together'.

One of the old guys frowns at me.

'You don't sound like you're local,' he says. 'You sound American.'

'I know,' I say. 'But I was born right here in Newquay.'

They wander away, mumbling something about 'Yanks' and I shout up to Makayla.

'I thought you already broke up with the Doberman?'

'Not officially. I was sending him a few memes here and there.'

'Why?'

'I still hadn't seen his puppy,' she says. 'But I have now. Bumped into them on the Barrowfields this morning.'

'What was it like?' I yell.

'The little fucker bit me,' she says, slamming the window.

*

'Even if the puppy hadn't bitten you like that,' I say, later, looking at the fresh graze on Makayla's hand. 'Even if it was the sweetest puppy in the world, the Doberman is no Irishman, is he? And maybe there was always gonna be too much ick to come back from. Ever since the soup incident, I guess.'

'Way past ick,' she says. 'He also told me what he did to one of his ex-girlfriends.'

'What did he do?' I say, concerned that Makayla might have been hanging out with some kind of a predator.

'The Doberman can't stand confrontation with women,' she says. 'So when he's angry with a woman he's involved with, he pulls some truly passive-aggressive bullshit.'

'Like what?'

'Like once, he was pissed off that his girlfriend had gone out drinking and danced with his mates all night, so in the morning – when she was hungover to hell, after puking her guts up – he was rubbing her back and he passed over her toothbrush. But he'd already put on the toothpaste.'

'That's... helpful?'

'No, because earlier he did a sweep of the windowsills in their flat and he put a dead, shrivelled-up little spider on the head of her toothbrush, underneath a big blob of Colgate.'

'He's a sociopath,' I say.

'I know. He might actually be. He was laughing as he was telling me this, describing spider legs foaming out between the poor woman's teeth.'

I put my hand over my mouth and try not to puke.

'There's no going back from that,' she says. 'I try not to judge the weirdos – mostly because I am one – but it turns out I do have a line. And putting a dead fucking spider on someone's toothbrush is my line.'

'Jesus Christ, Makayla. Next time give me a trigger warning.'

'Sorry,' she says. 'Hey. I've been meaning to ask about your father. It feels like with the book and Joseph, we haven't really spoken about it for a while. Have you got any news? Made any progress?'

'No,' I say. 'Demi's been talking to all the carpenter's friends, to see if they know anything, but nothing's coming to mind.'

'That sucks,' she says. 'They must be about the right age, too.'

I shrug. 'They're going to keep asking around. Daniel is on the case, too. He's been reaching out to people involved in the surf scene here. He really wants to help and he seems to have the knack of getting people to talk about their lives. About their memories of the nineties. I think he's been buying people a lot of drinks at the beach bar.'

'That's nice of him,' Makayla says, airily. 'Suspiciously nice. Sounds like he's trying to impress you with all that niceness.'

'That's just who he is. And we're just friends,' I say. 'Colleagues, in fact.'

'Sure you haven't caught any feelings?'

Have I? I wonder. Just because I keep thinking about him, or someone who resembles him, it doesn't mean I've caught feelings. It just means I find him interesting. That I enjoy his company.

True, it makes me feel all warm and fuzzy when I know he's coming over. And maybe I feel a tiny bolt of lightning strike my chest every time I glance up and catch his gaze. But that doesn't mean anything. That just means I've been contaminated by all the big mushy feelings I've been writing about in the book.

'Of course not. It's strictly business.'

'Right then,' Makayla says, picking up her fancy crystal wineglass of water and tilting it in my direction. 'Time to brush my teeth.'

Forty-One

There's a knock on my bedroom door and I come out of a weird dream about a shoal of yellow fish swimming around me in a giant cored pineapple and nibbling the hard skin off my feet.

'You have a visitor,' I hear Demi say, and she adds, hastily, 'Not your husband.'

Then I hear Makayla's voice. 'It's the other Coder.'

I sit up and rub my eyes. What are they talking about? Another dog?

'Candice, it's me,' a man's deep voice says.

I jump out of bed and move to the door, not sure if I'm still dreaming.

The other coder. My brother.

He's in Demi's house, wearing a worried expression, along with wrinkled khaki pants and a black *South Park* T-shirt that details 'The Many Deaths of Kenny'.

I can't believe my eyes. He's really here?

'Ricky?' I say, as he leans forward for an awkward hug. Makayla and Demi both give me their 'Is this okay?' looks and I nod. I motion Ricky through to the room and smooth out the eiderdown for him to sit. I take the chair by the window.

'Is it okay that I'm here?' he says, tentatively, as if he read their looks too. 'Are you mad at me?'

'I'm a little mad at you,' I say. More than a little. Even if he thought he was doing the right thing, he broke a promise and gave Joseph my address, believed his bullshit about wanting to make things right with me.

'I figured. Your friends are so nice, by the way. But I feel like they got my whole life story in the two minutes we chatted in the hall.'

I smile. 'They're good at that. But how are you even here, Ricky?' I say.

'I'm supposed to be in Germany, for ISC Hamburg. My colleague got Covid so they offered her slot to me at the last minute.'

'ISC Hamburg?' I say, my head fuzzy from sleep.

'Conference for High Performance Computing, Machine Learning and Data Analytics. It's kind of a big deal in my industry.'

He tucks his shaggy hair behind his ears, the way he always does when he's coding or concentrating on something he finds difficult.

'Okay, so why aren't you in Hamburg right now?'

'Because I ditched a day and took a flight and a bunch of trains to be here. I'm so sorry, Candice. I should never have told Joseph where you were.'

'So, you know he really came here?'

'Yeah, he finally picked up my call and told me what happened. His version, anyhow.'

Ricky frowns, as if trying to remember the particulars of this conversation is uncomfortable for him.

'What did he tell you?'

'That some Irish guy in dinosaur pants hit him or something? I don't know. He wasn't making a lot of sense, but he called you a whole bunch of names and I knew whatever went down had to have been bad, knew I had to come here and see you.'

I exhale and feel the tears building behind my eyes. I can't believe Ricky is here. My whip-smart brother who understands computer code so well but has always struggled with people has ditched his big deal conference to check I'm okay.

'Can we go for a walk?' he says. 'It's been a minute since I was here.'

'I'd love that,' I say.

Ricky has always said he was too young to remember much about our life in Newquay, because there were so many beaches back home in Oahu and they all got mixed up in his head, but he thought he remembered a cinema on a military base, where he could take as much warm butter as he wanted for his popcorn, and being excited to go to a zoo every week to visit some lions that he gave the names of the *ThunderCats*.

Showing him around Newquay now, I can't help feeling proud – both of my brother, who I introduce to every acquaintance I meet, and of this town. I can feel Ricky's surprise that so many people know me here. I'd always valued my anonymity back home. I hadn't wanted to talk to strangers, but being in a foreign country has brought me out of myself, stopped me being afraid to talk to folks

I don't know. I've built a network here. I'm part of a community.

When we get to Fistral parking lot, he stops and looks up at the Headland Hotel.

'I remember that place,' he says. 'Mom and Dad took me there, maybe for someone's wedding or something.'

'It's where that movie *The Witches* was filmed.'

'No kidding,' he says. 'This is different,' he adds, waving his hand towards the large complex of surf shops and restaurants. 'I think it was kind of natural and undeveloped when we lived here.'

'What else do you remember?' I say, hoping there might be some clue my mother gave him about my biological father, that he'll remember now he's back here.

He frowns, trying hard to recall the past.

'There was a white bird that washed up dead. It was big, all tangled up in kelp and it smelled bad. I thought it was an albatross.'

'I don't think they get those here. Maybe a gannet?'

'Yeah, maybe. Dad started telling me about an old poem or a story about a sailor who got cursed after killing an albatross.'

'*The Rime of the Ancient Mariner*,' I say. 'Samuel Taylor Coleridge.'

'That was it,' he says, looking at me in surprise. 'But something about that poem made Mom cry and then they argued, screamed at each other, right here on the beach. Argued so badly that a woman came over and checked I was okay. She bought me an ice cream cone and talked with me until they finally stopped shouting at each other. Our folks were so unhappy, Candice.'

I nod. Some of their arguments lasted for days, their resentment for weeks.

'Can you remember why they were fighting that day?' I ask, desperate to know more. 'What was it about the poem that made them angry?'

He runs his fingers through his hair and closes his eyes.

'It was something about why the sailor killed the bird. They kept talking about it, even after we left the beach. For a long time after. Weeks. Dad didn't see why anyone would do something like that, kill a beautiful thing for no good reason. But Mom said something weird.'

He's straining to recollect. Maybe it's not that he was too young to remember, maybe it's that he's tried to block out the memories of what happened here.

'Weird how, Ricky?' I say. 'Please.'

He looks at me, his eyes wide with the pain of remembering.

'She said something about how that albatross was a big red button with the words "Do Not Press". How the wrongness of the thing just makes you want to do it even more. I think maybe that was the thing that made Dad so angry.'

'You don't think Dad *knew* Mom had cheated on him, do you?' I say. 'Mom swore to me that she never told him.'

'I think he maybe had an idea,' Ricky says, pressing the palms of his hands into his eye sockets.

He gets quiet, maybe thinking about things he doesn't want to share with me. Hard memories this place is bringing back.

'But maybe that doesn't even matter any more,' he says, softly. 'They're gone and we have to figure out a way to go forward.'

We both wipe away tears and I hug him, burying my face into the shoulder of his *South Park* T-shirt.

'I love you,' I say. 'I'm so glad you're here.'

'I have to go today,' he says. 'I can't even stay overnight. I have to be back at the conference tomorrow.'

'Can you stay for lunch?' I say.

He checks his wristwatch.

'I have three hours before I have to check in for my flight from Newquay to Gatwick. Is that enough time?'

I nod. 'That's plenty enough time and, when we're done, I'll give you a ride to the airport.'

He smiles. 'Now where's good here for ice cream? I'm buying you the biggest cone they have.'

'The place where I usually "bus tables" is closed for renovation,' I say, giving him a pointed look because he's voiced his disapproval of my working in a café once too often. 'But I know a place that does Cornish clotted cream cones if that interests you?'

'Clotted cream?' he says, looking very interested. 'What is that?'

'We don't have it at home. Traditional clotted cream is unpasteurised and therefore very illegal in the US. It's a huge thing here though. You'll love it.'

He grins and follows me to the ice cream van. I may only have three more hours with my brother, but I'm going to make the most of every minute.

Forty-Two

Another week passes without drama, and I'm mostly over the shock of seeing Joseph, and then Ricky, in quick succession. Alexis has wanted to push hard at the book, so I've been writing with him every day. Today though, we're back to location-scouting. He's started a full read-through of the draft and realised he's missing several short but crucial scenes and needs new locations to set them in.

The Gannel estuary at low tide is a wide expanse of golden sand, overlooked by seventies-style luxury homes and modern McMansions that sell on the market for two million pounds, while most local folks work for minimum wage. The first time I saw this place, the sun was shining, the water was turquoise, and I thought it could have been the French Riviera. Ornamental gardens spin up the riverbank on one side, while farmland dotted with grazing cattle and sheep covers the other. I've only ever been here at full tide, to paddleboard with other locals who come and let the current from the flooding tide sweep them inland, before taking them back out to where they started once the tide flips. The most blissfully lazy paddleboarding experience of my life.

I think of Demi spending so many of her childhood years in a trailer park on the banks of this river mouth. A community of women, single mothers mostly, who helped each other through the hardest times, their children living a free-range life, without wealth except what Mother Nature offered them. After-school evenings swimming in the river, first kisses in the light of the sun setting over the water, and sports with every kid on the sand flats. Friendships forged for life, a shared understanding that though they had suffered, they had also received gifts they would carry with them forever. These are the lives I want to write about, the stories I want to unravel, the women I want to bring to life in my own books. One day. When the time is right. When my backbone is strong enough for the weight of all the disappointment and rejection Alexis talks about so often, and so vividly.

Daniel and Alexis have gone ahead, while I sit on a huge outlet pipe that leads into the water, where little kids use white nets full of raw chicken to catch crabs by the dozen and stare at them in their little clear buckets until they're ready for the release part of the operation.

I'm watching a pure white wading bird stalk along the trickle at the centre of the riverbed, when I notice that Daniel has crouched down and is looking at something on the sand, motioning for Alexis to come and see. Then he's kneeling in the wet sand and digging at something with his fingers.

By the time I get over there, he's nearly finished digging a trench between a deeper pool and a much smaller, shallow one.

'What's going on here?' I ask, curious.

'Daniel noticed a minnow stuck in this tiny puddle here,'

Alexis says, using his cell phone to snap a photo of Daniel digging the trench. 'For Facebook,' he explains.

'*Mate*. Don't put that on Facebook,' Daniel says, groaning. 'I've got a wet patch on the back of my trousers.'

'Huh,' Alexis says. 'Wet Patch was my first nickname at boarding school – they got progressively nicer as I got better-looking.'

'A minnow?' I ask, trying to get back on topic.

'Might not be a minnow,' Daniel says to me. 'Whatever sort of fish it is, it's tiny. Size of a Haribo.'

'Okay... and?'

'It was trapped,' he says, as if this explains things. 'The sun was drying out the puddle and the tide isn't due to turn for another few hours.'

'Couldn't you just, um, fish it out of there and put it in the larger pool?' I say.

'Didn't want to risk hurting the little fella,' Daniel says, looking up at me with clear eyes. He's not embarrassed about this rescue mission, he's happy. I want to get down there with him. I want to help him do this.

But I'm too late. He finishes the last section of the trench, water flows between the two pools and there, as we watch, a tiny little fish swims beneath our shadows to safety.

'Well, look at that,' I say. 'You saved a life.'

'My hero,' Alexis says, wryly, turning to Daniel, but my stomach flips, because yeah, he might have saved the life of something that weighs less than a fraction of a gram, but he saw something in trouble and he helped it, and that means something to me.

'Patrick Swayze level of swoon right here,' Daniel says, pointing to his chest.

We walk a little further upriver until we reach a wooden loveseat that somebody has placed here for hikers to rest and admire the view. Or maybe to do other things, it occurs to me.

But this is more than just a bench. It's a wooden rowboat, cut in half across the middle and stood on end, the arch of the bow giving shelter from the rain to the lovers tangled up together underneath.

In a split-second, I see Bryce and Janie here, but an instant later it segues into an image of myself with a curly-haired man, my legs wrapped around his waist, as he kisses my neck. My fingers are working his fly, unbuttoning. I feel the warmth of him straining against my hand and wonder, briefly, how romance novelists deal with the problem of sexual terminology, specifically when referencing balls. My eyes fix on the white-painted hull of the rowboat, which forms the back of the loveseat. Kids have graffitied it with their tags, subtly, but they're there. I move in closer to read them.

I hear the crunch of shoes on shingle and suddenly Daniel is with me.

Was he the man I was imagining kissing me just then?

Yes.

Why? Because he got on his knees to save a one-inch fish? That small act of kindness shouldn't reduce me to a pool of jelly. It must be the novel. All the writing and thinking about lovers is taking over my brain and sweeping me away on waves of romance.

'I've seen more impressive graffiti...' Daniel says, getting closer. 'What does that one say? I can't figure out the lettering.'

He touches his finger to the old timber, and I read out the words to him.

'This word is "Deez",' I say, moving his finger. 'And this one is "Nutz".'

'Deez Nutz?' He looks at me, delighted, and I think perhaps I've discovered the key to the problem of writing about balls after all.

'I want to check out the other bank of the river,' Alexis says, catching up to us.

'There's a path beneath the trees,' I say. 'Do you want me to show you?'

'It's okay. I'd prefer to be alone when making the notes for this scene. If you don't mind.'

'No problem,' I say.

'I'll walk back to my cottage when I've finished. I have the muse with me now, and I don't want to drive her away with idle conversation.'

'Whatever works for you, mate,' Daniel says, as I go sit on the loveseat.

Alexis leaves, taking his shoes off and walking barefoot across the sand flats. Daniel turns and looks at me and there's a moment when he's weighing this. To come and sit with me or walk on alone?

I drop my gaze to my sneakers, try to will him to come over, to just know that I need him to sit here with me.

When I look up, he's standing right in front of me. I give him a rueful glance and he sits down on the wooden seat next to me.

'Alexis really rates you,' he says.

'Alexis thinks I can be useful to him. There's a difference.'

'It's more than that. He keeps talking about you. You've really got in his head.'

'It's about the book. He told me that our collaboration has helped him find his passion for the story. That's all.'

'I don't know – I think he might have feelings for you.'

'You're reading too much into this,' I say firmly.

'Maybe you're right. It could just be that he's grateful for how much you've helped him this summer. His productivity really increased when you came on the scene.'

'On the scene?' I say. 'Is that bad wordplay?'

'Turn of phrase,' he says. 'I'm sorry. I don't know why I brought this up.'

He looks at me, really looks at me.

'What is this outfit you're wearing?' he says, motioning to the sleeveless brown wrap-over tunic I've teamed with beige linen trousers.

'It's summer chic,' I say. 'It's my classiest outfit.'

'It's nice. You look like Luke Skywalker.'

'You totally nailed my aesthetic,' I say, smiling. 'Are you a big fan of *Star Wars*?'

'Alexis is. It's shameful to admit, I suppose, but I was always way more into *Star Trek*.'

'Wrong choice,' I say. 'Given the option, do you want to watch the people on your TV screen warring or trekking?'

He thinks about this. 'Wars definitely have the greater potential for dramatic tension… But I love a bit of nature, so I'm probably still going to go for the trekking. Especially intergalactic trekking on alien planets.'

'You showed your workings,' I say. 'I'll let it stand.'

'So, about Alexis. He hasn't been unusual with you lately?'

'He's always unusual. He's not into me, though. And

there's really no need to have this conversation. I'm not interested in dating anyone right now.'

His face falls and my stomach clenches. Either he really cares about the dating life of his client or there's some other reason he's disappointed, and I really hope it's not the first thing.

'I still haven't got a contract,' I say, tentatively.

'I know,' he says. 'And I'm so sorry. Alexis's editor at the publishing house is on holiday, so I haven't been able to get hold of her to discuss it, but Alexis assures me he spoke with her before she left for Tuscany and it's all in hand.'

'He's not going to screw me over, is he?' I say. 'I can trust Alexis on this?'

'No…' Daniel begins.

'Is that no he's not going to screw me over, or no I can't trust him?' I ask.

'Um,' he says, 'Alexis is in a weird place at the moment, but I have your back, Candice. I promise.'

'Okay,' I say, meeting his gaze, believing him.

Forty-Three

The next day, Alexis wants to write alone. He tells me he wants first crack at writing the book's ending and he doesn't want me to know anything about it until he's drafted the entire finale. Which means I get a day off.

Makayla and I are sitting on the rocks overlooking the Cribbar reef, where the big waves break in winter, so huge that international big wave surfers come here to ride them. The ocean is calm today, though, and there's a pod of dolphins feeding on the shoals of fish that have come in close to shore. I didn't even notice they were there until one of them flipped a somersault a few feet from shore and almost gave me a heart attack. But they've been moving up and down the bay for hours, coming so close at high tide that we've made eye contact with several that were spy-hopping in the water, staring at us as we stared at them, leaving us with the unnerving feeling that we were communing with equals.

I try to be present in the moment, because what's happening is amazing – the first time I've even seen wild dolphins in Cornwall – but my mind keeps drifting to Daniel. I haven't yet checked in with him today, and I wonder if he'll message me or stop by. The few days when he hasn't come to Demi's place, I've felt strangely restless, as if something is not quite right in the world. As if something is... missing.

'Wow, look at this one,' Makayla says. She's taking photos and videos on her phone for Instagram, and for her sister in Spain, who has been collecting dolphin paraphernalia since she was in kindergarten.

My phone beeps with a message and my heart leaps as I see it's from Daniel.

He says he's found some old footage of Fistral Beach surf contests from the nineties on YouTube. He forwards me several links, with the words:

A couple of them look like you. Never know. Could be something?

I've looked at all this footage on YouTube already. I've driven myself crazy with it, trying to see my nose or eyes in the grainy footage uploaded to the site. Even so, the fact that Daniel has done this, tried to help me in this way, fills me with gratitude. I don't know if I've ever met somebody this helpful before.

He's caught at least a dozen spiders in Demi's house. He didn't even have to be asked. Just trapped them in a wineglass and set them outside in the flower garden. Joseph would have either raised a shoe or, if he couldn't reach the target, taken out the vacuum cleaner.

I message him back.

Thank you.

No worries. I've got a quiet day. I'm working on getting you a contract too. Alexis has a meeting set up with his publishing team and then we'll get everything sorted out.

Appreciate it.

'Who was that?' Makayla asks.

'Just Daniel.'

'No "just" about it.'

'Huh?' I say, glancing at her. 'What does that mean?'

'Oh, nothing...' she says, airily.

I hear a cough and turn to see a striking guy with long red hair wound into a topknot. He's carrying a fishing rod and a bucket of something that squirms. He looks at me with vacant eyes and then shoots Makayla a sharp look.

Makayla seems to have frozen, her eyes wide.

'That's him,' she hisses.

'Who are we talking about?'

She exhales and tries to calm herself. 'The fisherman with the manbun is the Poet.'

He's walking aimlessly now, as if suddenly not sure where he wants to go.

Another guy, tall and wide-shouldered, wearing a beige bucket hat, three-quarter-length combat pants and carrying an open messenger bag of beer bottles that clanks with every step he takes, is walking from the opposite direction and also holding a fishing rod. He stops to talk to the first fisherman.

'Oh, fuck me,' Makayla says, paling even more and pulling her hood up over her hair, like a disguise. 'Someone up there has a warped sense of humour.'

'What now?'

'The other fisherman,' she says, covering her eyes. 'Is the Doberman.'

'How many fishermen have you dated, Makayla?'

'They're hobbyists, not professionals!' she objects. 'One line-caught fish costs eight quid in Morrisons. Whereas here, they cost fuck all.'

'Okay, no judgement.'

'I felt judgement,' she says, and then adds, 'Poor little fishies. Last time I was in the Doberman's flat, a mackerel resurrected in the sink and started flopping around.'

'I hope you told him to put it in some water,' I say.

'I did, but he did not.'

'What did he do?'

'He got out the mallet.'

The Doberman points to the path leading around the other side of the headland, where licensed coasteering groups go cliff-jumping and gully-swimming for a hefty fee, and local kids learn to swim for free.

The Poet goes on his way, glancing back at Makayla with rueful eyes as the Doberman yells, 'Go find 'em, brother!'

Then another dolphin jumps, and Makayla turns to me and says, 'Ply me with wine now, please,' and I top up her plastic cup with Zinfandel rosé from my water bottle.

'Are you okay in there?' I ask a moment later, refilling her glass, since she slammed the contents of the first. She's staring at the sky, lost in thought, her mouth set in a resolute line. It worries me when she gets like this, makes me realise that there's pain within her that I can't reach, can't help to diminish.

'What are you thinking?' I say.

'You don't want to know.'

'I do. You can tell me anything, Makayla.'

'That cloud,' she says, pointing ten degrees above the horizon. 'Looks like a banana.'

Forty-Four

Five days later and the ocean is still flat. The surfers here talk about flat spells that last for weeks, while they pace around like caged tigers, getting progressively more frustrated, dreaming of the gorgeous waves of fall. I've been in the ocean to swim a few times a week, or to glide up and down the bay on a stand-up paddleboard, but there's been no swell, no set waves and nobody is coming to learn to surf. Likewise, the café is still closed, undergoing final renovations, although Demi is planning big things for the reopening party.

'Hey there,' I say, relieved when Daniel calls. 'Does Alexis want me to come over?'

'He's still working on the ending. It's taking longer than he thought. He doesn't want you to see it until he's cracked the denouement.'

'Oh. So why are you calling?'

'Cruffins. When can you be ready?'

'Five minutes,' I say.

*

'What the heck is a cruffin?' I ask, when Daniel pulls up to Demi's house.

'Check it out,' he says, getting out of the car and opening up Instagram. 'My social media feed is full of them. There's a bakery van that's opened up just down the road. We have to go try them.'

He shows me a picture of what looks like a muffin but instead of cake mix, it appears to be made from croissant pastry. It's covered in gooey caramel, which judging by the other photos – the ones of sticky people eating them – goes straight down the middle of the pastry. It's the most delicious-looking thing I have ever seen.

'Where do we go to buy these pastries?' I say. 'Because I think I need one in order to continue living.'

'It's not far.'

'Let's take my van.'

'We can take my rental car.'

'It's fine,' I say. 'I'll drive. I just need to get gas before we go.'

'Okay, but I insist on paying for the fuel.'

'What are you, a millionaire?'

'In negative numbers. But, as we've established *thoroughly* now, I'm putting this trip down as a business expense, which makes it tax-deductible.'

'In that case, you can fill up the tank,' I say. 'Sure we shouldn't ask Alexis if he wants to take a break and come along?'

I don't know why I say this, because as the words come out of my mouth, I know for sure that I really don't want Alexis to come. I want it to be just Daniel and me.

'No, he's going to be drafting all day long and maybe through the night too. We'll just make notes on anything interesting that we encounter.'

'He won't mind?'

'Nah. He'll be glad to get rid of me. No writer wants their agent breathing down their neck when they're trying to knock out a cracking ending.'

*

We stand in line for our pastries for almost forty minutes, but they are worth every moment of the wait.

I finish mine before Daniel.

'Hungry?' he asks.

'Not particularly. I am thirsty, though.'

'There's a pub near here called The Bucket of Blood,' he says. 'Shall we check it out?'

'That's a messed-up name for a bar,' I say, making a face.

'Yep. It's old and there's a whole story that goes with it.'

'Spill.'

'I'll tell you when we get there.'

Ten minutes later, we arrive in the parking lot, which only has a handful of other vehicles. We walk around the front of the old building and go through an ancient-looking wooden door. It's dark inside and there are low wooden beams everywhere, with signs advising customers to watch their heads. I'm just reading one of the painted signs when Daniel cracks his head on one of the beams with a very loud bang.

'Ow,' he says.

'Nobody does it twice,' the bartender says, cheerfully, as Daniel crouches down like Quasimodo the rest of the way to our table.

'So what's the story with the name of this place?' I ask Daniel once we have our drinks.

'Are you sure you're ready for this? It's gory.'

'Shoot.'

'Okay. Imagine you're a serving wench at a tavern,' he says.

'Not so hard to imagine,' I say, narrowing my eyes at him.

'Right. But there's no running water in this tavern – cos, olden times – so you scurry over to the well.'

'Why am I scurrying? Am I a rodent?'

'You stride over to the well.'

I give him a thumbs-up.

'And lower your bucket down, down, down, until it reaches the water.'

'My bucket is way down there.'

'You swish it around until it's all heavy.'

'Done.'

'Then you wind it up and catch a glimpse of the contents.'

'Which is – let me guess – blood.'

'Yes. Because some murderous git dumped a body down there the night before, and you've just dropped your bucket onto a dead smuggler's head.'

'What a truly lovely story.'

'I thought so.'

'Terrible murder protocol, though,' I point out.

'It was hundreds of years ago. Times were different then. No forensic evidence to worry about.'

'I don't know…' I say. 'It still doesn't seem very smart. I'm no CSI but that seems like the very first place a body would be discovered, in a situation where there is no running water and people have to drink, like, literally every day.'

'Look, nobody likes a pedant,' he says. 'Feel free to poke holes in the plot of Alexis's first draft but nobody mocks The Bucket of Blood murderer. That's just not cricket.'

I smile. Daniel seems to be getting happier by the day. More relaxed. Less frowny.

When we've drunk our lager shandies and munched our way through matching bowls of curly fries, I turn to him and say, 'Where now?'

'We've done cruffins and chips,' he says. 'I could use a walk. There's a beach somewhere around here.'

But when we get there, the word 'beach' undersells it by a mile. It's a vast expanse of golden sand backed by a wilderness of sand dune craters, so empty we could be walking on the surface of the moon.

'So, this is something,' I say.

'We *should* have brought Alexis,' Daniel says. 'He has to set something here.'

'It's so empty,' I say, spinning the whole three-sixty. 'Why aren't there tourists? Where is everybody?'

'Newquay?' he says. 'This is off the beaten track, I guess. Let's keep going,' he says, and we walk until we're standing at the foot of a colossal sand dune.

'I feel we have to climb it,' he says, looking at his feet. He's wearing a pair of Nike sliders.

'It's too steep to climb in those,' I say, motioning to my own thong sandals. 'We're gonna have to go bareback.'

He looks taken aback. 'I mean bare*foot*,' I say, feeling my eyes widen because I've said something so ridiculous. 'Not bareback.'

'Yeah, that's, uh, something different, isn't it?' Daniel says, awkwardly.

'Doesn't it just mean riding a horse without a saddle?' I ask, innocently, and he grins.

We take off our shoes and climb to the top, my thighs burning from the steepness of the incline, which is when I notice that Daniel is staring off into the distance, to where a lighthouse stands on a rocky island, waves lapping against it.

'It's *the* lighthouse,' I say. 'Did you know?'

'It's certainly a lighthouse,' he answers.

'It's the one that Virginia Woolf wrote about in her novel *To the Lighthouse*.'

'What the fuck? Really?' he says, seemingly staggered by this information.

'Unless every source on the internet is lying to me.'

'Woolf came here?'

'She had a vacation home over in St Ives. Talland House. You can go rent it, if you have the money. Have a vacation of your own there.'

'I'll start saving up,' he says. 'Or... put it on the MasterCard.'

'It's probably booked up for, like, five years straight,' I point out. 'But you can dream.'

'Have you read much Woolf?' he asks.

'Of course. It was mandatory at college.'

'What did you think?' he asks.

'I think she'd have been a lot more chill on Prozac.'

He smiles.

'You're not what I expected,' he says.

'Ditto,' I say. 'I was expecting a big-shot agent with no sense of humour and great taste in fashion.'

'Fair,' he says. 'I do have a great sense of humour.'

There's a moment when he catches my eye, and I think I maybe want the distance between us to disappear, to get sucked away so that our bodies are touching. Chest to chest, pelvis to pelvis.

It can't be that way, though, because this is a professional relationship. If it's growing into a friendship, it has to be platonic. He knows Alexis got naked with me, and Alexis is his star writer. He wouldn't do anything to jeopardise his relationship with his star writer. And beyond that, it's clear they're friends. What kind of man would make a move on a woman his friend had just sort of almost dated? A douchebag. And Daniel is not that.

I must have it wrong; I must have gotten the wrong impression.

But in my van, we touched hands for too long. That happened. He held me steady in the waves of the cove by the poppy fields. We watched wild foxes together on the midnight beach. He came to look for me with a flashlight when I had a headache and went to swim in the ocean, afraid I might be hurt. He took Joseph away when I needed him to. He's trying to help me find my father.

Daniel leans forward and takes my hand.

'Candice...' he says, his voice so soft I can only just hear it.

My phone buzzes and I look down to see Alexis's name. I flip the phone around to show Daniel the screen. We've hit a patch of cell reception and message after message comes through. Questions about Cornwall, about surfing, about *Bridgerton*, about the qualities I find attractive in a romantic partner, about what it feels like to be head over heels in love.

'I should reply,' I say. 'Shouldn't I?'

'Go ahead. I'll meet you down there,' Daniel says, waving his hand vaguely towards the wide sweep of marram grass below us.

He picks his way down the narrow trail in the centre of the dune, past the rabbit skulls and empty snail shells, and I can tell just by his shoulders that he's feeling the same way about this as me. Catching feelings is a mistake.

I reply to one message, the one about *Bridgerton*, and Alexis calls me.

'Are you busy?' he asks.

'Not really,' I say, feeling the heat come into my cheeks.

'Having a chill-out day?'

'Something like that.'

'I'm driving myself nuts with this book. I've read the last three chapters so many times that it feels like the words are burnt into the surface of my brain. I still can't get it right. Do you think we could go out for a surf later? I need to get out of my head. You can catch your own waves. I don't need you to push me onto them any more.'

'Conditions are still bad,' I say, wondering whether Alexis has been practising without me.

'I don't mind,' he says. 'I'll practise paddle technique. We'll have a paddle battle across the whole bay if you like. Say, seven o'clock?'

I look at my watch. It's already past six and it's going to take us thirty minutes to find our way back through the dunes, assuming we don't get lost, and another thirty to drive back to Newquay.

'Can we make it seven thirty?'

'Great. It's a date,' he says, and I blink.

There's a heaviness in my chest that wasn't there before.

I always want to get into the water, no matter what the conditions, but right now I don't want to be with Alexis. I don't want to see his face and I don't want him to look at mine.

When I catch up with Daniel, he's pulled himself together a little, but he doesn't ask about Alexis. He doesn't seem to want to speak to me at all.

Something comes into my head. Anne Elliot and Captain Wentworth in *Persuasion*. One of the first things Alexis asked me was about the essence of romance. How I'd told him that for me – and maybe Jane Austen, too – it boiled down to two people longing for each other, not able to have each other, suffering in silence. They share this huge intense thing that they can't talk about. And nobody knows about it, except them.

As we climb into my van, our eyes meet for a split second. The rest of the way we keep our eyes on the road.

*

Back at Demi's house, I'm pulling my wetsuit from its hanger in the garden when my phone buzzes. It's a message from Alexis. Yet another one.

Forget the sea. Can't face it. Can we meet to talk? I need a friend.

I reply right away.

Where?

*

We meet in the centre of town, in the circular amphitheatre across from the movie theatre. Alexis arrives before me, and I see him slumped on the flagstone steps. He meets my gaze, but he doesn't look like himself. There's something missing. That glint of self-assurance in his eyes is gone.

I sit down next to him.

'What's going on?' I ask, quietly.

'I don't know. I'm having second thoughts about the entire book.'

'Why?'

'I've been doing a read-through, leading up the final chapter, and it's like nothing I've ever written before. It's not me.'

'So? It's a collaboration. Plenty of writers work in a duo. You're broadening your style and your appeal.'

'When I think of my parents reading it, or any of my ex-girlfriends, I want to curl up and die.'

'Should I call Daniel?'

'No, I don't want him to know about this.'

'Why?'

'Because he's my agent. He's not my friend. Not really.'

I exhale. Something is happening here that I do not understand, and if I don't handle this the right way, I can feel that everything is going to break bad. That Alexis is going to split and I won't see him again. Which would suck, and not only because I still haven't signed a goddamn contract. Although, I have at least been paid the first week at my day rate, which is worth more than a month of work at the café.

'What can I do?' I say. 'What do you need?'

'It's the book,' he says. 'It's messing me up. I've sent Daniel my latest pages and he says they're fine, but I know they're not. I'm selling out. I'm writing bullshit. Stuff I don't believe in. Just because I think it will be successful in the market.'

'Creatives have to eat too,' I say, trying to get him to crack a smile, trying to break this awful tension.

'I don't like what this is doing to me. The whole plotline about soulmates is making me feel inadequate, as if all my choices have been wrong.'

'Inadequate?'

'Inadequate and alone. I don't know why I can't relate to other people, but I just can't seem to get there. There's always this gulf between me and them.'

'Maybe that's okay,' I say. 'Maybe you don't need to share everything with another person.'

'I'm just wired wrong, really wrong, and writing a romance is making me realise that. It's making me unhappy.'

'So, stop. Take a break from this book and go write something else.'

'I can't. I signed a contract. If I don't deliver the manuscript on time, I'd be in breach. I'd have to give every penny back.'

'Then at least talk to Daniel. Or maybe some kind of writer therapist. It could help.'

He shakes his head. 'It won't, though. Nothing will. I know myself.'

And he really thinks he does. He thinks he can lay out all the options in his head, assess them and dismiss them before he even tries something new.

'This is my problem,' he says, scratching viciously at his shoulder. 'I shouldn't have dragged you into it.'

'I wanted to be involved. I've loved working with you and Daniel. I'm actually thinking of writing my own novel.'

'What?' he says, his chin disappearing into his neck as if he's personally affronted by the idea.

'I have this idea for a love story about a young pro-surfer guy from Hawaii – from up in my neighbourhood on the North Shore – who comes to Newquay and falls for a local girl. He sees her talent and encourages her to compete professionally. Both their lives change forever. Something like that…'

'You think you can just write this book alone?' he says.

'I know the Hawaiian junior surf scene – I competed in it. And I'm starting to know Newquay. I also know romance novels.'

'So, you'll write it, and you think it'll just be published?' he says, his eyes narrowing.

'Maybe. It happens. Isn't that how it happened for you?'

'Why would you want to, though?' he says, bitterly. 'Writing books is shit.'

'You don't really feel that way, Alexis, otherwise you'd have a different career. You'd go back to journalism.'

'You don't know what you're getting yourself into,' he snaps. 'If you really wanted to write that Bildungsroman surfer love story, we could maybe do something together, but you honestly wouldn't want to go it alone. There's so much more to it than you realise. It's not just sitting down in a café with a notepad.'

'No kidding,' I say, thinking of all the help Alexis has needed this summer, how many people in this town have offered him practical and emotional support. How much of that he's gotten from me. I've written and reworked huge sections of his novel, cut the passages that didn't fit the genre, helped to tighten the pace and develop characters. I took Bryce the dirtbag and turned him into a hero. I made Janie a heroine that readers will root for.

'Look, I'm not trying to crush your dreams here, Candice. I'm just saying it's not as simple as you think. Maybe if we both worked together on something new, if I left Janie and Bryce behind and offered my publisher this instead, it might get somewhere, but that's just a maybe. There's no guarantees.'

'I'm not asking you to write it with me, Alexis,' I say, standing up and feeling a flush of shame, because maybe he's right – who do I think I'm kidding? But, on the other hand, he's yet another guy telling me I can't do something, and I've had enough of that to last a lifetime. 'I'm doing this on my own.'

'Then you're an idiot. Your manuscript will just get rejected by agents and publishers, over and over, and it'll be a waste of your time, your talent, and it'll break your heart. Everything about publishing is a massive headfuck. All of it.'

'Then maybe you're the one who shouldn't be writing books, Alexis,' I say, turning my back on him and walking into the throng of tourists, where I know he won't follow.

Forty-Five

The day passes, and then I receive a text message from Alexis.

> I am so sorry, Candice. I was an absolute arsehole yesterday. Please forgive me.

> Don't worry. It's fine.

> It's not fine. Please let me take you out for lunch. To say thank you for everything you've done. And also sorry. Maybe tomorrow, if you're free?

I leave him on Read for an hour before I reply. Which is stupid, because, for better or worse, we're colleagues and I can't avoid him. I have to put his harsh words behind me and move past this.

> Sure. In the meantime, could I read your ebook? The one you published secretly on Amazon?

Because now that he's made me feel horrible about my

first shot at writing something alone, I'd like to see his. Weeks ago, I asked Daniel if he could get me a copy of *Exclosure*, but he couldn't find the document in his files, and said Alexis would happily email one over to me if I reminded him. I've been so busy that I haven't thought to ask him. Until now.

Exclosure? If you're sure… It's pretty gruesome, though. A bit *American Psycho*.

I'd love to read it.

Okay, I'll email you the document.

And he does. It comes through one minute later. I make it three pages before I decide I need a breather, because, while exquisitely written, the voice is so sinister and the imagery so vivid that I know it's going to give me nightmares.
I text him back.

So I read three pages of *Exclosure*. You write beautifully but your main character is going to haunt me forever if I keep reading.

Yeah, I'd stop if I were you. I'm afraid he doesn't get any more likeable as the story progresses. The first agent I sent it to called it 'gratuitously nasty', and I think she was trying to be kind. See you tomorrow. Let's say mid-morning?

Great. See you then.

*

The next day, I'm back at Alexis's place, standing outside his front door again, heart fluttering. We're getting close to the finish line and, at the end of this process, there will be a book on shelves that I helped to write. And if I do a good enough job, if I don't screw this up, that book could have my name on it, too.

'Hi,' he says. 'You're right on time.' He speaks with the hint of an American accent and I wonder if he's making fun of me, but I don't think so. I think whatever is happening to his accent, it's unconscious, like most of what I've noticed about him.

He doesn't invite me inside today. Instead, he takes a new notebook out of his messenger bag and says, 'I need to write a new passage on surfing as therapy. I've been out a few times and it's definitely made me feel more care-free in the moment, but I can't say it's made any lasting improvement to my mental health.'

'You've been surfing alone? Without an instructor?' I say, surprised. Beginners do, all the time, even though it isn't advised, but Alexis seems so by-the-book. 'Or did you employ a new instructor?'

The thought makes me cringe a little. True, he'd gotten injured when he went out with me, but what were the odds of him stomping on a weever fish?

'I went on my own. Only when the waves weren't too terrifying. Eight pounds for an hour's board-hire from the place on the beach seems very reasonable. Although,

I usually find I've swallowed quite enough seawater after forty minutes.'

'You paid to rent a board? I could have loaned you one of mine. Dropped it off at the cottage whenever you wanted,' I say, a little hurt that he hasn't asked for my help. Maybe he feels he's paying me enough already, but I'd have thrown in surf tuition as part of my rate.

'Oh, I know you would, but to be honest I didn't fancy having to lug a board from the cottage all the way around the headland to Fistral.'

'My grandma could make that walk in ten minutes.'

'I don't want to look like some poseur, as if I think I'm Keanu Reeves in *Point Break*.'

He laughs uproariously at this, like he's cracked quite the joke.

'Keanu Reeves wasn't much of a surfer in that movie. Patrick Swayze, on the other hand…'

He rolls his eyes, clearly done with Patrick Swayze appreciation. 'Do you actually believe in all that stuff about surfing being transformative? Do you think it can heal the broken people?'

'Um,' I say, 'it's a little early for the philosophy of surfing.'

'You must have an opinion,' he says, tilting his pencil in my direction.

'I guess I feel that surfing forces you to be in the moment. It stops you obsessing about the past or worrying about the future. You have to be in that moment alone, all your senses firing, all your judgement and reason focused on that wave, how to ride it and how to stop it hurting you.'

'You're talking about the adrenaline rush,' he says.

'Not just that, although that is something. I'm talking about the feeling of being really, truly whole. All the parts of your body and mind, your entire self, lining up and working together.'

His pencil scratches as he writes this down, and I wonder if at the end he's added a helpful little note for himself, like, 'Insert some kind of surfy self-help bullshit here.'

The way he hangs off my words is actually a little disconcerting. He's looking at me as if I'm an ancient stone tablet in the British Museum. Something completely other and inexplicable that he's determined to find the cipher for, even if it takes forever, even if it kills us both.

'I don't know a lot about this stuff,' I say. 'And I can't speak for other surfers, but when I'm in the water, I feel most like me. Or the me I want to be.'

'Oh, that rhymes,' he says, happily writing it all down, as he stands there, still not inviting me inside the cottage.

When he's done, he steps aside and motions to two bicycles leaning against the wall of the tiny garden outside.

'I hired them,' he says.

'Just the two? Isn't Daniel coming?' I say.

'He's got some work calls. Big agency meeting he has to dial into. Anyway, I thought the bikes would bring a new element to our lunch.'

'I guess that's true,' I say, looking them over. They seem great. Top-of-the-range mountain bikes.

'What do you think?' he asks.

I shrug. 'Decent way to work up an appetite.'

'And you take in so much more. You experience all the sensory things you miss in a car, which is obviously important to me, since I'm still trying to get a feel for the essence of the place.'

'You know,' I say, giving him a look. 'You didn't even ask if I could ride a bike.'

He looks surprised.

'I just assumed you'd know your way around one, being American.'

'That's quite the assumption. And I prefer to think of myself as Hawaiian, not American, FYI. Because there is a distinction.'

'I sense I've caused you offence but I'm not sure why,' he says.

'There's pride that comes with being Hawaiian,' I say, feeling a knot in my stomach. 'The surfing world considers Hawaii its own sovereign surfing nation. Hawaiian surfers compete for Hawaii, not the USA.'

'Why? Because it's so far away from the mainland?'

'It's complicated but that's part of it. Hawaiians were the founding fathers of surfing. Duke Kahanamoku, who popularised surfing as a sport, was actually Hawaiian nobility, born into a noble family just a few years before the overthrow of the Hawaiian kingdom. Hawaii didn't even get made a state until 1959. There's still a lot of sensitivity, a lot of hurt. It's not so long ago that it all happened.'

'Interesting. I never really thought about Hawaii like that. I've always sort of thought of it as a paradise holiday place. One big resort, you know? A bit like this town, just on a much bigger scale.'

'I would not express that opinion if you went there,' I say. 'Besides, I was kidding. I can ride a bike – I just didn't think that's what I'd be doing today. Will we make it in time for our reservation?'

'Loads of time,' he says, motioning to the door. He goes ahead and I notice he has a loaded backpack with him.

'Just a few snacks and waters,' he says, noticing my eyeline. 'I even managed to get us some root beer at the health food shop in town. Since you're American and all.'

'Yeah, you aren't going to be finishing that root beer.'

'Not good?'

'It's fine, but I've never met an English person who liked it. To you guys, I guess it tastes like cough medicine. But thank you for the sweet thought. What else do you have in that backpack?'

He thinks. 'First aid kit, bicycle pump, sunscreen, and my Leatherman multi-tool.'

'Huh, so this is like a bug-out bag?'

'What's that?' he says.

'You know, like an emergency survival kit for when the zombie apocalypse hits. Very popular with guys in the Deep South, who like to be prepared for every eventuality. Except they would have guns also.'

*

He's right about the views. The landscape here is breathtaking, every corner revealing a new vista of blue. What Alexis didn't mention, however, is that the place we're going is six miles away and those little winding Cornish lanes, which at first gave me extreme nausea whenever I tried to drive them, are also extremely unsafe for cyclists.

Mostly this is because of lost holidaymakers consulting

their satnavs or yelling at kids in the back seats of rental cars. After the third hairpin turn that nearly proves fatal, I stop in a turnout, which happens to have a world-class view of the ocean looking towards Watergate Bay.

I leave Alexis to cycle on and wonder when he'll notice that I'm no longer behind him. Pretty soon, it turns out. Within two minutes, he's biking back to me, a look of total concern on his face.

'What's wrong?' he says. 'Did you get a puncture?'

'I don't love this,' I reply, turning to look at the water some more.

'Biking?'

'Risking my life every time a vehicle blasts by me way too fast.'

'Some parts of this road are a bit dicey, I suppose,' he says, as if this is a thing that has only just occurred to him in direct response to my mentioning it. 'This ride is not quite as romantic as I'd hoped.'

I shoot him a look.

'In terms of research. For a new scene in the book, I mean,' he clarifies. 'But it's not exactly Marilyn Monroe and Arthur Miller in chic knitwear, out for some soothing cycling in the countryside, is it?' he says, wiping sweat from his brow.

'What's that?' I say, something catching my eye out on the water.

'Hmm?' he says, looking in completely the wrong direction.

'Something's on fire out there,' I say, pointing. What had been a tiny little wisp of white when I first noticed it has turned into a thick plume of smoke, which seems to be growing wider and darker by the second.

He follows my gaze and there's no mistaking it.

'That boat seems to be on fire,' he says, calmly.

'Seems to be,' I say. 'And it's not just a boat. It's a yacht. A big one. Man, I hope nobody's hurt.'

But we can see the lifeboats coming over the side already. Tiny little figures bailing. Leaving the inferno behind them.

'I hope the captain doesn't feel the need to go down with the ship,' Alexis says, in a tone I can't identify. Almost – but this can't be right – amused.

'Who says the ship is going down?' I say. 'They might put out the fire. That could happen.'

But even as I say it, it strikes me that the wind is feeling brisker. It's fanning the flames.

There's also a tightness in my chest that wasn't there two minutes ago. Then my eyes start to sting.

'Fuck it. *Fumes*,' Alexis says, covering his mouth. 'We need to get away from here. It's only going to get worse.'

The smoke has thickened and darkened further still, with every moment while we've watched, and we've already watched too long.

'Is this a bad time to tell you I have asthma?' he says, squeezing his eyes shut.

He's not looking so hot. His breathing is raspy and there's a visible pallor to his face.

'Do you have your asthma pump with you?' I ask, assuming he will because he has so much other shit in his bag.

He rummages in the backpack, then shakes his head. 'Can't find it.'

He doesn't say anything else, not wanting to breathe in more smoke.

'Wait here,' I say. 'I'll wave someone down to give us a ride back.'

I stand at the roadside, with my arm out, waiting for someone to stop but nobody does, and then the traffic ceases completely. No vehicles come from either direction.

'We have a problem,' I say.

'Fantastic,' he croaks.

'Nobody's driving by.'

He coughs into his elbow, panic in his eyes.

'Police must have closed the road because of the emergency. You sure you don't have your pump?' I say, looking at his backpack.

'Thought I had my spare in the front pocket, but it's not there. How bad are these fumes for them to close the road? Must be actual toxic fucking vapours.'

He coughs again into the wrist of his long-sleeve T-shirt.

I'm trying not to panic but I can see he's definitely finding it harder to breathe and the bay is now cloven – half turquoise, but half charcoal too, hidden under clouds of smoke.

'This is bad,' I say. 'We have to get you someplace inside. Like now.'

He nods desperately, his eyes wide with fear. But there's something else. He's trusting me to make this situation better. To get him to safety.

'We passed a hotel a quarter-mile back. We'll walk it if you can't ride.'

Alexis can't ride. We leave the bikes by the roadside, and I can only hope they won't get stolen. His eyes are streaming, and he can't take a breath without choking.

It feels like the longest walk of my life but the further we get around the bend in the road, the easier he breathes.

*

The desk in the guesthouse, when we finally reach it after ten minutes of trudging along the road, is just a dining table on a threadbare Turkish rug. An older woman with black hair and a crooked smile says, 'Good afternoon. What a thing to be happening in the bay! Do you have a booking?'

She has a thick Scottish accent and I struggle to understand her.

'No, but no cabs are running and we need to get away from the fumes,' I say. 'My friend is having breathing difficulties. I don't suppose you have an asthma pump?'

'You mean, like, an inhaler?' she says, looking doubtful. 'A puffer?'

'Yes, that's exactly what I mean,' I say.

'We have loads of them in lost property, but we're not really allowed to hand that out to guests unless they're the ones who lost it.'

'Look, my friend here is probably going to have an asthma attack if you don't give him one of those inhalers right now. The road is closed, and an ambulance is going to take too long to get here. Can you please help us?'

She takes a look at Alexis, who is not in good shape, and pulls a woven basket from under the table, which contains a whole heap of miscellaneous items, from phone chargers to hairbrushes. But there are also asthma pumps in a variety of colours. Alexis snatches up a blue one and breathes deeply as he sucks down the drugs that he needs to calm his lungs, that he needs to live.

Then he goes and sinks back into an armchair at the foot of a set of stairs and leans forward, knees apart, just breathing and looking at the floor tile.

'We'll take any room you have left,' he says. 'Any room.'

'We have a few cancellations, funnily enough. Can't imagine why,' she says, wryly, relieved now that Alexis is not going to have an asthma attack right in front of her, feeling maybe that she saved this gorgeous guy's life, which she really might have.

'Great. We'll take whatever you can give us.'

'You have a choice of a double with a farmland view or a suite with a sea view.'

'Take the suite,' Alexis croaks in a husky voice from his chair across the room. 'Then at least we can watch the burning boat.'

'You want to watch that?' I ask, trying to keep judgement out of my voice. Is he one of those rubberneckers who like to stop at road traffic accidents to gawp at people being cut out of wreckage?

'Keep an eye,' he says, and I get it. He wants to keep an eye on the situation. The rescue operation. The smoke plumes. He wants to see when things start to improve. Because if it doesn't improve soon, we're going to have to be here together overnight.

'Okay,' I say.

He hands over some kind of platinum card without blinking, fills out some paperwork and the woman passes him the room key.

'Come on,' he says, the strength coming back into him now. I try to offer him my arm, but he won't take it.

'I'm all right,' he says. 'Just a dickhead for not making sure I had an inhaler when I brought so much other crap.'

'Don't beat yourself up,' I say. 'It's human to make mistakes.'

'I don't know what's wrong with me. My head's been all over the place since I got here.'

We walk slowly around the corners of this old guesthouse and up flights of stairs because the elevator is out of service and neither of us says a thing.

He takes the old-fashioned key out of his pocket, opens the door and holds it for me, which is the first time we make real eye contact since arriving at this place.

'So, this is not a fun time for you,' I say.

'Or you,' he answers, absentmindedly now, his eyes roving over the suite, which is outdated with upholstery designed in shades of maroon and gold. A lot of stripes. A couple of darker patches on the wall-to-wall carpet.

There's a *Sights of Cornwall* book on the end table with a selection of pamphlets advertising Newquay Zoo, something called a 'Pirate Experience' and Bodmin Jail.

'Who would want to walk around a jail for fun on their day off?' I say, trying to lighten the atmosphere.

'People do,' he says. 'If you build it, they will come…' and then adds, 'Particularly true of a prison, I should think.'

I laugh at his joke, try to remain calm about all this.

There are twin armchairs set in a bay window, with a view over the ocean, where the boat is still burning furiously.

'It's drifting,' Alexis says.

'Aren't we all?' I reply, too late, so that it seems as if I am thinking this is a real statement I've made.

'Yes,' he says, his eyes still fixed on the choking fumes that could maybe kill him if he was outside right now. 'Do you have people waiting for you in Hawaii?' he asks.

'Just my brother. I don't count Joseph. Clearly. And my grandmother's in Florida.'

'That's all?'

'I mean, I have friends too.'

He nods. 'Of course. You'll make friends wherever you go. It's always easy for people like you.'

'People like me?'

'Extroverts.'

'I am not an extrovert,' I say, making a face, as if he's just insulted me.

'I heard you chatting to people in the café all day. You're a natural people person.'

'I chat to people all day because it's my job. It's exhausting. I do it because that's what I have to do to get a paycheque.'

He doesn't answer but I can tell he doesn't believe me. He doesn't understand how much that veneer of sociability takes out of me. He doesn't know how sometimes I can barely talk or think after being around so many people.

'Do you have anyone back home in London?' I ask him, because why shouldn't I, when he's crossed a line and asked about my life.

'I had a fiancée, once,' he says. 'She jilted me at the altar.'

'I'm sorry to hear that,' I say. '*Literally* at the altar?'

'Yep. Had second thoughts in the Rolls-Royce.'

'Shit,' I say. 'That's… awful.'

He sighs. 'I'm still not sure what happened. She seemed happy enough.'

I had thought he was just completely self-absorbed. But maybe he was absorbed in thinking of something else. Somebody else.

'I think I need to grab a shower,' Alexis says, getting to his feet. 'The smoke in my hair and clothes is making my chest feel weird again. I can wait if you want to go first, though.'

'Go right ahead.'

I go to the closet and swing open the doors. 'They have robes,' I say. 'We can run your clothes under the bathroom faucet, use the tiny soaps to get out the worst of the chemical stink and dry them on the heated towel rail.'

'Okay,' he says, wandering into the bathroom as if in some sort of trance. Which he could be, after inhaling toxic fumes.

I hear the toilet flush and the water begin to run. Then I'm on my own for nearly an hour. He takes the longest shower I have ever known any man to take. If showering were an Olympic sport, he'd be in line for the gold medal.

When he eventually emerges, his hair slicked back from his face like some Prohibition-era gangster, he says, 'Sorry, I couldn't seem to make myself get out. You know, when the water is burning hot, and you feel like you need to stay under it forever.'

I take a moment to think about this.

'I'm more of a cool water person.'

He nods. 'All the surfing. Cool water is where you're comfortable. Are you hungry?'

'I could eat.'

'Do you think this hotel has room service?' he says. 'Or is it not that kind of place?'

I go to the coffee table and pick up a black, leather-bound book.

'There's a menu. What shall I order for you?'

'Some kind of meat and salad. I'm trying to get back on the healthy eating wagon now the book is almost done. What about you?'

'Um, I was going to order a cheeseburger and fries.'

'Okay then.'

But, just like everything else on this day, there winds up being a problem. The roads to the entire area have been closed down, several of the lunch kitchen staff have not been able to make their shifts and the late-morning delivery truck hasn't made it through the roadblocks.

'We're not going to be able to Uber any food either, if the roads are closed,' Alexis says, groaning. 'Fuuuck. I can't actually believe this.'

'Is fasting suddenly a problem?' I ask.

'Yes. Because now that I know there's no possibility of food, I have to eat. The fast thing only works for me if it's a choice I'm making for the good of my digestive system and metabolism. Otherwise, it feels like starvation.'

'Is there nowhere in walking distance that might be open? Maybe I can tie some fabric over my mouth and walk to pick something up?'

'I don't know. I had a five-star restaurant in mind,' he says, gloomily. 'I didn't research takeaway options.'

I consult my phone and see that there is one place showing as currently open within a one-mile radius, which I hope will be doable even with toxic smoke in the air.

'What is it?' Alexis asks me, looking over my shoulder at my phone screen. I can feel his breath on my neck, and it sends a shiver of something I can't quite identify through me.

'It's called Fishionista – so I'm guessing it's a Chinese takeout.'

'Ha ha,' he says, in a grouchy voice. 'A chippy. This healthy meal I was planning, to get me back on the nutritional straight and narrow, is going to turn into a chip shop dinner. Amazing.'

'What's your order?'

He thinks for a long minute. 'I won't order fish because of the batter. Maybe a saveloy?'

'A what now?'

'You know, a long sausage thing.'

'Like a footlong dog?'

'Yes, but no bread. Just the meat.'

I bite my tongue. 'Just the meat. Anything else?'

'I'm trying to think what side dish would be high enough in protein.' He rubs his fingers through his damp hair, massaging his scalp. 'Right, I'll have a tub of mushy peas as well.'

'Mushy peas? That sounds not delicious.'

'They're actually very nice. A lot nicer than avocado. You can try mine – you'll be converted. Well, if you can get over the way they look.'

'What do they look like?'

'There's no putting a good spin on it,' he says. 'They look like a tub of snot.'

*

I get lost a few times trying to find my way along the maze of winding lanes and the GPS on my phone seems just as confused as me. There is nobody around at all, which is eerie, given Cornwall has been busting at the seams with holidaymakers since Easter.

There's a moment, right after I've collected our order, when I consider just walking the three miles back into Newquay and leaving Alexis alone in the guesthouse, but I don't know for sure that he's okay with his asthma and, sooner or later, he'll be expecting me to come back to the maroon suite and present him with a sausage, no bun. I would be bailing on him. Leaving him saveloyless and alone. And I'd have to see him day after day as we finished the book and there would be weirdness between us because I'd be the research assistant, slash co-writer, slash waitress who left him stranded in a guesthouse, hungry and alone, when he was still in the woods with a potentially life-ending condition.

I have to go back.

I walk down the centre of the road, smoke-scented wind in my hair and sun burning the skin of my nose.

The Scottish woman is no longer at the reception desk, but I can hear her voice in some distant part of the guesthouse, talking to a man and whooping with laughter like he's Ricky Gervais.

The meal in the polystyrene containers I'm carrying is emanating a rich odour of fast food that seems to fill the space and, as I walk up the stairs, I imagine it leaving a fragrant trail behind me to lure in any hungry zombie tourists stranded in this quarter.

The door to our room is locked and Alexis has to come let me in.

He seems to have set up camp in one of the armchairs by the window. He's made coffee, munched a bunch of the free oat cookies and scribbled something on the guesthouse notepad.

I can't help wondering what he's written on that notepad. A to-do list? New ideas for additional scenes? Maybe something about the catastrophe in the bay?

'You're quiet,' he says.

'Just a little out of breath from the walk. It was further than I thought. Did I take forever?'

'You were quick, but I'm sorry for making you go. My stupid fucking lungs have always let me down.'

'It's really no trouble. I have to eat too. So, they had a savalong...'

'Sorry?'

'The sausage thing you wanted?'

'Oh, a saveloy.'

'That's the one. I also got a little container of the squished-up pea thing you asked for.' I hand him his order. 'Is that okay, did I get the right thing?'

He nods, as he inspects the cartons. 'Thank you. Did they have your burger?'

'And then some. I also ordered fries, sausage in batter and some pickles.'

'Nicely done,' he says, looking impressed. 'My fiancée used to always order a gigantic pickled onion.'

There's a silence that I don't know how to fill. In the end, I just say, 'I went for the mini pickled cucumbers.'

I hold up one of my pickles to show him.

'Nice-looking gherkin you have there,' he says.

'That is a weird word. Why do British people call it that?'

'I think it's just the name of that type of cucumber, but I don't actually know.'

'I also got a pickled egg, but I'm not sure I'm brave enough to eat that.'

'You've never tried one before?' he asks, sounding quite shocked.

'I mean, I've seen the huge jars of them in backwater bars in the south of the US, but I've never felt the need to order one.'

'They're not bad. Salty. Briny. Sulphuric overtones. Perfect ocean snack.'

'Okay, I'm going in...'

'Hey, look at that,' he says, scrolling his phone. 'The name "gherkin" derives from the Dutch word "gurken", which means a small, pickled cucumber. Every day's a school day.'

'And what else have you learnt today, Alexis?'

'Not to ask women on dates that involve cycling?'

'This was a date? I thought it was a thank you.'

'Figure of speech.'

★

When we've eaten our food, we scrub our clothes with hand soap, twisting out the water together over the bathtub, each of us at different ends of the wet clothing. We leave everything to dry on the towel rail, which is when the awkwardness hits. Mostly because all we have left is our underwear.

There's a queen-size bed in the centre of the room and Alexis goes to lie on it, in his boxers, facing the ceiling. He's turned the light out but left the drapes open, the tall window a theatre to the drama of the rescue operation on the water. But I'm not watching that any more. I'm looking at him and thinking of how Makayla was so keen to get me to hook up with him, so worried about my being touch-deprived.

Maybe what I should do is walk out the door. I could find a seat in a quiet part of the hotel, and hang out there, alone.

But that would be weird. Instead, I stand up, walk to the linen cupboard, pull out one of the fluffy folded robes and put it on, walk back to the head of the bed and sit down next to him.

We don't say anything, we just lie there looking at the old-fashioned popcorn ceiling together, the plaster stippled into a texture that's less like popcorn and more like smallpox.

When I roll over to look at him, I catch a waft of scent.

'What is that... fragrance?'

'Bad?' Alexis says.

'Floral.'

'I washed my hair with the hand soap as well as the hotel shampoo.'

'You smell like the summer meadow from a detergent advertisement,' I say.

He smiles. 'You can smell adverts?'

'The scratch 'n' sniff versions, sure.'

'So, what now?' he asks, quietly.

'Now we wait.'

Sitting in silence, I can hear the people in the next room crashing around, and flicking the channel on their TV.

I must have lain down because I'm on the edge of sleep when there's a knock at the door. I can't move. The room is so hot from the central heating, which we haven't figured out how to turn down, and I feel almost hungover, but we haven't drunk anything. Alexis puts on a robe and goes to the door, the skin of his legs glistening with sweat.

The woman from the desk is there, black hair loose around her shoulders now, instead of scraped back into a bun.

'Got a bit of an update for you, love,' she says to Alexis. 'No taxis are running yet. No Ubers. No traffic of any kind. Police are turning back people on foot, telling them it's unsafe. It's like the end of the world out there. It's like the zombie apocalypse, just without the zombies.'

'Jesus,' Alexis says, as if this is a disappointment, which stings a little. Is it really so bad to be here with me?

'You'll have to stay the night. Breakfast is between 7.30 and 9 a.m. There won't be many fried eggs, because the delivery didn't come, so better get there early if you want one.'

He thanks her and closes the door.

'I think we're staying the night in this place,' he says. 'Sorry. I know you probably want to get home.'

'It's fine. I'm good,' I say, and wonder if it's time to message Daniel about this. But it would only worry him, or worse.

I'm just thinking about how badly Daniel could misinterpret the situation, when Alexis leans forward and kisses me.

I recoil and push my hand into his chest.

'No,' I say, horrified. 'What are you doing?'

'You don't want to?' he says, sounding genuinely surprised. 'Could be a nice final bit of research for the book...'

I feel my stomach lurch with disgust.

He still sees me this way? After all the time we've spent working together as co-writers – I'd thought as equals – I'm still nothing more than useful research material? A fucking muse for when he has writer's block?

'Hey, douchebag – I'm not sleeping with you for a book,' I say, trying to sound tough, but feeling as if he's punched me in the gut.

'Why not?' he says, in that way he has of making everything seem like a writer's natural curiosity.

'Because I don't want to, okay?'

'Okay, it's just... well, you're here. I'm here. There's nothing else to do. I mean, I know you've been flirting with Daniel but it's not like that's going anywhere. He's my literary agent, for fuck's sake. He's here for me.'

'I know that,' I say, my throat so tight I can barely swallow, because it's true, isn't it. Daniel is here for Alexis, not for me, and when Alexis leaves, he'll leave too.

'Okay, sorry,' he says. 'I got the wrong end of the stick. Maybe the toxic fumes have gone to my head.'

'Go to sleep, Alexis,' I say, and wait until he's snoring before I allow myself to cry as quietly as I can into a throw pillow.

*

I'm so exhausted that I don't wake up until the next day, when I hear Alexis in the shower again. He returns from the bathroom, towel wrapped around his waist, hair washed again, only with shampoo this time, and looks surprised to see me. Almost as if he forgot I was ever here.

'So, that might be my weirdest day in Cornwall so far,' he says. 'From burning superyacht to asthma attack, to spending an unexpected night in a hotel with my co-writer.'

'Mine too,' I say, wincing a little at the memory of him coming onto me. The thought of it still turns my stomach. But he's acting like it never happened.

'Are you hungry?' he asks.

I'm not, particularly. I'm still full of greasy French fries and burger, but what else are we going to do?

Our clothes are still damp when we get ready to go down to breakfast.

We reach for them on the towel rail, but somehow, I wind up with Alexis's jeans instead of my cut-offs. I pass them back, our hands bumping.

'Horizontal jean transfer,' he says, laughing at his own joke. At least I think it's a joke.

'Should I know what that is?'

'No. It's very uncool.'

'You have to tell me now.'

He takes a breath.

'It's when one organism encounters another and sort of steals genes from it. Like if a guy meets a girl with freckles and red hair and thinks, *Sexy*, and then he also gets freckles and red hair. But on a more micro-organism level.'

'Were you a science journalist in your former career?' I say. 'Because Demi will have questions.'

'No. I've just been reading a book about different types

of fungus. It helps me get to sleep. It's the only thing that does at the moment.'

'Before bed you're reading a book about *mushrooms*? No wonder you haven't been feeling the romance. What do you dream about after reading something like that?'

'Slime moulds, last night – although technically they're no longer considered fungi. They've been reclassified.'

'As what?'

'I'm not exactly sure. They're simple organisms that sort of club together and go on the rampage, consuming everything in their path... A bit like a stag party.'

I manage a half-smile.

'You know, from here on out, every time I see a bachelor party, I'm going to be thinking *slime moulds*.'

'They're actually very striking,' he says. 'Sort of technicoloured, like neon crystals. Or pretty little alien fruits.'

'Ah, so this is more of a bachelor*ette* party.'

*

The breakfast room is only half-full, but there's a line for the hot buffet. Alexis cuts the line and goes straight to the fried eggs section.

'Pre-ordered,' he says, when an older couple in the queue begin to tut.

'You just cut the line like it was no big deal. Like it wasn't even there,' I say.

'The receptionist said they were low on eggs,' he says, as if this explains anything at all.

'But people were waiting, Alexis. At least six people were waiting.'

'I know, but they don't need the protein like I do.'

It's a unique experience breakfasting with Alexis, especially as everyone in this dining hall keeps treating us like a married couple, like we've been together for years, because who else would come to a place like this? This is no motel, and no fancy Four Seasons. It's not for people having a casual liaison. It's a guesthouse for people who've made a commitment to each other.

Two different elderly couples ask us if we are on honeymoon in the time Alexis takes to eat his eggs.

'You've got the honeymoon glow,' one old man says, smirking, before getting hit on the arm by his wife, as if she's swatting away a fly.

The cringeworthiness of it all is almost too much for me. Alexis seems oblivious to any discomfort. He just tells me a story, in this very quiet breakfast hall, about how the word honeymoon comes from an old Scandinavian practice of drinking some kind of fermented honey mead during the first month or 'moon' after the wedding, in the hope that this will help in getting the bride knocked up.

'Cool story,' I say, hearing my own teeth come together with an audible clack.

*

We check out the moment that we've finished eating, and have the receptionist call us a mini-bus taxi back into town, stopping to pick up our rental bikes on the way, which have thankfully not been stolen. But there's no conversation. At one point I think I recognise the two women who did the HIIT workout beside my van, jogging on the spot at a crosswalk, ponytails swishing in tandem, but I don't tell the story to Alexis. I'm keeping that one for me.

I still feel tearful. I know rationally that I've done nothing wrong, but the place where my shame lives is flashing lights and blaring sirens. Sooner or later, Daniel is going to hear about this sleepover with Alexis.

We sit in silence, waiting until we can get away from each other.

*

'How mad was that boat fire yesterday?' Makayla says, not even seeming to know that I didn't come home last night. Perhaps she went to bed early or thought I'd slept in the van.

'Crazy,' I say. 'Do you know what happened?'

'Mechanical failure is what they're saying. It's been all over the national news. Imagine if it was an insurance job, though? It could have been.'

'That would be some insurance payout,' I say. 'It shut down the whole area.'

'So,' she says. 'Who were you with last night?'

'Who says I was with anyone?'

'That massive hickey on your neck is saying it loud and clear.'

'What?' I say, touching my throat.

'You're too easy,' she says, smiling. 'So... Daniel?'

'No. We're just colleagues.'

'Sure you are,' she says. 'And the Poet is a poet.'

My phone dings with a message.

Daniel.

Have you seen Alexis? He didn't come home.

I stare at the phone in my hand. I don't want to lie, but I don't want to tell the whole truth, either.

He's fine. He had an asthma situation but he seems okay now. He should be home soon.

Daniel's reply, which comes after ten minutes, is the shortest message he's ever sent me. No jokes. No emojis.

Okay thanks.

Forty-Six

The café is still undergoing final renovations but Demi's planning for the reopening party. I'm at a loose end, because the ocean is still flat, and I haven't heard from either Daniel or Alexis since we got home from the hotel – something I'm trying not to overthink, but which keeps gnawing at me like woodworm. So, when Demi asks if I fancy some manual labour to keep my hands busy and stop me pacing around her house, I say yes before I even know what she wants me to do.

Paint the shack, is her answer, since I did such a bang-up job on my homemade signage, and she's having the local paper come to take photos of the café's remodel.

The shack is built of slats, overlaid like a fence, and there are so many edges and surfaces that it's going to take a while. The paint is sea green and so bright that the midday sun hits on it and dazzles me, but at least she sprang for the expensive 'eco' stuff that doesn't reek or give people stomach issues for two days after.

I have my earbuds in so that I can listen to Carrie Underwood singing about a tired mom's stealth drinking and secret smoking, which makes me think of my own mom. I could never listen to this on speaker back home. Joseph despised country tunes, so I had to pretend to hate them too, in case he thought I was disputing his superior taste in music. But I feel those tunes in my soul – the sadness of them, the anger, the longing.

I look down, startled by a skittery movement coming toward me. It's a spider, one that I've somehow managed to cover in paint. It seems disorientated, as if it doesn't have any idea where it's going, and I have the terrible thought that I've painted over all eight eyes and made it blind. But when I look a little closer, it seems like I've maybe just painted its butt.

I take my glass of sun-warmed water and carefully pour it over the little guy. It washes him sideways. Maybe some paint comes off its booty, but I doubt it.

The ground here slopes a little and I have to reach up on tiptoes to hit the top part of the wood. I've only finished a little of the area when I hear a person clearing their throat.

I turn to see him standing a way off, like he's worried to get closer, in case I flick paint at him.

'Can I help you with something, Daniel?' I ask, smiling.

'You have good painting technique,' he says. 'It's very *Karate Kid*.'

'Where's Alexis?' I ask.

'Still writing.'

'He's finally nailing the draft?'

'Seems to be,' he says, looking uncomfortable. 'Do you want a hand with the painting? I suspect that the repetitious movements might be soothing to me. Or maybe I'll learn some new fighting moves.'

'You sure? I still have about two miles of wood to get through.'

'Solidarity?' he says. 'Helping a person in need?'

'Okay. Thanks. You might want to change out of your shirt.'

He's wearing a blue soccer shirt that looks brand new and extremely counterfeit. There's a good trade in them at the local car boot sales, according to Makayla. Maybe a gift from Kristoff. Instead of going back to the cottage to change into some ancient holey shirt, he takes off the soccer shirt and throws it onto the sand.

He has tattoos across his well-defined chest and upper arms. Tattoos that mostly appear to represent Celtic art and one of which is a woman's name.

'Who's Emily?' I say, looking at a spot above his left pectoral. 'Favourite Brontë?'

'First girlfriend,' he says, sheepishly.

'Aww,' I say. 'You're totally a romantic.'

'I thought about trying to change the wording to "Family", but figured that's even weirder. I'll probably just block it out with a manly skull and crossbones when I get around to it.'

'You should keep it,' I say. 'It's part of your story. It's cute.'

'Just what every man wants to be,' he says, looking amused.

'Anyhow, change into something old and ruined is what I meant. You could have borrowed one of my "dad chic" shirts. Your top half is going to get covered in paint now; you're going to spend tonight picking paint drops out of your belly button.'

I feel my face flush as my gaze lingers on his navel area.

He smiles at me. 'Or I could find a person to do that for me.'

'Lucky person,' I say.

'Anyway, I need to catch some rays. Gotta get that Vitamin D.'

Daniel looks like he's been getting enough sun on him already, his already tanned skin darker from the week's heatwave, but I'm not his mother to tell him to go slap on the factor fifty sunblock. If he wants to go full radiation burns, that's his call.

I turn and feel him following me around to the back of the shack, and I'm suddenly weirdly aware of the fit of my shorts. Are they riding up my thighs, digging in and revealing my underwear? I don't know; he definitely isn't saying anything about it, but I can feel his eyes on me.

I go into the shack and grab another can of paint. It has four little metal clips around the rim, which need to be prised off with a screwdriver. Daniel takes it and tries to open it.

I don't help him do this, but I watch him out of the corner of my eye. He tries to pull off the clips with his bare hands and the metal shoots straight up beneath his fingernail.

'Owie,' I say, kind of mesmerised by the drop of blood oozing from his nail.

'Shit, fuck, shit,' he says, then seems to remember something and takes a teensy key-fob penknife out of his cargo shorts pocket and has the clips off in a flash.

'Sucks you didn't remember that ten seconds ago,' I say, handing him a smaller brush for painting all the awkward, hard to reach places.

'Hmm, I'm not really thinking straight,' he says, smiling wanly.

Does he think something happened last night between Alexis and me? Did Alexis tell him about it? Misrepresent it in some way?

There's no obvious way to bring up the subject and he isn't asking anything about our guesthouse adventure, so maybe I should just leave the topic alone.

I turn my back to him and start up the tunes on my phone speaker. If he sticks this out, between us, we'll have the painting done in a day, and Demi will have one less thing to worry about.

I've barely finished this thought when Daniel asks a question about my taste in music, which leads to a three-hour conversation about obscure bands and country singers.

Demi comes an hour before sundown to bring us pizza and drinks and to tell us we've done enough and should stop, but we don't. We're so close now that we can't bear to walk away until we have every inch of this covered.

We work until the sun goes down, and then some more by the fading light. The wind drops, the evening birds fly above us, and the bats begin to dart, at which point Daniel says we need to do another complete coat, which is ridiculous, but the instructions on the paint can apparently say it's essential.

'What's the point of doing it, if you don't do it right?' he asks, and for a moment I think he's being skeevy in some way, but he is literally just talking about paint. But maybe also life.

At 11.20 p.m. it's pitch black but still humid, and my arms are on fire with the strain of raising them over my head for so long, but Daniel is absorbed in the task, working only from the light cast by his phone, which he's slotted into an iPhone bicep band that he says he uses for running and dawn beachcombing. He's got it set to flashlight mode and his jaw is tense with determination.

I call to him, but he has earbuds in now so we're not making a noise disturbance, and he doesn't hear. I have to go up to him and touch him on the shoulder before he registers my presence. Then, paintbrush still in his hand, he looks at me for a few whole seconds, the longest stretch of eye contact yet. He takes off my cap and kisses me gently on the forehead.

'Okay,' I say, totally confused by this head-kiss, which is pretty much the last thing I'm expecting from him.

'Thanks for today,' he says.

'Why? I should be thanking you for helping me. Which I am. You were super helpful. You were great.'

'I needed this,' he says. 'Really.'

'Thankless manual labour?'

'I needed to accomplish something visible, you know? I needed to see something that I made better.'

'I get it,' I say.

'Alexis is not the only one who's been failing at something this year. I got a bollocking yesterday at the agency meeting for not selling any manuscripts to publishers lately.'

'Define lately.'

'Five months… If I don't make another sale soon, they'll replace me.'

'I'm sorry. That sounds like a lot of pressure.'

'I'm just thankful that Alexis didn't break his contract. That would've been the end of me, I think.'

I nod, but don't know what to say. It hurts to think of Daniel failing, when I know he tries so hard, when I know how much he loves the books he represents.

'I think there's rain coming,' he says.

'I hope not,' I say, looking to the horizon. 'This is quick-dry paint, but that rain had better hold off another three hours, else Demi's patio is going to be Jackson Pollocked.'

'I don't think it's going to hold off,' he says, looking at the sky. 'I think it's coming soon.'

'Fantastic,' I say, already imagining the clean-up operation tomorrow, scrubbing flagstones with methylated spirit.

'Do you want to walk through town?' he says, suddenly.

'You want to walk through town in the dark, in the rain?'

'I can see it easier when there's nobody around,' he says.

'No tourists standing in front of the storefronts and blocking your view?'

'More feel it than see it, I suppose. I can feel the history better. In the old fishermen's cottages, in the grand banks of the high street. You can almost hear the hooves of the horses that used to pull carts down the streets.'

'Huh, so you really are a romantic, Daniel. At least, you're sounding suspiciously like one right now.'

'Maybe,' he says, shrugging. 'I definitely entered a melancholy state when I read the ending of *The Lord of the Rings*.'

'You did? Why?'

'I was overwhelmed by the beauty of Aragorn and Arwen's love story.'

'How old were you?'

'Nine.'

'You did not read *The Lord of the Rings* when you were nine,' I say.

'My dad was really into watching sport,' he explains. 'All sports, not just football and rugby, which I did actually enjoy – and he was out of work for years so there was basically nothing *but* sport on TV. I think that's probably what turned me into a reader.'

'Your dad decided all the shows you watched?'

Daniel nods. 'He didn't want us rotting our brains with too much telly. He said if he put on stuff he knew we'd hate, we'd do something else. Formula One races, golf tournaments, snooker games that put me to sleep. Tennis. Darts. Badminton. Ski fucking Sunday. The only thing he wouldn't watch was basketball, because he couldn't stand the timeouts. All that stopping and starting did his head in. Boxing was probably the worst, though. My brothers still take the piss because I always had tears in my eyes whenever the losing boxer got hammered. To be fair, they generally looked like Carrie after she'd been doused with that pail of pig's blood.'

I reach up to touch him on the cheek. 'That's pretty sweet of you, you know.'

'Oh yeah, that story gets me all the ladies.'

'You tell it a lot, huh?'

'Are you mad? I'm mortified that I just told you. Please don't sell me out to the *Daily Mail* if I ever get on *Love Island*.'

'I can't promise that. It's just too juicy a tale,' I say, grabbing my jacket from the shack. 'All right, Chatty Cathy – are we walking or standing around here gabbing all night?'

*

Daniel and I walk through the streets of town without speaking, because a storm is coming and the wind is loud, and we look through the windows of the fishermen's cottages we pass. A tall man is rocking a tiny baby, singing something we can't hear. A woman is ironing laundry in front of a flickering TV.

A few night-joggers weave around us, checking in with their fitness apps, and then it goes completely quiet, and we don't see anyone.

We stop for a breather in a playground, just as the rain starts. Everything looks old, all the colours dull and faded. There are no children around now. There's just the storm wind and us.

We sit side by side on the swing-set, watching the gulls wheel above our heads, as if they're enjoying the drama of the storm, too.

Daniel waits until the rain is coming down hard before he stands up and reaches his arms into the night sky, as if there's something about the rain that he wants. Needs. I stand up too and he looks at me, and leans forward to brush away a piece of leaf, the size of a baby's fingernail, from the shoulder of my jacket.

When I look up again, he places his hands gently on the curve of my waist and meets my gaze. I can feel his strength drawing me toward him and I can hardly breathe.

Our lips are about to touch, when a flash of lightning cleaves the sky and a thunderclap erupts what seems like right over our heads.

The moment is over.

We're running for cover when his phone rings.

It's Alexis. He tells Daniel that the old coastguard's lookout – the whitewashed shelter at the top of the headland, just a hundred feet from the cottage – has been struck by lightning.

Of all the places in Newquay that lightning could have hit, it was the lookout. A message from the gods, my mom would have told me, absolutely believing it.

Look out.

Forty-Seven

The next day, the thing I sensed was going to happen, finally happens.

Because hurt people hurt people?

Nope.

Because Alexis is a dick.

I notice a crowd of people taking photos of the lightning-scorched lookout as I take the path down to the cottage, where Daniel has been staying the past few days on account of a tourist surge in the Travelodge. I'm happy to tell Daniel the paint has bonded to the wood and there's no clean-up operation necessary, and to officially invite him and Alexis to the Demigorgons reopening party, with an invitation that Makayla has hand-drawn just for them, featuring three women who look suspiciously like Demi, Makayla and me, but with snakes for hair.

But when I get there, Daniel's rental car is gone, nobody answers the door and the downstairs shades are pulled – all except one. I go to look through the living room window, putting my hands against the glass to shade my eyes from the sun's glare, and see that Alexis's chaotic and garbage-strewn workspace is now clean. All his papers and books have gone. All his takeout cartons and beer bottles have been disposed of. There's nothing in there at all. The cottage is empty, completely fucking cored, and Alexis is in the wind.

And so, it seems, is Daniel.

After everything we've shared, all the places we've visited, all the evenings we've worked together into the night, lovely, kind, funny Daniel has ghosted me?

I sit on the rocks and look out to the ocean where the waves are still raging from the storm, and salt-wind is blowing so fierce that I couldn't stop my tears even if I wanted to. I put my face in my arms, feeling the wind buffeting against my bare skin, and crash into a wave of desolation that completely sinks me. I weep for my mother, my father, for Joseph and Issy, for everything I left in Hawaii, for the writing career I could have had and now won't, and for this kind Englishman who I seem to have lost, too.

When I get hold of myself enough to at least breathe properly, I realise I've had things wrong from the start. I've let myself think that vulnerability is a flaw. I've let myself believe that it was my own fault that Joseph hurt me so badly, because I let my guard down and gave him an opportunity to hurt me. But I realise now that I've been wrong – all this time I've been wrong. I couldn't make Joseph take a different path, no matter what I did, and I can't go through life protecting my heart with a Faraday cage. Those sparks of electricity I felt with Daniel hit their mark, and even if he's gone now, even if those weeks with him are all I'll get, it wasn't wrong, or shameful, to want that connection.

'The cottage is completely empty,' I say to Makayla when I get back to Demi's house. I hand her back her beautifully drawn invitation and she gapes, for once lost for words. 'I've just been down there and Alexis is gone. No sign of Daniel either.'

Daniel has left with his client. Of course he's left with his client. What else was he going to do? Stay in this provincial little beach town for me?

I could text him. I could call. But that will only make things harder, for both of us.

So I do the opposite. I bring up his number on my phone and hit 'Block'.

Forty-Eight

The parking lot is full when I arrive in my best dress for the party. All the regular customers are here, as well as a bunch of Demi's family and friends and some tourists she got chatting with on her walk up the beach.

Looking at the café, I can't help thinking how weird it will be to go back to working here after this crazy summer of writing a book that never even belonged to me. After weeks of dreaming up scenarios for fictional lovers. After soaking my soul in romance for so long that it dissolved all the self-protective sense out of me.

A teenage boy is handing out lines of black electrical tape and giving them to partygoers to cover their licence plates – so they won't have to pay for parking, and they won't get caught by the extremely zealous parking eye camera that monitors the entrance and exit of the parking lot.

Makayla and Demi are meeting me here as they've come early to set up the place with silver streamers and balloons, as well as to have pre-drinks with their boyfriends. They invited me to attend, but I didn't want to be the fifth wheel.

I don't allow myself to think of Daniel and Alexis, who Makayla will now only refer to as 'The DFLs' – to mean

Dead Fucking Loss rather than *Down From London* – because she is furious.

I'm not thinking about them. They won't ruin this moment. This isn't about them.

Instead, I think about how much this town feels like home, and how even if I haven't managed to do what I came here for, haven't found my birth father, maybe that's okay, because maybe what I have found is even better. In Demi and Makayla, I've found a mother and a sister.

So many of the café customers used to ask me how I wound up in Newquay. They'd ask me why I chose to come to this surf beach out of all the amazing surf beaches in Europe.

I'd say I'd seen it in a magazine. On a list of top ten surf destinations to visit for a beach vacation. And that was true. I had. But that wasn't the reason I came here.

How could I turn around and tell those strangers that I was here because my husband had betrayed me in the worst way?

How could I tell them I was trying to find my biological father, who my mom had lied about right until she couldn't any more? That by working in this small café at the heart of Fistral Beach, I was secretly hoping to run into him one day, because he had been right here. In 1992, when I had been conceived, he was a lifeguard on this beach.

The problem, though, was that my mom didn't know his name.

It started a couple of years ago, when the emotional distance between Joseph and me was so great that we didn't even spend our evenings in the same room. I read in the bedroom, and he scrolled the internet on his phone in the living room. I could feel him drawing away from me and, even though I didn't know who he was pulling toward, I think I knew even then that there was somebody.

I decided to write up our family tree as a hobby, a thing I'd present to my mom on her birthday – maybe framed, even.

Once I'd joined the genealogy site, it seemed natural to take an ancestry DNA test to find out where my ancestors were from. I didn't think about the consequences. It was just something to take Joseph off my mind because he was so angry, so bitter, and I wanted something happy, something that was just for me.

It took three months for the results to come in and, when they did, they showed the strangest thing. One half of my ethnicity estimate was Northern European, which fine, that made sense, but what didn't make sense was that I had a whole heap of relatives in the south-west of England. Hundreds of them.

Subcategory: Cornwall.

Once I had the results to show my mom, she didn't even try to deny it. She swore me to secrecy, made me promise I wouldn't tell Ricky – a promise I later broke when I came here – or even Joseph, but she told me everything, which wasn't much, in fact, because she'd only hung out with the guy for a couple of hours and the sea wind was so loud that day that she hadn't caught his name when he introduced himself and, once he'd kissed her, it had seemed rude to ask something like that. All she remembered of my biological father was that he had blue eyes that made her go weak at the knees, a line of freckles across his nose, and hair like a hippie. Real surfer-boy hair. The hair you see in movies about beach bums chasing the endless summer.

His name, she thought, maybe began with an R or a L. It might have been Ray, she thought. Or Lee. Or Liam. But then again it could have been Ian. Or Kai. It was something short, for sure.

Knowing the truth felt like an insult to the man who'd raised me – even though we were never close, even though he was dead eighteen years by then, even though my mom assured me he never knew the truth.

It felt like I'd betrayed everyone by taking that test, by forcing my mom's back to the wall.

Going to visit my biological father's hometown with a view to maybe locating him was a whole other level of wrong.

It was out of the question. It had to be out of the question. But when my mom died, the idea of a second father burnt in me like torchlight, even through all my grief. It wouldn't let up. I just needed to know who he was. To see his face, hear his voice. Just one time. Then I would go home; but I couldn't rest until I had done this thing. I needed it for me.

And, even if I failed, I wanted to learn about the place where half my ancestors had lived their lives.

My mom never came back to Cornwall, not even when she was in London for her thirtieth birthday trip. Seeing this beach again would have been too hard on her. Reminding her of her secrets, her lies, her youth – all of which would have brought pain that she did not wish to carry. It was easier to pretend that one evening's roll in the sand had never happened. That my dad had been my biological father, even though she knew that was impossible, because she was already three weeks late for her period by the time she even slept with my dad again, and they hadn't shared a bed in the longest time.

I don't want to think my dad did the math; maybe he just thought I came early. Did he have a right to know that my mom had been impregnated by a stranger from Cornwall who she'd never seen again? Maybe he did have a right, so that he could make a different choice, but he never got it. And in the end, they stayed together even though they weren't happy. Right up until my father left for the rig, they made the choice that sticking together was better than living apart, even when so much was already wrong between them. Should one split-second decision undo that choice? Should it bring everything else into question?

Maybe.

*

There are so many men in their fifties in this town who my father could be. It could be the guy who helped me throw stranded pilchards back into the ocean, it could be Matt, head of the Fistral lifeguards team, or Clive the council trash collector who drives the tractor along the beach each morning. It could be the carpenter. But it isn't any of them, and part of me senses that when I finally meet my father, I'll somehow just *know*.

The party finishes up and people take their doggy bags of leftover canapés and cake with them. Eileen the Avon lady takes three whole trays of crudités, which haven't been touched by the guests, with the intention of batch-cooking enough soup to take her through the winter. She loads them into the trunk of her car, which is stuffed full of white paper bags for her next Avon delivery run.

Demi comes over to me, looking hesitant.

'Are you okay?' she says. 'You look upset.'

I turn to her. 'I think I've made a decision.'

'Oh?' she says, narrowing her eyes.

'About my future.'

'You're not leaving us, are you?' she says, panic in her voice.

'It's about the shack. I'm giving you back the keys.'

'You're giving up on your surf tuition business?'

'It's not what I want to do. I don't think it was ever what I wanted to do. I think I was just trying to prove something to Joseph, and I don't need to do that any more.'

'Good for you, love,' Demi says. 'So now what?'

'I think I'm supposed to do something else, but I don't know if I'm brave enough to try.'

'Of course you are,' she says. 'You're a dauntless spirit, Candice. I could tell that the first time I met you. Shoot your shot.'

'I have this idea for a novel. My own novel.'

'Shit, Candice,' Makayla says, appearing from the kitchen, holding half an unpeeled carrot, which she's munching on like a rabbit. 'You have to go for it. You'll be *amaaazing*.'

'I don't know about that,' I say, already feeling a little pressure. 'But I want to try. Do you mind that I don't want to use the shack any more, Demi?'

'Mind? It was the shelter for the *bins*. I was going to demolish it with a sledgehammer, before you asked for the key.'

'Could we do that now, do you think?' I say.

'Well, actually. . . I do still have the sledgehammer out back,' she says. 'But you don't want to do it now, do you? Wearing your pretty dress? And right after you've just painted the thing?'

'I really, really do,' I say.

★

Demi returns with a two-pound sledgehammer, and we walk outside, where the carpenter is smoking a cigarette.

'Budge over, mate. We're doing some demolition,' Makayla says.

'Um, you won't be,' I say. 'Not with a broken leg.'

'Okay, I'll film it for Instagram.'

'Not for Instagram,' I say, groaning.

'For posterity then,' she says.

'If you need more hammers, I have loads of them in the van,' the carpenter says.

★

It takes us thirty minutes to bring down the freshly painted shack, as tourists watch, and some lend a hand. When it's down, the carpenter saws the wood into small pieces, while Demi oversees the removal of any parts containing nails, and then writes a sign in Sharpie on a huge piece of cardboard, which says: 'FREE WOOD FOR FREE SPIRITS'.

All the wood goes within the hour and, as the sun gets lower in the sky, the beach is covered in little fires, more than I've ever seen here or on any other beach, for that matter.

And that's when my father comes, attracted by so many flames.

400

He's walking the cliffs as he does every day, from his house up on Pentire headland, coming every morning and night down to the beach to see what the tide has washed up, what it's left for him to find. Some days he brings his metal detector and sometimes he searches eyes-only.

Like today.

I see him here, only a little grey visible in his beard, and long hair, loose around his shoulders. Sparkling eyes. And I get that feeling again, of recognition. He looks at me sharply, and then our chef Jeremy comes out.

'Elliott,' he says. 'You made it. I thought you weren't going to come, you antisocial bastard.'

'I wasn't, but I saw the fires and wondered what was happening. Thought it might have been hippies. Or witches.'

'I think the witches are all up at a convention in the Headland Hotel,' I say, smiling.

'That's right,' he says. 'We all used to hang about outside when they were filming the original Roald Dahl movie there in the late eighties. We were desperate to get a photo with Angelica Huston or Rowan Atkinson.'

'Did you manage it?' I ask, warming to this man, with his vivid blue eyes.

'Nope, not even one,' he says, sighing. 'But my mum worked there as a chambermaid and got me some autographs. She said Jack Nicholson kept sending Anjelica enormous bouquets of flowers, which set off Mum's hay fever horrendously.'

'Candice,' Jeremy says, 'this is my husband, Elliott.'

'Did you say Janice?' Elliott says, looking at me again.

'Candice,' I say. 'But Janice was my mother's name.'

'You're American and your mother was called... Janice?'

he says, still staring at me with an intensity that goes through me.

'She lived in Newquay for four years,' I say. '1991 through 1995. You knew her?'

'I think so. But only for one night,' he says, slowly. 'Back before I'd worked some things out. Worked myself out.'

He reaches out a hand to me and I realise I know him. He was there with the crowd looking at the rare birds.

'I think we've met before,' I say. 'You were looking at those crows with the red beaks. You said there were more of them around than people think.'

'Cornish choughs,' he says. 'Yes, I remember. I was with Jeremy's sister that day. She told me off for teasing her about her skills of observation.'

'*No one likes a smart ass*,' I say, my fingers making quote marks as I remember her words, which had made me think of Makayla – the very smartest of smart asses.

'Yeah, that sounds like Anne,' Jeremy says.

'You also said choughs and crows are part of the same family,' I say, hesitantly, so much emotion rising within me that I couldn't stop the tide, even if I tried.

'I did,' he says, tears falling too. 'Like us, so it turns out.'

'Fucking hell,' Jeremy says, shaking his head in wonder, but smiling at me.

'I can't believe it,' Elliott says. 'You're the spitting image of Janice.'

'And you,' I say, holding his hands in mine, 'are my father.'

★

We sit down, drink the red wine that Demi brings, and talk all the way through our tears.

'I spent thirty years looking for treasure on this beach,' he says later, looking into my eyes, the lines around his own radiating outwards like sunbeams. 'Never found anything good.'

'No?'

He shakes his head. 'Lots of ring pulls and fishing weights, bits of scrap metal – once found a tiny brass bell that fell off an old ship – but I never found anything worth getting excited about. No treasure.'

I nod, wondering where he's going with this.

'Until today,' he says, patting my hand. 'Today I found you.'

*

Jeremy and Elliott are going to leave for the dunes together, to talk, but everyone exchanges numbers before we separate.

'I can't believe I didn't ask you about my father,' I say to Jeremy, before he goes. 'I'm an asshole.'

'You made your assumptions,' he says, pursing his lips before flashing me a smile.

'I really did,' I say, and he nods.

'I slept with a lot of women before I came out, you know. Way more than Elliott. I could have been your father, for all you knew,' Jeremy says, kissing me on the cheek. 'Wouldn't that have been something?'

'Well, you're not,' Elliott says, firmly. 'Go find your own long-lost daughter and stop trying to steal mine. By the way, Candice, you didn't happen to run into a detectorist on the beach this summer, did you? A man about my age, who helped you chuck stranded pilchards back into the water?'

'I did, as it happens,' I say. 'Why – who was he?'

Jeremy laughs. 'Only Elliott's mortal enemy.'

'Derek is not my enemy, even if he did detect a gold sovereign on a Cornish beach – the only person I've ever known who has,' Elliott says.

'You search together?' I ask.

'Absolutely not. But he is one of four members who attend my monthly detectorist club. He mentioned he'd met a young American girl on the beach, who was very keen on attempting the impossible, which he said made him think of me.'

'That's Newquay for you,' Demi says. 'Everybody knows everybody. If you want to be anonymous, forget it, because somebody knows you and they're probably telling someone else your business right at this very moment.'

'I can't wait to tell him that the girl he met is my daughter,' Elliott says, grinning. 'He doesn't even have a cat.'

*

I watch Elliott and Jeremy as they walk the dune path holding hands, until I can't see them any more. Demi and Makayla have followed the carpenter and Travis to the beach bar for celebratory tequilas, but I tell them I'm beat and need an early night. All I want to do is crawl into bed and fall asleep to the sound of the waves.

Except, when I turn to look towards the beach, I see a figure standing there, waiting for me to notice him. Not Alexis. Not Joseph.

'Daniel,' I say.

'Alexis made me drive him back to London,' he says. 'The arsehole.'

'He is really... something.'

'I tried to call you, but you blocked my number,' he says.

'I sure did,' I say. 'Wait – you drove him all the way to London and came right back down?'

'Yep. Twelve-hour round-trip. Few near misses with kamikaze rabbits. And I can no longer feel my left buttock – those car seats are brutal. Remind me never to buy a bloody BMW.'

We both get quiet, look out at all the little fires dotted along the beach, which are still burning, but lower now. And at the fancy drone, which is back, high in the sky, like the spaceship from *E.T.*

'So, I found my father,' I say.

'You did? Who is he?'

'His name is Elliott, but he used to go by Lee in the nineties. He told me he thought that name sounded "straighter", and also,' I say, nodding at the drone, 'less like that whiny kid from *E.T.*'

Daniel looks down at his shoes, awkward, as if not knowing what to say.

'I'm so sorry about Alexis bailing,' he says.

'Did he say anything to you about a guesthouse?' I ask, because I'm burning to know the answer.

'He did mention you'd been to one, but I didn't like to ask questions...'

'It was nothing. We shared a bed but only to sleep.'

'It's fine. None of my business at all,' he says, but he looks so relieved. 'So... you don't have feelings for him?'

'No, and he doesn't for me, either. Really.'

He shuts his eyes for a few seconds, exhales.

'So, I guess Alexis no longer wants me as a co-writer?' I say, grimly. 'Now the work is done?'

'He's being a dick. We've had words. Some of them slightly... heated.'

'Oh?' I say, trying to imagine that conversation.

'He's not going to screw you over. I won't allow that to happen. I've made myself very clear to him. If he lies about or fails to disclose your involvement, I'll set his publisher straight. He has one day to come clean himself, and then I'm picking up the phone and calling his editor.'

'Thank you,' I say, exhaling in huge relief and gratitude.

Then I begin to tell him all about the coming-of-age love story I've started to write. Set here. Inspired by this warm and wonderful beach community, which has given me so much, which has given me everything I needed. I let him hear the pitch line and show him the blurb I have written on my cell phone.

'It's good. Maybe even some TV adaptation potential, too,' he says. 'Write it the best you can, and it just might sell. I'll do whatever I can to help you.'

'Don't worry, I won't ask you to be my agent,' I say. 'I don't want any special favours. This needs to be something I do on my own.'

'Good, because I haven't had the best luck in selling things lately. You'll want to go for a more successful literary agent. Someone hot right now. Someone who's mentioned in *The Bookseller* more than once a year... On a good year.'

'You think you could point me in the right direction?' I say, hesitantly, because I still don't know what he's doing here. What this means.

'Sure, I can give you some names. There are some amazing agents who are really kicking arse – who are looking for stories just like yours.'

'Really?'

'One of them is my university nemesis. Biggest advance I've ever secured a client? Five figures. Her biggest advance for a client? Seven figures. She has incredible taste.'

'But she's your nemesis?'

'Well, not really. It's just that at university she was always number one whenever I scraped my way up to number two. She represents some fantastic books now and she's always on the lookout for strong new voices. You can say I recommended her, although I'm not sure that would help. She finds me irritating. Says my sense of humour needs work.'

I smile. 'You don't say.'

'It's fine,' he says, looking sheepish. 'I know constructive criticism when I hear it.'

'On that... Would you change anything in my synopsis?'

'There is one change you could make,' he says. 'As a special favour to me.'

'Anything,' I say.

'Promise you'll name the local knobhead bad boy after me.'

'You want me to do that?' I say, grinning.

He shrugs. 'Might give me some street cred at the agency Christmas party.'

His phone rings and he takes it out of his back pocket. Shows me the display.

Alexis.

There's a moment when I think he's going to take the call. Then he clicks decline, turns the phone to silent and slides it into the back pocket of his pants.

'That can wait,' he says. 'I'm off the clock.'

I smile so hard my face aches. 'People are saying there's going to be an incredible sunset tonight. And then there's some planetary alignment thing happening.'

'I saw on the news,' he says. 'A planetary conjunction.'

I bring up the details on my cell phone and read to him that Mercury, Venus, Mars, Jupiter and Saturn are going to be visible to the naked eye.

'Saturn's going to be first, at midnight,' I say. 'We should be able to see her clearly, because her rings are going to make her extra-bright. Mercury will be the last to appear, around 3.30 a.m.'

'So... this is definitely a night to remember,' he says, looking at me.

'The first time in a thousand years that they've even appeared in that part of the sky together,' I say, still reading from my phone. 'The last time was AD 949. There was no new quay here then. It hadn't even been considered. It was just ancient smelters looking up at the sky.'

'Want to walk down to the water's edge?' he says. 'Watch the sun go down?'

'Yes,' I say, and we stand together, saltwater lapping our shoes as the sun dips into the ocean, just like the lovers I saw here before, standing here waiting for the sun to set, for the right moment to do something.

At the moment the sun dips into the sea, Daniel turns and kisses me, and we don't go back to my van until the sun has set, the sky has darkened, and all the planets are shining above us.

Forty-Nine

Daniel and I are sitting on Adirondack chairs on Lusty Glaze beach, a little tipsy from several glasses of Cornwall's finest sparkling wine.

'You know, this is the only place in Cornwall where you can actually get married on the sand?' I say to him, as he takes my hand and kisses my wrist, like he's not even aware he's doing it.

'It was the perfect place,' Daniel says. 'But definitely not an Austen wedding.'

'Austen's characters would love this place,' I say, confidently, looking around at the happy tourists in swimwear, playing volleyball.

'Wouldn't they be horrified by all the flesh on show?' he asks, as a guy in very tight trunks walks past, accompanied by a girl in a white string bikini.

I give this some thought.

'I don't think they'd care about cleavage – breasts weren't that big a deal back in the day. They weren't sexualised in the same way. If you were a lady, you could totally have your portrait taken with your bosoms up and at 'em, and major cleavage was standard for eveningwear, but yeah, all these naked thighs would cause a scandal.'

He looks down at his own muscular thighs and gives them a reassuring pat.

'That's a shame,' he says. 'These are my only good feature.'

'They're not,' I say.

'What's wrong with them?' he says, a little hurt.

'I just meant you have plenty of other excellent features.'

He grins and checks his wristwatch.

'How long do we have before the bride and groom are done with photos?'

I point to the water, where two electric-blue jet skis are coming around the cliff. 'That's them now.'

'Shall we go ahead and give them a minute alone?' he says.

I nod. 'It's finally time to climb up one hundred and thirty-three steps and make our way to the reception. Totally worth it though.'

'Yeah,' he says. 'I've heard the wedding band is pretty good.'

'I heard they've won four Grammys...'

He rubs his chin. 'I heard that too. Come on, I'll give you a piggy-back,' he says. 'These thighs can take it.'

Fifty

The dress code for Demi and Percy's wedding is eighties with a *Stranger Things* twist, because Demi finally got around to watching it and wound up loving it more than any other TV show she's ever seen.

'Isn't it kind of quick to be getting married?' I'd asked her.

'Yes, but it feels right. He's been married a few times; I've been married a few times. We figure we've both made enough crappy prototypes to get the final version right this time. Plus, you should see him hang a door. Flawless.'

'Is your daughter coming back for the ceremony?'

'She's trekking in the Himalayas, but she's hoping to get home in the next month.'

After her post-vows, jet ski-riding photoshoot with Percy, Demi dries off and gets back into her bridal gown, which is a multicoloured jumpsuit, a look only strengthened by her plastic hoop earrings and rows of matching bangles. Most of the guests, including Daniel and me, are wearing variations of double denim with neon prints. There is not a heeled shoe in sight, because everybody is rocking their favourite sneakers with sports socks pulled right up to their shins.

Coder is wearing a *Stranger Things* Demogorgon costume, which is one of the cutest things I've ever seen, his little face poking out the middle of what looks more like a large red hibiscus flower than a monster's mouth, and he's lapping up the extra attention his attire is getting him.

Daniel and I have come to the cliff overlooking Bedruthan Steps – a cab ride that should have taken fifteen minutes from Lusty Glaze Beach but actually took more than an hour because of the crazy traffic chaos. We're earlier than the rest of the guests, who have likely also been caught up in the road mayhem, but they'll be here soon enough, because in a little while the entertainment will start, and the evening could not be more beautiful.

We're sharing artisanal snacks, and he is holding up the largest potato chip I have ever seen.

'I think we should at least take a photo,' he says. 'If not offer it to a museum.'

I take the potato chip from him and eat it.

'Wow,' he says. 'I can't believe you just ate the Robert Wadlow of crisps.'

I give him a quizzical look and he explains. 'Wadlow was a shade over eight-feet-eleven-inches tall. Tallest human on record.'

'How do you know that?' I say, eating a regular-sized potato chip.

'As a child, I was quite interested in him.'

'That's a little strange, Daniel.'

'I felt bad for the guy. Early death from an infected scratch on the ankle. And he died when he was just a whisker away from hitting nine feet tall. It's like getting all A-stars on your exams and one A – without the star. You've done amazingly well, no one can dispute that, but you didn't quite hit perfection.'

'Being nine feet tall is perfection?'

'To my seven-year-old self, absolutely.'

'And now?' I ask.

He leans over and kisses me right between my cleavage, hanging out there for a moment – exactly like a genuine tit limpet.

*

'Bedruthan was supposed to be a giant who used the huge rock stacks in the sea as stepping stones across the bay,' I tell Daniel, later, as we lie back on our blanket and throw pillows, waiting for the music to start.

'Another Robert Wadlow, was he?' Daniel says, lazily. 'Bigger than your average Cornishman?'

'He was a complete fabrication. A myth made up by the Victorians to bring more holidaymakers here. The rock stacks are just rock stacks. There's no "stepping stones" mentioned in any ancient Cornish legends. No giant called Bedruthan. It's all made up.'

'So why does the area name include Steps?' he asks, looking out at the ocean.

'There was a cliff staircase leading to the beach...'

'Those Victorians,' he says. 'Always so full of shit.'

'Marketing is everything,' I say. 'At least that's what Anya says.'

Anya, my literary agent. Not Daniel's superstar nemesis Victoria, but a junior associate within her agency, who

Victoria passed my three chapters and synopsis to after deciding they weren't right for her own groaningly full list of superstar clients. Anya is hungry to find new commercial stories and make a name for herself. I met her in London for a coffee and signed right there and then. I don't know if she'll be able to sell the story I want to tell, of surf romance, but I knew just from meeting her that she's the right agent for me. Mostly because she was wearing a tiny lapel pin of Patrick Swayze.

'Anya's onto something,' Daniel says. 'The key is to figure out your hook, and then hammer the general public over the head with it.'

'I don't think I want to hammer my readers over the head with a hook,' I say. 'That sounds more like a horror novel.'

'Alexis will probably write that next,' he says, sighing.

Alexis, my colleague and co-writer on *Touch Light*, but only because Daniel fought for me tooth and nail. He wouldn't give in, even when Alexis argued that it would be better for me to start my publishing career with a fresh project that had no affiliation to him, which was just a way of saying he didn't want to split royalties, although he was happy to split the work.

'I guess he won't have a co-writer next time around?' I say.

'He wasn't exactly keen last time, but he needed one. You did as much work on that book as he did. You gave Janie a voice. Alexis didn't know what to do with her. He would probably have had her lounging in bed all afternoon playing with her own nipples.'

I think of all the nights I spent wondering what Janie would say, or think, or do in a particular situation. How her life would fit into this small town I've come to know and love.

'But I hadn't signed a contract at that point. He could have denied I had any input.'

'Yeah, but to be honest, in the end he thought having a female co-writer on a romance novel might be a good look for him. Good for sales. And his reputation as a feminist.'

'Is Alexis a feminist?'

'Some days…'

Daniel told Alexis that if he screwed me over, he would no longer represent him. And he'd tell the truth to anyone who asked why. Even though Alexis was Daniel's only client who brought in any real money.

'Thank you for risking everything for me,' I say, because I feel the weight of what he's done for me, what he was willing to lose for me.

He shrugs. 'It was the right thing to do.'

'In what universe?'

'I don't know. Maybe in some universe where I'm falling in love with you.'

'And… that's not this one?' I say, my heart thudding in my chest.

He grimaces. 'Sorry. I'm shockingly shit at romance.'

'Verbally, maybe,' I say. 'But that's okay, because you have other skills.'

*

Daniel's kissing me and his hand is in my shirt, when we hear an exaggerated cough and look up to see Makayla and Travis walking towards us.

'Oh hi, I wondered where you'd gotten to,' I say, sitting up.

'You're the dimbos in the wrong place. Everyone else is over there,' Makayla says, pointing into the distance.

'I thought we were just early,' I say, clapping my hand over my mouth. 'Why didn't you call me?'

'Couldn't get through,' she says, patting down her red and white puffball skirt, which she's teamed with a white lace crop top. It's a novelty seeing Makayla wearing something other than her new range of printed slogan T-shirts, which she's been wearing constantly as a marketing tactic and selling in huge numbers at car boot sales all over Cornwall, along with her sea glass jewellery. She has two main designs, one aimed primarily at the bachelor party market and one aimed more at bachelorettes, although she says there's been a surprising amount of crossover. Her second range is basically the same as the first, except with the slogan in a thick red circle with a red diagonal line crossed through. Her new venture has been so successful, with such overwhelming enthusiasm from her customers, that she's actually looking into trademarking her slogan – which is 'Tit Limpet'.

'There's an extra fifty thousand people up here on the cliffs, if you haven't noticed,' she says. 'The network is down.'

'Is Demi here yet?'

'She's the one who sent us to look for you – should have known you'd be making out like teenagers. And guess what? Demi's daughter, Sennen, is here. So much for trekking in the Himalayas.'

'Wow, she made it?' I say, sitting straighter, because I've

wanted to meet Sennen ever since I met Demi and now I'm going to.

'Yes, she couldn't make the ceremony as her flight got delayed but she's just in time for the after-party. She's got the eighties thing right, but seems to have missed the *Stranger Things* part of the memo.'

'How do you mean?' Daniel asks.

'She's the one wearing a black and white stripy suit. She's come as Michael Keaton in *Beetlejuice*.'

I laugh. These wedding photos are really going to be something.

'Your father and Jeremy just arrived too, and they've changed into evening attire. Matching muscle vests and parachute pants. It's a strong visual. Very Vanilla Ice.'

Earsplitting screams start what seems like three feet away.

'Wow, listen to the crowd,' Makayla says, leading us over stiles and through fields to where all the other excited wedding guests have gathered and are waiting on lawn chairs and beach blankets. I spot Demi laughing with her daughter in a gazebo lit by string-lights and candles set in storm lanterns.

'I guess the band just walked on stage,' Daniel says, sounding excited.

And then Kings of Leon is playing Boardmasters, and we are listening for free with the hundreds of other local people who've had the same idea and are sitting on the coast stretching away to either side of us with their plaid blankets, picnic baskets and bottles of beer. The night is so incredibly still, without a breath of wind, that we can hear every twang of a guitar string.

They open with 'The Bucket', which makes me think of

Alexis, sitting in the Fistral Beach lifeguard hut with his envenomated foot jammed into a steaming pail of water.

Maybe the Fates were giving me a message that they had their own way of dealing with him.

The last email I received from Alexis had the subject line: *A Letter of Proper Submission.*

A quote I instantly recognised from *Sense and Sensibility.* The letter that Edward Ferrars refused to write in apology to his awful mother, after she'd disinherited him for sticking to his guns and making his own life choices. I wasn't sure how to take this subject line because I couldn't imagine Alexis being submissive to anyone, least of all me, no matter how badly he'd behaved.

It turned out that 'submission' just referred to the manuscript, the latest draft of which he'd finally resubmitted to his publisher under both our names.

'Listen,' Makayla says, wrenching me back to the present and dragging me to my feet. 'They're playing "Fans". You *have* to dance to this, Candice. Especially since you're going to have some of your own one day.'

'I don't know about fans,' I say, flushing. 'But I hope that I'll have readers. Even if they hate what I write, and say it everywhere, I'll be grateful to them for taking time out of their lives to read my writing.'

'Really?' Makayla sniffs. 'Because I'd want to poke them in the eye.'

'*Really.*'

'So dance to the song in honour of them,' she says, twirling in a slow circle, and I give in.

'We're really dancing on a clifftop?' I say. 'What is this – a movie?'

'It could be,' Daniel says, pondering.

When the band plays 'Revelry', Daniel takes me by the hand and raises it, as if we're dancing a reel at a ball in an Austen novel, and Travis does the same to Makayla. His move ripples through the gathering until almost everyone is up on their feet, including Jeremy and my father – a crowd of revellers like a scene from *Bridgerton*, except the revellers are wearing the most garish eighties clothing imaginable.

When we sit down for a breather and a sip of champagne, Makayla turns to me and says, 'You're a real local now you're listening to Boardies for free.'

'How long will it take before I get to be a local?' Daniel asks, looking hopeful.

Because he's living here now too, renting his own room from Demi, and commuting to London with all the other business folks when he needs to – which isn't all that often, now so much of his work is remote. I'll go with him sometimes too, when my writing takes me to the city – leaving via the Newquay to Gatwick plane, which departs at 7 a.m. every day, flying so close over the water that passengers sometimes see whales during take-off and landing.

Daniel's plan is to wind down his agenting over the next few years, not take any new clients, and relocate permanently to Newquay. When Kristoff found out that Daniel worked bar jobs through college, he offered him all the shifts he wants, which should help a little with the credit cards and get him settled into the community that stays here through the long winter, battling Atlantic rainstorms and the tail ends of hurricanes.

He has a side hustle in mind too, as almost everybody does

in this town. Daniel's eldest brother, who worked twenty years in casting, travelling all over the world for shows and movies, is planning to use his connections and experience of the industry to open his own production company based in Cornwall to take advantage of the spectacular views and British film tax incentives – and probably to score free drinks whenever Daniel is working a bar shift. I imagine a lot of their business meetings will be held huddled together in oceanside bars during the quiet winter months. Together they'll build their company from the ground up. Daniel will head the creative side, his experience as a literary agent and access to a rich network of writers and their stories invaluable.

I hear the first few bars of the next song and realise it's 'Wait For Me'.

And, man, it feels like I waited a really long time to meet Daniel.

'All this lyrical resonance is making me feel like I'm back at college, sitting in Poetry class,' I say, smiling at him.

'But, will you, though?' he says.

'Will I what?'

'Wait for me, while I'm working out my new life?'

'I might,' I say, smiling. 'Just don't ask me to take one in the temple for you.'

'Huh? What does that mean?' he says, confusion clouding his eyes.

Makayla snorts champagne out of her nose and grips my wrist, her whole body trembling with laughter.

Travis looks at Daniel and they both shake their heads.

'Do you understand what they're laughing about, mate?' Travis asks.

'Nope,' Daniel says. 'I think we're just going to have to live with that.'

★

We lie back under the blaze of the setting sun, people we love around us, and listen. During the last ten minutes of the set, a sea fog rolls in, and the music gets softer and more muted.

'So are you going to write about this moment in your book?' Daniel says, reaching out to hold my hand. 'It's pretty special.'

'Hell yeah,' I say, kissing him.

Acknowledgements

This book came like a gift at a time when I was feeling very down about my writing. Rachel, thank you for taking a chance on me. I've never had so much fun writing a novel and I am forever in your debt. Thanks also to Bianca, Rhian and Felicity.

I'd also like to thank the following people, who have shown me so much kindness.

Jon, for everything. Including taking me to Torquay while I was writing the book, even if the whole area was shut down by the authorities as soon as we arrived, on account of a superyacht fire in the harbour filling the air with dangerous toxic fumes. I'm very glad you remembered to pack your inhaler.

Katy Moran and Kat Devereaux, for reading early drafts and giving me much appreciated words of encouragement.

Rachel Lamb, for so many adventures.

My Hyena group pals, Rachel, Rachel and Lerryn, for wisdom and laughs.

Moira, for lending me your sourdough starter story, which still makes me smile.

Mum and Dad, for incredible love and support, always.

Dad, for watching so much sport on the TV and making me a reader.

Richard and Paul, for cheering me on when I needed it.

My writing group friends. You know who you are and what you mean to me.

My friend Jo, for lending me forty quid so we could travel to London and see Pearl Jam back in 1996 at Wembley Arena. What a night. Also, Kings of Leon for that epic Boardmasters gig in summer 2022, which I listened to from my back garden, as I was too skint to buy a ticket.

Finally, my girls. I love you more than I can ever say.

About the Author

TAYLOR COLE grew up on a council estate in Devon and is of Armenian heritage, via her maternal grandmother who survived the Armenian genocide as a child refugee. When she was twenty-one, Taylor left university to run away to Cyprus and live in a men's barrack block with her military boyfriend, but returned the next year to finish her BA in English, which she followed with a master's degree in Creative Writing. She lives in Newquay with the military boyfriend-turned-husband, two daughters and an eighty-year-old tortoise called Shelley who was found wandering the streets of Plymouth in 1958.